T

Feeling s................ beneath her skirt, Paulette clutched the front of Declan's jacket tightly. He wouldn't really kiss her, would he?

Time seemed to stop, suspended around them, enveloping them in a special world all their own.

And then, with slow deliberateness, he leaned down and kissed her while his muscled arms encircled her shoulders and drew her against the length of his body.

His mouth, warm and soft, covered hers thoroughly, and Paulette melted at the supremely intimate contact. This man, this virtual stranger, whom she had only met once before, was kissing her.

She should have been surprised by it, appalled by it. Outraged even. But oddly enough, Declan kissing her was not completely unexpected. On some level, she had been thinking about kissing him since the moment she met him. That fact was the most shocking to her.

And now . . .

Not sure what was happening to her, she did not care. She only knew that she did not want this man to stop kissing her.

And he didn't . . .

Books by Kaitlin O'Riley

SECRETS OF A DUCHESS

ONE SINFUL NIGHT

WHEN HIS KISS IS WICKED

DESIRE IN HIS EYES

IT HAPPENED ONE CHRISTMAS

TO TEMPT AN IRISH ROGUE

YOURS FOR ETERNITY
(with Hannah Howell and Alexandra Ivy)

AN INVITATION TO SIN
(with Jo Beverley, Sally MacKenzie and Vanessa Kelly)

Published by Kensington Publishing Corporation

To Tempt An Irish Rogue

KAITLIN O'RILEY

ZEBRA BOOKS
KENSINGTON PUBLISHING CORP.
http://www.kensingtonbooks.com

ZEBRA BOOKS are published by

Kensington Publishing Corp.
119 West 40th Street
New York, NY 10018

All Kensington titles, imprints, and distributed lines are
available at special quantity discounts for bulk purchases for
sales promotion, premiums, fund-raising, educational, or
institutional use.

Special book excerpts or customized printings can also be
created to fit specific needs. For details, write or phone the
office of the Kensington Special Sales Manager: Attn.: Special
Sales Department. Kensington Publishing Corp., 119 West
40th Street, New York, NY 10018. Phone: 1-800-221-2647.

Zebra and the Z logo Reg. U.S. Pat. & TM Off.

ISBN-13: 978-1-4201-1240-5
ISBN-10: 1-4201-1240-6

First Printing: November 2012

10 9 8 7 6 5 4 3 2 1

Printed in the United States of America

To Maureen,
the most incredible sister and aunt.
Thank you for everything.
I love you!

Acknowledgments

I am fortunate to have many amazing people in my life. This past year has been particularly challenging for me and I would have been lost without them.

Thanks go as always to my family: Jane Milmore (for critiquing everything), Shelley Jensen (for being there), Maureen Milmore (for being a betty), Janet Wheeler (for being a bud), Scott Wheeler (for techno-savvy), Adrienne Barbeau (for the beginning), Billy Van Zandt (for eagle eyes), Jeff Babey (for the laughs), Laurence Cogger (for the French), Kim McCafferty (for keeping me sane), and Yvonne Deane (for keeping me positive). I give a very special thank you to Jennifer and Greg Malins for helping to make my life infinitely better this year.

Thank you to all my CH friends (especially Cela, Melanie, Gretchen, Lynn, Jensie, and Jill) for always supporting me and making work more fun.

I wish to thank the lovely Rebecca Zaccagnino for my beautiful website design and the talented Dennis Greco for bringing the places in my stories to life with his gorgeous artwork.

And I give thanks to Jane Dystel and John Scognamiglio for making my writing journey the pleasure that it is.

Lastly, I thank all my readers who love the Hamilton sisters as much as I do.

Note to Riley

I still can't believe you're taller than I am.
Thank you for being so much fun to be with.
I love you more than you know.

Thomas Hamilton
(1820 - 1869)

Colette Elizabeth
(b. 1849)
"When His Kiss Is Wicked"

Juliette Sara
(b. 1850)
"Desire In His Eyes"

Lise Anna
(b. 18..)
"It Happe... Christ..."

m. 1870

m. 1871

Lucien Sinclair
Earl of Waverly
(b. 1845)

Harrison Fleming
(b. 1841)

Quin Roxb...
(b. 18...

Phillip
(b. 1871)

Simon
(b. 1873)

Sara
(b. 1873)

Ham...
Family

Genevieve
La Brecque
(b. 1830)

m. 1849

...ette
...belle
...853)
...ned One
...mas"

Paulette
Victoria
(b. 1856)
"To Tempt An
Irish Rogue"

Yvette
Katherine
(b. 1858)
BOOK #5

m. 1874

...nton
...bury
...846)

...ilton
...r Tree

Chapter 1

Impressions

London
August 1876

The bells above the entrance of Hamilton's Book Shoppe jingled as the front door opened and the drizzling summer rain drifted in momentarily. It had been a slow afternoon with little business and Paulette Hamilton looked up in eager anticipation at the customer who had ventured out on such a dreary August day. A tall gentleman stepped into the shop, holding an umbrella in one hand and clutching the hand of a reluctant little girl in the other.

"Welcome to Hamilton's!" Paulette greeted the customers with an animated smile. New customers always made her happy.

As the gentleman folded his wet umbrella, Paulette took careful note of him, which was a habit of hers. Ever curious and observant, she couldn't help but pay attention to the customers in her store. This gentleman was mature, tall and rather broad and wore expensive, well-made clothes. Beneath his elegant black hat, strands of chocolate-colored hair were visible. He was handsome enough, she supposed, in a dark, brooding sort of way, but she had never favored that look. Paulette usually found herself drawn to golden, fair-haired heroes. At least she did in all the books that she read.

Using her best shopkeeper's voice, she asked, "How may I help you this afternoon?"

"My little daughter here would like a new book," he explained, indicating the child hiding with shyness behind him.

The rich, melodic timbre of his words, laced with the notes of a vaguely familiar accent, filled the air around her. Unable to resist the magnetic attraction of his voice, Paulette suddenly eyed him with keener interest as he looked toward the little girl.

The man possessed an aquiline nose, a strong jaw, and a lean face with dark eyebrows. He was clean-shaven, but she could easily imagine a thin black mustache upon him, giving him the look of a wicked pirate. He seemed tense, almost as if he held his feelings tightly in check, but the slightest disturbance could set him loose in a fury. His full mouth was set in a grim line. In fact, he had a look about his face that conveyed the distinct impression that he had not smiled in a long, long while.

Something about the man unsettled her and the dark intensity about him brought to mind the words "sinister" or "dangerous."

A little shiver raced through her.

Feeling slightly nervous in his presence and somewhat relieved knowing that her assistant was close at hand in the back room, Paulette silently reprimanded herself for being so foolish as to think of herself in any kind of danger. She had never felt this way about a customer before. Why on earth would she think that this man would cause her any harm? Perhaps she had read one too many gothic romance novels lately!

Her attention was drawn to the little girl, who still attempted to hide behind the man's dark trousers. The child could not have been more than four years old, with a sweet, chubby face framed by golden curls mostly covered under a wide-brimmed bonnet.

Paulette knew exactly what the little girl wanted. Hamilton's carried the best children's books in the city and because of that she had dealt with all manner of children in the shop before, from the most well-behaved to the most spoiled, so she was no stranger to bashful children either. This shy-looking girl would be easy to please.

"Well, you are quite a lucky young lady for your father to give you such a special treat," Paulette began, favoring the girl with a warm grin. "We have some lovely fairy-tale books with the most beautiful pictures in them. Would you like me to show them to you?"

Peeking out from behind her father's leg, the little girl nodded in agreement. She did not make a sound, but her cherubic face lit with excitement.

"Thank you," the gentleman said, seeming a bit relieved by Paulette's suggestion.

"Why don't you both come with me to the children's section of the shop?" she suggested brightly.

They followed her to the rear of the store, where she and Colette had designed an inviting space for their smallest customers. They'd had shelves built at a lower height and miniature-sized tables and chairs to better fit little bodies. A brightly colored area rug covered the wooden floor, lending warmth to the section of books on display. Paulette immediately located their most popular-selling book, a gorgeously illustrated volume of fairy tales. She placed the book on the table and motioned for the child to join her while she sat herself on one of the tiny chairs as well.

"I think you might like this one."

The little girl glanced up hesitantly at her father, seeking his permission. He patted her head in encouragement. "It's all right, darlin'."

She moved slowly forward, taking hesitant steps to the table where Paulette waited for her. When she reached the small table, the girl stopped and stared at Paulette in expectation.

"Do you have a favorite story?" Paulette questioned.

The little girl shook her head, her expression extraordinarily serious for one so young.

"Do you like the story of *Sleeping Beauty*?"

The child gave the slightest nod of assent.

"That story has always been a favorite of mine." Opening the thick volume, Paulette turned to the page that had an elaborate and richly drawn illustration of a grand castle tower covered with an overgrown tangle of thorn-laden vines and a profusion of red roses. The little girl's eyes widened and a small gasp of awe escaped her.

Paulette asked, "Isn't this picture beautiful?"

Again, the girl merely nodded. She had not uttered one word since entering the shop.

"I'm Miss Hamilton," Paulette said, hoping to coax a response from her. "What is your name?"

The child blinked at her and shrugged her tiny shoulders.

"What is your name?" she repeated.

The little girl still did not respond. Paulette had never seen such a withdrawn child. Did she not speak at all? Paulette was usually able to cajole bashful children into an easy conversation by this point. But not this girl. From what she sensed, it was not merely shyness that kept the girl from speaking. Was there something the matter with her? Perhaps she was she a mute? Paulette's natural curiosity piqued and she wished to ask the gentleman about it, but it was certainly not her place to ask such intimate questions of a stranger.

The girl's father finally answered for her. "Her name is Mara."

Aware that the man's eyes had been focused on her during the entire exchange with his daughter, Paulette glanced up at him.

They held each other's gaze for longer than two strangers normally would. His deep green eyes were fringed with thick dark lashes that were startlingly long for a man. A tingling sensation raced through her and in that instant, Paulette was almost knocked off the tiny chair upon which she sat.

He was not as old as she had first thought him to be and that surprised her. Although she guessed he was not yet thirty, aged weariness had settled in his eyes. Struck by the sadness she saw within the emerald depths, she sensed that a profound heartache dwelled within this man. What had happened to him? Paulette was at a complete loss to explain the sudden surge of intense feelings that rushed through her as he looked back at her.

Somehow he seemed less forbidding than he had a moment ago.

"And your name, sir?" she managed to ask, suddenly needing to know.

"Forgive me, Miss Hamilton," he acknowledged her with a slight bow, removing his hat. "I am Declan Reeves."

Of course. The accent. Now she recognized it. He must be from Ireland. Wondering what had brought him to London, Paulette forced her gaze away from his mysteriously sad eyes and turned her attention back to the child. His child.

"Mara is such a pretty name," she murmured to the little girl. Paulette was more than aware that the man's eyes were still on her. The intensity of his gaze made her uncomfortable. Her hand moved to smooth her own golden-blond hair.

Again the child did not say a word. She merely looked at Paulette with somber green eyes that now seemed remarkably like her father's. Mara reached out a hand and slowly began turning the pages in the book of fairy tales, mesmerized by the colorful illustrations.

"Her mother named her." His voice, smooth and melodic, spilled around her, sending a shiver of a different kind through Paulette.

The mother. Of course there would be a mother, this man's wife.

Paulette rose from the tiny chair, brushing her striped skirts with her hands in a nervous gesture. "I think Mara likes the fairy-tale book." She returned to being the efficient bookseller once more. "Is there anything else I can get for you today, Mr. Reeves?"

She found herself staring into his emerald eyes again and Declan Reeves answered her question with a desperate look of longing that caused her heart to constrict in her chest. He seemed to be asking her for something. Anything, and she wanted desperately to give it to him but she was not even sure what it was. She held her breath.

Why did this man unsettle her so?

Shaking herself from her overactive imagination, for surely she could only have imagined what had just passed between them, Paulette straightened her shoulders. She should thank them for coming and get on with business.

Instead, she then blurted out, "Does your daughter not speak?"

Paulette immediately regretted her impolite question. Why couldn't she keep her mouth closed? Her sisters were always telling her to mind her own business. She really tried to, but for the most part Paulette could not help herself and always said what she thought. And yes, once in a while she overheard conversations she shouldn't, but that was not her fault. She was simply very aware of what was going on around her.

Still it was quite rude of her to ask such an intrusive question. Feeling remorseful, she was about to apologize to him for her bad manners.

"She doesn't speak anymore." He shook his head, sadness emanating from him. "She hasn't spoken a single word since her mother passed away."

"Oh, I see," Paulette murmured. His daughter had been struck dumb with grief at losing her mother. How tragic! This poor little girl, losing her mother so young! And this man had lost his wife.

Heart pounding, she eyed Declan Reeves anew as it suddenly dawned on her.

He was not a married man.

Once again chiding herself for such a ridiculous musing, she frowned. Paulette didn't even like the man! Aside from being a complete stranger, he was too dark, too sad, and too mysterious for her taste. She preferred lighter, happier, and generally more outgoing males. Declan Reeves was definitely none of those things.

"Thank you for choosing the perfect book for Mara," he said. "It's sometimes difficult to know what she likes."

"All little girls love fairy tales," Paulette said, feeling flustered, still aware that his intense eyes were upon her. She felt incredibly self-conscious, wondering how she appeared to him, in her striped work dress. Earlier that morning, she had piled her blond hair upon her head without much thought, as she usually did. Paulette knew she was not unattractive, yet she wished she knew what this man thought while he stared at her so intently.

"Yes, well, thank you again."

"You're most welcome. Can I help you with anything else?"

"Thank you, no."

"In that case, I shall get the bill for you."

"Perhaps, I could look about for a moment first?" he asked.

"Why yes, of course," she said with a nod. "I shall be up front if you have need of me."

Yet again the man gave her a dark look of longing that Paulette felt to the tips of her toes. The fact that he was a widower and staring at her in such a pointed manner left her breathless. She gave him a faint smile and made her way to the safety of the counter, sighing deeply with relief.

The bells jingled and another customer entered the bookshop. Paulette busied herself assisting Mrs. Abbott in finding a volume of poetry, yet all the while she was keenly aware of Declan Reeves milling about the shelves and his silent daughter still flipping through the pages in the book of fairy tales.

A half hour had passed and Paulette stood behind the counter waiting for him to pay for his purchase. The man finally made his way toward her, with Mara following behind, clutching the book in her arms.

"Did you find what you were looking for?" she asked.

He raised a dark brow in her direction. "Do you always ask such leading questions, Miss Hamilton?"

"I beg your pardon?" What on earth did the man

mean? Paulette hadn't asked him anything different from the questions she posed to all her other customers. It was her duty, for goodness sake!

He shook his head with a rueful glance, his eyes dark and shuttered. "Never mind."

Paulette straightened her shoulders again. She was usually very good at reading people, but this man's manner left her disconcerted and unnerved. "Well then, I assume that will be all."

"Yes, thank you."

Ignoring his brooding countenance, she collected his payment without comment, while offering a smile at his little girl instead. "Are you happy with your book, Mara?"

Mara glanced up at her with wide green eyes. Her winsome little face, seeming even more innocent and precious framed by the wide brim of her bonnet, filled with happiness and expressed what she would not say with words. She loved the book.

She smiled at the sweet girl. "I am so pleased that you like it." Paulette glanced back up at Declan Reeves, relying on her shopkeeper role to steady her. "Please keep me in mind if you should need anything else."

Their gazes met and something forceful and charged raced through her as she looked into his green eyes, so deep and impenetrable. She shivered slightly at the intensity.

"I'm sure I shall," he said with a glance that sent more quivers through her.

Flustered, Paulette blinked and looked away, shuffling a stack of papers on the counter in a businesslike manner, suddenly at a loss for something to say in response. It seemed he responded to every innocent comment she made as if she meant something else entirely.

She managed to mumble, "Thank you for coming to Hamilton's."

"No, it is I who should thank you, Miss Hamilton."

She looked up as he turned to the door, ushering his silent daughter out of the shop and into the misty afternoon.

Chapter 2

Rumors

"How were things at the shop today?" Colette Hamilton Sinclair asked. "I meant to stop by this afternoon but then Phillip came down with a bit of a fever."

Paulette sat having dinner with her two sisters and her brother-in-law in the elegant dining hall of Devon House later that evening.

"It was a good day all in all, taking into account the rain." Paulette's thoughts drifted back to the magnetic dark-haired man and his silent daughter who had been in the shop that day. "The strangest gentleman came in to buy books for his daughter. I think he was from Ireland. His little daughter was so sweet but she hasn't spoken a word since her mother died."

"How sad," murmured her younger sister Yvette, who was seated across the table from her. "Was he a handsome man?"

Of course Yvette would want to know what he looked like! That's all she cared about. Whereas Paulette found the subtler qualities in a person more interesting. She wrinkled her nose at the thought of the Irish gentleman.

"He was not what I would describe as handsome, but he was not unattractive either," she began, recalling the brooding dark looks and unreadable expression. But he had those deep green eyes and full mouth. "Yet . . . I suppose he was handsome."

"From Ireland, did you say?" Colette, her oldest sister, asked, sounding a bit intrigued, her blue eyes sparkling. "What was his name?"

"Declan Reeves."

"Declan Reeves?" Lucien Sinclair echoed, pausing with his fork in the air and taking a marked interest in the conversation. Colette's husband's dark brows furrowed and he glanced sharply at Paulette. "Are you sure he said the name Declan Reeves?"

"Yes, I'm positive." Paulette nodded, wondering what could have captured her brother-in-law's attention. "His daughter's name was Mara. She had to be about four years old, and so pretty. But dreadfully sad. Why do you ask?"

Lucien set his fork down. "I just read something in the paper about him yesterday. He's Lord Something-or-other, but it must be the same fellow."

Now it was Paulette's turn to question. "What did the paper say about him?"

"Nothing good, as I recall," Lucien explained. "I won't slander a man's name based on gossip, but there are those who are suspicious of him and the manner in which his wife died."

A cold shiver raced down Paulette's spine and she suddenly sat up straighter in her chair. The uncomfortable feeling she had in the shop when she met the man now did not seem so far-fetched. There had been something dark and rather sinister about Mr. Reeves. She dared to ask, "How did his wife die?"

"There was mention of a fire, I believe," Lucien said

with a slight shrug of his shoulders. "I don't know all the details as I was just skimming the article in the *Times* and didn't pay much attention to it, but the name stuck in my head for some reason."

Paulette's heart ached at the thought of the little blond girl who would not speak and a wave of sadness washed over her. The child had lost her mother in a fire and it must have been quite traumatic for her. Was there a possibility that her father was responsible for her mother's death?

"Well, let's talk about something more cheerful, shall we?" Yvette added while wrinkling her nose. "I don't care for morbid stories."

"No, I'm sure you'd rather discuss fashion and handsome gentlemen," Paulette pointed out, oddly relieved to be changing the topic of conversation. Although she wished to know more about the mysterious and brooding Declan Reeves, learning that he might very well have killed his wife left her feeling unnerved. But somehow, after seeing how kindly he treated his little daughter, she did not think him capable of such an act, no matter how forbidding he looked.

"There's absolutely nothing wrong with talking about pretty clothes. Or handsome gentlemen," Yvette countered with an enigmatic smile. With her blond hair styled in an attempt to appear older than she was, she added, "And one of these days I'm going to be wed to the richest and handsomest gentleman of all."

Lucien gave her an amused look. "And just who would that be?"

Yvette paused in deep thought. "I'm sure I don't know. I have yet to meet anyone who catches my fancy." Her dainty chin went up defensively. "I'm still looking."

"And you keep looking until you find him, Yvette."
Lucien gave his youngest sister-in-law an indulgent smile.

"I have every intention of doing so." Yvette disregarded
the skeptical looks of her two sisters. "Mark my words."

"Well, I've no doubt you will when you are old
enough," Colette said. "You are only eighteen, Yvette."
As the eldest sister, Colette had taken over the role of
parent to her younger siblings after their father died and
their mother had been unable to care for them.

"Yes, I'm eighteen now and old enough," Yvette responded eagerly, tossing her blond curls with an air of
superiority. "And Paulette is twenty-one."

"I'm *almost* twenty-one," Paulette amended, as always
careful of the little details. She wouldn't reach her
twenty-first birthday until September.

Ignoring her correction, Yvette pointed to Paulette.
"*She* should be married by now!"

"Don't drag me into this," Paulette protested. "I'm
not interested in getting married."

"Oh, you always say that, Paulette, and I don't believe
you one single bit." Yvette tossed her head emphatically.
"Every girl wants to get married."

"Well, you're quite mistaken on that account." Paulette
was in no rush to have some man telling her what to do
night and day. She was quite happy with her life the way
it was, thank you very much. Paulette loved living with
her sister and her husband at Devon House and working at the bookshop. Colette and Lucien were much
more permissive than her own parents ever would have
been and they allowed her the freedom to manage the
shop and to be her own person.

Ever since Colette had married Lucien Sinclair, their
lives had changed for the better and Lucien's generosity
had allowed them to keep the bookshop. Even though
their widowed mother, Genevieve Hamilton, had decided

to leave London and live in Brighton, Lucien Sinclair had invited all Colette's sisters to live at Devon House. Her older sisters Juliette and Lisette were both married now, leaving only Paulette and Yvette still living with Lucien and Colette.

Last year Simon Sinclair, Lucien's father, died, making Lucien the Marquis of Stancliff, and Colette the Marchioness of Stancliff. Given their titled positions the two of them always had many social obligations, but Colette still managed to raise her two sons and take care of things at the bookshop with Paulette.

More than content with the way her life was currently arranged, Paulette had no interest in rushing into a marriage with just anyone. She had already made up her mind that she would wed only if she could find someone just like Lucien Sinclair. In her eyes he was a perfect husband to Colette. Yet Paulette harbored a secret doubt she would ever find a man who would let her do exactly as she liked.

"So, no," she continued with certainty, "I've no wish to marry."

Yvette looked horrified and turned to her eldest sister for support. "Colette, you cannot allow Paulette to spend the rest of her life alone in the bookshop!"

Colette, her blue eyes filled with kindness, gave Yvette a look of understanding, but did not agree with her. "Paulette can do as she wishes. Just as you can."

Vindicated, Paulette smiled in smug triumph at her younger sister. Honestly! She had more important things to do than worry about finding a husband. She was about to open a new shop, for heaven's sake! The business of marriage required more time than she was willing to take away from the importance of managing the bookshop. And Colette understood her on this matter better than her other sisters did.

Yvette could just keep her romantic dreams and aspirations for a lofty marriage. Paulette would marry some day, perhaps, if she met someone special enough, but she certainly wasn't on the hunt for a husband like so many girls her age were. Luckily there was no pressure for her to marry right away. Colette and Lucien were in agreement with her, so Paulette was free to do as she liked, knowing full well that she was fortunate indeed. Most girls were not so blessed.

Yvette let out an anguished little squeal, blinking back tears. "But if Paulette doesn't marry, then I cannot!"

All eyes turned to her in surprise and, once again, Lucien laughed. "Where on earth did you get that idea?"

Yvette's expression filled with worry. "I can't marry before my older sister does, Lucien. It isn't right! And if Paulette doesn't ever marry, then what's to become of me?"

Paulette really tried her best to contain her laughter but failed. The giggles just escaped. Yvette's worry seemed quite ridiculous to her.

Lucien and Colette both began speaking at the same time. "Yvette, you don't have to wait for Paulette to marry first!"

"I don't?" Yvette blinked in surprise. "I thought it was common knowledge that sisters had to get married in order of their age."

"Maybe that is true in some households, but I can assure you, Yvette, you can marry, or not, whenever you wish to, regardless of what our little Paulette here decides to do," Lucien explained. An unspoken look of understanding passed between him and his wife.

"Thank you for taking that pressure off me, Lucien," Paulette said, grateful beyond measure that Colette had married such a reasonable man. Lucien had always understood her motives and actions and Paulette loved that about him. The last thing she needed was Yvette breathing down her neck to hurry up and wed some fool, just so she could plan her own grand wedding. "Besides," Paulette pointed out with her calm reasoning, "there's no one that you want to marry at the moment, is there?"

"Well, no . . ." Yvette stammered helplessly. "But it's the principle of it all." She released a weary sigh. "However, if Paulette is not worried about being a spinster—"

"Who said anything about me being a spinster?" Paulette cried in indignation. Honestly! Maybe she would marry someday. At some point. If she met someone truly special. Paulette was not averse to marriage. Hadn't she seen her three older sisters marry quite happily? It was for that very reason that she would not be rushed into anything.

"Well, you don't want to have a Season and you don't go to parties or have gentleman callers. You don't seem interested in the least in finding a husband," Yvette pointed out. "It just stands to reason that—"

"Please stop!" Colette held up her hands. "I've had quite enough of this conversation for one evening. Suffice it to say that both of you can marry whomever and whenever you choose."

"Thank you!" Paulette was more than happy to end the conversation. She loved Yvette, but her endless pursuit of a fiancé was a bit taxing. Whereas Paulette had loftier goals in mind.

Lucien deftly changed the subject. "Have you been by to see the new shop yet?"

Filled with excitement at the prospect of the new shop, Paulette answered, "No, I haven't seen it yet. But Quinton said that it should be finished in the next few weeks. Then we shall be able to begin installing the furniture and books. I'm hoping we can open by the end of October."

Hamilton's Book Shoppe was doing so well that she

and Colette had decided to open another, larger book-store on the other side of town. They had been preparing for months and the newly constructed building was almost ready.

"We're going to have a grand opening celebration," Colette added. "And Juliette will be returning home in time to be a part of it."

"It's going to be the best bookshop in London!" Paulette declared. She couldn't wait for the new store to open!

Chapter 3

Blame

Declan Reeves sighed heavily as he entered the elegant townhouse he had just rented for his stay in London. How long he stayed depended on a number of things. He had simply needed to get away from Ireland for a while. Away from memories and sadness. Away from everything that he had ever known.

Away from anything that reminded him of her.

But more than anything else he had needed to get Mara away. His daughter needed a fresh start. He hoped that the change in environment would be good for her. And he prayed that it would prompt her to speak again.

He glanced down at the little girl who walked beside him, her tiny hand clinging tightly to his. His daughter's heart was broken and he did not know how to mend it.

As they walked through the foyer of the house, he stopped and knelt beside her, looking into her pretty green eyes. "Mara, darlin', are you happy with your new book?"

She gave him a smile and nodded.

Declan longed for her to laugh and giggle. To squeal with delight as she used to whenever he entered a room.

She had been so bright and spirited before, full of life and energy. Now it was as if she were a shell of her former self. Hollow on the inside. He had no idea how to reach her.

With this trip to London, he hoped that a complete change of scenery, at a place with no memories associated with her mother, would jolt her out of her silence. Mara had not uttered a word since the night her mother died. And those last words would haunt him forever. He heard them in his sleep every night.

And so did Mara. Some nights she woke up screaming uncontrollably, her face a mask of terror streaked with tears, sobs wracking her little body. He'd rush to her room and hold her until her screams ceased and she fell back to sleep out of abject weariness.

They'd only been in London a few days, so perhaps it was too soon to expect her to change. Then again, perhaps London wouldn't help at all. Perhaps he'd been foolish to leave behind all the girl had ever known. But he'd had to give it try. Lord knew they both needed a respite from all that was going on back home.

A petite, kind-faced woman came bustling into the foyer. "I see you've returned, Lord Cashelmore. Shall I take Lady Mara upstairs now?"

He glanced briefly at the lady he had recently hired to watch over his daughter and nodded in agreement, before turning his attention back to Mara. She stared at him, her eyes fixed upon something within him. As had become her custom, she spoke to him without words. He touched her soft, baby cheek with his hand and placed a gentle kiss upon her forehead. "You go on up with Mrs. Martin now and I'll be up to see you for supper and then we'll read your book together."

As she always did when he gave her instructions, Mara

nodded her head obediently. She took the woman's outstretched hand and followed her up the stairs.

Ignoring the familiar ache in his chest, Declan stood silently and watched them go. It was a moment or two before he finally walked to his study and threw off his hat and cape. He moved to stand before the window and stared out at the misty afternoon. Dreary and depressing. There was no other way to describe the day. There was not a single bright spot to lighten the dark afternoon.

Except for the girl in the bookshop.

Miss Hamilton. Something about her had caught his attention. Her bright energy and obvious intelligence. Her incredible patience in dealing with Mara. Her obvious joy and pride in her store. Her sparkling blue eyes that had glanced at him with such suspicion, then avid interest, followed by a nervous shyness. Every emotion she had was easily seen in her delicate features. It was strange, but their eyes had held for a moment and something unspoken passed between them. He felt instantly drawn to her.

But he supposed there was nothing unusual in that. She was more than merely attractive. The girl was quite beautiful. One doesn't expect to find such a beauty working in a bookshop.

What was more unusual was that he found himself still thinking about her. He hadn't thought of a woman in that way since . . . Margaret Ryan.

He shook himself at the memory of her beautiful face, her silver-blond hair.

Would there ever be a time that he thought of Margaret without overwhelming grief and guilt? Would he ever be able to put all the anger and horror behind him? Would he ever have a normal life again?

At least that was his goal in coming to London. To find some sense of normalcy in his life. And Mara's.

Maybe once they had found a measure of peace he could stomach returning to Dublin and facing Margaret's acrimonious family and the past that haunted him.

A knock on his study door startled him.

"Come in," he called, turning from the rainy scene outside the window.

The door opened and his new butler, another of the number of house staff he just hired, entered. The butler, Roberts, was a tall, lanky man of about fifty. "Lord Cashelmore, a Mr. O'Rourke is here to see you."

Declan sighed inwardly with relief. Perfect. Gerald was just the person he needed to see, although he hadn't expected him to arrive so soon. Declan had left Dublin so abruptly and he sent only a terse note informing Gerald that he was going to London. "Please send him in, Roberts."

"Very good, sir." The door closed as the butler hurried off to retrieve Declan's guest.

Declan moved to the sideboard where there was a decanter of Irish whiskey. If he knew anything at all about his cousin, Declan knew that Gerald would expect a drink when he arrived. He lifted the lid of the crystal decanter and poured a shot of the amber liquid into a glass. He turned as the door opened.

"So you found me," Declan said by way of greeting.

"Yes, and the weather is as depressing here as it is back home," Gerald O'Rourke announced as he entered the study.

Declan smiled at his cousin, noting with surprise that Gerald had more gray in his hair since the last time he'd seen him. The man was far too young to be so gray, but then his only cousin had always looked older than his years. "It's good to see you, Gerald." He handed him the glass of whiskey.

Gerald's florid face smiled broadly, accepting the

drink. "You're a good man, Declan." He downed the whiskey in one neat gulp and placed the empty glass on the table. He glanced around. "So, it's a nice place you've got yourself here."

"It'll do for now."

Declan had no idea how long he would stay in London or if he would move on to some other place. Perhaps he would never go back to Ireland. The very prospect of returning to his native land filled him with an unbearable sadness.

"How is Mara these days?"

"She's fine," Declan murmured. He hated having to admit that his daughter had still not recovered.

"Is she . . . is she talking yet?" Gerald's eyes flickered as he glanced at Declan.

Declan shook his head regretfully. "No, not yet."

He wished he could have said yes. What a joy that would be! To have his beautiful daughter speaking again. To hear the sweet sound of her voice in his ears. He dreamed of it. When he wasn't having nightmares about her mother.

Gerald shrugged carelessly. "Oh, I'm sure she'll start talking one of these days. It was a lot for a little girl to go through."

"It's been almost a year," Declan muttered.

Almost a year ago his wife burned to death in front of their daughter's eyes, screaming for her. Almost a year since Mara had uttered a single word. "Papa." It was all she would say for hours after the horrific scene. Then a blank expression shuttered her childish features and she said no more. Declan had tried everything he could think of to reach her. The finest doctors, the best care. But it seemed Mara only retreated further into her own little world, not venturing forth into the real one. Not uttering a sound.

"Still, children are funny creatures." Gerald gave a half smile. "Mark my words, one day she'll just surprise you and ask for a biscuit or something equally inconsequential."

Declan said nothing, but in his heart he hoped for nothing else. "How are things back home?" The heaviness in his chest began to tighten.

A shadow crossed Gerald's round face. "Not good. You left so unexpectedly, without word to anyone. By the time I got your note you were already gone, Declan." He paused. "They think you ran away to escape the consequences."

Declan sighed heavily. "Well, they are partly true anyway." He had run away, but not for the reason everyone assumed.

His mouth forming a grim line, Gerald continued, "It's gotten worse since you left."

"How could it possibly be worse?" Declan scoffed.

Since Margaret died, Declan had watched in muted shock as the comforting words and sympathies on the death of his wife transformed into something else entirely. He'd endured months of dubious glances, cold shoulders, suspicious murmurings, whispers behind his back, blatant accusations, and outright blame. That was the reason he had left. He had had to protect Mara. She didn't need to hear any of that ugliness. Especially from her own family.

Declan stood and went to the sideboard. Pouring himself a glass of Irish whiskey, he stared at the amber liquid as it floated in the crystal. With a quick motion of his wrist, the whiskey swirled in the glass faster and faster. He stilled his hand, watching the liquid spin wildly then slowly wind down. Not wanting to drink it after all, he set the glass down and turned back to face Gerald and what he had to say.

"Some say that you are planning to marry again," Gerald continued. "That's why you came to London."

Declan laughed with derision. "I can assure you that marriage is the last thing I'm seeking out at the moment!"

"Having a new mother might be good for Mara," Gerald suggested with a shrug of his shoulders.

"I don't think so. I will never marry again. In case you hadn't noticed, my first marriage did not end all that well." Declan could not hide the bitterness in his voice. He was not cut out for marriage, as his disastrous union with Margaret proved beyond a shadow of a doubt. He never wanted the responsibility of a wife again, even if there was a woman out there who was not terrified of the idea of wedding him. For after all of the rumors about him, who would want to marry him anyway? Marriage had been nothing short of a disaster for him and Declan took the blame for all of it. But he had no interest in marrying ever again.

"I understand that. But it's more than rumors and innuendo now, Declan. It's far more serious than the gossips' tongues wagging behind their fans." Gerald paused. He gave Declan a pointed look. "There are some who are demanding an inquest."

The heaviness in his chest grew even weightier. Declan had half expected this news, but never quite believed it would actually happen.

"How can they still think I had anything to do with Margaret's death?"

Gerald hesitated, running his hand across his round face, before answering. "It doesn't look good, Declan, what happened that night."

"Do you think I'm responsible?" Declan demanded, anger and frustration coursing through his veins. "Do you honestly think I killed my wife? That I deliberately set the fire that night?"

"No! No!" Gerald put his hands up. "Of course not! Heavens, no! I'd never think such a thing about you, Declan. You know that. I'm your cousin, your best friend. I'm on your side. Alice and I will always stand by you. I'm just telling you what they're saying in Dublin. I came to warn you."

"Warn me?" Declan asked of his cousin. Gerald was his only living relative and had been his trusted friend and advisor since he was a boy. If Gerald had come to London to warn him, Declan knew it was serious.

"Well, yes. As I said, it doesn't look good. Taking Mara to London with you didn't help matters. It only inflamed their suspicions. I think they may call you in. They're building a case against you. You never did have an alibi that night."

"Jesus, Gerald! You know why I brought Mara to London! And you of all people know where I was when the fire started!" Declan would never forget a single detail of that horrendous night for as long as he lived.

"I know that, yes. But no one else believes you." Gerald gave another helpless shrug. "And they certainly don't believe the likes of me."

"The Ryans need someone to blame and they are going to blame me no matter what the truth is, because they don't care about the truth. They've never cared for me, never wanted Margaret to marry me in the first place. Now they just want to blame Margaret's death on my head and be rid of me. They only want to take Mara from me."

"You may be right." Again Gerald hesitated. "Maybe London isn't far enough away."

"What are you suggesting? That I flee to America?" Declan scorned the idea of hiding.

Gerald gave him a helpless look. "Would you prefer to spend the rest of your life in the gaol?"

"It's not going to come to that. I'm innocent." Declan shook his head defiantly. He would not go to prison for murdering his wife. It was impossible. Unthinkable. "And I will not skulk away in shame as if I've committed a crime when I haven't," he declared.

"It's your neck," Gerald offered. "I just thought you should know that the situation has become more serious and it might be wise to take your leave while you still have the opportunity."

"They can say I'm guilty, but that does not mean that I am. Besides, they have no proof of anything. Jesus, Gerald, I'm only twenty-five years old! I refuse to give up my inheritance, my title, and my home to take the blame for something I had no part in."

Gerald grew quiet, his graying brows furrowed. "Then come home and face them. You're not proving your innocence by hiding here in London."

"I'm not hiding! I'm here because of my daughter. And Margaret's family knows this. They're angry I took Mara away from them, which is another reason they are lashing out at me while I'm not there to defend myself. If the Ryans had any proof at all they would have had me arrested already."

"So you're staying here in London then?" Gerald asked.

Declan nodded. "For the time being, yes."

"Any idea how long that might be?"

Declan released a very long sigh. "As long as it takes."

Chapter 4

Attraction

Paulette pulled up the shade that covered the door to Hamilton's Book Shoppe, turned the "Closed" sign to read "Open," and smiled as the morning sun greeted her. Finally! A bit of good weather after the rainy spell they'd had the last few days! She glanced around the tidy shop, pleased with its attractive and inviting appearance. She and Colette had worked tirelessly to make the shop a success and her pride in her family's business filled her with joy.

She could barely recall the cramped, dusty, and disorganized place it had been when their father had been alive and handled everything, before she and Colette had transformed the shop. But she distinctly remembered being a very little girl and her father lifting her up to the top of the ladder so she could reach a book for him. Paulette had loved being up that high. She had loved the smell of the books. A beautiful mix of leather, paper, and ink. And when her father had allowed her to assist him, she adored helping customers choose the perfect book.

Running her hand along the glass-covered counter,

she savored this early morning quiet when she first opened the store and she was the only one there. The shop truly belonged to her then and it was her favorite time of the day. She reveled in being the first one up and out of the house and busy at the shop. It made her feel as if she were ahead of everyone else.

The bell over the door jingled merrily. "Good morning, Miss Paulette!"

She smiled at the red-haired young man who entered the shop. "Good morning, Tom. How are you today?"

"I'm just fine on this gorgeous morning." His freckled face grinned broadly and he placed a cloth-lined basket on the counter. "My mother sent these over to you."

"Oh, I can smell them from here!" Paulette squealed with delight. Mrs. Alcott made the most heavenly short-bread biscuits and she knew they were Paulette's favorite. Tom Alcott and his mother had lived in the rooms above the bookshop for the last few years and had been the caretakers of sorts.

Her older sister, Lisette Hamilton Roxbury, had helped to save Tom and his mother from the slums of St. Giles and had given them work and lodging at Hamilton's Book Shoppe. It had been a perfect arrangement all around. Although about six months ago, Mrs. Alcott and Tom finally moved to one of the houses that Quinton Roxbury had designed. Paulette had not yet found anyone to take the Alcotts' place and the living quarters upstairs, where the Hamilton sisters had been born and raised, were still unused.

"Please thank your mother for me," Paulette said, reaching beneath the red-checkered cloth and retrieving a shortbread biscuit. She couldn't wait to have one.

"She knows how much you like them."

"Thank her for me, please." Paulette grinned. "I miss having you both here."

"We miss it too, but we love the new house. And with Mother getting married soon, the house is a better place for us."

Paulette nodded as she ate the cookie, delighting in the sweet buttery flavor. She was happy that Anna Alcott was finally getting remarried, after all the heartache she'd been through in her life. Jack Harris, a grocer, was a fine man and would take care of her and her son. Thirteen-year-old Tom still helped out in the bookshop when he wasn't in school.

"Do you have anything for me to do today?" Tom asked.

Wiping the crumbs from her lips, Paulette nodded. "Yes, if you could just take that package over there to the printer I would appreciate it." She pointed to the shelf near the door.

"That's it?"

"For now, yes. Get going to school or you'll be late." She smiled at him. Tom was a good boy and she didn't want him to miss a minute of his education.

"Thank you, Miss Paulette." He flashed her one of his broad grins, grabbed the package wrapped in brown paper, and moved to the door. "I'll drop this off on my way to school."

"Thank you, Tom. And good-bye."

Alone in the shop once more, Paulette stepped behind the counter and sat upon one of the high stools. Her assistant, Lizzie Parker, wouldn't arrive for another hour. She took another cookie from the basket. Taking a bite, she opened the thick accounts ledger, bound in red leather, and glanced at the long columns of figures.

Hamilton's Book Shoppe was doing very well and she was certain the new shop would do even better. With quick efficiency she added up each column, her numbers neatly arranged in her precise handwriting. Without thinking she grabbed another cookie from the basket and popped it into her mouth. Heavenly. She had to stop herself or she would eat the entire basket!

The bells above the door jingled and she glanced over to see who entered the shop. Her heart did a little flutter at the sight of Declan Reeves. His tall form blocked the sunlight and for the briefest moment outlined him in silhouette. Paulette had trouble swallowing the last of the shortbread.

"Good morning."

His lyrical voice sent a shiver through her. Unable to speak, she nodded her head and managed a weak smile in greeting. The cookie suddenly felt like sawdust in her mouth. She forced herself to choke it down.

"It's nice to see the sun again. Don't you agree, Miss Hamilton?"

"Why, yes." How her lips formed the words, she had no idea. Her heart was beating ridiculously fast. For lack of anything else to say, she offered, "It's quite early yet."

He responded, "I prefer to start my days early."

"So do I."

An awkward silence ensued as they stood there, staring at each other. The usual bookseller patter that always came to her so naturally abandoned her in his presence.

Declan Reeves was much handsomer than she remembered. Younger looking, too. Perhaps it was the morning light. He seemed less foreboding and for some reason that made her even more nervous. Why was he back in the shop so soon? Was it only two days ago that he had been in the bookshop with his daughter? His daughter! Now she had something to talk about!

"Where is your little girl?" she asked, surprised by the

normal tone of her voice. She wished she had a cool glass of water.

"She's at home with her nurse."

The lyrical sound of his Irish accent made Paulette's pulse quicken. "Did she enjoy the book of fairy tales I selected for her?"

"Yes, thank you very much. Mara loves it. I've read it to her at least a hundred times before bed the past two nights."

The image of this man reading a story to his little girl made her heart flip over in her chest.

"I'm so glad," she murmured. "Are you looking for another book for her?"

"Perhaps." His emerald green eyes settled on her. "But I was also looking for myself."

"Oh?"

"Yes."

She tried to swallow but her mouth was too dry. "And what is it you would like?"

His eyes widened the slightest bit, but he didn't answer.

"Would you care to browse?" she suggested weakly.

His intense glance lingered on her longer than anyone would deem proper. Her cheeks grew warm and a funny feeling filled her chest.

"Would you mind if I did?" Mr. Reeves questioned, one of his dark eyebrows raised.

"Not at all. Feel free to wander about the store." She waved her hand in an attempt to appear casual and light-hearted. "If you decide you need my assistance, please let me know."

"I promise I will, Miss Hamilton."

Paulette surreptitiously watched him turn and make his way down one of the rows of tall shelves lined neatly with books of all sorts. He was in the philosophy section. Interesting, she thought.

He was very tall, she noted, almost as tall as the highest shelves. And he walked with definite purpose, with his hands clasped behind his back. It was strange. He had the mannerisms of a much older man, yet he was quite young. Close to her own age perhaps. She was dying to ask him how old he was, but knew it was impolite. He disappeared around the corner shelf at the end of the row and she lost sight of him.

Rousing herself, she wondered at her nervousness. The man had flustered her and she did not know why that should be so. In an effort to calm herself, she reached for the water pitcher and filled a cup with the cool liquid. She downed the water quickly.

Once again the bell jingled and the shop door opened. A trim young woman with a bright yellow bonnet covering her black hair entered. "Good morning, Paulette."

"Hello, Lizzie." Grateful that her assistant had arrived and she was no longer alone with the enigmatic Mr. Reeves in the shop, Paulette smiled. "You're early this morning."

Lizzie Parker and her brother Daniel had been assisting in the bookshop for the last few years, but recently Paulette had trained Lizzie to manage it completely, to take her place when the new shop opened. Paulette and Colette would need to spend most of their time in the new store.

"It's such a glorious morning, I got an early start. Oooh! I see Tom Alcott has been by already with his mother's shortbread!" Lizzie's face lit up in delight.

"Yes, please take the basket away from me before I devour all of them," Paulette said, suddenly unable to stomach the thought of another shortbread biscuit. It was strange that she lost her appetite the minute Declan Reeves had entered the shop.

"Oh, I'll take them from you gladly and have some with my tea!" Lizzie took the basket in her hand. "I shall bring them to the back room to fortify me as I sort through those crates of—" Lizzie suddenly eyed the tall form of Mr. Reeves meandering through the shop. He voice dropped to a whisper. "Who is that?"

Paulette couldn't help glancing in his general direction. "A gentleman from Ireland who was in two days ago with his daughter," she explained quietly as that flutter of nervousness rushed through her again at the thought of Declan Reeves. "He's browsing."

"So I can see." Lizzie's eyes narrowed. "Isn't it a bit early for customers?"

"We're open, aren't we?" Paulette countered, but her thoughts had been exactly the same as Lizzie's. Even though the shop opened early, most customers didn't usually come in until closer to noon. He had arrived rather early.

Lizzie shrugged, and with basket in hand, she walked toward the rear of the shop, calling, "You know where I'll be."

With Lizzie in the back room, Paulette felt comforted knowing she was no longer alone in the shop with the Irish gentleman. Glancing around, he was out of view again and she wondered what he was looking at now. She picked up the quill pen and dipped it in the ink and tried to resume her accounting. But she could not focus on the columns of numbers in the ledger as she ought to. Her thoughts kept drifting back to Declan Reeves. Where was he? She could not see him. Was he reading a book? It was too quiet in the shop. The minutes ticked by. She could no longer see or hear him.

What was he doing?

Perhaps he needed help selecting a book. Feeling braver than she had earlier, she decided to offer him her assistance. Taking a fortifying breath, Paulette made her way toward the row where she had last spied him. Walking with determination and purpose, she moved down the aisle.

Just as she rounded the corner, she stopped short. For there was Mr. Reeves. In order to prevent herself from slamming into the wall that was his body, she unthinkingly placed her hands upon his chest. Her fingers rested on the black buttons on the front of his black jacket and she could feel the beating of his heart beneath her hands. She was so close she could smell the clean scent of the soap he used. So close she could count the threads in the fabric of his jacket. Staring at his broad chest, she paused for a moment, filled with trepidation. Then she forced herself to look up at his face, tilting her head back to be able to see.

He was looking down at her, a bemused expression on his handsome face.

"Oh, pardon me!" she found herself babbling. "I just wondered if you needed my help."

Declan Reeves grinned at her then. She had not seen the man smile before and the beauty of it almost took her breath away. It dazzled her, confounded her, because it changed his face completely. He no longer seemed dark and brooding in the least. There was a youthful exuberance in his expression that captivated her. She stared at him in mute fascination for what seemed like a very long time. The green of his eyes was quite rich and clear, without even the tiniest flecks of gold to mar the pureness of the color. It was like peering at two perfect emeralds.

"Yes, I would like that." His melodic voice cut through her little reverie.

"You would like what?" she asked breathlessly, the question she asked him only a moment ago now forgotten. Her eyes still locked with his and her hands continued to rest familiarly on his chest. The warmth from his body surged through her palms, along her arms and into the whole of her being.

"Yes, I would like you to help me," he said.

"Of course." She did not move, did not dare to breathe. Her gaze held steady, the odd connection between them intensifying.

The charming grin left his face, replaced by an expression of distinct longing and Paulette suddenly understood they were not speaking of books but something else entirely. The man was alone and hurting, suffering in his soul. The pain was evident in the depths of his eyes, the anguish in his face.

Bowing his head toward her, he whispered low, "You'll help me then?"

The aching appeal in his voice asked for more than assistance in the bookshop and Paulette's heart skipped a beat. He needed her. Whatever he wanted, whatever he needed, at this moment she would give it to him. Without hesitation she answered, "Yes," knowing she had just agreed to something she could not name.

He moved his head closer to her, close enough to kiss her, close enough to feel his breath on her cheek.

Feeling slightly faint and her knees shaking beneath her skirt, she clutched the front of his jacket tightly with her fingers for support. He wouldn't really kiss her, would he? She stared at his full lips, which were perilously and deliciously close to her own.

Time seemed to stop, suspended around them, enveloping them in a special world all their own.

And then, with slow deliberateness, he leaned down and kissed her while his muscled arms encircled her shoulders and drew her against the length of his body.

His mouth, warm and soft, covered hers thoroughly, and Paulette melted at the supremely intimate contact. With female intuition surging within her, she leaned into his embrace, seeking more.

This man, this virtual stranger, whom she had met only met once before, was kissing her. Paulette had never kissed anyone before! Had never met anyone she wanted to kiss before. And now . . . well now, she was allowing a man she barely knew to kiss her!

It was heavenly. Being held by him. Being kissed by him.

She should have been surprised by it, appalled by it. Outraged, even. But oddly enough, Declan kissing her was not completely unexpected. On some level she had been thinking about kissing him since the moment she met him. That fact was the most shocking to her.

And now . . .

Now there was only intense sensation after sensation that rocked her to the core. The utterly male scent of him filled her head, leaving her slightly dizzy. The smoothness of his freshly shaven skin against her cheeks sent waves of heat through her veins. His strong arms wrapped around her so securely she felt nothing could ever harm her while in his embrace. And his mouth. Oh, God, his mouth . . .

Warm and soft and firm all at once, his lips moved over hers, gently at first then growing more insistent. More demanding. Her mouth opened, an unspoken invitation, and his heated tongue slipped inside. A slow, languid, yearning ache began to blossom within her, moving like warm honey through her entire body.

Not sure what was happening to her, Paulette truly

did not care. She knew only that she did not want this man to stop kissing her.

And he didn't stop.

Mouth against mouth, she felt she was devouring him while being devoured by him at the same time. It was blissful. That deep yearning continued to grow within her, a longing for him. For more. She wanted to melt into him.

Vaguely she was aware of the jingling of the bells above the shop door, but she wanted nothing to interrupt the magical sensations she felt while kissing Declan Reeves.

"Paulette!"

With utter gentleness and great reluctance, he released her. "Are you Paulette?" he asked so softly, his breath hot against her ear.

Was she Paulette? Heavens above! The man did not even know her given name! Her face turned scarlet, her cheeks burning. She could only nod.

"Someone is calling you, lass."

"It's my sister," she managed to murmur, cringing at the thought of Colette finding her this way.

"Then go to her." He gave her a warm smile.

Barely recovering from his smile, his kiss, she removed her hands from his chest. On trembling legs she turned around and made her way to front of the shop, stunned by what had just happened to her.

"Oh, there you are!" Colette said, as she glanced through the ledger on the counter. "You left the house before I could catch you this morning. I can only stay for a little while. Simon has a fever now. Phillip just recovered and now, of course, Simon comes down with the same illness! So let's go over these figures, while I'm here." She suddenly paused and gazed at her sister, her expression perplexed. "Whatever is the matter with you, Paulette?"

Unconsciously, Paulette's hand flew to her cheek and the skin was warm to the touch. Was it so obvious? Could her sister discern that she had just been kissing a complete stranger behind the bookshelves? Did it show on her face? Did she appear disheveled?

Paulette had no idea what had come over her to do such a thing! Certainly she had never behaved in such a scandalous manner before. How had she allowed that man to kiss her when he hadn't even known her name? And he had not even apologized for such an affront on her person, come to think of it.

"Nothing is the matter," she managed to squeak out, wondering how she could keep what had just happened to her a secret for long. Had the man who had kissed her senseless not been nearby she may have blurted out to her sister what she had just done. "Why do you ask?"

"You have a peculiar expression on your face. Almost as if you've seen—oh! Good morning, sir. Forgive me, I didn't realize we had a customer here already." Colette's brow furrowed as she watched Mr. Reeves walk from behind the bookshelf. Her eyes darted suspiciously to Paulette.

"Good morning, madam," Declan said, appearing surprisingly relaxed in his manner. "Miss Hamilton was helping me select a book for my daughter."

"Oh, I see," Colette murmured, but it was clear that she did not understand what had happened between the two of them.

Paulette barely found her voice to do the introductions. "Colette, this is Mr. Declan Reeves, from Ireland. Mr. Reeves, this is my sister, the Marchioness of Stancliff."

"It is a pleasure to meet you, Lady Stancliff. I'm afraid

I did not introduce myself properly to your sister. I am also the Earl of Cashelmore."

Once again, Colette's blue eyes flashed between the two of them.

Paulette held her breath. Could Colette know that they had just been kissing? She said a little prayer to herself that her sister could not. And since when was he *Lord Cashelmore*? Why had he not introduced himself as such when she met him two days ago? Instead he used plain Mr. Reeves. The man was a complete mystery!

"It is nice to meet you, Lord Cashelmore." Colette gave him a slight nod of her head in acknowledgment. "I trust my sister has been able to help you find what you are looking for?"

"Yes, she has." Mr. Reeves stared at the two of them, his gaze lingering on Paulette at his words. "And may I add that the two of you could never be mistaken for anything other than sisters? You both look astonishingly alike."

If Paulette had a pound for every time someone remarked on how much she and her sisters resembled each other, she would have a mountain of money in the bank. It never failed to amaze her how people marveled over their looks. Sisters were related, for heaven's sake. Of course they would look alike! When meeting someone who knew nothing about her family, she usually liked to watch their eyes widen when she mentioned the next bit of the Hamilton tree. But Paulette was still too overwhelmed to speak. So she let Colette take care of it.

"There are three more of us, Lord Cashelmore."

"Five?" His eyes widened in astonishment. "There are five of you? All girls?"

They both nodded, accustomed to this type of questioning about their family.

Paulette simply wished to stop the dizzy breathlessness that filled her. She gazed at Mr. Reeves as he stood before them. He really was quite handsome, although that rather dark and foreboding look had returned to his face. How was he able to change his countenance like that? Had she truly just allowed him to kiss her senseless only a few moments ago and now they stood here exchanging pleasantries with her sister?

"And do you all look this much alike?" he questioned.

"More or less," Colette said by way of hurried explanation with a wave of her hand.

He seemed intrigued. "And this is obviously your family's bookshop. Do you all work here together?"

"Yes, at one time or another." Colette seemed more intent on learning about the man in the shop than discussing her sisters. "I seem to recall hearing your name before, Lord Cashelmore, but I can't quite place it."

"I'm not sure where you would have heard about me," he said. "I've only just arrived from Ireland last week."

Colette gave him an appraising glance. "I understand you have a daughter?"

"Yes," Declan said. "She is four years old. Your sister met her the other day and helped me find a book for her. Do you have children, Lady Stancliff?"

Colette's face lit up and she beamed proudly. "Yes, I have two sons. Phillip is five and Simon is two and a half."

Paulette listened in amazement as Declan Reeves expertly steered the conversation away from himself, while he and Colette chatted about raising children. She had wanted her sister to continue to ask him questions because she was more than a little curious about the man who just kissed her and was now disappointed that the topic had changed to their children.

But she knew exactly why his name was familiar to her sister.

Paulette recalled quite well where Colette had heard Mr. Reeves's name mentioned before and wondered if her sister would remember. It was during supper at Devon House the night before last. After Paulette told them about their visit to the bookshop, Lucien recalled reading about him in the paper and recounted for them how Mr. Reeves was under suspicion for the death of his wife.

A different kind of shiver raced down her spine.

No wonder he deflected the conversation from himself. She continued to stare at him, wondering if it were possible that the man was guilty of murdering his wife. Even though he looked a bit roguish, Paulette could not reconcile the man who cared for his daughter so sweetly with a man who would commit murder. In her mind it didn't make sense.

But could she reconcile herself to the thought that she may very well have just kissed a murderer? Her heart pounded wildly as she stared at the handsome gentleman in front of her.

"Paulette?"

Startled by the sound of her name, Paulette blinked and looked at her sister. "Yes?"

Colette eyed her with some concern. "Paulette, Lord Cashelmore asked you a question."

Paulette looked back at Declan Reeves, feeling like a simpleton. What had he asked her? "I'm so sorry. Please forgive me. I was woolgathering, apparently, and I confess that I did not hear what you just said."

"I merely asked if you would help me select another book for Mara now?"

"Oh, yes, of course," she responded, thankful to have

something familiar to do. This she could handle. "We shall go to the children's section."

She felt Colette's eyes on her as she and the Irish gentleman walked away from the counter and was infinitely grateful that her sister was not capable of mind reading.

Chapter 5

Wondering

As he followed Miss Hamilton to the children's section of the bookshop, Declan knew she was more than a little flustered and he was the cause of her discomfort. The poor girl's cheeks were still pink and she had barely been able to follow the conversation he had just had with her sister.

And Lady Stancliff had apparently heard the rumors about what happened to his wife and his involvement in the sordid affair, but had been too polite to say anything in front of him. For that he was thankful. For some reason, he desperately did not want Miss Hamilton to know about the ugly rumors. He had come to London to escape the gossips and accusations and having to explain himself.

He had no wish to have to explain his past to someone as completely enchanting as Miss Hamilton.

Miss Hamilton. Paulette. Her name was Paulette. He liked thinking of her as Paulette. The name suited her.

Had he truly been so brazen as to kiss her passionately behind a bookshelf? What had possessed him to do such a thing with a woman he didn't even know? It had been the strangest and yet most romantic encounter he had ever had. As soon as Paulette put her hands on his chest, as soon as she touched him, he felt connected to her somehow. Being so close to her did something to him. A part of him that was frozen inside seemed to melt. He suddenly wanted to bare his soul to her and it terrified him. To keep himself from confiding in her, he kissed her instead. And then kissing her was all he could think about. Ah, what a grand kiss it had been though! She was sweet and eager. And had tasted faintly of shortbread, funnily enough.

But more importantly she had kissed him back. God, just recalling it made him want to kiss her again.

Yet guilt plucked at him, for he should not have taken such liberties with her.

When they reached the children's section with its colorful child-sized furniture, which he recalled from his last visit, she spun around and faced him. Her blue eyes sparkled in her delicate face, her sweet mouth a line of anguish.

"Mr. Reeves. I mean Lord Cashelmore . . . Oh, I don't even know how to address you now." There was a note of panic in her voice.

He placed a gentle hand on her shoulder in an attempt to calm her. "It doesn't matter. Call me whatever you wish, Miss Hamilton."

She stared at his hand on her shoulder. With a nod of her head, she gently placed her hand over his.

The moment her hand, so soft and small, touched his, Declan could not breathe. Surprised by the intensity of their contact, he slowly pulled his hand away. "Call me Declan if you like."

Her eyes met his and she whispered, "You mustn't kiss me like that again, Declan."

"Mustn't I, Miss Hamilton?"

"No."

He grinned. "Now you see, if you had said, 'You must not kiss me again, Lord Cashelmore.' Or even, 'You must not kiss me again, Mr. Reeves,' I might be more inclined to believe that you did not wish for me to kiss you in the future. But you just called me by the more familiar, Declan, which leads to me to assume quite naturally that you would wish for me to kiss you again at another more convenient time perhaps."

Paulette smiled at him and that pleased him, for he knew then that he'd read her correctly.

"Ah, there you are incorrect, sir. I only used your given name because having already . . . kissed . . . it seemed rather foolish to refer to you so formally. It does not imply that I wish for another encounter as such nor that I grant you leave to do so again."

"In that case, however," he countered in triumph, "I would then have leave to call you Paulette."

She hesitated for the slightest instant before agreeing. "But of course."

"And if I were to kiss you again, you would protest?" He raised an eyebrow, waiting for her response.

"I . . . Well, I . . . You . . ." Her face turned red as she grew adorably flustered.

They both knew that if he kissed her again she would not protest and she couldn't pretend otherwise. An incredible sense of triumph raced through him as he used her given name to drive his point home. "Yes, I can see that, Paulette."

She opened her mouth to speak but stopped herself. A long moment passed before her demeanor changed and she suddenly changed into the efficient little shopkeeper. "Well, I believe I know the perfect book for your daughter."

Declan watched in fascination as Paulette Hamilton moved gracefully to a small corner shelf of the children's section and selected a thin volume bound in dark green and brought it back to him. He took the book from her and read the title, *Mother Goose's Melodies*. Flipping the pages, he saw that it was beautifully illustrated in color. He smiled at her in admiration. "Mara will love this."

She placed her hands on her hips and stated, "Now, for your needs."

Her words sent an unexpected thrill through him. Her shopkeeper questions always seemed to him to have a double meaning that escaped her. "I beg your pardon?"

"Don't you want a book as well?"

"A book. Oh, yes. Of course."

She eyed him critically, her gaze raking him up and down. Without a word she walked away from him and toward the larger bookshelves in the main area of the shop. Was she going to choose a book for him without asking him what he liked? This he had to see. He followed behind her, admiring the way the finely made, pale blue and white striped summer gown clung to her petite frame.

Paulette seemed extremely skilled at her job for one so young. She could only be twenty. Not much younger than himself after all. Still, there was a maturity about her that he found lacking in so many girls her age. She managed the bookshop quite well. He'd never seen a shop like it and as he glanced around, it suddenly occurred to him why.

The arrangement of not only the shelves, but the books themselves, lent an airy and open feel to the space that was unheard of in other stores. No shelf was full.

He usually felt a bit claustrophobic in most bookshops he'd visited. The shelves crammed with books, and stacks of books everywhere, were overwhelming and difficult to sort through or find anything. But not here. The attractive orderliness of Hamilton's was remarkable. The shop was warm and inviting overall, with comfortable seating areas and eye-catching book displays.

He was quite impressed with Hamilton's Book Shoppe. And Paulette most of all.

He should apologize for kissing her. But she did not seem angry or put out with him. In truth, he was not sorry he kissed her. Not at all. In fact, he wanted to kiss her again, but Paulette Hamilton was not someone to trifle with, and he was in no position to become involved with a girl like her. He knew better than to kiss her. He still didn't know what had come over him.

Paulette faced him with a look of triumph in her eyes. "Here. This is for you."

He took the book from her hands and stared at her face. "Do you know every book in this store?"

She gave a nod of her head. "Most of them."

"Have you read all of them?" he questioned her.

"Most of them," she repeated, holding his gaze. A smile played at the corner of her lips.

He glanced down at the book in his hand and read the title. *The Law and the Lady*. "What's this?"

"It's a novel I think you might find rather interesting."

"Have you read it?"

"How would I know that you might find it interesting if I hadn't?'

Flashing her a grin, he smiled. "Just checking."

"Is there anything else I can do for you?"

Once again, her little shopkeeper phrases begged to be answered in another way. He stopped himself from saying what he really wanted her to do for him, for his mind was spinning with possibilities that he dared not mention to her. "No, I think that will be all, Paulette."

"Miss Hamilton," she corrected him.

He shook his head. "In the presence of others I shall call you Miss Hamilton. However, when we are alone I shall call you Paulette."

"Alone?" she asked, her voice a little breathless. "When would we ever be alone together, Mr. Reeves?"

"That remains to be seen, Paulette. And it's Declan in private."

"I see," she said, when she obviously didn't, and turned to walk to the front of the shop.

He followed behind her to the counter where her sister still stood, eyeing them with interest. Although she had darker hair, Colette Sinclair looked so much like Paulette it was a little unnerving.

"I'd like to buy these two," he said, giving the books to her and paying for his purchase. "Your sister was most helpful, Lady Stancliff."

"I'm so pleased you are happy with Paulette's selection," Colette said as she expertly wrapped the books in brown paper and tied them with green ribbon. "She is very good at knowing what people will like."

He glanced at Paulette, who stood quietly beside her sister. With his eyes on hers, he added, "Yes, she certainly is. I'm sure I shall be returning for more books."

"Thank you, Lord Cashelmore," Paulette said. "Please come again."

Declan smiled at both sisters, tipping his hat to them, and, taking his prettily wrapped package of books in his hands, he left Hamilton's Book Shoppe feeling quite a bit happier than he had before he entered.

Chapter 6

Confidences

"What was all that about?" Colette turned on her as soon as Declan Reeves left the shop.

"What do you mean?" Paulette attempted to remain calm and failed utterly.

"Oh, for heaven's sake, Paulette! I've got eyes, haven't I? What was going on between you and Lord Cashelmore?"

Paulette had never been very good at keeping secrets and she certainly couldn't keep this one to herself another moment. "Oh, Colette, he kissed me!"

"He did what?!"

The shock on her older sister's face, the sister who acted as a mother to her for most of her life, left Paulette feeling more embarrassed than she had ever felt about anything. She admired and looked up to Colette. The thought that she might have done something to disappoint or scandalize her was very sobering.

"He . . . I . . . Well, we kissed each other."

Colette's mouth opened but no sound came out.

Paulette began to babble. "I don't know how it

happened really. One minute he was looking for books and I went to help him. We almost bumped into each other and I put my hands out to stop myself from slamming into him and then we exchanged a few words and the next thing I knew he was kissing me and I was kissing him back and then you came into the shop and called my name . . ."

Her sister stared at her in astonishment. "But you just met him. He's a complete stranger!"

"Yes, I know, but I've met his daughter already and he's been here twice now so he doesn't seem so much like a stranger and now you know him too so he's not entirely unfamiliar—"

"Oh, hello, Colette," Lizzie Parker called as she ventured from where she had been working in the back room, completely unaware of the little drama that had unfolded while she had been taking inventory. "We're missing a set of books that we ordered from Blackwell's. I'm going to stop by their office now and while I'm there I'll see that they send the correct order to the new shop." She paused and looked between Paulette and Colette. "Am I interrupting something?"

Paulette answered first, grateful for her assistant's timely intrusion. She had almost forgotten that the girl was there, so caught up was she in all that had happened with Declan Reeves. "Not at all, Lizzie. Thank you for taking care of that order. I'm sure it's just an oversight on Blackwell's part."

Lizzie nodded. "Yes, that's what I thought as well."

"Thank you, Lizzie," Colette added.

"I shall be back before lunch." And with that, Lizzie Parker left the shop, leaving Colette and Paulette alone.

Colette wasted no time. "What are you thinking? The man is a complete and total stranger!"

"I can't explain it, but it felt like we knew each other.

I know he's a stranger, but he didn't feel like a stranger when he was kissing me!" Paulette cried, the pitch of her voice increasing.

"That is exactly my point!" Colette exclaimed in frustration. "How can you be kissing a man you don't even know?"

Paulette did something she didn't normally do. She burst into tears.

Colette's manner changed from one of outrage to one of concern. "I'm not angry with you, Paulette. I'm angry with that man for taking advantage of you. Don't cry." She patted Paulette's shoulder in comfort. "I'm not angry with you."

"Yes, you are." Paulette reached into the pocket of her dress and took out a handkerchief and began wiping her eyes. Goodness! How had the day taken such a dramatic turn, and it wasn't even noon yet! She had been at the shop early, ready for a busy day, happy with her little basket of shortbread cookies. And then *he* had come in. He kissed her and she kissed him back. It was heavenly. It was madness. It sounded ridiculous even to her. Somehow everything had changed and now she was crying like a silly fool.

"I'm not angry. I'm just very concerned about you." Colette sighed in resignation. "This behavior is so unlike you and something about that man worries me and I can't place my finger on what it is."

"Lucien mentioned him during supper the other night," Paulette confessed with a sniffle. "Declan Reeves is suspected of murdering his wife in Ireland."

"Oh, dear God in heaven!" Colette gasped, placing her hand over her heart. "That's where I've heard his name before! Oh, Paulette, you must stay away from him!"

The bell over the shop door rang and two customers

entered the store. Two young gentlemen, obviously university students, stood before them.

"Welcome to Hamilton's!" Colette called brightly through clenched teeth. "How can we help you today?"

Paulette quickly turned her back and tried to compose herself, taking a deep breath and dabbing her eyes with a handkerchief.

The taller of the two men answered, "We need a book for our history class. Here is the title." He handed a piece of paper with handwriting on it to Colette.

"Oh, yes. I believe we have that textbook in the history section, just over there. Do you see the sign?" Colette pointed out to them the placard hanging from green ribbon with the word "History" elegantly painted in black. "Look on the third shelf and I shall be right with you."

The two students walked away and Colette hissed at her, "You must stay away from that man, Paulette. He might be very dangerous."

"I was not planning to see him again," Paulette responded, sounding somewhat defensive.

"Good! We'll discuss this at home later. Don't forget that Lisette is joining us at Devon House this evening."

Colette moved around the counter, on her way to help the two students, when the door opened and an elderly lady entered the shop. The quiet of the morning ended and Paulette gratefully lost herself in the usual business of selling books. They were so busy for a good portion of the day that she pushed the tempting thoughts of Declan Reeves, the Earl of Cashelmore, and his kisses to the back of her mind and occupied herself with the needs of the bookshop. They did brisk business that day and Paulette was thankful that Lizzie returned to help when Colette left early to take care of her son.

When Lizzie finally departed at the end of the day,

Paulette was left to close up the shop. Alone once more, the events of the morning and her kiss with Declan all came back to her. Certain a discussion with Colette awaited her at Devon House, Paulette was in no hurry to go home even though Lisette was visiting. As the long, lazy rays of the sun sunk low in the August sky, the shop was shrouded in stillness and Paulette soaked up the silence.

She sat on one of the two high stools behind the front counter and stared at the ledger in front of her that accounted for the day's sales in her neat handwriting. Long columns of numbers swam before her eyes. She usually tallied them up with a skill and efficiency that surprised most people. Now, however, Paulette couldn't add together two plus two. Just as she had that morning, she simply could not focus on the figures.

Her mind could only think of Declan Reeves and how it felt to be kissed by him.

The novelty of her first kiss filled her with wonder. She had definitely enjoyed the experience and would not mind kissing him again. But was it kissing Declan specifically or would it be the same kissing some other man? She had never had a beau or anyone call on her before. Not that men weren't attracted to her. To the contrary, there had been a few gentlemen who expressed their interest in calling on her to Lucien, but Paulette had refused them. So she had to assume it was only Declan she'd wanted to kiss.

He said he would return to the shop. As she recalled his remark her heart fluttered. He intended to see her alone and call her by her name. And part of her was thrilled by that knowledge.

The other part of her was terrified. Absolutely terrified. What did she really know about Declan Reeves? He was a widower. He was from Ireland and a member of the aristocracy, although that hardly mattered to her. Seemingly, he was a caring father who read to his young daughter. He liked books. Oh, and the man was quite skilled at kissing.

And he may have murdered his wife.

Paulette had always believed herself to be an expert judge of character. She knew Lucien Sinclair was a good man as soon as she met him, and she had been right about that. She had always distrusted her Uncle Randall and had been proven correct on that account time and again. Instinctively she felt that Declan Reeves was not a murderer. Perhaps there had been some sort of accident and he was inadvertently responsible. He could not have killed a woman on purpose. Knowingly. She was sure of that.

At least she hoped she was.

A gentle tapping on the shop door caught her attention. Glancing at the door she saw that she had flipped the sign to "Closed" but had not drawn the shade. As if she had conjured him up by her thoughts alone, standing outside the door was Declan Reeves.

Suddenly Paulette's legs were shaking so much she could barely stand. She stumbled to the door to let him in, feeling dizzy with giddiness at his sudden appearance.

"Hello," she said as she stepped back to allow him to enter.

"Hello, Paulette," he said, and her heart raced at the sound of her name on his lips. They were most definitely alone in the shop. "These are for you."

He handed her a small bouquet of lily of the valley.

"Oh my!" She accepted the flowers with a delighted squeal, breathing in their sweet scent. "They are my favorite. Thank you!"

"I thought I should bring you something by way of an apology for kissing you."

"Oh." She moved behind the counter again, feeling much safer behind it.

There was a moment of awkward silence.

"After I left this morning I got to thinking that it really was not well done of me," he said, shaking his head. "Kissing you like that . . . Well, it is not something I usually do."

"Nor I," Paulette said softly, placing the fragrant bouquet into a jar of water.

"Of course, I didn't mean to insinuate that you did," he began. He sighed heavily. "I just thought I ought to tell you that I apologize for my behavior."

"Thank you. I accept your apology."

He made a move toward the door. "Well, then, I wish you a good—"

"Did Mara like the book of nursery rhymes?" Paulette asked hurriedly before he had a chance to leave.

Declan paused, then stepped back. "Yes, she did. Thank you for selecting it. She hasn't put it down. She's fascinated by the pictures."

"Mara seems like a sweet girl." Paulette slowly sat on the high stool.

"Ah, that she is."

"How long has it been since she's spoken?" Paulette found herself asking.

A dark shadow passed across his features. "It's almost been a year. A very long year."

"She misses her mother very much, doesn't she?"

"Yes."

Never one to hide what she was thinking, Paulette decided since they were on the subject, she would ask him straight out. "How did your wife die?"

"There was a terrible fire."

Now was the time. She held her breath and asked him the question that had haunted her all day long. "Is it as the rumors say? Did you cause her death?"

A faint smile played at the corners of his mouth and his eyes glittered. With careful steps he came around to her side of the counter. His tall form loomed over her. "I have the oddest feeling you would be disappointed if I said no, Paulette."

"I beg your pardon?" Her voice squeaked a little in spite of herself.

"Do you find it exciting to think you were kissed by a murderer?"

"Heavens no!" she gasped, panic racing through her. "How can you ask such a question?"

"Well, what do you think, Paulette?" His voice dropped to a harsh whisper. "You have obviously read the accusations in the papers that people are casting upon me. Do you think I killed my wife?"

Her heart hammering, Paulette did not pause in the slightest in answering him. "No, I don't believe you could do such a terrible thing."

Declan seemed a bit surprised. And then very relieved. He moved to sit on one of the stools beside her. "Thank you for that."

"You still didn't answer the question though," she pointed out. Her nerves tingled at his nearness to her.

His eyes met hers with a steady gaze. "No, Paulette. I did not kill my wife nor did I have anything to do with her death. Although there are people who would dearly love to believe otherwise."

The honesty in his voice and the sincerity in his eyes confirmed what she had felt in her heart. Declan had not killed his wife. Paulette felt more than a little relieved by his response, too.

"But why?" she questioned him. "Why do people blame you for her death, Declan?"

"Because sometimes it's easier to blame a person for something that has happened than to accept the reality."

"Which is . . ." she prompted him to continue.

His mouth set in a grim line. "A very long story for another time perhaps."

Paulette sat silent for a moment. "Thank you for telling me as much as you did. My questions were a bit presumptuous."

"No, your questions were honest and I appreciate that. Most people don't have the nerve to ask me to my face. They'd rather whisper and spread rumors behind my back."

"That must be a dreadful feeling."

"It is."

"Is that why you left Ireland?"

"Yes, partly. And I also wanted Mara to see some doctors here in London."

Paulette thought of the little blond-haired girl with her father's eyes. "I hope the doctors can help her."

"Thank you. I do, too."

"Where in Ireland are you from?"

"Dublin."

"Is it very different from London?"

"Not very. In some ways they are very much alike. Then again, most large cities are the same."

"I wouldn't know. I've never been anywhere except here," Paulette said with a sigh.

"All large cities seem to be the same. Crowded, noisy, and dirty."

Paulette laughed at his remark. "I've heard people say that. How long are you planning to stay in London?"

"I'm not sure yet. Now it's my turn," Declan said, with a grin.

"Your turn for what?"

"My turn to ask you questions."

Paulette smiled. "Oh, I guess that's only fair."

He placed his hand under his chin, resting his elbow on the counter. "Why aren't you married, Paulette? A beautiful girl like you?"

Surprised by his question, she was also caught off guard by his compliment. "I haven't met anyone I want to marry."

"Why is that, do you think?"

"I honestly don't know."

"But you're happy here, working in the bookshop with your sisters?"

"Yes, very much so."

"How old are you?"

"I'll be twenty-one next month. How old are you?" she asked.

Declan shook his head. "Oh, no. My turn is not over. No questions from you yet. But if you must know, I'm five and twenty."

"Oh." He was much closer to her in age than she had originally thought. "You must have married very young! Why, Mara is four years old, isn't she?"

"Paulette?"

"Yes?"

"You're interrupting my turn."

"I'm sorry. I promise I won't interrupt again. Please continue."

"Thank you." He paused a moment before asking, "Why did you let me kiss you this morning?"

Why *had* she let him kiss you? She'd been asking herself that same question all day and had only been able to come up with one response.

"Because I couldn't help it. I'd never been kissed before and I—"

"Do you mean to tell me that no man has kissed you before me?" Declan was clearly astonished. "Before today?"

"No." Flooded with embarrassment, Paulette felt her cheeks grow warm. Why did speaking about kissing her seem more mortifying than his actually kissing her? She had no idea, but she liked sitting here with him, talking. He was surprisingly easy to converse with.

"Well, thank you, Paulette. That was an honor I didn't know I had. Now I feel even more regretful over kissing you though."

"Oh, don't regret it!" she cried out. "I thought our kiss was wonderful! Didn't you?"

"You're a funny little thing, aren't you?" He looked amused by her. "Do you always say exactly what you're thinking?"

"Not deliberately." She paused, feeling slightly panicked. "Didn't you think it was wonderful? Kissing me?"

"Yes, I did," Declan admitted, his emerald eyes glittering as he looked at her. "Perhaps too much."

"Why too much?"

He laughed. "You're asking the questions again, lass."

"Well, I can't help it," she said, waving her hands in exasperation. "When is it my turn again?"

"When you've answered my questions."

"Aren't you done yet?"

He chuckled. "You can't help yourself, can you?"

"No. I'm sorry. Please continue."

"Thank you. Now I forgot what I was going to ask you."

"Was it about kissing me?"

"Ah, yes . . . Our kiss today. Let's go back to that. You liked it, did you?"

"Yes, I did. It was magical."

"Yes, it was, lass." His eyes glittered as he paused for a

moment. Then he leaned closer to her. "Are you afraid of me, Paulette?"

"Yes, maybe a little," she admitted, adding hastily, "but not because people say that you're a murderer."

"Then why are you afraid of me?"

"Because I let you kiss me. And I have never let anyone do that before. That's what scares me."

He nodded. "I think I understand that."

"So what happens now?" Paulette could not help but ask. She liked talking to him and watching the expressions on his face and hearing the soft Irish brogue on his lips.

"What do you mean?"

Feeling a bit self-conscious she asked, "What happens with us now? Are you my suitor now? Are you going to call on me? I'm not sure how all this is supposed to work."

He chuckled again and gave her a funny look. "I don't know. I hadn't thought that far ahead, to tell you the truth, Paulette." He paused as if in deep thought. "I didn't come to London seeking a romance or a new wife, if that's what you're thinking. I should tell you straight out that I'm not interested in ever getting married again. My first marriage did not end well, and I don't believe I made a particularly good husband. That being said, I have no idea what I'm doing here with you, kissing you and bringing you flowers. It gives the impression that I am courting you when I barely know who you are."

Paulette fought an impulse to reach out and touch his cheek, which was shadowed in stubble now. Did she want him to be her beau? Since she had never had one, she didn't know what that would be like. A part of her wished crazily that he would say yes, he wanted to call on her, yet the other half of her was terrified by the very idea. Instead, she merely said, "I barely know you either. Yet here we are."

"Yes," he whispered, "here we are."

Yes, there they were, alone in the closed bookshop.

"We could be friends," she suggested.

"I don't know anyone in London and knowing what the papers are saying about me I doubt anyone would be my friend. It would be good to have you as a friend, Paulette."

She smiled brightly, loving the sound of his accented voice. "I would like that, too."

He reached out and covered her hand with his as it rested on the counter.

Paulette held her breath, enjoying the warmth of his skin touching hers. They were silent for a few moments. With her heart pounding, she glanced over at him, but he was staring at her hand in his. Slowly he raised her hand to his lips, placing a gentle kiss on top of her fingers.

Shivers of delight spread through her and Paulette grew dizzy with sensation.

He said in a low voice, "I should be going home now. It's getting late."

She nodded in agreement, although reluctantly.

Still holding her hand, he asked, "May I escort you home, Paulette?"

Paulette had more than a few tasks still to complete in the bookshop before she should leave for the night, but she ignored them completely.

"Yes, I would like that."

He released her hand and within minutes she had the shop locked up and they were walking along the streets of Mayfair. The beautiful summer day had given way to a pleasant summer evening and a large harvest moon glowed golden in the night sky. As Declan escorted her to Devon House, Paulette's heart filled with a completely unfamiliar emotion. An excitement bubbled within her at the thought of being with this man. This man who seemed to genuinely like her. The novelty of the experience buoyed her spirits in a new way.

"You grew up in this neighborhood?" he asked.

"Yes, we lived above the bookshop."

"You and your sisters?"

"Yes, but we almost lost the shop when my father passed away. My sister Colette, whom you met this morning, she's the oldest. She and I worked the hardest to reorganize and improve the store. When she married Lucien Sinclair, we all moved in to Devon House with her, because our mother moved down to Brighton then. My sister Juliette is the second oldest, and is married to a sea captain and lives in America. She has a daughter about Mara's age. My sister Lisette lives here in London with her husband, Quinton Roxbury. He's a renowned architect and may be running for parliament next year. Now there's just my younger sister, Yvette, and myself, living at Devon House with Colette and Lucien and their two sons."

"You're the fourth sister, I gather."

"Yes. Three older, one younger. I'm stuck in the middle."

"I don't know that that's such a bad place to be," he said thoughtfully. "It seems you have a wonderful family and you're lucky to have a family that loves you. I haven't any siblings, although I always wished for a brother to play with when I was younger. I do have my cousin Gerald whom I'm close with, but it's not the same."

"I can't even imagine what being an only child is like."

"There's good and bad to it, just as I'm sure there is with being in a large family."

"My family is very important to me."

"I can tell that about you."

Paulette smiled at him. "Well, here we are." They had reached the massively grand, white house that was her home. "Thank you for walking with me."

"You are most welcome."

"Would you like to come in and meet the rest of my family? My sister Lisette is visiting tonight."

"Perhaps another time." He shook his head. "I should get back home to Mara. She gets anxious if I've been away from her for too long."

"Yes, of course. I understand."

They stood on the street in front of Devon House and looked at each other, neither one quite knowing what to say or do next. Declan reached out and took her hand in his and Paulette's heart skipped a beat as she looked up at him. How had she ever thought he seemed old and forbidding? Now he only looked incredibly handsome. She wished he would kiss her again. Even though doing so outside on the street would not be wise.

"I really should go," he said, but he did not let go of her hand.

"Yes."

"It's been an interesting day, Paulette."

"Interesting is a bit of an understatement."

He chuckled. "I suppose you are right, at that. In either case thank you for a most understated day."

Smiling at him, she could not help but ask, "Will we see each other again?"

Declan paused briefly. "Would you like to meet me in Green Park at noon on Sunday? I promised Mara I would take her."

Without a second thought, Paulette accepted his invitation. "That would be lovely."

As he did in the bookshop, Declan lifted her hand to

his lips and placed a kiss on her hand. "I'll see you then. Good night, Paulette."

"Good night." Paulette watched as he walked from her, his tall form making long even strides down the sidewalk. She watched until she could no longer see him in the darkening night.

Chapter 7

Silence

Papa was late and she was growing weary of waiting for him.

Mara Reeves sat on the wide, cushioned window seat in the nursery, tracing the patterns of the big cabbage roses on the chintz fabric with her fingers. The large pink rose swirled perfectly into the smaller red rose, the waves of color blending into each other in a continuous swirl, over and over. Pink, red, pink.

She liked patterns and colors. Bright colors. Like the colors in the new books Papa brought her. The stories were not what interested her, even though she listened politely when Papa read to her, like a good girl should. She just loved sitting beside him, listening to the soothing sound of his voice and looking at the pretty pictures.

She wished he would come home already.

"Well, Lady Mara, why don't you come over here and have your supper? There's chicken and the potatoes that you like."

Mara looked up at the sound of Mrs. Martin's voice. She was comfortable sitting on the window seat and not hungry in the least. But she swung her little legs over the edge of the cushioned seat and jumped to the floor. The carpet under her booted feet had a pattern of ivy and green vines interlaced with colorful flowers and Mara made sure she only stepped on the large blue flowers. That was the rule.

She made her way across the length of the nursery, taking care only to put her feet on the designated blossoms.

"What are you doing there, sweetheart? Is it a game?" Mrs. Martin smiled, her grin warm and encouraging. "It looks quite fun."

Mara didn't answer her nanny, but continued to the table set for the two of them. She climbed onto her chair and placed the heavy cloth napkin on her lap. Mrs. Martin sat across from her. After saying grace, the woman gave her a nod, and Mara picked up the silver fork and took a bite of her potatoes.

She wished Papa would come home. He'd been gone longer than usual that day and that worried her. He always came to see her before supper and she didn't like that he hadn't done so tonight. That's why she'd been sitting on the window seat, so she could watch out the window for him. But she grew bored of waiting and became entranced with the flower patterns on the cushion.

"Do you like the chicken, Lady Mara? It's my favorite. And the potatoes are tasty, aren't they?"

Mara took another bite by way of response. It wasn't her favorite, but it was fine. She liked the potpies better. The kind with the crispy crust.

"I'm glad you like your supper. Eat all your food so you grow up nice and healthy."

Mara wasn't sure she wanted to grow up. Grown-ups did not seem as if they liked being grown-ups very much, from what she could tell. But she didn't say that to Mrs. Martin. Of course, Mara didn't say anything.

Mrs. Martin was very kind to her and even though she'd only known her for a short time, Mara liked her well enough. In fact she liked her much more than her nurse back home in Ireland, who had always acted very cross. Her life in Ireland seemed very far away to her now. It was strange traveling all that way from her home in Dublin, across the sea on a ship, to London. Being on the ship was rather exciting and she wasn't too afraid, as long as Papa held her tightly when they were on the deck.

Where *was* Papa?

Unable to eat another mouthful, no matter how much Mrs. Martin attempted to cajole her, Mara set down her fork and wiped her mouth with her napkin and placed it on the table beside her plate as she had been taught to do.

"You certainly are a calm and obedient child, for all that you won't speak a word," Mrs. Martin remarked as she continued to eat her own supper. "I must say this is the easiest position I've ever had. For a four-year-old you don't cause a speck of trouble, little Lady Mara. You may be excused."

Mara climbed down from her chair and stepped only on the blue flowers all the way back to the window seat. Once back in her perch, she crawled on her knees to the windowsill and peered out. It was growing dark and still no sign of Papa. Her heart thumped loudly in her little chest. *Come home, Papa*, the voice in her head repeated, *Come home now.*

She pressed her face close to the windowpane and blew on the glass, her fingers making patterns in the condensation. Over and over she blew her warm breath on the glass, and drew patterns until they faded quickly and she had to begin again.

She mostly drew faces. Two eyes, a nose, and a mouth. Sometimes the face smiled. Sometimes it didn't. She didn't know why, except that's what she always drew.

A big golden moon was rising in the sky. It was the biggest moon Mara had ever seen in her whole life. Captivated by the beauty of it, she stopped drawing faces on the glass and leaned her forehead against the cool pane. She stared at the giant orb glowing in the night. So far away. So far from anything she had ever known. She guessed the moon was as close to heaven as one could possibly get.

Everyone told her Mama was in heaven. Could Mama jump on the moon from heaven? Was Mama up there now, searching for her? She could barely remember what Mama looked like anymore. She just had images, a rose scent and silver blond hair. She had gone away such a long time ago. But Mara still missed her, still wanted her.

But thinking of Mama brought back ugly images of the last time she saw her. And Mara hated to think of the evening that gave her nightmares. It was too terrifying. The all-consuming fear and dread. Voices shouting in anger. Papa's voice calling for her. Sickening black smoke. The blistering heat. The brilliant flames and crackling wood. The agonizing screams.

Mama's screams.

Tears welled in her eyes and she pulled away from the window and the big glowing moon. Where was Papa?

Then she heard his voice and her heart leapt. Papa was home! He'd come back to her.

"Good evening, Mrs. Martin. How was she today?"

"The same, Lord Cashelmore. She's the most obedient child I've ever laid eyes on. She didn't eat much tonight, but she hasn't eaten more than a few mouthfuls of anything since I've been with you. But as I always say, children will eat when they're hungry."

The blue flower pattern forgotten, Mara fairly flew across the carpet and flung herself into her father's arms.

He laughed in surprise, but he lifted her in his strong arms and held her tight. "My goodness, Mara, darlin'!"

"I'll leave you two alone for a bit." Mrs. Martin excused herself from the nursery.

Mara clung to Papa, breathing in the familiar scent of him, and buried her head in his neck. He patted her back as he rocked her in the way that she liked. He carried her over to the window seat and sat down, resting Mara on his lap.

"What is it, darlin'?"

She stared into his eyes and touched his cheek with her fingers. His cheek was scratchy against her hand, but she liked that feeling.

"Did you think I wasn't coming back?"

She nodded.

"Mara, I will always be here for you." He gave her a squeeze and kissed the top of her head.

Now that Papa was home, her fear abated somewhat.

"Were you crying? Don't cry, Mara. Look," he said, pointing out the window. "Have you seen the moon? Look how grand it is."

Mara had already seen the moon. She only wanted to be with Papa now. She pressed her forehead against his.

"Ah, darlin' . . . Why won't you talk to me?"

She always felt bad when he asked her this. It was not as though she didn't want to talk to Papa. She simply could not. No matter how hard she tried. Every time she attempted to speak, it felt like a giant hand gripped her. Cold and icy, its fingers closed tightly around her chest, pulling and drawing her down. She could not speak. The words simply wouldn't come out anymore.

They were gone and she couldn't find them. The words were lost and scrambled in her head and she couldn't make sense of them. She was too afraid of what would happen if she ever did make sense of them. Too afraid of what she might say.

Papa held her tight and that helped her feel safe. She rested her head on his chest, her eyes growing sleepy as Papa rocked her.

"One day you'll talk again, Mara. I know you will," he whispered. "I know you will."

The last thing she recalled before falling asleep was wishing that one day she would talk again, too.

Chapter 8

Mysteries

"And Quinton is having such success that we think he shall run for parliament next year," Lisette Hamilton Roxbury explained excitedly to her sisters later that same evening. With her husband out of town on business, Lisette was spending the night at Devon House.

After Colette had put her sons to bed, the four Hamilton sisters had gathered in Lisette's former bedroom. In her nightclothes, Paulette lounged on the large canopy bed with Lisette beside her. Colette and Yvette were curled up on the velvet divan.

However, Paulette had difficulty paying attention to any of the conversation. Her sisters had been chattering for nearly an hour and Paulette was only vaguely aware of what was being said. Her mind was completely occupied with thoughts of Declan Reeves and all that had happened between them in the bookshop today.

Relieved that Colette had not questioned her about kissing Mr. Reeves, Paulette remained more or less quiet throughout the evening.

"That's very exciting news," Colette said with enthusiasm. "Quinton is so capable and has such good ideas, he can't not be elected."

"That's what we're hoping." Lisette beamed with pride. "I'm counting on you girls to help us with the campaign. It's going to be a very busy year."

"Well, aren't you going to have a baby soon?" Yvette asked.

The room grew unnaturally quiet.

The sudden silence caught Paulette's attention. What had just been said? Had she missed something important? Were they waiting for her to respond? Noting that Colette and Yvette were staring at Lisette, relief flooded her. Then she realized Lisette was crying.

"Yvette," Colette scolded lightly. "Why did you have to bring that up?"

"What did I do?" Yvette asked with innocent eyes.

Wiping her tears with a lace-trimmed handkerchief, Lisette jumped to her youngest sister's defense. "No, it's all right. Don't worry, Yvette. It's the question everyone is thinking but not saying aloud for fear of upsetting me, and the one I don't have an answer for." Tears spilled down Lisette's cheeks and her auburn hair hung loose around her shoulders, making her appear young and vulnerable. "I don't know why I haven't had a baby yet. I'm afraid something might be wrong with me."

Rousing herself from her own worries at the sight of her sister's tears, Paulette wrapped her arm around Lisette's shoulder, giving her a comforting squeeze. "Oh, don't cry. I'm sure everything is fine."

Lisette sniffled, a few tears still escaping. "But it's not. I'll have been married three years in January and still no baby. Quinton's brothers' wives have been making snide remarks about my being barren. Mother even said something to me when I saw her last week. And I know Quinton feels terrible about it too, but is too kind to say so."

"You shouldn't worry about it. I'm sure it will happen soon enough," Paulette said. She really had no knowledge of these things, but thought it was best to be positive.

"It will," Colette added, coming to join them on the bed. "It will happen when you least expect it and the time is right, I promise. Maybe you've been too distracted with all of Quinton's building projects and his political career and simply getting used to being a wife. You've been through a lot of change and that can cause nervous tension which is quite unhealthy for babies."

"Colette is right," Paulette said. "There's nothing wrong with you, Lisette. Just be patient and relax."

"And really, just enjoy the time you have without children right now," Colette continued. "I love my two sons dearly, don't misunderstand me, but there is a part of me that wishes that I hadn't had them so soon. Lucien and I had very little time alone together just the two of us before Phillip came along."

"Perhaps you're right," Lisette said, giving a half-hearted attempt at a smile.

"Are you quite sure you are doing it correctly?"

Three pairs of eyes turned to stare at Yvette in astonishment.

Still sitting on the divan, their youngest sister looked back at them in exasperation and held her hands up. "What?"

"Yvette! How can you ask something like that?" Colette asked, her voice rising in pitch.

"I'm not a child anymore," Yvette pointed out to them. "I know about those types of things."

Lisette actually laughed a little, breaking the sudden silence. "Yes, I'm sure we're doing it correctly, Yvette."

"Honestly, Yvette, what is the matter with you?" Paulette

couldn't help but say. Her younger sister could be so vexing at times.

"It's a valid question," Yvette sniffed with an injured air. "You don't have to take that tone with me, Paulette. It's not as if you're a married woman and an expert on the subject!"

"Well, neither are you!" Paulette retorted. Still, it stung a bit to think that she was less of an expert on the subject than Yvette was. And she was until this morning when Declan Reeves had kissed her. Kissing him had changed everything and now it seemed that she had a different perspective on the world. But Yvette didn't know that.

It was strange to be having this discussion with her sisters about intimacies between a husband and wife. They'd never done so before, but that was because they had always thought she and Yvette were too young, she supposed. Of course, Paulette knew how babies were made since she had secretly read a medical text in the bookshop years ago. *A Complete Study of the Human Anatomy and All Its Functions,* by Doctor T. Everett, had described the events in explicit detail. It still seemed odd to think that Colette had engaged in the act with Lucien, and her sister Juliette with Captain Fleming. And here they were discussing whether Lisette and Quinton knew how to perform the act properly.

Yvette turned up her nose in indignation. "I'm eighteen now so you can't send me to my room anymore just because you think I'm too young to hear about such things."

Colette sighed in resignation. "No one is sending you to your room, Yvette. Now hush. This isn't about you."

Lisette shook her head and sniffled. "No, it's all right. Yvette is old enough to speak her mind."

Yvette smiled smugly, tossing her blond curls.

"Well, there is nothing wrong with you, Lisette," Colette continued, ignoring Yvette. "Trust me. Just enjoy being alone with your husband for a while longer. You are young and healthy. A baby will come in time."

"I'm sure you're right," Lisette said softly. "We'll keep trying. . . ."

"What is it really like? To do that with your husband?"

Paulette was stunned the question had come out of her own mouth. Now three pairs of eyes were staring at her. Colette's mouth dropped open and Lisette's cheeks turned red.

Yvette's face lit up and she clasped her hands together in glee. She rushed to join them on the bed, pushing in beside them. "Tell us, please. And don't just say we have to wait until we're married to find out. I despise that answer, which is what *Maman* always says when I ask her."

Colette and Lisette remained mute.

"What's the point of having older sisters if they won't share their experience and wisdom with us?" Paulette cajoled. The need to know about the great mysteries of life pulled at her, now more than ever before. How did it begin? What did it feel like? Was it awkward and embarrassing? How long did it take?

Declan Reeve's kisses that morning had left her wanting more. And that frightened her because she didn't know what to do about it. Something about that man had changed her. She didn't feel at all like her usual self.

Colette rolled her eyes heavenward and there was a moment of silence. "I didn't have anyone to tell me a thing about it. I had to find out for myself."

"Me, too," Lisette added. "I learned everything from secretly reading a medical textbook in the shop."

"So did I!" Colette exclaimed.

"I did, too," Yvette confessed with awe.

Paulette chimed in, "It seems Doctor T. Everett's book was helpful to all of us."

"I suppose the book never sold because we were all so busy reading it," Colette giggled.

And they laughed at the idea of all of them surreptitiously reading the same medical book to find out about sex.

Looking thoughtfully at her sisters, Paulette asked, "But don't you wish you *had* had someone to talk to about those things? Wouldn't it have been nicer if you had talked to each other first?"

Yvette chimed in, "I'd share with all of you if I were the oldest and had done it first."

"If Juliette were here, you know she would tell us," Paulette pointed out. Their sister Juliette was unusually outspoken and Paulette had no doubt that her second oldest sister would not hesitate in divulging intimate details about the marriage bed.

"They're right," Lisette conceded with a meaningful look at Colette. "We should tell them."

"Oh, fine then. What is it that you wish to know?" Colette asked in resignation.

Again there was a slight pause. Paulette exchanged triumphant glances with her younger sister. Yvette grinned with glee. She was finally going to obtain some actual information about the unspoken and mysterious aspects of romance.

Paulette asked first. "What is it like? Of course, we're aware of the technicalities, so to speak, but how is it really?"

Lisette, the shiest of the sisters, surprised them by answering before Colette. "It's absolutely lovely. It's the most magical and the most indescribable expression of love."

Colette grinned bashfully but agreed wholeheartedly. "It is."

"So it is something you enjoy doing with your husband then?" Paulette asked, more intrigued by this response than she expected.

Without hesitation Colette and Lisette answered in unison, "Yes."

"Well . . . What exactly makes something like that enjoyable?" Yvette questioned, her expression quite puzzled. "Because it certainly doesn't seem like it would feel good. It sounds as if it would be painful, embarrassing, and awkward. Even messy."

"Well, I suppose it could be all of those things," Colette began with a laugh. "But I think it depends on a number of factors. Perhaps for some women it's not enjoyable because they don't have husbands who love them. However, if two people truly love each other, the feelings are more intense and that is what I think makes all the difference."

"I couldn't imagine doing it with anyone else but Quinton," Lisette added for emphasis.

"I can't imagine doing that with anyone!" Yvette gave a little shudder of distaste.

On the other hand Paulette could easily picture herself being with Declan Reeves. Suddenly she could see herself naked in a bed, with Declan kissing her. Her heart flipped over in her chest at the thought of doing such a thing. She'd never been able to envision herself even kissing anyone before, let alone doing *that*.

And she certainly never thought about being with a man who had already been married and had a child.

"Oh, you will be able to when you meet the right man for you," Colette explained. "But it's nothing you have to worry about now."

"It has a lot to do with kissing, doesn't it?"

Paulette's question garnered her a sharply suspicious look from Colette, but it was Lisette who answered her.

"Oh, yes, good kissing is quite important. There was a very distinct difference in the way that Henry kissed me and the way that Quinton kissed me."

"And what was that?" Yvette asked, fascinated.

"I can't describe it exactly. When Henry kissed me it was nice, but I didn't feel anything special and I had no desire to kiss him. But with Quinton . . ." A joyous smile spread across Lisette's face. "We couldn't *not* kiss each other and when he kissed me, I couldn't breathe or think."

"That's how it was for me with Lucien," Colette explained. "I think I knew after kissing him that he was the one for me. And the kissing naturally led to doing those other things, but it didn't feel uncomfortable or strange because it was Lucien and somehow you want to do it."

Yvette appeared to be completely enraptured by the worldly advice of her older sisters, while Paulette's head was spinning. She had just met Declan Reeves and he was a stranger to her, but there was something about him that drew her to him. And if what her sisters were saying was true, and they had no cause to be untruthful, then Paulette's feelings for Declan were more emotional than she even realized.

"I've only been kissed twice and neither of them made me feel the way you described," Yvette stated in disappointment.

"And just who have you been kissing?" Colette demanded to know.

"Tad Vogels and Donald Dow."

"You shouldn't be too free with your favors, Yvette," Lisette advised, with a frown. "That's how you'll get a reputation."

"I can't help it if they all want to kiss me!" Yvette cried. "They begged me to let them have a kiss. Besides, they were just little kisses. Nothing like you described. They are probably more along the lines of Henry kisses rather than Quinton- or Lucien-type kisses."

"Oh, my Lord, we've created a monster," Lisette groaned at her little sister's words.

"We need to get someone to kiss poor Paulette!" Yvette declared, ignoring Lisette's disapproval. "That's what we need to do!"

"Leave her alone," Colette said, defending her. "Paulette is fine as she is. She'll get kissed when the time is right."

Paulette couldn't look at Colette but silently blessed her for not divulging what happened in the bookshop with Declan Reeves that very morning.

Yvette shook her head. "I certainly hope so."

"You both will fall in love when the time is right and things will happen and you won't worry because you will be with the man you love," Lisette added.

"And you waited until you were married, of course?" Paulette suddenly asked.

A very long, uncomfortable silence ensued. Both Colette and Lisette averted their eyes and turned varying shades of pink. Yvette began to giggle.

Paulette realized that her sisters' lack of response was their answer. They had not waited until marriage before doing such things with Lucien and Quinton, and that surprised her.

"But that doesn't mean that *you* should not wait." Colette rose from the bed, effectively ending their intimate discussion. "Let's all go to bed now and allow Lisette to get some sleep."

As they hugged each other good night, Lisette said, "Thank you all for making me feel a bit better. I apologize for being so emotional about it, but I want children so desperately. It's just that every month my heart is broken again. . . . And the worry has been on my mind for some time now. I don't know what to do. . . ."

"You can always talk to us," Paulette said, giving her sister one last hug before rising from the bed. "We love you very much. And Quinton. And we'll do whatever you need us to do to help with his campaign for parliament."

As she made her way to her own room, Paulette grabbed Colette's hand. "Thank you," she whispered so Yvette wouldn't hear.

"We'll talk about it later." Colette winked at her. "But make sure you let me know if he comes into the shop again, all right?"

Paulette nodded woodenly, hating that she had just lied to her sister.

Chapter 9

Deception

Dropping his heavy portmanteau on the floor of the hallway, Gerald O'Rourke cursed under his breath.

"What did he say?" asked Alice O'Rourke, his wife of two years, her pretty face full of concern. She lay sprawled on the sofa and raised herself up languidly on her elbow to look at him. Clad in nothing but a thin, white, silk robe, her long chestnut hair piled atop her head, Alice was an enticing sight indeed.

Although he usually gave in to the temptation of his young wife's charms, Gerald was too angry to be interested at the moment.

"He's not coming back. Not anytime soon, at least."

"Did you suggest he go to America?" she asked.

"Yes, I suggested he go to America," Gerald snapped at her in irritation. "But he's not planning on going there, either."

Alice released a heavy sigh and sat up, her long legs peeking between the opening in her silk robe. "Well then, we shall simply have to wait for them to arrest him.

They must do it at some point. They've waited long enough."

Gerald poured himself a drink before he even removed his jacket. The small but elegantly furnished Dublin house he shared with his wife was stifling on this sweltering August night. He could barely breathe. "They've waited this long because they don't have enough evidence." He wiped his brow with the back of his hand. "Jesus, Alice, it's as hot as an oven in here."

"It's summer," she replied with a careless shrug, standing and walking toward him.

"Can you open a damned window at least? Let some air in?"

"They're all open, Gerald."

He gritted his teeth. He hated the house, hated the heat, hated the city, and hated his cousin, Declan Reeves, most of all. Frustrated with the way his trip to London ended, Gerald wanted to punch something, or someone, to release the anger welling within him.

"Well, it sure as hell doesn't feel like it," he ground out bitterly.

"Calm down, have your drink, and tell me how things went." Alice helped him out of his jacket, tossing it on the chair, and loosening his neckcloth.

Gerald released a weary sigh as he lowered himself onto the sofa, heat clinging to him and perspiration dripping down his back. "Sometimes I feel like it is never going to go our way."

"It will, just be more patient. The tide will turn," Alice murmured in a soothing tone, caressing his cheek. "It always does. We know they are getting close to bringing him in. We only need to hurry things along."

"And just how do we do that, Alice?" he snapped sarcastically. "I don't know what else to do. I thought for sure he'd want to take Mara and just leave for good, start over in America, and never come back. It would be the best move for him. And us."

But Declan Reeves had never done anything that Gerald thought he should have done or would have done in his position. Declan married the wrong type of woman when he was too young and never heeded Gerald's advice. And look how it ended.

"Is Mara talking yet?" Alice questioned.

"No. I didn't even see her, but he says no. It's a strange thing that that child won't speak."

Alice's elegant dark brows furrowed. "I'm still not sure if it helps or hurts us."

"She saw me there that night, so her not speaking definitely helps us." Once again he could not hide the sarcasm in his tone.

"Even if she did say you were there, at this point who would believe her? She's merely a frightened child and it's been almost a year since it happened. You could attribute her words to a bad dream. Nothing the girl said would make a difference now."

"It sure as hell would, if she can say I was in the house during the fire."

Gerald shuddered, recalling how events spiraled out of his control that night. The acrid smell of smoke and burning flesh were permanently seared into his memory. Nothing had turned out as it should have that fateful evening. But being spotted by his cousin's young daughter was definitely not in his plans. Her sweet little face, full of terror and tears, would haunt him until the day he died.

"In either case, I left your brother, Brinks, in London to keep an eye on Declan and to keep me informed on what is happening there. He'll send me regular updates. And perhaps persuade Declan to return home, in fear if need be."

"He'll do a good job of it." Alice moved to stand behind him as he sat on the sofa. She began to massage his shoulders in an attempt to ease some of the tension that had been growing within him. Alice had magic fingers and she was quite skilled with them in more than one area. It was one of the reasons he had married her.

At the age of thirty-five and believing he would remain a bachelor his whole life, he'd surprised himself and everyone else by marrying twenty-year-old Alice Kennedy only two years ago. Looking the way he did, Gerald was damned lucky to have found someone as young and beautiful as Alice Kennedy to marry him. Alice was intelligent, ambitious, and accomplished in the bedroom, and Gerald would do anything to please her. He'd met her one day at a horse race in Galway and he'd been instantly attracted to her, and even more surprising, she to him. Alice understood him and what he wanted. She was shrewd enough to know that Gerald could get her what she wanted, too, which was out of the miserable life of poverty she had been born into. Perhaps her past was a bit tarnished and she had come from unsavory beginnings, but what did that matter in the end? The girl polished up nicely. Alice was his wife now and belonged to him. She would be the Countess of Cashelmore one day very, very soon.

"Gerald, we've discussed this over and over again," Alice said pragmatically. "You can't even be sure she recognized you. It was dark and chaotic that night and she's just a frightened little girl. A baby still. If she hasn't said anything about seeing you there by now, she won't. Relax and let nature take its course. Margaret's family is angry and powerful enough to bring Declan down without our involvement. The Ryans will never allow Declan to remain free if they think he is responsible for Margaret's death. And they truly think he is. Our work is done. Now we just wait."

"I'm tired of waiting," Gerald grumbled. "I've been waiting to be the Earl of Cashelmore my whole damn life."

"Just be patient, darling. All we have to do is quietly keep fanning the rumors and declaring outrage that Declan Reeves walks free while his wife lies in her cold grave at Cashelmore." She gave him a conspiratorial smile. "We just keep stirring the pot."

Closing his eyes, Gerald finally relaxed as Alice continued to knead his shoulders and neck with her expert fingers. The tension and anger slowly began to recede from his tired muscles. The liquor probably helped with that as well, as he downed the last of his whiskey.

Ever since he was a child he railed against the accident of his birth. His mother had been the younger sister of the Earl. Declan, as the only son of the Earl of Cashelmore, was the one to inherit the title, the estate, and all the money. As the only other surviving male member of the family, if Declan were out of the way, it would all belong to Gerald.

"He doesn't suspect you, does he?" Alice questioned, biting her lip.

"No. Not at all. Which makes him too stupid to live. If I were him, I would certainly suspect me. But not Declan. He was genuinely happy to see me and regards me as his brother. The bloody fool." Gerald's lip curled in disgust. He'd been pretending to be his younger cousin's friend for years, gaining his confidence and trust. "He hasn't a clue how I really feel about him. He even asked me to keep an eye on Cashelmore for him while he's in London indefinitely."

"Good!" she declared, digging her fingers hard into his flesh. "When he's finally in prison, it will make for an easy transition for us to assume control. I'd get over there first thing in the morning and start managing the

estate. Your trip to London was not in vain then, Gerald."
Alice laughed in triumph. "You have his permission to
take over Cashelmore Manor. It's the perfect start, my
darling!"

Still, there was something about the whole situation
that bothered Gerald. "I don't like being his servant and
that's exactly what this feels like."

"Don't be an idiot." She smacked the back of his neck.
"If he wants you to watch over the estate for him,
wouldn't we be better able to do that if we moved in to
Cashelmore?"

"Yes," he agreed reluctantly, still feeling frustrated and
stifled by the unfortunate circumstances of birth that
had ruled his life.

"You're being short-sighted. Stop pouting, Gerald,
and take control."

He reached up and grabbed both of Alice's hands
tightly, preventing her from rubbing his shoulders.
"Take control?" he questioned, his voice growing low. He
swung around and pulled her over the back of the sofa
until she was lying beneath him. "Take control? Is that
what you said, Alice?"

Her brown eyes glittered with excitement as he positioned himself over her. "Yes," she demanded. "Take
control."

His mouth came down hard over hers then, and in the
steamy heat of the evening he ripped off Alice's silk robe.

Chapter 10

Beginnings

Declan held Mara's hand as they walked along the path in Green Park on Sunday afternoon. He'd asked Paulette Hamilton to meet him there, and somehow he knew it would be safer if he brought his daughter along.

They were lucky to have another gorgeous summer day, with the sun bright in the clear blue sky. The park was bustling with people enjoying the fine weather. Children ran and shrieked, playing in the grass, while youthful ladies, shielded from the sun with pastel parasols, walked on the arms of young men. Mara skipped beside her father, wearing her wide-brimmed sunbonnet and a pink and lace embroidered dress, her golden curls bouncing as she held his hand tightly.

Mara had been so frightened the night he went to see Paulette, simply because he came home later than usual. That worried Declan. Perhaps taking Mara from her home in Dublin and all she had known had been the wrong choice and caused her to be too fearful. But looking at her now, she seemed as happy as could be. Yet somehow, he knew she would never truly be happy again until she released the fears that gripped her so tightly and she could speak once more.

And there was Paulette Hamilton.

She sat on a bench under the shade of a tall, silver maple tree. In a gown of pale lavender and a straw sun hat bedecked with lavender ribbons, she looked as pretty as a picture. Paulette smiled and gave a little wave as they approached.

"Good afternoon!" he called to her.

Beside him, Mara came to a complete stop, causing Declan to pause and look at her in surprise.

"What is it, Mara?" He knelt down, so he could be at eye-level with her. "You remember Miss Hamilton? From the bookshop? She showed you the fairy-tale book. I thought you'd like to see her again."

His daughter gave him a look that shook him to the tip of his boots. It was as if she were older and wiser and knew, *just knew*, that he had not brought her to the park to see Miss Hamilton. She saw completely through his simple ruse. Mara knew that Declan was the one who wanted to see Miss Hamilton. She eyed him most carefully, but did not protest. Mara let go of his hand and walked over to the bench without him.

Declan watched in fascination as Paulette greeted his daughter with a warm smile.

"Good afternoon, Mara. Do you remember me? I'm Miss Hamilton. I have something for you."

Mara nodded and took a step closer to Paulette.

Paulette picked up a package, wrapped in brown paper and tied in dark green ribbon, which rested on the bench beside her. She handed it to Mara. With hesitant fingers, his daughter held out her hand, accepting Paulette's gift with a questioning gaze.

He and Paulette exchanged a glance and again he was struck by just how beautiful she was. A gentle breeze wafted under the brim of her sun hat and ruffled the edges of her blond hair. She looked fresh and young and full of life. He moved toward the bench where she sat.

Paulette focused her attention back to Mara, encouraging her. "You can unwrap it. It's a little present. Here. I'll help you. Come sit up here by me." She patted the bench in invitation and Mara scrambled to get herself seated, clutching the small package in her hand.

Together they untied the green ribbon and unwrapped the brown paper, revealing a book, *Beauty and the Beast.*

"It's a toy book," Paulette explained with excitement, helping Mara turn to the first page. "Look, when we pull the little tab right here, the picture moves."

Mara was fascinated. With great care, her little fingers tugged on the tab and they watched the colorful picture change its scene. Her mouth opened in surprised delight. Even Declan was intrigued.

"Isn't that clever!" he cried, looking over them.

"We just got a new shipment of these toy books into the store yesterday and I had a feeling that Mara would like one."

"Thank you for thinking of her," Declan whispered, touched by her thoughtfulness in bringing something for his daughter.

"You're welcome." Paulette glanced up at him and smiled. "She's a very sweet child."

"Mara, thank Miss Hamilton, please." His daughter might not speak, but he still expected her to have manners enough to thank someone for a gift.

The child looked up at Paulette with wide eyes and smiled. Mara gave Paulette a genuinely happy smile. Declan nodded his approval.

"I'm so happy you like it, Mara. I thought of you the

moment I first saw this book." Paulette leaned over and demonstrated another section. "Look at this page. If you pull this tab, you can make the beast dance. Isn't that funny? But you have to be very gentle with it. You don't want to tear it."

With great care, Mara's tiny fingers tugged and the beast moved on the page. A small giggle escaped her. Completely mesmerized, the child made the motion over and over again on the same page of the book.

Stunned, Declan knelt beside the bench and stared at his daughter. Mara had just laughed! He hadn't heard that sweet sound in almost a year. The beauty of her fleeting giggle filled him with a joyous hope that none of the expert doctors he consulted had given him. He knew with a certainty in his heart that Mara would speak again when she was ready. He patted her head and she blithely ignored him, enraptured with the novelty of a book with colorful pictures of a beast that danced.

"Is everything all right?" Paulette asked, her delicate brows drawn in concern.

"Everything is wonderful, lass," he said. Rising to his feet, he held out his hand to Paulette. She clasped his hand and rose from the bench. They took a few steps away, leaving Mara completely engrossed in her new book.

"It's good to see you again, Paulette," he said. Was it only two nights ago that they spoke in the shop? Only the day before yesterday that he had kissed her so passionately behind the bookshelves? He hadn't stopped thinking about her since then. Paulette was so different from any girl he'd met before. And she was entirely different from Margaret.

"It's good to see you, too." She flushed slightly, suddenly shy with him. "Declan."

As he still clasped her hand in his, all he could think

about was kissing her. He wanted to pull her into his arms and kiss her sweet mouth right then and there in the beauty of the day. He certainly couldn't do so in front of so many strangers, let alone his daughter. Instead, he did all that he could do. He gave her gloved fingers a light squeeze.

Paulette grinned up at him and squeezed his fingers back. "Shall we walk?"

"Yes, let's." He turned back to the bench. "Come along now, Mara."

Mara closed the book with great reluctance, holding it close to her chest, and slid off the bench, her little boots landing on the ground with a thud. She skipped over to them, and sidled up to Paulette. She placed her hand in Paulette's.

"I think she likes you," Declan whispered in Paulette's ear.

"I like her too, so it's mutual," Paulette said, grinning.

He offered Paulette his arm and they walked along the meandering path slowly so Mara could keep up with them.

"I have a question for you," he asked.

"And what is that?"

"I've been wondering about all the French names."

Paulette's lyrical laughter lightened the air around him, filling his chest with an emotion he did not recognize. A deep coldness within him suddenly melted, filling him with a warm sense of peace he hadn't experienced before.

"Oh, that's because of my mother," she explained. "She's French."

"Ah, now it all makes sense." He nodded in understanding. "I suspected as much."

"But we all have English middle names."

"And yours would be?"

"Victoria."

"For the queen."

"Yes. I am very queenly, am I not?" Paulette laughed sweetly.

"Yes, I can see the name suits you." He winked at her playfully. "So all your sisters work in the bookshop as well?"

"Well, most of us that is. Juliette, the second oldest, and Yvette, the baby, never had much interest in the shop and spent the least amount of time there. Lisette has always been a great help, but it's mainly been just Colette and me. We took over the shop after our father passed away. We redesigned the store and changed everything from the layout to what types of books we sold. Our bookshop is doing so well, we're opening another store."

"Is that right?" Looking at her with increasing admiration, he liked the idea of Paulette's business being successful. Even though he knew the bookstore belonged to all of the Hamilton sisters, in his mind the shop was Paulette's alone.

"Yes, we should be ready to open by the end of October. My brother-in-law, Quinton Roxbury, the one married to Lisette, designed the new store for us. We helped to design it. I've never been able to give my ideas for a building as it was being built before and that was the most exciting part of it. Everything is being crafted especially to our specifications and requirements. It will be quite modern and beautiful."

"I would love to come see it sometime."

"Oh, I'd love for you to see it! They are very near to completion and the construction should be done soon. Quinton thinks I'll be able to look over the finished space within the next week. Then we shall have the furniture installed and the book inventory stocked and hire new employees."

"Will it be called Hamilton's as well?" he asked, intrigued by her passion for her work. She was fairly brimming with enthusiasm, making her look even more beautiful with her eyes alight with excitement.

"Oh that's a secret for now. Only Colette and I know the name of the new shop and we're saving it as a surprise for the opening day."

"Can I have a hint?" he asked, giving her a mischievous smile.

She laughed but wouldn't give him one.

"I've also started reading the book you chose for me." He gave her a knowing look. *"The Law and the Lady."*

"And what do you think of it?"

"I think you are trying to tell me something with that story, lass."

Again Paulette's sweet laughter warmed his heart. "Perhaps I am. Let me know what you think when you finish it."

Walking with Mara and Paulette on his arm, Declan had the impression that people who passed by them assumed they were a happy, young family. He could not recall that he and Margaret had ever walked in a park together with their daughter. Being in London was such a contrast to the depressing environment they had been living in with Margaret back at Cashelmore Manor. The grief during the past year was terrible enough, but the anger and tension in his marriage had been unbearable.

He had no other option but to get away from Ireland, for Mara's sake as well as his own. And each day he spent out of that sickening atmosphere strengthened his resolve that he had made the right choice. Mara seemed a little happier. And he felt lighter than he had in years. In fact, since the day he married Margaret.

The simple pleasure of walking in a park on a summer day in the company of a beautiful girl renewed his sense of hope that he could get out of the tangled nightmare his life had become.

The three of them continued strolling through the shady park, pausing from time to time for Mara to look at some flowers. His daughter picked a handful of daisies and Declan ended up carrying the book for her. They walked out of the park to a nearby restaurant that Paulette was familiar with, which she declared served the best ice cream in the city. Seated at a small outdoor table, they enjoyed their vanilla dessert served in pretty glass dishes. Mara was especially taken with the creamy sweetness and ate more than Declan had seen her consume in her life.

"I think she likes her ice cream," Paulette commented, with an amused smile.

"Mara darlin', you have some ice cream on your nose," Declan pointed out, reaching over with his cloth napkin to wipe the cold treat from her tiny face.

Before he could do so, Mara wiped at the vanilla ice cream with the tip of one of her chubby fingers, then shoved it in her mouth to lick off the cream. A delighted giggle escaped her once again and his heart constricted in his chest. He knew in that moment that taking her away from all the sadness at home in Cashelmore was for the best, no matter what Margaret's family said.

That made twice in one day that Mara had laughed. She had made a typical childish show of delight and he nearly burst with the joy of it. And all they had done was walk in the park, look at a picture book, and have some ice cream. The normalcy and ordinariness of the sunny day outdoors must have prompted the change in her.

"You're having a good time, aren't you, darlin'?" he asked her with great affection. He loved her so.

Mara looked up at him with her wide green eyes and smiled.

"Paulette Hamilton!"

Startled, Declan and Paulette both turned at the sound of her name. A tall and extremely good-looking gentleman with dark hair stood before them. On his arm was a gorgeous blond woman, dressed in a gown with outrageous pink ruffles.

"Paulette, it is you!" the man exclaimed in surprise. "What are you doing here, little minx?"

Declan's brow raised in question. Who was this man who addressed Paulette so familiarly?

"Jeffrey!" Paulette cried in disbelief, her expression one of complete astonishment. Declan noted a bit of nervousness in her expression as well.

"What a surprise to see you here!" Paulette continued. "When did you get back from France?"

"Just yesterday. And I have presents for all of you. But first let me introduce you to my friend, Miss Francine Hunter. Miss Hunter, I'd like you to meet Miss Paulette Hamilton and . . . ?" The man glanced rather skeptically at Declan. He had a proprietary air about him that instantly put Declan on edge.

"I'm pleased to meet you, Miss Hunter," Paulette said with a note of amusement in her voice. "This is the Earl of Cashelmore, from Ireland, and his daughter, Lady Mara Reeves. And Lord Cashelmore, this is a dear family friend, Lord Jeffrey Eddington."

Declan exchanged a handshake with the man, wondering what claim he seemed to have over Paulette.

"Are you here in London on holiday, Lord Cashelmore?" Lord Eddington asked.

Declan bristled under the other man's intense regard. "No, not a holiday."

"Then you are planning to stay here?"

"I'm not sure how long I'll be here," Declan responded tersely. The man's tone had a critical edge to it. There was not a doubt in his mind that Lord Eddington glanced disapprovingly between Paulette and Declan.

Mara stared up at the handsome stranger with wide eyes.

Then Eddington asked, "You have a very sweet daughter, Lord Cashelmore. May I ask why your wife is not with you on this fine afternoon?"

"Oh, Jeffrey!" Paulette whispered hurriedly. "Lord Cashelmore is a widower."

Declan glared at Eddington, daring him to say anything more. He and Paulette were not doing anything untoward and he didn't like this man insinuating that they were.

"I beg your pardon. I had no idea," Eddington said, his expression one of genuine regret. "My condolences to you and your daughter."

Declan nodded, barely acknowledging his remark of sympathy, and the atmosphere around them grew quite tense. How dared this man, who was obviously carousing with a lower-class woman, for the girl had to be a dancer or an actress judging from her dress alone, question him in such a way? Who was he to Paulette? Clearly he was not a blood relative for she would have introduced him as such. Yet he had the effrontery to act as if he were her older brother.

"We were just treating Mara to some ice cream after a walk in the park," Paulette murmured in an attempt to break the awkward silence. "Have you had the ice cream here before, Miss Hunter? It's quite good."

The woman shook her head. "No, but I've heard it's delicious."

Lord Eddington said, "We were just walking to the theater. Miss Hunter has a show this afternoon. But it was wonderful to run into you, Paulette. It's rare that I ever see you outside of the bookshop. Please be sure to tell Lucien and your sisters that I'll be around to Devon House sometime tomorrow." He turned his attention to Declan. "Lord Cashelmore, it was a pleasure meeting you and your adorable daughter. Enjoy your stay in London. Perhaps we shall meet again?"

Declan shrugged noncommittally. "Perhaps. It was nice meeting you, Miss Hunter. Lord Eddington. Enjoy the show."

As the two walked away, Declan handed the picture book to Mara, who hurriedly opened it and immersed herself in the colorful pages once again. Then he turned to Paulette. "Who *was* that?"

"I just introduced you," she said matter-of-factly. "He's Lord Eddington."

"No, I meant who is he to you? He acted very protectively toward you."

"Yes, well, he's been like a brother to us since Colette married Lucien Sinclair. Lucien and Jeffrey grew up together and are like brothers," Paulette explained. "So we accepted Jeffrey as a part of our family, too. He's very sweet and charming, and he's great fun."

"And clearly not married."

Paulette laughed. "Jeffrey? No, he's not married yet! But plenty of women want him to be!"

"He certainly wasn't happy at finding you here with me. He made that very plain."

"He doesn't even know you. But he's known me since I was a young girl, and he is protective of all us Hamilton girls, and I think he was just surprised to see me out with . . ." Paulette fumbled for the right word. ". . . Out with . . . well, surprised to see me out."

"With someone like me," Declan finished for her.

"With anyone, I suppose." Her cheeks flushed prettily.

"I'm sure it looked to Jeffrey as though you and I are . . . you and I . . ."

Not for the first time Declan wondered what he was doing with this girl. Perhaps this Eddington character had every right to be suspicious of him. For what were his intentions with Paulette? He sure as hell didn't know.

"Does your family know you're here in the park with me right now?" he questioned.

He sensed the hesitation in her before she answered.

"Well, no, not actually," she confided, her expression a bit anguished. "I told them I was walking in the park, but I didn't necessarily mention that I would be meeting you there."

"Why not?"

She grew thoughtful and her voice changed to a whisper. "I don't know. Maybe I was afraid they wouldn't approve."

Declan glanced at Mara, who was still engrossed in the toy book on the table in front of her. He lowered his voice as well. "Because of the rumors about me?"

Paulette nodded, her eyes downcast.

His heart raced. "But you don't believe those rumors, do you?"

She looked up to meet his eyes. "I told you the other night that I don't believe them."

"Wouldn't your family believe me if you said that you believed me?"

"I suppose they would." She didn't seem very sure of her answer. Paulette bit her lip. "Jeffrey is sure to tell them about seeing us here."

"And that concerns you?"

"Only for the fact that I wish I could tell them myself, when I was ready to share such information. It's just that now I shall be subjected to far too many questions that I don't know how to answer."

Their gazes locked, and for a moment they were lost in thought. They both had questions. Lord knew Declan was filled with a multitude of questions where Paulette was concerned. And he had no answers for her either. He had placed her in an uncomfortable position.

"I wish I knew how to answer them for you, Paulette."

"You could probably answer some of them for me at some point. But now is neither the time or the place."

"I agree," he said.

A dainty, little snore distracted them both. Mara had fallen fast asleep, her head resting on the table over the opened book.

"It must be past her nap time, the sweet thing," Paulette whispered. "We should get her home."

Declan noted the use of the word "we" in her remark and did not know what to make of it. Instead he stood and lifted the sleeping child in his arms. Mara's head lolled against his shoulder. Paulette gathered up the picture book, Mara's daisy bouquet, and her reticule, and they left the little restaurant together.

"Do you live far from here?" she asked.

"Not at all. Just down the block," he said, as Paulette fell in step beside him.

They walked back to his townhouse and he felt oddly comforted by Paulette's presence. His butler, Roberts, greeted them in the foyer and Mrs. Martin hurried in, clucking over the sleepy child.

"Oh my, someone is just worn out!"

Declan made the introductions rather hastily, as he noted that Mrs. Martin eyed Paulette with avid curiosity. While Roberts escorted Paulette to the parlor, Declan carried Mara upstairs to the nursery and then let Mrs. Martin put her to bed for a much-needed nap. He returned to the main parlor to find Paulette waiting for him, seated on the rose-patterned sofa. She had removed her lavender beribboned hat and her gloves and looked more at home here than he would have imagined.

They were quite alone in his formal parlor as he closed the door behind him.

"This is a very nice house, Declan," she said.

He gave a cursory glance around the room. "It'll do for now. Can I get you anything? Shall I ring for some tea?"

She shook her head. "No, I'm fine, thank you."

"I should thank you for being so kind to Mara. She loves that book." After a slight hesitation he moved to sit beside Paulette on the sofa. The sweet floral scent of her perfume wafted to him. She smelled delicious. "Being in London has already been an improvement for Mara. She actually laughed for the first time since her mother died. It was just a brief giggle, but it meant the world to me."

"It made you hopeful that she'll speak again?"

"Yes." He liked how Paulette knew what he was thinking. "She was happy today in the park. I think she finally felt safe and forgot the horror of that night for a little while. It exhausted her too, apparently."

"I'm sure it did, but when she has more days like today, she will eventually come out of her shell." She smiled brightly at him, her pretty face beaming. "Have you thought about other children?"

"Excuse me?" Her question startled him.

At one time, when he and Margaret were first married, he had wanted a large, boisterous family with lots of children. Something he never had growing up. But now . . . Now he had his hands full dealing with only Mara. Another child was the furthest thing from his thoughts, which saddened him, too. Nothing in his life had turned out as he had planned.

Paulette looked confused and became a bit flustered. "Forgive me. I meant to say have you thought about having other children over to play with Mara? It seems as though she spends her days alone or only with adults. Being with children her own age might engage her enough to talk."

Declan was astonished by Paulette's simple idea. "I'd never thought of that, to tell you the truth. Maybe because I don't know any other children. Not one doctor has ever given me that suggestion before, but what you say makes complete sense. If Mara had a playmate or two her own age, maybe that would help."

"It's too bad that my niece Sara isn't here. She's about Mara's age and would be a perfect playmate to her. But she lives in America with my sister Juliette. However, Colette's two sons, Phillip and Simon, are darling little boys. They would play with Mara and not scare her. They're all close enough in age. Maybe we could introduce them at the bookshop one afternoon?"

"That would be a grand idea, Paulette. I think Mara would like that and it wouldn't feel so forced. Thank you." On impulse he took her hand in his and gave her a gentle squeeze. Her hand felt warm and her fingers intertwined with his.

"You're welcome."

Declan looked into her blue eyes, seeing the honesty, intelligence, and warmth within her. Paulette's golden blond hair had come loose from the pins during their walk home and few stray tendrils fell charmingly around her delicate face. He still held her hand in his and she did not pull away.

"You are very beautiful, Paulette Hamilton."

"Thank you . . . Ah, about those questions that I am bound to be asked by my family," she whispered, her voice a bit breathless. "Might we discuss those answers now?"

She regarded him with a yearning that he recognized

quite clearly. Suddenly his heart pounded like a hammer in his chest. The familiar tension grew between them, as he still held her hand, their fingers interlocked together.

"Of course."

She remained silent, her gaze fixed intently with his.

He moved closer to her, inhaling the sweet scent of her hair. He lifted her hand to his lips, feeling the smoothness of her skin against his mouth. He pressed a kiss to her fingers. "You have questions?" he whispered.

She blinked in confusion. "I'm sorry?" Her words were barely audible.

He moved his head closer to hers. "You wanted me to answer something?"

"I . . . I don't . . . recall . . ."

He could almost touch her cheek with his lips, he was so close to her. Her skin looked so incredibly soft and he longed to touch it.

She licked her lips slowly, her tongue skimming the full curves. Declan's heart slammed into his chest, his eyes fixed on her mouth.

The air became warm around them. She did not speak. She stared at him.

Before he could consider what he was about to do, he leaned into her and covered her sweet mouth with his.

The effect was immediate.

As if waiting for him to do just that, Paulette practically melted into him, her body pliant and soft, her arms wrapped around his shoulders. He breathed in the flowery scent of her, basking in the feel of her lips against his. She kissed him back eagerly, which only enflamed his growing desire for her. When her mouth opened he dipped his tongue inside, the sensation almost causing him to lose his mind when she touched her tongue to his. With his arm around her he pulled her closer, pressing his chest against hers.

They kissed. And kissed. And kissed. Declan felt he could kiss her for days on end and never get enough of her.

Her breathing became shallow and so did his.

Releasing her hand, he traced a path up her arm, along her shoulder, and around to the back of her neck, his fingers sliding into her silky blond tresses. He tilted her head back as he kissed her even more deeply. God, but he could easily drown in her. She was all soft skin and warm sighs. He caught his breath as her hands splayed through his hair.

Wanting more, he slowly maneuvered them both until she was reclining on the sofa and he positioned himself over the length of her body. She was perfectly proportioned, and fit him as if she were made for him and no one else. He caressed her cheek, kissing her over and over again.

He couldn't seem to stop his other hand as it moved over Paulette, touching, caressing, and feeling every inch of her body through the silk of her lavender summer gown. He cupped her breasts, his fingers sliding below the edge of her gown, seeking the warm flesh of her naked body against his skin. She arched into his hand, her kisses growing more demanding. Over and over, they kissed each other. Time seemed to stand still, suspended, and the rest of the world fell away.

Declan forgot they were in his parlor. Forgot that his daughter was upstairs sleeping. Forgot that they were in a house full of servants. He forgot about his past, about Ireland. All that mattered was Paulette. All he could focus on was the incredibly lovely and sweet girl in his arms.

He continued to kiss her and caress her, his longing for her only increasing the more he kissed her. His hand roamed the curves of her body as he pressed himself against her wanting more. Her breathing became more frantic as she embraced him.

A small moan of pleasure escaped her and Declan shuddered with an unfulfilled need of his own.

He hadn't been with a woman since Margaret and it had been far too long.

Now he wanted Paulette more than he wanted anything in his life. It was madness. Where had she even come from? He barely knew her. He hadn't come to London to become involved with an innocent like Paulette Hamilton. A girl like her expected marriage and he was through with marriage. He wasn't any good at it.

Warring between the urgent need within him and the consequences that slaking his need would warrant, Declan growled low in his throat and tried to pull away.

Paulette clung to him, unwilling to let him go, making his decision even more of a struggle of wills. It would be so easy to give in to her. . . . But if he didn't stop now, they would go too far. And then there would be no turning back. As much as he wanted her, wanted to feel her naked body beneath him, Declan could not do it.

"Paulette." Her name was a ragged whisper. He kissed her cheek.

"Declan, please, stop," she whimpered, on the verge of tears. "Please. I can't take any more. We must stop. I can't . . . I can't even breathe."

That did it. With great reluctance, he released her. "I'm sorry, lass, I'm sorry," he murmured. He eased himself off of her, taking deep breaths to regain control of his body. Of his raging emotions.

Declan helped her to sit up. God but she looked tempting, her dress half undone, her eyes heavy with desire, and her long golden-blond hair spilling around her shoulders. If not for the sheer panic on her face, he would have lowered her back down on the sofa and finished what he'd started.

"Forgive me, Paulette."

"I just need a minute"—her hands fluttered to her heated cheeks—"to catch my breath."

Declan did, too. What the hell was he thinking? He should never have been alone with her in the house, should not have kissed her, should not have touched her—

"I promise that next time I won't be such a little fool about it," she said, closing her eyes and breathing in.

"Excuse me?" He stared at her. *Next time?*

She opened her blue eyes and looked at him. "The next time we do this, I promise I won't ask you to stop."

Declan felt all the air being sucked out of his lungs. "Good God, Paulette, what are you saying?"

"I didn't really want to stop just now, but I couldn't breathe. I thought I was going to faint from the sheer pleasure of it all. I've never felt so light-headed and dizzy before. But I think next time I'll know more what to expect and won't be so—"

"Stop it," he interrupted her, stunned by her words and still fighting the temptation to kiss her mouth again. "There can't be a next time, Paulette. There shouldn't have been this time. It was wrong of me to kiss you in the first place. I'm glad we stopped when we did. If it went any further, we would have to—" He cut off his own words.

"Oh, I see," she whispered, nodding her head slowly. The shadows of a smile played on her mouth. "You think you'd have to marry me, if we . . . if we did anything. But you don't understand, Declan. I'm happy running the bookshop and I don't want a husband. I don't wish to get married! So you see, next time we—"

"Please stop, Paulette, you're killing me." There was only so much a man could take. And having this beautiful woman willingly state that she wanted to have him was almost Declan's undoing. "You don't know what you're saying."

She began putting the front of her dress to rights. "Yes, I do."

He stood up, holding his hand out to help her from the sofa. "No. You don't. But I'll tell you this, Paulette Hamilton. You are the most beautiful and most desirable woman I have ever had the pleasure to know."

She frowned and did not rise from the sofa. "You sound as if you're saying good-bye to me."

"If I were a smart man, I would be." He flashed her a half-hearted grin. "But I'm not. I just think it's probably best if I took you home right now."

Her face shadowed with disappointment. "Oh."

"Fix your hair first." Although he liked the way she looked now with her hair long and loose, he certainly could not return her home that way.

And if he didn't bring her home right this minute, he would carry her upstairs to his bed and make love to her for hours. And that would be disastrous. For both of them.

Instead he ordered his carriage brought around.

Chapter 11

Letters

Paulette couldn't sleep at all that night. Her every thought was of Declan Reeves and the Sunday afternoon they spent together in the park and later at his house. Especially later at his house. He had been almost angry with her while he took her home in his carriage and she didn't know why he should be that way. She thought she had behaved most reasonably about the matter, considering how overwhelmed she was by it all.

The feelings she had for him were like nothing she had ever experienced before. She wanted to be with him. Wanted to know everything about him. She had so many questions for him she didn't even know where to begin.

She wasn't sure if these feelings meant that she was in love with Declan Reeves, but she was certainly fascinated with him. With his deep-throated, lyrical accent that made her insides melt. With his dark green eyes that caused her heart to skip a beat when he looked at her. With his tragic, haunted past that she wanted to heal. With his kisses that left her weak and shaking and yearning for more.

Ah, his kisses.

But Declan did kiss her one last time before she stepped from the carriage and that thrilled her. He had cupped her face in his hands and kissed her so deeply she thought she would faint right there in the carriage. Then he whispered, "I'll see you soon."

With her heart fluttering wildly, somehow she had managed to slip in the house unnoticed, with only Granger, the Devon House butler, raising an eyebrow at her disheveled appearance. By the time she appeared for supper an hour later, she had recovered enough to act as if she had not just spent the most wonderful day of her life with a handsome Irishman who had kissed her senseless. Luckily Colette and Lucien barely asked about her day in the park and Yvette was too consumed with deciding which new gown to wear to a ball the following week to notice her.

Now Paulette only hoped that Jeffrey Eddington wouldn't mention to Lucien or Colette that he had seen her with Declan Reeves in the park. Her plan was to speak to him and beg for his silence on the matter before he had a chance to tell her sister and brother-in-law. She prayed she could convince him, because she wasn't sure where Jeffrey would stand on the matter. He could be rather vexing that way.

It wasn't that she didn't want her sisters to know about Declan. In fact it was quite the opposite. She wanted to bring Declan home to meet them, but something held her back. They would be suspicious and wary of him. She only had to think of Colette's horrified face when she found out that Declan had kissed her in the bookshop.

Colette believed the rumors about him. She thought Declan had done something to harm his wife, while Paulette knew with every fiber of her being that those rumors couldn't possibly be true.

A man could not kiss her so sweetly and stop to protect her, if he were a murderer. A man could not carry
his sleeping daughter home from the park after confiding his wish for her not to be afraid of speaking, if he
had killed her mother. To Paulette's way of thinking, it
was simply impossible.

But until Declan's name was cleared or her sisters
could have a chance to know him as she did, Paulette did
not feel as though she should tell them what was happening. Paulette was having a romance, but not in the
traditional way that everyone else did, and her family
would never understand that. Colette would be too worried for her safety, thinking Paulette could be hurt next.
Lisette would be scandalized and anxious that Paulette's
association with a man suspected of murder could somehow hurt Quinton's burgeoning political career. Yvette
would be aghast at the thought of Paulette being with
someone presumed to have killed his wife. Her mother
would most likely faint in a dramatic fashion and take to
her bed for at least a week if not longer. And Lucien!
Her over-protective brother-in-law would never let her
out of the house when he found out about Paulette's involvement with Declan Reeves.

No one in her family would understand how she felt
about him.

Except Juliette.

Her sister Juliette wouldn't judge her or think her
daft for wanting to be with a man like Declan. She would
understand completely and encourage her to follow her
heart. Paulette now wished Juliette weren't so far away.
She and Juliette had had their differences over the years,
and Paulette spent her childhood antagonizing Juliette
about her lack of interest in books and the shop, but
they truly loved each other. They had just been reaching
a calm point in their relationship, when Juliette ran off

to New York and ended up married to the American, Harrison Fleming. Busy with her new family, Juliette came to visit London infrequently and Paulette missed her now more than ever.

Instinctively Paulette knew that Juliette was the only one who would support her current situation. She thought about writing to her, explaining all that was happening with her and Declan Reeves. There was one thought that stopped her from doing just that. She was afraid that Juliette would then tell Colette everything and that was a risk that Paulette was unwilling to take at the moment.

Instead she spent a very restless night, with images of Declan Reeves in her mind, and barely slept at all.

Bright and early Monday morning, Paulette was back in the bookshop as usual, preparing for another busy day. Colette and Lizzie would not be in until later that afternoon, so she was alone in the store. Before the shop officially opened for the day, Paulette indulged herself in a fit of nostalgia and went upstairs to the living quarters where she had spent her childhood.

The rooms had been refurbished over the years when little Tom Alcott and his mother, Anna, had lived there, but the rooms were empty now. However, Paulette could still see everything the way it used to be. The long dining table where she and her sisters had supper with their parents every night. The faded velvet divan where her mother reclined and declared she had headaches. The place above the mantel where the family portrait used to hang. She opened the door to the tiny bedroom she had shared with Yvette and Lisette. There had been heavy pink floral wallpaper, decorated with birds and fruit, that had lined the walls in their room. Now it was painted a soft cream and was used as a small office.

Paulette sighed heavily, wondering at all the years,

all the time that had passed by and how her life had changed after her father died when she was fourteen. She missed her father. What would her life be like if her parents still lived above the bookshop? What would her father think about her and Declan Reeves? Although he was a calm and reasonable man, she doubted Thomas Hamilton would be overjoyed at his daughter becoming involved with a man suspected of murder.

Nor would her mother, if truth were told. Alive and well and living in Brighton, Genevieve Hamilton would most certainly show great displeasure at Paulette kissing a widower who was believed to have been the cause of his wife's death.

No, her parents would not approve of Declan Reeves, but they were not there to give their opinion.

Paulette was no longer a child sharing a bedroom with her sisters. Mature and independent, she lived her own life and made her own decisions. Well, for the most part anyway. She would be twenty-one next month and most girls her age were already married and having families of their own.

So what did it matter if she had a secret suitor? Nothing in her life—from being raised above a bookshop to suddenly living in one of the grandest homes in London and being the sister-in-law of the Marquis of Stancliff to being a woman in charge of a bookshop—was traditional. If she wanted to be with Declan Reeves, what was to stop her?

Aside from herself.

Declan had been the one to stop them from going further yesterday. Paulette would have continued most eagerly if she had been able to breathe properly. Perhaps that had been a blessing in disguise. She had mixed emotions about their passionate kissing on the sofa and how quickly they had almost lost control of their senses and their situation.

The moment Declan's lips met hers there was nothing she could do to stop it from happening, nor did she want to. The thrill of being kissed by him was unlike anything she had ever known. And she had wanted much more than kissing from him.

The clock on the mantel chimed nine, rousing her from her thoughts. Sighing, she returned downstairs to the shop. It was time to open the store.

She walked to the front door to flip the "Closed" sign to "Open." It was then that she noticed a letter on the floor. Someone must have slipped it under the door while she had been upstairs. Picking up the envelope, she noted that her name alone was scrawled across the front. Curiosity and excitement brimming within her, she walked back to the counter and broke the seal, wondering if it were a note from Declan.

Unfolding the paper, she frowned. It was most definitely not from Declan Reeves. Not sure who sent the missive, she shuddered as she read the threatening words:

This is a note to warn you. Stay away from Lord Cashelmore. He killed his wife. Heed this warning, by all means, if you wish to stay alive.

Stunned by the words on the page, Paulette felt sick to her stomach. Who on earth would send her such a horrid message?

The bell over the front door jingled, startling her, and Paulette looked up, panic racing through her veins like ice water.

"Jeffrey! Thank goodness it's you!" she exclaimed in

relief. For an instant she had a wild thought that whoever had delivered that note had come to the shop. But it was only Jeffrey. Dear, sweet, wonderful Jeffrey Eddington. Tall and handsome, with dark hair and laughing blue eyes, he stepped toward her with his charming grin.

"And it's good to see you too, Paulette, darling!" He gave her a calculating glance, his sunny smile disappearing. "You look as if you've seen a ghost."

Taking a deep breath, Paulette shook her head. "I'm fine. You simply startled me. What are you doing here?"

"I just stopped by Devon House to say good morning but no one was there. Granger told me that Lucien was out for the day, Yvette was at the dressmaker, and that you and Colette were at the shop. So of course I came here to see you both."

"Actually Colette went to the dressmaker with Yvette first. She'll be along later." Carefully, she slipped the note under the accounts ledger. She would look at it again more closely later.

"You're here alone?" he asked with a frown. "I never like it when you girls are alone in the shop. I don't know how Lucien allows it."

"Oh, Jeffrey, please," she said in exasperation. Paulette had had this conversation with Lucien too many times to count and had finally worn him down. She felt no need to go into it yet again with Lord Eddington.

"Well then. I guess you're left with me." He flashed her a grin. "It's just as well. I wanted to talk to you about yesterday."

"Oh?" she asked, trying to sound casual, but her stomach tightened in a knot at his words. Paulette had wanted to talk to Jeffrey about Declan Reeves, but now that the moment was at hand she felt inexplicably nervous.

Jeffrey eyed her with careful consideration. "What is the story with you and Cashelmore?"

"Story?"

"Yes, Paulette. The story. Can you explain to me why you were with him yesterday?"

"We're friends?" Her voice actually squeaked.

He tilted his head. "Are you asking me or telling me?"

"Telling you." She nodded her head vociferously. "Yes, I'm telling you. Lord Cashelmore and I are merely friends."

His eyes narrowed in skepticism. "Do you know anything about this man?"

Paulette shook her head as her heart sank. She knew exactly what he was thinking. "It's not true, Jeffrey."

"So you do know about him then." He released a heavy sigh. "I had hoped that you were unaware of his background, which would explain your association with him. But now I see that is not the case." He paused. "I'm surprised that you haven't more sense, Paulette."

"Jeffrey, Lord Cashelmore didn't have anything to do with his wife's death."

He gave her a meaningful look. "And just *how* do you know this?"

"Because I asked him and he told me."

"As if he would go around admitting he committed murder to anyone who asked?" He raised a dark brow in question.

Paulette paused at his insinuation. Jeffrey made a good point. She supposed if anyone asked Declan Reeves outright if he killed his wife, he would have to say no. It only made sense. One didn't go around telling everyone that he had murdered his wife. Still, deep down she just didn't believe it, couldn't believe it, of Declan. No man could kiss her so passionately and then have the resolve to stop, as he had at his house yesterday afternoon, or be so loving and gentle with his daughter and be the type responsible for another's death. Declan had showed restraint. She didn't think a murderer would be able act so responsibly with his passions.

"No, Jeffrey. I know he's telling me the truth. He's too wonderful and kind to his daughter to ever have hurt her mother in any way. I'm quite certain of that. It's all simply vicious gossip." Paulette grew surer of that fact every minute she spent with Declan Reeves.

Jeffrey gave her a doubtful glance. "So, you are friends with this man who is rumored to have killed his wife in Ireland. How close is your friendship, may I ask?"

"Well . . . we just met a few days ago. He's alone in London and here to help his daughter, who hasn't spoken since her mother died in a fire."

"And what does Lucien think of this 'friendship' of yours?"

Paulette hesitated again before answering. "He doesn't know about it."

"I gathered as much," he said regretfully.

"Jeffrey . . ." She faltered for a second. "I would appreciate it very much if you wouldn't mention that you saw me out with Lord Cashelmore to Lucien or Colette . . . or to anyone else for that matter."

He stared at her hard. "Before I agree to something like that, I need you to be completely truthful with me, Paulette. How serious is this?"

"What do you mean?" She wrung her hands together. Her mind flashed to their passionate kissing in his parlor yesterday afternoon and she felt her cheeks grow warm.

"Is this a romance or just a friendship?"

"Well, I don't know exactly—"

"Paulette, I've known you since you were fifteen years

old. And not once in all those years have I ever seen you out with a gentleman."

"You don't have to rub in that fact," she said in her defense.

"I'm not casting aspersions, sweet girl," he said kindly. He gave her an understanding look. "I'm merely stating a fact. I've never seen you express so much as a passing interest in romance, unlike your younger sister, who seems fixated on the subject. So imagine my great surprise yesterday to find you seated rather intimately with an attractive man and his daughter, like a happy little family. It seemed as if . . ."

"As if?"

He shook his head in disbelief. "As if . . . you cared for each other as more than mere friends."

"It did?" Paulette's heart flipped over. She wasn't even sure how she felt about Declan Reeves, but to have others assume they were having a romance felt quite odd.

"Yes, it did. So please explain to me why you are out with that man and not telling your family about it." He folded his arms across his chest and waited.

After a moment of silence, Paulette had no choice but to confide in Jeffrey as best she could. "I don't know if I can explain it very well."

"Try." He flashed a grin at her.

"Well . . . Lord Cashelmore came in the shop a few days ago to buy a book for his little daughter, Mara. That evening I mentioned his name to Lucien and he told me of the accusations that were printed in the paper. When Lord Cashelmore visited the shop again, we talked and I asked him directly if he had harmed his wife. He denied that he had anything to do with her death but said that there were some people who wished to blame him for it."

"Did he say who these people were?"

"No," she admitted reluctantly. "But I'm sure he would

if I asked him. Then he escorted me home and we made plans to walk in the park. I met him and Mara there on Sunday and that's when you saw us."

"And that's all?" Jeffrey seemed a bit skeptical by her accounting of events. "That's it? That's everything?"

"Yes, that's everything." Essentially that was all that had happened between her and Declan. Aside from the kisses, and she thought it best to leave out the kissing details.

"Have you feelings for him?" Jeffrey asked.

Had she feelings for him? There was no doubt that she had feelings for Declan Reeves. Wild, tumultuous, inexplicable feelings. It was just that she wasn't exactly positive what those feelings were. "I . . . I don't know."

"Are you planning to see him again?"

"Yes," she confessed with some reluctance. "He's coming back to the shop."

"I see." The expression on his face hardened.

"Oh, Jeffrey, please don't tell Lucien or Colette," she pleaded with him. "I promise I will tell them when I'm ready and when I figure out how I feel about him. In the meantime, they would only worry needlessly about me."

"I don't know . . ." He hesitated, obviously torn by the decision he had to make. "I don't like this situation, Paulette. I don't like it one bit."

She looked up at him beseechingly, her hands clasped together. "Please, Jeffrey."

"I don't understand why I always seem to be the one looking out for you girls and keeping all your secrets," he grumbled under his breath, shaking his head.

"What are you talking about?" she asked. Secrets? Now that was an interesting new development. Just who else was Jeffrey keeping secrets for? Colette? Or Juliette?

"Nothing." He brushed aside his comment as if he

hadn't said it. "I'm just concerned for your well-being. Admittedly, I don't know this Lord Cashelmore, but I don't like what I've heard about him. After I saw you with him yesterday, I was curious so I checked in with some of the authorities with whom I have connections. You may as well know that it's just a matter of time before formal charges are going to be brought against him, Paulette."

"But it's not true!" she protested. Feeling sick at the thought of Declan being charged with murdering his wife when he was innocent, she shivered.

"The authorities will bring him in before long. From what I could gather, it seems that there are those who say Lord Cashelmore's wife died accidentally, but others say that he had motive to want her dead and that he caused the fire deliberately."

Paulette felt tears sting her eyes. "Declan would never do such a thing!"

Jeffrey shook his head, his expression concerned. "You just met the man. You don't know anything about him, Paulette."

"Neither do you," she pointed out, growing a bit angry. "But I know him better than you do. And I'm telling you, Jeffrey, that Declan Reeves is not capable of killing someone. He's not the kind of man who would intentionally harm someone, let alone the mother of his child. He loves that little girl and is thoughtful and kind to her. And to me. He may seem forbidding at first, but once you come to know him, he's intelligent, and kind, and sweet, and funny, and—"

"Oh, good Lord, you've kissed him already, haven't you?" Jeffrey interrupted. His expression was one of abject misery.

Stunned that he read her so easily, Paulette remained

silent, feeling her cheeks burn. She could not deny the truth.

"What is it with you Hamilton sisters?" he said to himself, shaking his head again.

Ignoring the sudden turn in the conversation, Paulette continued. "He did not kill his wife, Jeffrey. I swear to you. He's here in London to help his daughter, not because he's hiding. He had nothing to do with her death. Declan is a good man. I know it and I'm an excellent judge of character."

"Well, being that I haven't kissed the man as you have, I can't say if he's dangerous or not," Jeffrey began sarcastically. "Is he a good man tarnished by tragic circumstances? Or is he a deceptive man who has possibly gotten away with murder? I can't say for certain. But I do know you, Paulette Hamilton. You're not a flighty girl, or an impressionable girl who is swayed by the slightest whim. You are one of the smartest and most practical women I've ever known. So . . . I'm going to trust you on this matter. If you trust him, I'll give you that much. But I don't like the situation at all, nor do I like the idea of keeping this from Lucien and Colette. But for the time being I won't say a word about it unless they ask me directly or unless I deem it necessary to inform them." He paused and looked at her intently. "You can continue to see your Lord Cashelmore. But I plan to keep an eye on you. And him. And I'm going to look into the matter more closely."

Relief flooded Paulette at his pronouncement. He wasn't going to tell her sister and brother-in-law. She was safe for a little while longer. "Thank you, Jeffrey."

He shook his head and muttered to himself. "How is it that once again I'm cast in the role of protector to you girls?"

"What are you talking about?" she asked.

"Nothing," he grumbled with a weary sigh. "But you need to be very careful, Paulette. Don't do anything foolish and make me regret this decision."

"I won't. I promise. Thank you, Jeffrey."

Sometimes Jeffrey was better than having a real brother. She didn't think a real brother would be quite so understanding. But she loved him as if he were her true brother and she had since the first time she met him. She remembered that Jeffrey had shown up unexpectedly at her and Colette's first reading group discussion at the bookshop. He had charmed them all that night with his wit and good humor. For a while, she and her sisters had believed there might be a romance between him and Juliette, and he had even followed Juliette to America when she ran away. But Juliette had married Captain Harrison Fleming and remained in the United States. And Jeffrey returned to London and continued to be an integral and beloved member of their family.

Paulette walked from around the counter and leaned up on tiptoe, placing a kiss on Jeffrey's cheek.

"Don't try and sweeten my mood with kisses, young lady. I'm not happy with this situation." His words were hard but his expression was soft.

"Yes, I am aware of how you feel and that makes me even more appreciative of you keeping your word."

"Be careful," he admonished.

"I will. I promise."

Paulette suddenly remembered the mysterious warning letter she received just before he arrived. For the flash of an instant she considered telling him about it and asking his advice, but if she showed the note to Jeffrey he would only become unhappier with the situation and most likely overreact and, worst of all, tell Lucien. She decided against mentioning it for now. Instead she changed the subject altogether. "How was the show last night with the fascinating Miss Hunter?"

Jeffrey gave her a lopsided grin. "Delightful."

"I'm glad to hear it." She smiled back at him.

The bell above the door jingled and some customers entered the shop. Their private conversation came to an unavoidable end. Jeffrey bid her farewell as Paulette had to assist her customers. Feeling a little remorseful that she had not told him about the letter, she soon found her thoughts occupied by the needs of the bookshop. It was a busy day, brightened later that afternoon by a visit from Declan Reeves and Mara.

He arrived holding his daughter's hand. Mara favored her with a warm smile and they spent an hour in the children's section. Paulette chatted with Declan as best she could when she was not helping shoppers.

And so it went. For an entire week, Declan and Mara came to visit the shop every day. It thrilled Paulette to know that Declan was coming to see her. And as luck would have it, Colette never seemed to be in the store when Declan stopped by. Although Lizzie Parker raised a questioning eyebrow at Declan's daily appearances at the shop, she didn't utter a single word and Paulette silently blessed her.

Paulette found herself anticipating his visits and taking more care with her appearance each morning. Unlike Yvette, Paulette had never given much thought to how she looked before. She had always dressed prettily enough and possessed a fairly fashionable wardrobe. But now she spent time pondering which color looked better with her fair complexion and which gown showed off her figure to its best advantage and which hairstyle was more flattering to her face.

Being attractive to Declan Reeves was suddenly very important to her as she looked forward to his visits each day. Something about him fascinated her. Perhaps it was his mysterious past. Perhaps it was the lyrical sound of his voice, the intensity of his green eyes, and the looks he gave her that made her knees go weak with desire. Or the memories of the kisses they shared. The ones she longed to experience again. Declan Reeves filled her thoughts during the day and her dreams at night.

And Paulette simply wanted to be with him any time and any way that she could.

Chapter 12

Temptation

Declan knew that Paulette would be closing up the shop about now and he struggled with his desire to see her and the fact that he knew he should stay away from her. He had taken Mara to Hamilton's Book Shoppe every afternoon that week on the pretense of obtaining books for his little girl. Which was partly true, because Mara enjoyed their visits and loved the books Paulette chose for her, and Mara now had a stack of picture books almost as tall as she was.

Yet he knew the true reason he was visiting the shop. He simply couldn't stay away from Paulette Hamilton. And today was no exception.

It wasn't just because she was beautiful, though she most definitely was. It wasn't just her intelligent blue eyes. It wasn't her delicate face and silky golden blond hair. It wasn't her sweet scent and soft skin. And it was more than her honesty and good nature. It was much more than her kindness and affection for Mara or her impressive business skills.

It was simply her. Just Paulette. Everything about her enchanted him.

And Paulette didn't deserve to be dragged into the tangled nightmare that had become his world.

During the last few years his life had certainly become one unending, inescapable hell.

He glanced down at the letter he had received yesterday morning. Someone had slipped it under his front door, his butler told him, for it hadn't come with the regular post. It was a warning letter of sorts. Threatening. He didn't need to reread it, for the short message was seared into his memory.

You killed Margaret. You will pay for her death. If not one way, then in another. Tread carefully. You may be next to die.

He wondered who would send such a note to him. Most likely it was someone from Margaret's family. It had to be one of her sisters. Ellen and Deirdre Ryan had never liked him and were no doubt furious that he had taken Mara from Ireland, but he couldn't believe that either of them would resort to harassing him in such a cowardly and underhanded way. Would they? He wasn't sure of anything anymore.

How had his once promising life come to this?

He had been born into wealth and privilege and had been happy for the first part of his life. Then his parents had died in a violent carriage accident when Declan was ten years old, leaving him alone. Raised by nannies and tutors on the grand estate of Cashelmore Manor outside of Dublin, he had only his cousin Gerald O'Rourke as family. At nineteen he married Margaret Ryan because he had been in love with her. Or so he thought at the time. Now he could see that it had been more lust than love. They had been desperate to have each other and

Declan had been too blinded by her to see the truth. His cousin Gerald had advised him against marrying Margaret, declaring the girl and her family nothing but trouble, but Declan had not heeded that advice. He'd given in to Margaret's pleading to marry and his own desires.

And what was not to want? Margaret was a desirable woman by any man's standards. With silver blond hair, intense green eyes, and a face that melted hearts, Margaret was a force to be reckoned with even as a young girl. Everyone was in love with her, in spite of her mercurial moods and incomprehensible whims. From a distinguished family in Dublin, she had a line of eligible suitors vying for her fair hand. Each of her sisters had married very advantageously and Margaret's parents had wanted their youngest daughter to wed the powerful Duke of Kilcarragh, who was more than agreeable to the arrangement, being quite taken with Margaret's beauty. But he was older than the eighteen-year-old by almost twenty years and she wanted no part of him. Known for his gray hair and his grand estate called Cheshire Court, the Duke of Kilcarragh was eager for the match. But Declan was who Margaret wanted to rescue her from the duke and her family's pressure to marry him.

So Declan and Margaret ran off to Galway, married in secret, and then faced the wrath of her family and that of the angry and humiliated Duke of Kilcarragh. The Ryan family had tried to have their union annulled but by then it was too late. Margaret was already carrying Declan's child.

Living at Cashelmore, Declan believed that the two of them had been happy enough in the beginning, in spite of all the drama that accompanied their marriage. When Mara was born, Declan was overjoyed to have a family. He instantly fell in love with his infant daughter and doted on her day and night. But things quickly fell apart between him and Margaret. She became more petulant and disenchanted with married life, especially after Mara was born, missing the attention and drama of being the most sought after woman in Dublin. She declared she would have no more children and barred Declan from her bed. It was no wonder their every conversation ended in a bitter argument.

Relations grew worse between them, until he and Margaret were barely on speaking terms and could only just tolerate each other's presence. She threatened daily that she was planning to leave him and return to her family. Rumors swirled that the Duke of Kilcarragh was still willing to marry her, but Declan had his suspicions that his wife was having an affair with someone else.

The events that led up to the night of the fire haunted him to this day. He may indirectly have been the cause of those events, but he never intended for Margaret to die that evening.

He hated to think of it, and felt regret about the hurtful words he had shouted at her before the fire began. The fire that destroyed his world at the house in Galway that night was still a mystery to him.

He and Margaret had gone to Galway on the western Irish coast last October in a desperate attempt at reconciling. They had spent their honeymoon there, after their elopement, and those few days had really been the only happy ones of their ill-fated marriage. Declan thought returning to the place with their daughter might help them recapture the feeling they once had for one another and it had been at his suggestion that they went. Margaret had been most unwilling and had argued with him bitterly against the trip. But she gave in reluctantly, pouting and complaining the entire journey there.

They stayed at Kenmare House, his mother's ancestral

home. A large and rambling old house, it was constructed mainly of wood and stone and set on a hill overlooking the sea. He had loved the house as a child because there were so many secret passages and stairways.

And then came that fateful, horrifying night. He tried to block out the dreadful memories of the wild flames and the scorching heat. The black smoke and Margaret's agonizing screams of pain. But worse than that had been Mara's petrified expression and hysterical sobs. The girl was shaking and calling for him. *"Papa! Papa!"* Even hours after he pulled her into his arms and held her, she still trembled and sobbed his name in fear. He heard her terrified cries even now echoing in his mind. How Mara came to be in that part of the house that late at night confounded him to this day, for he had put her to bed earlier that evening himself.

But everything that happened after that was a mystery and he had recounted all that he knew to the authorities. Now Declan took the threatening note that had appeared under his front door that morning and tossed it in the fire. He'd had enough of the accusations. At first he had not paid them any mind, for he knew he was innocent and he was too mired in grief to care much what others were saying about him. His focus was on Mara, who was suffering more than he could imagine. The child saw her mother burn to death in front of her eyes. Good God, he got sick every time he thought of what his sweet daughter had gone through that wretched night in Galway.

But as the months wore on, he finally pulled himself out of the dark cloud of mourning and shock for his young wife and the life they might have shared together, and worry over his poor daughter, still frightened out of her wits. It was then he took note of what was being said about him. While he had buried himself at Cashelmore,

Margaret's sisters had ostensibly come to help with Mara, but Declan soon realized they had gone to work with their whispering lies, spreading doubts to the authorities about what happened the night of the fire and Declan's part in it and, worst of all, trying to poison Mara against him.

When he had overheard Deirdre one afternoon in the nursery with Mara, saying that is was his fault that Margaret had died, he almost lost his mind. He ordered the woman from his house and made plans to leave Ireland then and there. Mara had been traumatized enough and the last thing she needed was being told her father was responsible for the nightmare that had altered her young life.

He had no doubt that Deirdre or Ellen had sent the note today.

All he wanted to do now was see Paulette Hamilton, for only she could erase the ugly thoughts and memories that the awful letter had elicited. Something about Paulette's nature soothed his soul and he wanted to be near her, hear her voice, and look into her eyes. He just needed to be with her.

Mara was already asleep in bed for the night, coming down with a cold and not feeling well, so she would not miss him if he left for a little while.

So Declan found himself going to Hamilton's Book Shoppe to see Paulette.

Chapter 13

Upstairs

It had been another bustling day at the shop and Paulette was helping the last of the customers with their purchase of some books of Shakespeare's plays. Lizzie had left a few minutes early to attend a special dinner for her mother's birthday, so Paulette was alone in the shop once again.

"I'm sure you'll enjoy these," she assured the woman, as she wrapped the books in brown paper and tied them with Hamilton's signature green ribbon.

"Thank you very much," the woman called, heading toward the door just as it opened.

The bells rang and Declan Reeves entered the shop. He tipped his hat to the woman as she passed by and then turned his attention to Paulette.

Her heart fluttered wildly at the sight of him. Declan had not come to the shop today and she had tried not to wonder why and to ignore how incredibly disappointed she was by not seeing him. Standing there now, he looked so tall and handsome it almost took her breath away. His brown hair was combed back from his clean-shaven face. His emerald eyes, framed by dark lashes, gazed at her. His mouth, with lips that had kissed her so passionately, broke into a devastating grin.

"Good evening, Paulette," he said.

"Hello, Declan." She could barely contain her joy at being with him again. "It's so nice to see you."

"Mara wasn't feeling well today, so we weren't able to come by this afternoon."

"Oh, I hope she's all right." Relief flooded her at his explanation.

"It's just a slight cold. She'll be fine. But I missed seeing you today and thought I might escort you home this evening."

A thrill of excitement raced through her at his words. He'd missed her! And he had come to see her! Filled with a giddy happiness, she grinned at him. "Oh, that would be lovely, Declan. I just have to close up. It won't take me long, I promise."

Not if she didn't finish the day's accounts, but she could do that tomorrow. There was no rush for her to be home either. Colette and Lucien had escorted Yvette to a musicale and would not return for hours. If Paulette were a bit late, she would not be missed because it wouldn't be the first time she had stayed late at the bookshop.

As she hurriedly locked the door, drew the blind, and turned the sign to "Closed," she could feel Declan's eyes upon her.

"Have I told you how impressed I am with your bookshop?" he asked.

Surprised by his words, she turned to look at him. "No, but I can assume from your frequent visits that you like it here well enough," she said rather flirtatiously.

His laughter, rich and musical, wrapped around her. Paulette's heart skipped a beat.

Then he said, "I honestly think you and your sisters have done amazing work here."

"Thank you." She beamed with pleasure at his compliment. The shop was her pride and joy and it thrilled her that he recognized how hard they worked to make it a special place.

"And you spent your whole life here?" he asked.

She began to close the account ledgers and straighten up the main counter while she spoke to him. "Yes. I suppose it was a bit unusual, living above a bookshop, but my father loved his books and I've helped in the shop ever since I can remember. We were happy here. Although not to say that I'm not happy now, but sometimes I miss those days, when it was just us five girls and Papa and *Maman.*"

"It sounds like you had a happy childhood."

"I did." Paulette couldn't help but smile. "We didn't always have much, but we had each other. We were happy upstairs."

"Does anyone live up there now?"

"Not any longer. We had a little family there for the past two years acting as caretakers and helping out in the shop. It was nice having them here. But they moved to a lovely house and now we're looking for a replacement." Recalling this moment later, Paulette would never understand what possessed her to utter the next words. "Would you like to see it?"

"Your former home upstairs?" His dark brows raised in surprise.

"Yes." Her eyes met his, and as hard as she tried Paulette could not read his thoughts, but his expression grew serious. A nest of butterflies fluttered in her stomach.

Without a word, Declan nodded his head in assent and the butterflies inside of her took flight.

She whispered, "Follow me then."

Paulette walked on shaky legs to the back of the shop toward the door that led to the living quarters above, with Declan behind her. It was silent as they ascended the stairs and entered the warm rooms over the shop. That afternoon had been very hot and the heat seemed to settle, as it usually did, in the quiet, unused space upstairs. Outside the sun was setting and the rooms were cast in still shadows.

She faced him, chattering a mile a minute, suddenly feeling ridiculous for bringing him up here. "Well, this is it. This is where I grew up. It's changed a lot in the last few years. This room has been repainted and given new rugs and furniture. It's much brighter and airier in here than when my mother decorated the place. She preferred darker colors and heavier fabrics. The bedrooms are over here. The largest was my parents' room, the middle one was Colette and Juliette's, and the third one belonged to Lisette, Yvette, and me."

He looked around with interest. "When I was a boy I always had a room to myself and wished I had someone to share it with, someone to talk to and play with. I think it's nice that you shared a room with your sisters."

Paulette gave him a rueful smile. "It was nice in some ways, not so nice in others."

He smiled back at her and her gaze locked with his.

Silently they stood there in the waning daylight, the shadows growing deeper around them. The heat seemed to increase by the second and Paulette found it difficult to draw a breath. She was afraid to move for she didn't know what consequences her movements might incur.

"It's so hot," she murmured, feeling her summer gown sticking to her body. Her head was spinning and she could barely think. She had never felt such oppressive heat.

He nodded in agreement, his gaze growing darker. He took a step toward her.

Her heart pounding in her chest, she inched closer to him. She felt that she was on the edge of doing something irrevocable and yet could not stop herself from doing so. She wanted to be with him.

"Paulette . . ." Her name was the softest whisper of a question on his lips. He rested his hands on her shoulders and the contact thrilled her.

"Yes," she whispered back, tilting her face up toward him, inviting him to kiss her, reveling in the feel of his strong hands on her.

And kiss her he certainly did.

Declan drew her into his arms, covering her mouth with his, and she was lost, completely and utterly lost. His lips, warm and firm, moved over hers with an increasing urgency. She opened her mouth and he slipped his tongue inside. She was more prepared for the sensation than she had been a week ago and now she kissed him back in eagerness, her tongue delving in his mouth. Her hands found their way around his neck, his skin hot to the touch. His masculine scent enveloped her.

They kissed for what seemed like forever, barely pausing for air. It felt as though Declan was going to devour her and she honestly didn't care if he did, the kissing was so heavenly. Heedless of the heat, Paulette pressed her body against his and the low groan that escaped his lips excited her and scared her at the same time.

His hands, fingers splayed, slid into her hair, releasing the pins that held it in place. One by one he dropped them to the floor. Her long hair fell in heavy golden waves around her. Still she kissed him with a ravenous hunger.

And he kissed her, just as lost as she was.

She never knew that kisses could be so all-consuming, so shattering to one's senses. His hands moved lower, running down her back, sliding over her bottom and pressing her against the hardness of him. She gasped into his mouth as a shiver of sheer, unadulterated pleasure surged through her body.

It was then she realized he was slowly unfastening the clasps on the back of her pink gown. A flutter of panic stole her breath for the briefest of moments, and then she wished he would hurry and remove her dress completely. The heat consumed her and she wanted nothing more than to be free of the clothing that restricted her from feeling Declan's skin against hers.

He began kissing her cheek, her chin, and down her throat to her chest. Paulette's breath came in shallow gasps as he dipped his head lower, between her breasts, as her loosened gown fell away from her chest. Trembling, she held his head, her fingers running through his thick, brown hair, wondering if he could feel the frantic pounding of her heart in her chest. It felt as if it would explode.

Lifting his head, Declan gave her a look of infinite longing before he gently spun her around to better undo the myriad of ties that held her complex wardrobe together. With her assistance, they removed her gown and layers of underclothing, freeing her from the stifling heat. In nothing but her thin chemise and stockings, she did not care that she was half naked in front of him. In fact she helped him remove his jacket and shirt, marveling at the bare expanse of his male chest. She caressed the smooth skin, warm and hard beneath her fingers. Unable to stop herself she pressed her lips against his chest, placing soft kisses upon him. But she grew shy at removing his trousers, which he did himself.

Almost ready to flee, she flung her arms around him to keep herself from running away and he resumed kissing her mouth. With their many layers of clothing no longer separating them, she was amazed that the heat between them only increased. His hands roamed her body, over the curve of her hips, and along to her thighs. Slowly he began sliding down the stocking of one leg. She stilled. The touch of his fingers on her inner thigh caused her to ache with desire. His hands glided the silky material down over thigh, her knee, her calf, her ankle, and, trembling, she lifted her foot as he slid the stocking over her toes. Ever so gently he removed the stocking from her other leg, caressing her bare skin with his fingers as he slipped the silk from her.

He drew her back into the circle of his arms, with only her lawn chemise between them now. They kissed and the warmth of his mouth on hers filled her with a sweet longing. Again, his hands moved over her body, down her back, along her waist, and over her hips until he found the edge of her chemise, her last vestige of modesty. Slowly he pushed the garment up the length of her. He stopped kissing her mouth long enough to lift the thin material over her head, tossing it to the floor. Completely revealed to each other, she was breathless. Now skin to skin, the contact was heady enough to make her grow faint as she stood with her naked body pressed against his.

The intimacy of it left her weak with a need she had no name for. She placed her hands against his bare chest, the position reminiscent of the first time they had kissed in the bookshop. The difference of touching his chest covered by a shirt and jacket that day and touching him bare-chested now was almost more than she could take. Light-headed with desire and wondrous sensations, she trembled. But she had made a promise to herself and to Declan that afternoon in his parlor when they had last kissed that she would not stop him the next time. And she meant it. She did not wish to end this.

Although now that she was completely naked in his arms, her resolve faltered somewhat.

He drew back from kissing her. Lifting her chin to make her look at him, he said in a low voice, "Good God, lass, you're more beautiful than I imagined. Have you any idea how much I want you?"

"I want you, too," she murmured, surprised that any intelligible words came out of her mouth.

Placing his hands on either side of her face, he drew her to him and kissed her so thoroughly she thought she would die from the pleasure of it. In one sure motion, he lifted her in his arms and walked toward one of the bedrooms, carrying her. Paulette wrapped her arms around his neck, grateful for his strength. Her own legs were too weak to take the steps forward. The deliberateness of his gesture filled her with a giddy joy. This was going to happen.

Everything she had read about and wondered about was finally going to happen to her. All she wanted was Declan. She was immersed in him. In the exquisite feel of his warm skin, the intimate touch of his hands, the male scent of his body, the heavenly taste of his mouth. The look of passion in his eyes.

They were in the small bedroom, the one that used to be Colette and Juliette's. The heat and the hushed stillness of the room wrapped around them like a heavy blanket. Declan gently set her down on the bed, then climbed in beside her, covering her body with the muscled length of his own. Feeling unnerved, she closed her eyes. He rained sweet, gentle kisses on her face, her eyes, her cheeks, her chin, and the tip of her nose.

"My sweet, sweet Paulette," he whispered.

She lost any remnants of fear or uneasiness at that

point, becoming unbelievably calm. The feel of Declan's body over hers had done that to her. It felt perfectly right and she hadn't expected that. Growing bolder with her hands, she explored his male form, caressing his back, the muscles pulled taut as he held himself above her. The strength in him comforted her, settled her. And filled her with a yearning need for him. Her hands slid lower over his the curve of his buttocks, pressing him close against her and he stilled instantly at the contact. She gasped in surprise at the feel of him naked and hard between her thighs.

Her eyes flew open then.

In the growing darkness, she could feel his eyes on her wanting to know if she was still willing. In response she kissed him and wrapped her arms around his broad shoulders, clinging to him.

"Declan." She breathed his name.

A low groan escaped him as he rose up. Then he entered her, causing Paulette to draw in her breath sharply at the fullness of him inside her, closing her eyes tightly once more. She held her breath, gripping his shoulders, waiting, not sure what was to come next. He kissed her and she could feel him trembling. Slowly . . . slowly he began to move within her, gentle thrusts at first, then becoming more forceful. Overwhelmed by sensations and emotions she didn't know existed before, she held on to him until she realized her hips were rising to meet his and a languorous, liquid heat began to spread through every muscle in her body.

Declan reached his hand between them just where their bodies were joined and touched her, almost causing her to jump out of her skin with the exquisite pleasure of it. As he stroked her, he still moved within her and if Paulette thought she couldn't breathe the last time he kissed her she surely couldn't breathe now. She thought she might die right then and there. Sensations overwhelmed her. Her breath came in short gasps and pants as he continued to pleasure her with his hand and body.

"Oh, Declan . . ." She had no words, no coherent thoughts, no sense of time or place.

Never had she dreamed of this. Certainly nothing in that old medical book had prepared her for *this*. For these utterly blissful sensations and the passionate desire that coursed through her. For the sense of fulfillment and wonder. For the timeless beauty of being so intimate with a man and feeling so thoroughly female.

As Declan continued to caress her, the touch of his hand combined with the movement of his body caused ripples of pleasure to sweep over her and she yearned for even more. She thought she would go mad with the longing as she arched against his hand and he continued to move within her. At last great waves of ecstasy surged through her, and she cried out his name into the darkness. He rose over her then, bracing both hands on either side of her and thrusting into her with an intensity that she craved and matched. As she shattered into what felt like a million tiny sparkling stars, he took his own pleasure, every muscle in his body flexing with an urgent need.

Quite dizzy and feeling faint, she lay beneath him, her arms around his neck.

"Dear God, Paulette," he whispered, kissing her cheek. Declan rolled to the side of her and flung his arm over his head, breathing heavy and slick with sweat.

In spite of the sweltering heat she could have stayed there forever, so content was she beside him, her legs intertwined with his. The room had grown quite dark, and only the dim glow from the streetlamps outside gave them any light.

It occurred to her then that her sisters had greatly understated how special intimacies between a man and woman truly were.

"I didn't know it would be like that," she said softly after a few moments.

"I didn't either, my love." He leaned in and kissed her cheek again, still a little out of breath. "I didn't either."

Her heart thrilled at the term of endearment he used. In complete and utter contentment, she rested her head upon his chest and he wrapped his arm around her, holding her close, his fingers idly stroking her hair. Feeling indescribably safe and happy, she sighed.

"It wasn't like that with your wife?" she asked.

"Paulette!" He almost choked in astonishment at her question.

She lifted her head to look at him in the dark. "I was simply curious. Am I not supposed to ask such things?"

"No, you're not supposed to ask such things, lass." He chuckled a little. "But in answer to your question, no, it wasn't like that with my wife at all."

"Oh," she responded for lack of anything better to say, placing her head back on his chest. Still, she couldn't help feeling a bit victorious at his answer. He thought that what they had done was just as special and magical as she did.

"Am I not supposed to ask you what I'm thinking?" she whispered.

"My sweet Paulette, you can ask me anything you like." He continued to run his fingers through her hair, the motion soothing and comforting to her.

Somehow, after being so intimate with him, Paulette needed to know more about the mysterious woman who had claimed his heart and married him. And had a child with him. "Would you tell me about her then?"

His hand stopped in mid-motion, tangled in her tresses. "About my wife?" He could not disguise the surprise in his voice.

"Yes. What was she like, Mara's mother? What was her name?"

He was silent for a moment. "I guess there is no dissuading you from this topic, is there?"

"No," she said, smiling.

A resigned sigh escaped him and he resumed stroking her hair absently. "Margaret Ryan was sweet and not unlike you in appearance. Blond and pretty. I believed I was in love with her and she with me, but now I see that she was rather immature for her age. Looking back, I know she married me only to spite her controlling family and then regretted it afterward."

"She wasn't really in love with you?" Surprised by this, Paulette sensed the hurt in him. She had just assumed his marriage had been a love match and she felt a sense of feminine triumph at this bit of information. She pressed a small kiss against his chest.

"Margaret might have thought she was in love with me at one point, but I don't think she ever knew what love meant. She used me to thwart her family and escape the marriage that was being arranged for her. It seemed I was younger and infinitely more preferable to the older duke they wanted to wed her to. So we ran off together and got married against her family's wishes. Very soon after that she reached the conclusion that she didn't wish to be married to me either, but by then it was too late. She was pregnant with Mara."

"I'm sorry. That sounds terribly sad," Paulette whispered in disbelief. She could not imagine being in such an unhappy marriage. Her parents had not had the happiest of unions, she knew, but since then she had only witnessed the love and joy of her sisters' marriages. She had never heard of anything so dreadful as Declan's marriage.

"It was more complicated than sad, to tell you the truth," he explained calmly. "I tried to make Margaret happy. I tried everything I could to make our marriage work, but she was just as determined to end it."

"End it?" Paulette could not keep the bewilderment out of her voice. "You mean she wanted a divorce?"

"Yes. And I was almost inclined to give her one."

Stunned by this revelation, she could only ask, "What happened then?"

"Then there was the fire."

Paulette paused for a minute, thinking about this woman, Margaret Ryan, who married him and then didn't want him and ended up dying tragically in a fire. "Will you tell me about the fire, Declan? What happened that night?"

Chapter 14

Past

Declan stared at the beautiful girl lying naked beside him in the darkness, her long hair spilling around them. Paulette had just given herself to him with an earnestness and honesty that touched his heart, so how could he deny her?

Yet he had never told anyone the intimate details of that terrible last night with Margaret.

It was uncomfortably warm in the little bedroom above the bookshop and Declan knew he should take Paulette home, but he didn't want to leave. Didn't want to leave her. It had been so long since he had a woman in his bed.

And he didn't even want to think about Margaret Ryan while he was in bed with Paulette Hamilton. Let alone talk about her.

It was hard not to compare Paulette to Margaret, especially when she had asked about his deceased wife. In essence there was no comparison, even though the two women were similar physically. They were worlds apart in personality. Where Margaret had been petulant and overindulged, used to getting her own way, Paulette was mature for her age and completely unspoiled. Margaret was petty and prone to jealous fits, where Paulette was reasonable and calm. In bed, Margaret had been timid and unresponsive. And Paulette . . . Paulette had been astonishingly passionate and eager to learn.

There was no comparing the two women. In fact he didn't like to think of them in the same breath. Paulette was with him now and that was all that mattered.

"Please, Declan." Paulette's soft voice interrupted his thoughts.

Her words tugged at him. He supposed Paulette deserved to know what happened. Deserved the truth from him. It was the least he could do for her. Oddly enough, at the sound of her soft plea, he suddenly found himself wanting to share with her the events of that fateful night. Wanting her to understand what had happened.

There in the darkness with Paulette in his arms, the words came from him much easier than he would have imagined.

"My marriage had deteriorated to a terrible state of affairs, so last October Margaret and I had gone to my mother's home in Galway, to try to reconcile with each other for Mara's sake," he began slowly. "I loved Kenmare House and we had spent a happy week there once, so I thought it would be good for us. But it was a disaster from the moment we arrived there. She locked me from her bedroom and sulked about, refusing to discuss anything with me. For weeks I suspected she had a lover, but I could never prove it until I found a letter she was sending to him."

"She was unfaithful to you?" Paulette asked incredulously. The shock and scorn in her voice touched him.

He nodded. "I didn't believe it at first. But I then I found her note, saying how much she loved him and couldn't wait to return to him. I shouldn't have read it, but I did and then I confronted her about him."

"Who was he?"

"A young lord from the estate that bordered Cashel-more. He was apparently smitten with her, head over heels, completely unaware of her true nature. I actually felt sorry for him, because he was as captivated by her as I had been once."

"Oh, Declan."

The sincerity in her voice calmed him as he continued to thread his fingers through Paulette's silky hair. She smelled so sweet. He took a deep breath before resuming his tale.

"As you can imagine, I was furious when I found the note. Later that night, I put Mara to bed and then went to speak to Margaret. I was going to tell her she could finally have her divorce. She had finally won. I would be well rid of her, as long as I kept my daughter. I went to Margaret's room, but she had locked herself in again and wouldn't talk to me. I pounded on the door and yelled to her . . ." He paused. "Now I'm ashamed to admit I screamed vile names at her."

The memory of what he said to his wife chilled him to this day. He'd been furious with her and called her a lying whore, among other choice expletives he didn't wish to share with Paulette. He added in a low tone, "I also threatened to kill her. I said I would shoot her."

Paulette said without hesitation, "I don't blame you."

Feeling a momentous relief at finally telling someone about the worst moments of his life, he kissed the top of Paulette's head, which rested so comfortably on his chest, grateful that she seemed to understand him. "I was livid enough to kill her that night. Instead I went back to my rooms and drank. I drank until I got so drunk I eventually passed out. I don't know how long I slept or what woke me exactly, but something did. Shouts perhaps. And an odd, glowing light outside my window. When I looked out, I could see that the entire north side of the house was in flames. I knew Margaret's bedroom was there, for she had chosen a room as far from mine as possible. My first thought was for Mara and I raced to her room, which was down the hall from mine. But her bed was empty. The servants were yelling and calling to each other to get out of the house, but no one had seen Mara. I knew I had to get out, but I couldn't leave without my daughter and I didn't know where she was."

He realized that Paulette was holding her breath. He gave her a little shake until she exhaled.

"Then what?" she whispered, her eyes wide.

"Then I ran through the rambling, burning house, looking for my wife and daughter. Just as I neared the hallway where Margaret's room was, I heard the screams. The torturous cries from Margaret and the shrill screams from Mara. I couldn't say which was louder, but they were both horrifying to hear. When I looked . . . The end of the hallway was engulfed in a wall of fire and Margaret was covered in flames, her hair, her nightgown . . . the smell of smoke and burning flesh was unbearable. While Mara . . . God, Mara stood transfixed not far from Margaret . . . watching her mother burn to death—"

Declan's voice caught and he couldn't continue. Just the thought of what Mara witnessed that night ripped him apart inside. He should have protected her better. That was his job as her father and he had failed to keep her from the nightmare she lived.

Paulette squeezed him and he held her tightly to him, needing to feel her closer to his body.

He took a deep breath and began again. "I wanted to save Margaret, I did. But a beam fell from the ceiling, barely missing Mara, and blocking the way to Margaret.

I had to get my daughter out of there. I screamed for Margaret to run but she couldn't even move. The flames were everywhere and the smoke became blinding. There was no way I could possibly save her by that point. She was beyond anyone's help. So I did the only thing I could do . . . I grabbed Mara in my arms and I ran from the burning house." He paused in silence. "And Margaret died."

"Oh, God, Declan," Paulette breathed, choking back a sob. "I'm sorry I brought this up and made you relive it. I'm so very sorry. It must be too painful for you to talk about. I had no idea what you and Mara went through . . . I didn't know . . ."

"I know you didn't, my love." Deeply touched by Paulette's concern and worry for him, Declan was unable to recall the last time anyone worried about his welfare. He kissed her soft cheek, loving the feel of her in his arms.

She hugged him tighter. "It's so dreadful. Now I'm not at all surprised that Mara won't speak."

"Oh, God but she screamed for what seemed like hours afterward. Only saying 'Papa' over and over again, until she fell asleep in my arms out of sheer exhaustion. She's never said another word since then."

"The poor little thing, losing her mother that way."

"My heart breaks for her," Declan added.

Paulette asked, "So then what happened?"

"I told the authorities everything that night, leaving out only the part about Margaret's lover, Lord Williams."

"Why?"

"I didn't want the scandal. I didn't ever want Mara to grow up and hear such terrible things about her mother. What she saw that night was hellish enough. She can at least cherish what good memories she has of her mother."

"Why are they blaming you for the fire then?" she questioned.

"One of Margaret's maids overheard me threaten to kill her earlier that evening and she told everyone. Margaret's family has always hated me for running off with her and it's easy to blame me. It was no secret to anyone that our marriage was in trouble. But I honestly don't know how the fire started or what Mara was doing in that part of the house so late at night. I was drinking in my room all evening and regret every minute that I was. Because of that I haven't had a single drop of liquor since. I could have easily lost Mara, too, if I had not woken up when I did. . . . I can't bear to think about what might have happened to her if I hadn't."

"Oh, Declan." She leaned forward and kissed him on the lips. "I'm so sorry, but I'm glad you shared this with me."

"Thank you for listening to me, lass." Surpsingly, it was good to talk about his past with her, as if some frozen part of him was slowly melting away.

"What are you going to do now?" Paulette asked softly.

"I haven't decided yet. The Ryans are mounting some sort of case against me and I suppose I shall have to return to Ireland to defend myself sooner rather than later. I just wish I knew how the fire started that night."

"Are there any clues?"

"It started in Margaret's room. That's all they know for certain. Was it a stray ember from the fireplace? Or something deliberate? No one can say for sure. But when they combine our failing marriage, the fact that Margaret was seeking a divorce, and my angry threats to kill her that night . . . all fingers point to me." He sighed heavily.

"But you didn't do it!" Paulette cried.

Her unwavering belief in his innocence made the wall

he had built around his heart begin to crumble. "Thank you for that, Paulette, but there are others who don't see it that way."

"They have no proof," she pointed out, then hesitated. "Do they?"

"No, which is why I haven't been arrested. But Margaret's sisters are determined to see me punished for her death. They started their accusations during the funeral and of course the whole countryside heard the rumors within days, but I was so consumed with worry over Mara that I ignored it all at first. I just thought it was their bitterness and that nothing would come of it, since I am innocent."

"Why did you leave Ireland?"

"I had to get Mara away from Margaret's sisters, Deirdre and Ellen. They wanted to turn my daughter against me and I couldn't allow that. I thought she could recover better away from any memories associated with that night last October and anything to do with Margaret."

When he left, Declan had no idea if his plan would work. Now he knew that leaving Ireland was the best thing he could have done for Mara. And looking at Paulette in his arms, for himself, too.

"But the rumors followed you here," Paulette said softly.

"Yes, they did."

"It must be dreadful having people give you strange looks and whisper about you when they know nothing about what really happened."

"I'm getting used to it," he said with a slight shrug. "And it doesn't matter much with strangers. I can't help what people who don't know me think. But it bothers me that your family might think that you were in danger because of me."

"I'd love for you to get to know my sisters and brothers-in-law," Paulette began, "because I know they would love you if they met you. They would know, just as I do, that you had nothing to do with your wife's death. They would know what a good person you are."

His heart constricted at her words. In such a short amount of time, this woman believed in him more than his own in-laws had. "How can you be so sure about me, Paulette?"

"I'm an excellent judge of character," she responded matter-of-factly, kissing him on the lips to emphasize her point.

"You knew about my past before I knew you did, and you gave me that book, *The Law and the Lady*, for a reason, didn't you?" he asked.

"Of course."

"You gave it to me the day I first kissed you."

"Have you finished reading it yet?"

"Yes." He'd read it almost immediately, intrigued by the type of book she would select for him and he was astounded. The story involved a woman married to a man who was accused of murdering his first wife. The woman, bright and independent, not unlike Paulette, so believed in her new husband's innocence that she set out to prove it.

"Well, what did you think of the book?" she asked.

"I found it fascinating," he said. "I liked how Valeria put together the clues to solve the case. It's unusual to have a strong female as a central character in a detective story."

"That's what I liked about it, too," Paulette agreed. "I stayed up all night when I was reading it. I've read quite a few of Wilkie Collins's works and enjoyed them."

Declan paused in reflection, pondering a thought that had been with him since he finished reading the book. "Was choosing that book for me that day your way of telling me that you believed me?"

"Yes, I suppose it was," she said, kissing him.

"Oh, Paulette." Declan held her to him, enjoying the feel of her and the new intimacy between them. It felt good to just be with her. They lay there together in the warmth of the darkened room and he held Paulette in his arms, not wanting to leave and wishing he could sleep with her next to him all night long. The thought startled him.

"It's getting late. I should take you home," he said at last. "Won't your sisters be worrying about you?"

"They won't be home for at least another hour, so I still have some time. But I suppose I should get going." She made a motion to rise from the bed, but he stilled her.

"Not yet," he whispered, drawing her back into the circle of his arms. "Paulette, about this evening—"

She placed a finger over his lips to stop him from speaking. "Shhh," she ordered in a sweet voice. "Don't say anything because there is nothing you have to say right now. This evening with you was perfect."

Unable to resist, he moved her hand and slowly covered her mouth with his. He could not get enough of her sweet lips. When he drew back, he smiled down at her and his heart flipped over in his chest. "If I don't get you home right now . . ."

With great reluctance they both rose from the bed. He found the lamp on the bedside table and lit it, its warm glow casting a small circle of light but enough to get dressed by. When he was clothed again, he helped fasten the back of Paulette's pink gown and watched while she fixed her hair. Together they straightened the bed covers and tidied up the room, before heading back down the stairs to the silent bookshop.

Before they left the shop, he took Paulette into his

arms one more time and kissed her. "May I come see you
again tomorrow afternoon?"

"Yes, please," she said, her smile lighting her face.

The night air had not cooled much, but they welcomed the slight breeze as they walked the quiet streets
together. He wished he could have held her hand in his
the whole way home to Devon House, but he knew better
than to do so. However he did manage to give her hand
a brief squeeze before she turned and hurried inside.

Once again, he stood on the corner watching Devon
House for some time before he made his way home.

Chapter 15

Expectations

"Honestly, Paulette, whatever is the matter with you today?" Colette asked in growing frustration.

"I'm sorry," Paulette muttered as she pulled her gaze from the carriage window. Lost in her own thoughts, reminiscing about the night before with Declan Reeves, she had not heard one word her sister had said to her.

"I've asked you twice about the invoice papers, but it's as if you haven't been listening to me." Colette frowned. "Are you not feeling well?"

"I suppose I'm simply tired. I didn't sleep very well," Paulette responded. And that was not a lie. After being with Declan, she had barely slept all night for thinking of him and all they had done together.

Paulette had soaked in a warm bath when she got home, grateful that she made it back to Devon House before Colette, Lucien, and Yvette returned from their evening out. She was even able to crawl into bed for the night without having to face her sisters, who would surely suspect something by the fixed smile on Paulette's face.

And she simply wasn't ready to have a discussion with them about it.

She had no idea how to explain what was going on between her and Declan Reeves. She only knew she was happier than she had ever been in her life. She felt very mature and sophisticated, harboring her secret love close to her heart.

Keeping a secret this momentous was no easy feat and she didn't know how long she could contain it to herself. Especially being alone in the carriage with Colette on their way to visit the site of their new bookshop. She was fairly bursting with the news.

"Are you quite sure?" Colette questioned, eyeing her with concern.

"Yes, quite."

"You know, we never did get a chance to talk about what happened between you and Lord Cashelmore in the shop that day."

"No, we didn't." Paulette felt a knot in her stomach. "But I can assure you that I'm fine."

"Well, I imagined that if you wished to discuss it with me, you would have said something sooner," Colette said. "He seemed like a nice enough gentleman when I spoke with him that morning. Still, you have to admit that a man under a cloud of suspicion is not someone we should become involved with. So when you didn't bring it up, I let it go. However, you seemed quite upset by him that day."

"I was at the time, yes, of course," Paulette began to explain. "However, I've not given it much thought since." Oh, how lies came so easily to her now, when the truth was that she'd not thought much about anything else except kissing Declan Reeves.

Her sister gave her a skeptical glance and asked her

the question Paulette had been dreading. "Has Lord Cashelmore returned to the shop again?"

Paulette hesitated for a moment. She hated to lie, even though she knew how her protective older sister was going to react to her answer. "Yes."

"He has?" Colette exclaimed in surprise. "Why haven't you told me? Has he bothered you? Shall I tell Lucien about him? That might be best—"

"Oh, no! There's nothing to worry about. Truly. Lord Cashelmore has been visiting with his little daughter. She loves the new toy books we have. He's been a perfect gentleman, Colette."

Colette shook her head, a frown on her pretty face. "I don't know about this. The entire situation makes me uncomfortable."

"He's actually a very pleasant gentleman. I believe all those accusations are just false and ugly rumors. You should see him with his daughter. He's a good father. You'd like him if you got to know him, Colette."

"But I don't know him," her sister pointed out. "And neither do you."

"I didn't think you would be so closed-minded."

Colette looked hurt. "What do you mean by that?"

"Exactly what I said," Paulette continued. "You're being very closed-minded to judge another person without all the facts and without knowing his true character."

"If his character were true, he wouldn't be accused of killing his wife in the first place. But that is beside the point. I don't care what Lord Cashelmore has or hasn't done. I just would prefer that he steer clear of you. I'd rather you not be hurt by being involved in any of his affairs."

"I'm not involved in his affairs, Colette. He's just a kind man who comes into the shop with his daughter."

"And he kissed you!"

Paulette kept her mouth closed at Colette's indignation. Her sister would faint if she knew what else Declan had done with her. Again her thoughts returned to the magical evening above the bookshop. Never had she felt more alive. It was as if she had been asleep her whole life and with one kiss Declan had awakened her.

"There's nothing to worry about, I can take care of myself," Paulette finally responded. It was the closest statement to the truth she could come up with.

"Well, I wouldn't be so sure of that," Colette retorted.

Although she understood her sister was only trying to protect her, Paulette still wished she would not be quite so maternal. With three older sisters, there were times in Paulette's life when it felt as if she had four mothers worrying over her or admonishing her or advising her when the one mother she had was more than enough. So it was with great relief she exclaimed, "Oh, let's not talk about this anymore. Look, we've arrived!"

The horse-drawn carriage came to a stop in front of a modern two-story building made of red brick, with wide, arched windows on either side of the grand main entrance. Six smaller arched windows graced the upper floor and three gabled windows peered from the pitched roof. The effect was graceful and charming. The sight took Paulette's breath away. The home of their new bookshop!

Davies, the Devon House footman, opened the door for them and helped them descend onto the busy London street crowded with people. The day was overcast and a little cooler than yesterday; the hot spell they had suffered all week had finally broken.

Quinton Roxbury, their handsome, blond brother-in-law, stepped forward to greet them. Married to their sister Lisette, he was also a renowned London architect who had designed the new bookshop for them.

"Good morning, ladies!" he called to them with an enthusiastic smile.

"Good morning, Quinton," Paulette responded excitedly. "Oh, the building looks wonderful! I love it already and we haven't even been inside!"

"And there is much to see!" Quinton took her arm and Colette's, escorting them toward the newly constructed store.

"Where is Lisette?" Colette asked, glancing around. "I know she wanted to be here."

"She'll be along soon. She had an appointment this morning," Quinton said. "I know you haven't seen the building yet, so this should be quite a treat for the both of you." He beamed proudly. "I hope you'll be pleased with it."

Paulette smiled at him. "I'm sure we will."

Releasing her arm, he opened the front door and let them in. Workmen were still painting and installing shelves and cloths were draped about, covering the hardwood floors, but it was a beautiful, modern space.

Paulette's excitement grew as she looked with awe at the new store. It was one thing to see the architectural drawings on paper and imagine how it might look, but it was quite another to actually see the new shop finished!

"Well, what do you think?" he asked.

"Oh, it's beautiful!" Colette and Paulette exclaimed in unison.

"I knew you would think so! Over here," Quinton began to explain to them, "is where you'll have—"

"Oh, please don't tell me!" Paulette interrupted, bursting with anticipation. "I feel like I've looked at those plans so many times I have them committed to memory! I know every inch of this shop as well as the old one! I know where everything is. Let me show you!"

Quinton and Colette laughed together, exchanging glances.

"It's true enough, Quinton," Colette conceded. "She probably knows more about it than either of us."

With an indulgent grin, Quinton bowed. "Well then, Paulette, be my guest."

Filled with enthusiasm and satisfaction, Paulette walked the length of the store, pointing out what each area of the building was intended for. She knew exactly where the front counter would be situated, where the bookshelves were to be arranged, where each section of books belonged, where the private reading rooms were located, where the seating areas were designated, where the stationery and pen-and-ink display cabinets would stand, and how the improved layout of the store would increase sales. She knew because she had helped in designing it.

Quinton applauded her. "Well done, Paulette! Your knowledge is quite impressive. Would you like to stay and direct the workers?"

"Oh, be careful, Quinton!" Colette cried in jest. "She's more than likely to take you up on that and be here with you all day!"

Paulette shook her head. "No, that won't be necessary, but thank you."

Surprisingly she had no desire to stay at the new shop all day. What she really wanted was to get back to Hamilton's as soon as possible. Declan would be sure to come by this afternoon. After all they had shared last night, she longed to see him again. In fact, she could think of nothing but Declan. She wished he were there now, so she could show him the shop she had helped to design.

He would share in her joy and excitement. She just knew he would.

"I've also arranged for you both to meet with the sign maker for the name to be placed on the front of the building." Quinton paused, giving them a hopeful expression. "You still don't wish to tell me?"

"No," Colette responded with a mysterious smile. "It's to be a surprise for us on opening day and will only be revealed then."

"I'm so sorry I'm late!" Lisette came rushing into the shop, appearing a bit harried. She stopped suddenly, looking about the room. "Oh, it's beautiful!"

"Isn't it, darling?" Wrapping his arm around Lisette's shoulder, Quinton hugged her to him.

"Have I missed it? Have you looked at the reading rooms yet?" Lisette asked, her face alight with interest.

They had also designed the shop to have two private spaces, one designated for reading clubs and one set up for reading lessons. Lisette had made it her mission to teach as many people as she could how to read.

They toured through the new shop one more time for Lisette's benefit.

Quinton then continued to discuss timelines and items that still needed to be completed before they could begin installing their book inventory. Colette and Paulette also needed to hire and train a larger staff and they had all agreed that they would only employ women. As they well knew, there were so few opportunities available for females that they decided that the Hamilton bookstores would be run entirely by women. Paulette was proud to be a part of something as important and innovative as providing employment and education for women, and had a busy schedule ahead of her in the coming weeks, preparing for the grand opening in October.

"Oh, before I forget, you've already received some mail here," Quinton said. "I suppose it has something to do with asking about available positions in the shop. I've even spoken to a few people who came in to inquire in person."

Quinton handed Paulette a small stack of letters while he, Colette, and Lisette continued to discuss lighting options and other decorative touches. Paulette riffled through the letters, realizing that Quinton was correct. It seemed most of the correspondence was in regard to seeking employment at the shop; however, she noted that one was addressed to her personally. Glancing about nervously, she saw that her sisters and brother-in-law were engrossed in conversation in one of the reading areas and paying her no mind.

She turned her body away from them anyway. Her heart rate increased as she broke the seal and opened the letter, a growing sense of alarm rising within her as she recognized the sprawling handwriting.

You've been warned already to stay away from Lord Cashelmore. You'll be sorry if you don't. Stay away. It's your only option if you wish to stay alive.

Quickly, she returned the letter to the envelope with a trembling hand and shoved it into her reticule. She wished she had a fire to burn it in. Once again someone had written to warn her about Declan Reeves. Who knew about the time she spent with him to begin with? Her own family wasn't even aware of how often she saw Declan! The only person who knew even the slightest hint of what was going on in her life was Jeffrey Eddington, and he was certainly not sending her intimidating notes. No, Jeffrey would come right out and forbid her to see Declan. And no doubt it would come to that if he knew about these threatening letters.

Who would want her to keep away from Declan Reeves? It had to be someone who knew of Declan's past. Someone who was keeping track of his comings and goings. And hers as well. For whoever it was also knew that she would be at the new building site today. She shivered at the thought. Was it the Irish authorities that wished to arrest him? No, that would be silly. What would they care if Declan was visiting a bookshop! No, these notes were personal and had to come from someone who was well acquainted with Declan. He said he didn't know anyone in London, so it had to be someone from Ireland. His family perhaps. Or his wife's family, which was more likely from what he had told her. Could there be another woman? Someone Declan had been romantically involved with? She didn't think so, but in any case, she didn't like that someone was spying on Declan. Spying on her. On them both.

She couldn't prevent the shiver that raced through her at the thought.

Now that she had received two such missives, she supposed she ought to inform Declan. The words were burned into her memory already.

You've been warned already to stay away from Lord Cashelmore. You'll be sorry if you don't. Stay away. It's your only option if you wish to stay alive.

For the briefest instant she thought about handing the note over to Colette and Quinton that very minute, and asking their help and advice on the matter. However, she immediately reconsidered. No. If she told them about the letters she would have to explain much more than she was ready to share. She was not prepared yet to divulge the extent of her relationship with Declan.

Paulette decided to keep the secret of the letters to herself.

Chapter 16

Pictures

Mara Reeves sat at a table with a set of paints in front of her. Mrs. Martin had thought she might like to paint and had laid out the paper and brushes and the little tin pots of colors on the large nursery table and had encouraged her to draw to her heart's content. Now Mrs. Martin puttered about the nursery, straightening up the growing collection of picture books Mara had accumulated.

Mara liked all her new books. And she especially liked going to the bookshop with Papa every day. She enjoyed walking with him, his hand clasped securely in hers, along the bustling London streets. She had to take very big steps and walk very fast to keep up with him, but she didn't mind. And she liked their visits to Hamilton's Book Shoppe.

It was nice and cheerful in the bookshop. It had little tables and chairs that fit her perfectly. And pretty Miss Hamilton would bring her such wonderful picture books and read to her in that soothing voice she had. Something about the bookshop made Papa happy, too. The heavy dark look in his eyes disappeared when they were in Hamilton's. He smiled more. A real smile that reached his eyes. That smile filled Mara with bubbles of excitement and almost made her forget the fear that gripped her heart and she would laugh out loud.

Now she stared at the paints in front of her. What was she supposed to do with this? She didn't particularly wish to paint pictures, but she didn't want to upset Mrs. Martin, who was very kind to her. Hesitantly she picked up a brush and dipped it in the blue paint. With the brush dripping she slid it across the clean white paper. As she usually did when she drew, she made a face. Two dots for eyes. A dot for a nose. And a curved line for a mouth. She made the face smiling this time. She dipped the brush in the red. And she retraced her steps by painting over the blue face, covering it in red. It turned the face a purplish color.

Pleased with the effect she created, Mara continued painting smiling faces and mixing different colors. When one sheet of paper was filled with her creations, she pushed it to the side and filled a second. The mix of colors fascinated her. Blue, red, purple. Yellow, blue, green. Yellow, red, orange. Blue, red, purple. Yellow, blue, green. Yellow, red, orange.

She heard Mrs. Martin humming a tune. It was a different tune than she usually sang, but Mara recognized it. She'd heard it before. A long time ago perhaps. It reminded her of Ireland. Of home. As she listened to the vaguely familiar melody, she continued her little paint drawings. Yellow, red, orange. Her swirling lines became thicker, heavier, darker, bolder. Yellow, red, orange.

So lost in creating her pictures was she, she didn't hear Papa come in to the nursery to see her. Startled to realize he was standing behind her, she dropped the paintbrush and stood up on the chair, wrapping her arms around his neck. He held her close.

"Mara, darlin'," he whispered. "What are you up to today? Painting pictures? Let's take a look!"

He released her, and she scrambled back down in her chair, pointing to the still-wet sheets of her paintings. She waited for Papa to exclaim over her colorful efforts. When he said nothing, she looked up at him. A most peculiar expression was on his face.

He turned to Mrs. Martin. "Did you give her these paints?"

Mrs. Martin walked toward them, smiling. "Yes. I thought it might be fun for her. She's been busily painting for the last half hour—oh, my goodness!" The woman covered her mouth with her hand as she looked at Mara's paintings.

Papa's brow furrowed. "I know. It's odd, isn't it?"

"Well, perhaps it's a way for her to express her feelings . . ."

Mara didn't like that they were discussing her as if she wasn't there. She stared at the paintings she had created. What was wrong with them? Lots of colorful faces. And she especially enjoyed the blue, red, purple and the yellow, blue, green waves. She had made rainbows, too.

Papa picked up one sheet of paper filled with swirls of yellow, red, and orange, and held it carefully.

"Flames. She painted flames." His voice was almost a whisper.

Mara stood up on the chair again. She hadn't painted flames. She didn't like fire. They were just pretty swirls, petals of bright orange, red, and yellow flowers. At least that was what she had intended.

Papa put the picture back down on the table and grabbed her to him. He hugged her tight, almost squeezing the breath out of her. She hoped she hadn't upset him. She hadn't meant to.

He released her, after kissing the top of her head, and asked, "Do you want to go to the bookshop today?"

She smiled and nodded her head eagerly.

Papa said, "You can paint again later if you want, when we come home."

"Let me get her cleaned up first, Lord Cashelmore," Mrs. Martin interjected. "You can't take her out looking like this!"

Obediently, Mara took Mrs. Martin's hand and allowed her to wash the sticky paint from her fingers. She had tried to be a good girl and be neat with the paint, but she found herself covered in red and yellow. Mrs. Martin made her change her dress, too.

Soon she was skipping along beside Papa on their way to the bookshop and Mara wondered what surprise Miss Hamilton would have for her today. She always seemed to know exactly what kind of book Mara liked. And she would much rather go to the bookshop with Papa than go to visit those dreadful doctors he dragged her to each week. They poked and prodded her with strange-looking instruments, peering into her mouth and ears and asking her silly questions, which of course she wouldn't answer. Then Papa and the doctors would whisper and talk about her as if she weren't there.

"What do you think?" Papa would ask each one of them.

"There doesn't seem to be anything physically wrong with her. She's been through a traumatic experience to be sure. I would think her problems are more psychosomatic in nature."

Then they would discuss various therapies. One angry-looking doctor asked Papa to leave Mara there with him, and that he would straighten Mara out soon enough. Thankfully, Papa disagreed. But they left each office with no more information than when they went in.

Sometimes, Mara simply wanted to whisper to Papa to stop taking her to doctors and she'd be just fine. But he never became cross or frustrated with her. He just hugged her and told her everything would be all right. And that's why she loved him so much.

They entered Hamilton's Book Shoppe and the bell over the door jingled. The very sound made Mara happy.

She was a bit disappointed when Miss Hamilton was not there at the counter to greet them. A familiar black-haired woman she had seen before stood in her place.

"Welcome to Hamilton's!" she called to them with a smile. "How can I help you today?"

"We were hoping Miss Hamilton could help us choose a book for Mara," Papa said, giving her hand a gentle squeeze.

"She's not here at the moment. I can assist you though," the lady offered.

Mara could hear the surprise and disappointment in Papa's voice as he said, "Oh, we won't trouble you. Do you mind if we browse in the children's section for a bit?"

"No, not at all." She nodded at them. "Please take your time."

Papa hesitated. "Do you know if Miss Hamilton will be in the shop at all today?"

The lady shook her head. "I'm not sure. She's with her sister, overseeing plans at the site of their new store."

"I see. Thank you very much."

She walked with Papa toward the back of the shop to the children's section. Mara let go of his hand and scurried to one of the little tables. Some picture books were stacked in the center of the table and Mara chose one. Papa came and knelt beside her. That heavy sad look was in his eyes again. She kissed his cheek and he smiled at her.

"Is this the book you want to read?"

She nodded.

"All right then." He propped himself on one of the little

chairs and Mara climbed onto his lap. Opening the book, he began to read to her, his voice soothing and calm.

"*A — Apple Pie and Other Nursery Tales*," he read the title of the leather-bound book. "A, Apple pie. B, Bit it. C, Cut it."

It was a book about the alphabet and Mara loved learning about her letters. She wanted to try writing them. Maybe she would try it with her paints later when they returned home. In the meantime, she listened to the story. Papa had gotten through the whole alphabet, read about the cats' tea party, this little pig went to market, the three bears, and was all the way into the story of Red Riding Hood, when Miss Hamilton rushed over to them.

"I was so afraid I'd missed you," she said, rather breathless. Her blue eyes were wide and she still held her reticule in her hand. Miss Hamilton barely noticed Mara, her eyes on Papa alone.

Papa gently lifted Mara off his lap, set her in her own chair, and slid the book over to her. He moved quickly to Miss Hamilton's side. That happy expression came over his face and it was the first time Mara associated it with Miss Hamilton. That intrigued her. She had thought the book-shop was making Papa happy, but now she thought it might be Miss Hamilton, too. Mara's mouth opened in awe.

The two of them whispered low, using voices that Mara knew meant they did not want her to know what they were talking about. But she could still hear them. She flipped the pages back to look at the pictures of the funny cats wearing suits again, but she listened intently to what Papa and Miss Hamilton were saying to each other.

"I was afraid I had missed you, too," he said, taking Miss Hamilton's hand in his. "You look so beautiful, Paulette. I hope you are you feeling well today."

"I'm wonderful." She beamed at him, her cheeks turning a warm pink. "Completely wonderful."

"No regrets about last night?"

"No. None whatsoever. It was truly lovely."

"I'm relieved to hear you say that. I've been worried that you—"

Their voices dropped even lower and they took a few steps away from her, their heads close together. Mara could no longer make out the words, although she could hear the murmur of their voices. It was just as well. They were talking in riddles, as grown-ups often did, about things that didn't make any sense. Mama had always talked in riddles and she never liked that. That's what was so good about Papa. He spoke to her as if she understood.

Sighing, Mara flipped the illustrated pages in her book, still surprised by the secret that she had just uncovered.

Miss Hamilton made Papa happy.

Chapter 17

Shadows

"Why should we care what happens to him? He killed our sister," Deirdre Ryan Hollingsworth uttered with distaste. Her once attractive face was pinched into a bitter frown, making her appear far older than her thirty-five years.

"I thought you might have some interest in what he is doing in London," Gerald O'Rourke remarked. He and Alice had invited Declan's in-laws to Cashelmore Manor for the week to see what information they could glean about the investigation. However, Margaret's two sisters had proven themselves to be as miserable as he had always declared them to be.

But then again, Gerald had always known that.

He had been somewhat fond of Declan's young wife at the start of it all. Margaret Ryan had been sweet and obliging, and quite nice to look at. But in a surprisingly short amount of time she had grown overly tiresome with her whining and complaining. Gerald had in all good conscience warned his cousin not to become involved with her and her horrid family before he wedded her.

The last thing Gerald needed was a nasty set of in-laws to deal with, as well as possible heirs. In any case, Declan was far too young to marry. But had Declan heeded Gerald's advice or warnings? No. He was too blinded by Margaret's silvery cool beauty to see any of the negative qualities she possessed. And she had quite a few of them.

So did her sisters, Deirdre and Ellen, sitting there looking more and more like a pair of old crows. They had both been attractive at one time, but it seemed their younger sister had inherited all of the beauty in the family.

"Well, then," Ellen Ryan Hanlon sniped. Her face was as lined and pinched with bitterness as Deirdre's. "What do you have to tell us about him? I thought that was why you dragged us back to Cashelmore Manor. To tell us something. I do hope it's important."

Gerald and his wife Alice exchanged looks across the elegant parlor where they sat having tea with the Ryan sisters.

Alice asked, "Have you no interest in your young niece?"

"Of course, I do!" Deirdre exclaimed sulkily. "I tried my best to keep her here! I offered to take care of her and raise her like my own. She is poor Margaret's only child. Of course I wanted her. But *he* wouldn't let me have her. 'There's no way in hell I would let a bitch like you take my daughter,' were his exact words to me, if you must know. I haven't seen or spoken to Declan Reeves since. He was off to London the next day with Mara and I've washed my hands of him completely."

"Yes, what happens to him now is up to the authorities," Ellen added with a smug grin, folding her long fingers primly in her lap. Her pale blond hair was pulled tightly back from her face and she wore a high-necked black gown, still in mourning for her sister.

"Well, what have you heard regarding Declan's standing?" Gerald asked, wishing he had some whiskey to settle his nerves. He needed liquor to deal with these women.

Ellen was only too happy to expound the news. "They're close to bringing charges against him."

Gerald made an effort to appear worried and anxious and not expose his delight. "That's shocking! Have you any idea when that will be?"

"It's not up to us," Deirdre interjected. She too wore a black silk mourning gown, her ash blond hair piled upon her head. "If it were up to us, he'd be swinging from a rope by now or at the very least behind bars already. However, the authorities assured us that it shouldn't be much longer. They are just waiting on some new evidence."

"What evidence?" Alice asked, her sharp brown eyes narrowing.

Gerald didn't like the sound of that at all. What new evidence could they have come upon? Kenmare House had been all but destroyed by the fire that night. He was lucky to have escaped unscathed himself. There was virtually nothing left of the place. Where could they have gotten new evidence from at this late stage? He tried to calm his quickening pulse. This could ruin everything. God, he wanted a drink.

He and Alice exchanged another knowing glance. His wife was more than aware of the risks involved in their venture to gain the title of Earl of Cashelmore. The title that rightfully belonged to him. At least in his eyes.

Ellen continued, "They've been investigating the ruins of Kenmare House for months and they have finally determined that the fire was deliberately set. Not accidental as they first presumed."

Gerald felt beads of perspiration breaking out down his back. He sipped his tea wishing there was whiskey in it.

"How would they know it was deliberately set?" Alice asked.

"Oh, I don't know, but they do," Ellen said. "I've known all along that fire was no accident. And who else had a motive to get rid of poor Margaret other than Declan?"

"No one, that's who!" Deirdre cried indignantly. "But they'll get him yet. Mark my words. Declan Reeves will be punished for murdering my sweet baby sister." Deirdre's hard eyes glittered in triumph.

"They're sure it was Declan then?" Gerald asked, hoping against hope the final event would happen sooner rather than later. So far there had been no suspicions of his involvement, which relieved him greatly. He wanted Declan in prison before the year was out. That was the plan for now. Then Cashelmore Manor and all that entailed would finally belong to Gerald.

"Of course!" Ellen joined in. "So go ahead and warn your cousin. He can run from the law, but he can't hide for long. They will bring him in."

"And once that fiend is in the gaol where he belongs, I'll finally get Mara," Deirdre couldn't help but add with an emphatic nod of her pinched face.

"What else did you have to tell us, Gerald?" Ellen questioned, her expression returning to its usual sour state. "About Declan? Did he say anything to you when you saw him in London?"

"I asked him if he were going to come home, and as you can see with me here overseeing Cashelmore, he is not planning on returning to Ireland anytime soon. I suggested it might be best for Mara if she comes home to be with her family, but he disagreed. He wants to keep her in London to consult with doctors who specialize in this sort of thing."

"Of course it would be best for Mara to come home and be with her family, instead of alone with him in London amidst strangers," said Deirdre, her voice dripping with scorn.

"Why would he come home anyway?" Ellen pointed out. "He knows they will take him into custody as soon as he does. In spite of all I say about him, Declan is not foolish enough to do that."

"Can they demand that he come home?" Alice asked, rising from her seat on the sofa and pouring more tea.

Gerald thought Alice looked as if she were born at Cashelmore, in her fashionable new gown of amber-colored silk. His wife was as beautiful and elegant as any countess, if not more so. She deserved to be the mistress of a home as grand as this and Gerald desperately wanted to be able to give that to her.

"If they gather the right evidence, they may very well demand that he return," Ellen answered.

"It's coming up on a year now since the fire," Deirdre said with a petulant frown. "I do wish they would hurry up."

"It pains me to be the one to tell you ladies this . . ." Gerald began, knowing very well this information would send the Ryan sisters out of their minds. "Sometimes I am ashamed of my cousin. It has been brought to my attention that Declan is . . . consorting . . . with a London shopgirl."

"Oh, dear God in heaven!" Ellen and Deirdre cried in unison.

Ellen looked as if she might faint. "It hasn't even been a year since poor Margaret has been in her grave and he's . . . with another woman," she added, her voice filled with disgust.

Deirdre slammed her bony hand on the table. "It's insulting to us and to Margaret! That's what it is!"

"It's a sad state of affairs," Ellen bemoaned, "when a man can murder his wife and then behave as if he hadn't a care in the world."

"Men can be that way," Alice added, shaking her head in feigned sympathy.

Gerald sighed. "Well, you know I feel just dreadful about what happened to sweet Margaret. I loved her like a sister. Even though Declan is my dearest cousin and only living relative, I must admit things look bad for him. Unfortunately all signs seem to point to him as the cause of Margaret's death. And when I think that poor young Mara might have perished too that night, I become sick to my stomach."

"As for myself, I feel as if I can't hold up my head, for the shame that Declan has brought upon our family." Alice managed to bring tears to her eyes, dabbing at them with a monogrammed handkerchief. Gerald wanted to applaud.

"Well, think how we must feel!" Ellen cried in outrage.

"I understand how you feel, for it pains me, too," Gerald said, his voice tinged with regret. "I would like to offer my services if you need help in getting Declan to return home. I will do the honorable thing here. Cousin or not. If he has committed a crime, and such a heinous crime at that, then he must pay for his actions." He paused dramatically. The Ryan sisters waited with bated breath. "While he is absent from his duties as the Earl of Cashelmore, he has left his affairs to me. I have full control of the estate and it is at your disposal, ladies, so please think of Cashelmore Manor as your home."

"Why, thank you, Gerald! You're an honorable gentleman, in spite of your embarrassment of a cousin!" Ellen declared emphatically.

"It's a comfort to know that not all of Mara's blood relatives are without decency," added Deirdre.

Which is exactly what Gerald wanted them to believe. That he was the honorable one in the family. He was winning the trust of the Ryan family. He was firmly ensconced at Cashelmore Manor, running the estate for Declan. He was receiving regular reports from London about his cousin's activities. Now he only had to wait. For the title and the fortune to become his.

Little did the Ryan sisters know how much Gerald had already done to implicate Declan in the death of his wife. The foolish old crows! And he would continue to do so, even if it meant spending time with the Ryans. Gerald didn't care. He would do whatever it took to make Cashelmore his.

One way or another.

Chapter 18

Falling

Declan held Paulette Hamilton close and she snuggled into him for warmth, her naked body pressed intimately against his.

The steamy August nights had given way to cooler September evenings, which was a much-welcomed relief. The autumn season was upon them.

As they lay together in the little bedroom above the bookshop, Declan wondered for the hundredth time what he was doing with this beautiful girl. She was so bright and beautiful, filled with determination and enthusiasm for all that she did. There was something about her that drew him in . . . like a siren's call. She had touched something deep within him, had melted the coldness that had surrounded his heart since his troubled marriage. This sweet, intelligent, wonderful girl. He simply could not stay away from her.

For the last six weeks they had continued to see each other secretly, and he had gone to the shop earlier that afternoon with Mara, as had become their daily routine.

Another custom was for Declan to arrive later each evening after the shop had closed and everyone was gone for the day, when they would tiptoe to the bedroom upstairs.

Although they had been most discreet, it was a miracle no one had found out about them yet, and Declan was determined to keep it that way. Paulette did not deserve to be ruined, nor did she deserve her reputation to be sullied by someone as tainted by scandal as he was. It was best if no one knew about the two of them.

Paulette sighed contentedly in his arms. "It gets better every time, doesn't it?"

He had to agree with her. And he did so by kissing her sweet mouth.

Declan supposed he should feel guilty about being with her this way and to a certain extent he did. But more often than not, guilt did not enter his mind. Because being with Paulette Hamilton felt more right than anything he had ever experienced in his life.

"Declan?" she whispered in the darkness.

"Yes, love?"

"There's something important I need to discuss with you."

She sounded very serious and his heart rate increased. He sat up a little, propping himself on the pillows behind his head. "What is it?"

"Well, I'm not sure exactly . . ." she began with hesitation. "I suppose I should have said something to you the first time, but I didn't wish to worry you and I didn't think it was all that important."

Declan's mind spun with possibilities of what his beautiful Paulette was hinting at. He had a sinking feeling he knew what was coming and he dreaded her next words, for he knew what he would have to say to her.

He could not marry her.

He would never get married again and he had been clear with her on that point from the start. Declan thought she understood that, because she had stated from the onset herself that she had no interest in marriage either. That had been part of his attraction to her. She was a lovely, intelligent, and independent woman not looking to be taken care of by a husband. Yet, here she was, suddenly hinting that they should wed.

And she was correct. He should make her his wife after all that they had done together these last weeks. She would make a perfect wife, if only he had met her first, before he had married Margaret Ryan. He felt riddled with guilt.

"Paulette, I—" he began, but her next words stopped him cold.

"I've been receiving some rather threatening letters, Declan."

His whole body jerked when her words registered. Threatening letters? His heart pounded so loud he thought it might burst out of his chest. This was far more terrifying than what he had expected her to say. Releasing her, he sat up straight and lit the lamp on the side table, casting a golden glow around them. "What are you talking about, Paulette?"

"Just what I said." She tried to be calm, but Declan could see the worry in her pretty blue eyes as she continued to explain. "Someone has been sending me letters, warning me to stay away from you. Isn't that strange?"

Trying to control his own worry, he drew Paulette back into his arms, her naked body warm against his, and pulled the blanket around them. Instinct immediately told him that she had been receiving letters from the same coward who had been delivering them to his own house.

The very idea that he had somehow involved Paulette in the ugliness of his problems in Ireland revolted him.

"Tell me everything," he demanded. "From the beginning. Don't leave out any details."

"I received the first one a number of weeks ago, just after our visit to Green Park," she said, her voice soft, but anxious. "And one has arrived each week since. All of them warning me to stay away from you and that I will be sorry if I don't. One even came to the new building while I was there. The latest one came today, just before you arrived with Mara."

Declan held his breath. "What did it say?"

"It said basically the same thing as the others, 'If you wish to stay alive, stay away from Lord Cashelmore. He's going to kill you, too.'"

Anger and fear for Paulette rose within him. It was one thing for someone to try to intimidate him. It was another matter altogether that they were trying to frighten Paulette. His Paulette. He pulled her tighter to him.

"I'm sorry, love. You shouldn't have to be exposed to something like that."

"It's not pleasant, but I'm not scared. I trust you, Declan, and I know you would never do anything to hurt me. And no one could ever scare me away from you. The letters are more of a nuisance than anything else. I just thought I should mention them to you because if someone knows about us . . . knows about you and me . . . I think that perhaps someone is . . ." She hesitated.

"Someone is what?"

"Well, it only stands to reason that someone is watching us."

Declan had had a feeling lately that someone was following him home from the bookshop each afternoon. He hadn't seen anyone specifically. It was just a sense that he had, and he had brushed it aside, thinking it ridiculous. But the idea that someone was watching and following Paulette as well made his blood run cold. If anything bad happened to her because of his involvement with her, he would never forgive himself.

"Who would care that you and I are together?" she asked. "Who would be watching us, Declan? And warning me to stay away from you?"

Only one possible thought came to his mind. "My first guess would be Margaret's family. I was sure that's who was sending the messages to me."

"You've been receiving them as well?" Paulette asked, her tone incredulous.

"Yes. But after learning that you have been receiving them too, now I'm not so sure it's Margaret's sisters. Although I wouldn't put much past them, threatening you seems a bit extreme, even for Deirdre and Ellen Ryan."

"Then who else would want me to stay away from you?"

"I'm not sure. But I'm sure as hell going to find out." He felt Paulette tremble slightly in his arms and he gave her a comforting squeeze. "I hadn't given much thought to the letters I've gotten. I've tossed them into the fire, to tell you the truth. I assumed it was merely Deirdre and Ellen's way of letting me know that they weren't going to forget about Margaret and that they were still pursuing their case of finding me guilty. Perhaps they thought it would scare me into returning to Ireland so they could get their hands on Mara. In either instance, I disregarded them. But now I'm going to do my own investigating. Do you still have your letters?"

"Yes. All of them. I'll give them to you."

"Can I ask why you didn't tell me about this sooner, Paulette?"

She gave him a funny look. "I'm not sure. I suppose I didn't want to worry you."

"You didn't want to worry me?" He echoed her words in disbelief. The woman was incredible. Because of him she was being threatened by a faceless, nameless person for weeks, and she didn't wish to burden him. He leaned down and kissed her, losing himself in the sweetness of her mouth, of her. Of Paulette. He withdrew and looked into her beautiful, innocent face.

"Well, I'll tell you right now, Miss Paulette Hamilton, you're not to keep anything from me again from here on out, whether you think it will worry me or not."

"I promise." She nodded in understanding.

They kissed to seal their promise.

"I should get home," she murmured finally, her voice filled with reluctance. "They weren't planning a late evening."

He and Paulette had scheduled their secret trysts above the bookshop to coincide when Lord and Lady Stancliff were out at a dinner party or a musicale or the opera, so Paulette's later-than-usual arrival home would not be noted. Their nights together were becoming more and more important to him.

She rose from the bed, standing gloriously naked before him. Her long golden hair fell in shimmering waves almost to her slender waist. His heart pounded. She looked so tempting, so gorgeous, he didn't want to let her go.

"Paulette?"

"Yes?"

With a devilish grin, he reached out a hand to her and pulled her back down to the bed. She fell willingly into his embrace, accepting his hungry kisses. Their need for each other growing, she straddled his hips, her eyes dark with desire. Paulette had become more and more comfortable and uninhibited in bed with him over the weeks, learning how to give and receive pleasure. He delighted in her nearness and the beauty of her. If anything happened to harm her, he would lose his mind. She had become more precious to him than he had realized.

With a fluid movement, she leaned into him, taking the length of him inside of her, and began moving her hips up and down in a deliberate and slow motion. And once again that evening, they made love, only this time it was intense and quick, knowing their time left together tonight was fleeting at best.

After dressing hurriedly and heading downstairs, they embraced one last time in the quiet of the empty bookshop. Declan held her tight in his arms again, feeling the beat of her heart next to his.

"I need you to do something for me, Paulette."

"Anything," she said, clinging to him.

"I don't want you to fight me on this." He had the distinct feeling that she would.

She pulled away and looked up at him, her delicate brows furrowed. "What is it, Declan?"

"I don't like the idea of you alone in the shop and someone out there watching you. I'm going to have one of my footman watch over you while you're at the shop and coming and going to Devon House." He saw the look of opposition appear on her pretty face.

"Why, that's utterly ridiculous!" she cried, on the verge of laughing out loud at his suggestion.

"No. It's not." His voice dropped, and she stilled at the seriousness of his tone.

"Declan, honestly, what would my family say if suddenly a burly footman was following me around?"

She had a point, but he didn't care. He refused to let anything or anyone harm her. And he didn't like knowing that someone lurked about the streets, keeping tabs on their whereabouts, especially Paulette's. "Then promise me that you'll ask your brother-in-law to have one of the Devon House footman escort you to and from the shop. He should be doing that anyway."

Declan would then hire someone else to watch over her without her knowing it anyway. He had to be sure that Paulette was safe.

"And just how would I explain my sudden desire for an escort?" She stepped back from his embrace, placing her hands on her hips, staring up at him. "I've never needed nor wanted one before and I've spent more hours than I care to recall having to justify myself to Lucien on this matter."

"You're a very clever girl, Paulette. I know you can think of something." He gave her a warning glance. "But you need an escort. Either your brother-in-law sees to it or I shall provide a burly footman of my own."

"Declan," she began in protest.

"Don't 'Declan' me, love. I'm not changing my mind on this. I can have a footman watch you or your brother-in-law can. The choice is yours, but it begins first thing tomorrow and ends when I find out who is threatening you and put a stop to it."

She drew a breath. "Is this really necessary?"

"Yes."

She had the good sense to recognize that he was not about to budge on this issue.

"Fine," she relented, however unwillingly. "Have it your way. I'll speak to Lucien tonight. But you do realize that we give up all our freedom with one of the Devon House footmen overseeing my every move, don't you? There will be no more of *these* nights above the shop."

"Yes. I realize that." There was a long pause during which neither of them spoke. It was a sacrifice, however difficult, that he was willing to make for Paulette's safety. "First thing tomorrow, do you understand me?"

"Yes, sir," she said, giving him a little salute with her hand.

He pulled her back into his arms and gave her a final kiss before they left the shop. They had both taken to walking home from the bookshop, since it gave them more time together and kept less people from knowing what was going on between them. As usual, he walked her to the corner of Devon House and watched her until she made it safely inside.

Declan stood there on the street for some time afterward, picturing her inside the house. Wondering what she was doing. Wishing he could spend the rest of the night with her beside him.

With a heavy sigh and a careful glance around the neighborhood, he turned and made his way home, keeping a close eye out for anything suspicious. He was not entirely sure when the feeling that he was being watched had first occurred, but now he would be paying much better attention as he went about his business.

It was a cool night, with a hint of colder nights to come in the air, and the coolness felt good against his skin. It braced him. Made him realize even more the seriousness of the situation.

Someone was threatening Paulette, and warning her to stay away from him.

He would not have her in danger on his account. Even if it meant not seeing her anymore . . .

Perhaps it was for the best. Having a footman watch over Paulette would definitely put an end to his nighttime trysts with her. It would also give them time to cool down, for what they were doing was beyond reckless. He was carrying on an affair with an unmarried young woman, for Christ's sake! He knew better than that. Paulette Hamilton was not the type to have an affair. She deserved an honest proposal of marriage.

But he was not the one to give it to her. She deserved far better than someone like him.

Paulette should marry a decent man. A good man. One who was not encumbered by murder accusations or rejected by society for something he hadn't done.

He liked to think of Paulette being happily married, living in an elegant home with children and still managing a bookshop or two. He could imagine it all too easily and he wanted that happiness for her, wished to see her contented and fulfilled with her life. But for all the world he could not picture the man who would be her husband. The very thought of another man taking Paulette to his bed not only filled him with jealousy but made him feel quite ill.

But what sickened him more was the thought of any harm coming to her.

It all came back to one thing. Who was sending those damned notes?

When he reached home, he glanced around carefully, but not too obviously, before ascending the steps outside his townhouse. Seeing nothing out of the ordinary, he entered the house.

His butler, Roberts, greeted him as he stepped into the foyer. "Good evening, my lord. Can I get you anything?"

"No, thank you, Roberts. Has Mara gone to bed already?" He knew his daughter was asleep by now, but it was his habit to ask anyway.

"I believe so, sir."

Declan took the stairs two at a time, hurrying to the nursery. That was the only disadvantage to the precious nights he spent with Paulette above the bookshop. He missed putting Mara to bed on those evenings. But she had been so much better lately, he didn't feel terribly guilty about it.

He tiptoed into her pink bedroom, which adjoined the nursery. Mara slept peacefully, her little hands clutching a stuffed puppy. He kissed her cheek gently, so as not to wake her, before he stepped out of the room. In the nursery, he noticed more of her new paintings laid out on the table to dry.

More fire depictions.

Another picture of swirling flames that Mara had created with her little pots of paint. Declan didn't know whether it was good for her to do this or not. None of the expert doctors he had visited seemed to be able to answer any of his questions regarding the mystery of his daughter's silence.

He knew the fire and the death of her mother had traumatized her. That fact was indisputable. It was how to cure her that left him in the dark.

Although he had to admit that since coming to London almost two months ago, there had been a definite change in Mara. She did seem happier, lighter. She smiled more often and even giggled on a few occasions. She did not seem to be as nervous and anxious as she had been while they were in Ireland. Her nightmares had all but ceased in the last weeks.

He had to thank Mrs. Martin for all that she had done to help Mara. The woman had been a godsend. Considering that he left every single one of his former servants in Ireland, wanting no reminders of the horrific fire to follow Mara, he came to London alone and had to begin hiring new staff the day he arrived. He had interviewed three women for the position of nurse to Mara. The first one had a prim hardness about her that he hadn't liked. The second looked as if she enjoyed alcohol more than she should. Then there was Mrs. Martin, a kind widow in her forties, with grown children of her own. She had a calm practicality about her that appealed to him. When he had explained the situation, she hadn't been horrified or frightened.

She spoke to Mara kindly, and not as if the child were a mute idiot as some people did. She had old-fashioned common sense that seemed to work wonders on his daughter whereas the directives from the medical community fell flat. Mrs. Martin had insisted on getting Mara out of the black mourning clothes and wearing bright colors again to lift the child's spirits.

"There's nothing more depressing than seeing children in black," Mrs. Martin declared and Declan had to agree with her. The sight of Mara in pretty pastels again raised his spirits as well.

It had also been Mrs. Martin's inspiration to give Mara the paints. "The poor child must have so many frightening thoughts bottled up inside that she's afraid to speak, Lord Cashelmore. Maybe the painting is a way for her to release them without talking," Mrs. Martin had suggested.

At first the paintings worried him, but seeing that Mara seemed to be improving a little more each day, he worried less about her depiction of flames. He tended to agree with Mrs. Martin's advice more and more.

And with Paulette's. Both women seemed to have a positive effect on his daughter and for that he was profoundly grateful.

Now, just when things were getting better in his life, someone was threatening it. More than anything, he needed to discover the source behind the intimidating notes.

Chapter 19

Suspicions

Paulette came home from the shop, escorted by Davies, one of the Devon House footmen, whom Lucien appointed to be her bodyguard after she told him that she felt uncomfortable walking alone. Lucien was thrilled to finally have someone watching over his independent-minded sister-in-law and all too willing to provide an escort for her. Although she had known Davies for years and he was just as nice as could be, Paulette was not at all happy with the situation.

She detested her lack of freedom and the sense of inconvenience. But most of all, she desperately missed being alone with Declan. The end of their secret nights in the bookshop and their forced separation was harder to bear than she had anticipated. It had been over three weeks since she had told him about the letters and she was beginning to regret having done so. Although she understood that he wanted to protect her, she resented having to be escorted everywhere she went.

Even though she had to grudgingly admit that she did feel safer having Davies with her at the store.

Paulette most definitely did not like the idea of some mysterious person watching her movements from the shadows and knowing about her trysts with Declan. And threatening her. But she now had even more to worry about than the specter of danger.

"You're home early," Yvette remarked idly, as she preened in front of the oval cheval glass mirror in the sitting room that adjoined their two bedrooms. She was dressed in a gorgeous, wine-colored bustle gown of silk shot with gold, and her blond hair had been styled elegantly upon her head. Her younger sister looked stunning.

"Yes," Paulette grumbled rather than said, removing her cloak and tossing it on a chintz-covered chair in the corner. Yes, she was home early. What point was there to staying late at the shop if Declan would not be coming to see her? She flopped down on the sofa near the fireplace, where a warm fire was burning brightly, which comforted her. The October evenings had grown decidedly colder, but Paulette didn't mind. The chilly weather matched her low spirits.

"Well, why don't you change into something pretty and come with me to the Sheridans' party tonight?" Yvette suggested, looking at her through the mirror's reflection, her face alight with excitement.

"I don't think so . . ." Paulette began, shaking her head. The last thing she wanted to do was gad about with a bunch of people she had no interest in talking to. "I'm tired."

"Oh, please come, Paulette! You never come out with me. You'll have fun, I promise. They say that Lord Barrington will be there, so it's sure to be a fun party."

"After working in the shop all day, I'm not in the mood for a party."

Paulette was much more than a little tired. It was already October and the opening of the new shop was in less than two weeks. She had been doing a million and one things to prepare for the opening, as well as interviewing the final candidates for the positions in both shops. She and Colette had a more difficult time than they had anticipated in selecting the best employees. It was exhausting work, but they finally had enough women hired and their training began tomorrow. Usually, anything to do with the bookshop inspired her and gave her so much energy, but now she was simply tired. All Paulette wanted to do was take a hot bath, have some soup, and crawl into bed for the night.

"All you ever do is work, Paulette! You didn't even want to celebrate your twenty-first birthday last month," her younger sister exclaimed, frowning in disappointment. "There will be lots of exciting people at this party and some very handsome young men. Aren't you interested in having a suitor? Don't you ever want to have any fun?"

"Of course I do," Paulette protested weakly, curling up on the sofa. "It's just a busy time with the new bookshop right now. Once the new store opens, things will settle down and everything will get back to normal."

Yvette made a face, her expression full of disbelief. "You just use the shop as an excuse. The new store opening won't change anything. You still won't come out with my friends and me."

"That's not true."

"Yes, it is." Yvette crossed her arms, giving her a calculating look.

"All right," Paulette conceded out of weariness. She

wrapped a blanket around her shoulders and laid her head on the sofa cushion. "Perhaps it is a little bit true."

"I just don't understand you sometimes." There was a note of sadness in Yvette's voice.

"You don't have to understand me," Paulette said with a tired smile. "You look very pretty tonight, Yvette."

Her sister came and sat on the edge of the sofa. "Are you all right, Paulette?"

Paulette lifted her head from the cushion in surprise. "Yes, of course, I'm all right. Why do you ask?"

"I don't know. . . . You just haven't seemed yourself lately."

"In what way?"

"You've been very distracted and almost day-dreamy. And don't say it's because of the bookshop. I grew up with you in the bookshop and this is just not the same." Yvette shook her elegantly coiffed head in protest.

"Well, that is the reason," Paulette said, feeling a trifle guilty. She *had* been working non-stop preparing the new store.

"No. It's not. You've changed somehow. It's like there's a spark lit within you . . . I know that sounds silly, but I can't put my finger on it. Colette and I were talking about it just yesterday, because she's noticed it, too." Yvette laughed a little. "If it weren't so ridiculous a notion, I'd say you were in love!"

Paulette's mouth dropped open at her sister's words and she could feel the redness creeping into her cheeks. Was it so obvious?

"Paulette?"

"Yes?"

Yvette's voice was filled with awe. "You're not in love with someone, are you?"

After weeks and weeks of keeping Declan Reeves a

secret, Paulette could no longer maintain her silence. She felt she would burst if she didn't tell someone about the man who consumed her every thought. "Oh Yvette, do you promise not to tell anyone? Especially Colette?"

Yvette's eyes grew wide and she nodded her head in excited anticipation. "I swear I won't tell a soul."

"You promise?"

"Yes! I just said I wouldn't say a word." Yvette almost squealed in delight. "Oh good heavens, Paulette, have you truly met someone? Are you in love? Who is he?"

"He is someone who came in to the bookshop."

"Oh, I knew I was right! How divine!" Yvette exclaimed happily. "I want to know everything! You must tell me all the details!"

Suddenly tears welled in Paulette's eyes. She could not hold them back. Mortified, she whispered, "But it's such a dreadful mess!"

"Please don't cry, Paulette!" Yvette handed her a silk handkerchief, her expression one of deep concern. "Well, now, you simply must tell me what is going on."

Paulette could not stop the flow of tears, but she wiped at them with Yvette's handkerchief. "I don't even know where to start or how to explain it. It's all so complicated."

"Well, why don't you start by telling me who he is first?" Yvette suggested, her pretty face lit with enthusiasm. "What is his name? What does he look like?"

Paulette sniffled, still wiping at her tears. "I met him in August. His name is Declan Reeves, and he's the Earl of Cashelmore and he's—"

"An earl! Oh, Paulette, this is so exciting! I never imagined you with an earl! Tell me more! Is he handsome?"

Paulette nodded, taking a bit of pride in the fact that Declan Reeves was so handsome and that he was attracted to her. "Yes, he's very handsome, even by your standards. He's twenty-five years old. He's a widow from Ireland and he has a daughter. She's only four years old and very sweet."

"A young, handsome Irish earl!" Yvette clapped her hands together in glee. "Paulette, you've completely astonished me! Why on earth are you keeping someone like him a secret from us all?"

Now came the difficult part. She took a deep breath. "Because Colette and Lucien wouldn't approve of him."

Yvette frowned in confusion. "Why on earth wouldn't they approve of him? He sounds divine."

"Yes, well, that's the thing. There is a bit of a problem." Paulette paused, hesitant to reveal Declan's plight. There was no way to avoid telling her sister at this point. "Lord Cashelmore has been accused of killing his wife."

If she had just shoved Yvette off the sofa, her younger sister could not have been more dumbfounded. Her blue eyes widened and her mouth opened in awe. Her hand flew to her heart. "Good heavens!"

"But I swear to you that he didn't have anything to do with her death!" Paulette hurried to add in Declan's defense. "He couldn't have. We've discussed it and he wouldn't lie to me. He's the most wonderful man, caring and kind. And he is so sweet to his daughter."

"Oh, how romantic!" Yvette cried in surprised delight, clasping her hands together. "A forbidden love! It's even better than I could have imagined!"

Feeling relieved at her reaction, Paulette should have known that Yvette would brush aside any cloud of suspicion against Declan. Yvette lived for romance. And Declan Reeves already had too many points in his favor. The danger and forbidden elements only added to his appeal in Yvette's eyes.

"Has he kissed you yet?" Yvette asked, a mischievous twinkle in her eyes.

"Yes." Paulette nodded, feeling a bit embarrassed.

"How could you not tell me this part?" Yvette shook her head in a mixture of disbelief and glee. "How was it? What did you think of kissing?"

"I can't even describe to you how wonderful it is."

Yvette squealed in delight, clapping her hands. "I can't believe you've kissed someone. Finally!"

"And that's not all," Paulette murmured very low.

Her face stricken with awe, Yvette grabbed Paulette's hand in hers. "Oh, Paulette, tell me please. What else have you done?"

"Everything."

Eyes wide, her sister gasped. "Everything?"

Paulette nodded somberly, her cheeks flaming.

"Oh, Paulette," Yvette said, breathlessly. "I don't even know what to say."

The room grew quiet and the fire crackled in the hearth.

"Everything, truly?" Yvette asked once more, eyeing her intensely.

"Yes." Embarrassed, Paulette suddenly wished she hadn't said anything at all.

"What is it like?" Yvette asked in wonder.

"It's even better than Lisette and Colette had said it was."

"Oh my! Paulette, this is so unlike you. You have a secret love!" Yvette giggled, covering her mouth with her hand.

"I never expected this to happen to me either. But it has."

"I'm so happy for you I could cry!" She paused and gave her a look. "When are you going to get married?"

Paulette whispered low. "We're not going to marry."

"What!? Why in heaven's name not?" Yvette demanded in confusion.

"Because neither of us wishes to get married."

"But Paulette, what are you— How can you just— He has to marry you now!" Yvette cried in indignation.

"No, he doesn't," she said softly. "And I'm happy with the way things are between us."

"Then why were you crying just now?"

The tears welled up in Paulette's eyes again. "Because I miss him, and I can't see him when I want to and I'm tired of keeping all of these secrets." She sobbed like a little girl, releasing all the pent-up emotions of the past weeks.

"Well, why can't you see him anymore?" Yvette asked.

Paulette then launched into the tale of the mysterious and threatening letters and how Declan insisted she have an escort wherever she go and how she missed him, but was worried about whoever was watching them.

"Then just tell Colette and Lucien the truth," Yvette suggested. "I'm sure they will understand. If you love him so much, then we are sure to love him as well."

Paulette shook her head, wiping her eyes with the handkerchief again. She felt a bit foolish, but it felt good to clear her conscience a little. "No, I don't think they will understand at all. They will think I have gone completely mad. Colette has already met Declan and warned me to stay away from him. And Jeffrey is already suspicious of him and—"

"Jeffrey!" Yvette exclaimed, her eyes narrowing. "Jeffrey Eddington? What does he have to do with any of this? How does he know about your Irish earl?"

"I was in Green Park with Declan and his daughter one Sunday afternoon and Jeffrey saw us together. He doesn't approve of Declan and thinks he may have killed his wife," Paulette explained. "I begged him not to tell anyone and he promised he wouldn't. But if Jeffrey does not trust him, then Lucien won't trust him either. Neither will Colette. If they knew about the letters, they would never let me leave Devon House, let alone see Declan."

"Yes, I see your point." Yvette nodded in agreement, patting Paulette's shoulder in comfort. "But still, Paulette, you can't go on like this . . ."

"I know," she sniffled, trying to catch her breath. Crying this way was so unlike her, but then she had not been herself from the moment Declan Reeves first walked into the bookshop.

"What are you going to do?"

"I don't know. Declan insists on finding out who is sending the notes and he won't see me again until he thinks it's safe for us."

"Well, you must do something soon. Let's figure this out, shall we?" Yvette made an effort to cheer her. "What are your options?"

"I don't know if I have any options, for it may just be worse than you know, Yvette."

Yvette's expression grew worried. "What do you mean?"

A long silence ensued, as Paulette gathered the courage to reveal the most recent secret that had tormented her. "I am almost certain that I am carrying Lord Cashelmore's child."

Yvette's shock left her completely speechless, her face frozen in utter disbelief tinged with horrified panic.

Paulette had harbored her suspicions for days now, but she had no way of knowing for sure. In all actuality, the consequence of a baby should not be unexpected, considering all that she and Declan had done together in the little bedroom above the bookshop, although he had even taken some precautions to prevent such an occurrence. Still she had not thought it could happen to her until certain physical symptoms could no longer be ignored. She had consulted some medical texts in the shop and all signs pointed to a pregnancy. The heavy burden of this secret left her sleepless for the last few nights.

She would have to tell Declan soon but thought she should get official confirmation from a doctor first. All she had now were her suspicions and the desperate hope that she was wrong.

Yvette still sat with her mouth agape in stunned amazement, when the door to their sitting room flew open and their two little nephews raced to them. Phillip and Simon Sinclair, dressed in their nightclothes, clamored for goodnight kisses from their aunts. The boys climbed upon the sofa where Paulette and Yvette sat and snuggled onto their laps.

Paulette took a deep breath and tried to laugh at the antics of the two boys.

"Kisses, Auntie Paulette!" demanded Simon, wrapping his baby arms around Paulette's neck and pressing wet kisses on her nose. She giggled and hugged him to her. Then Phillip, a little more sedate than his younger brother, claimed his kiss from her.

"The boys were so happy you were both still home this evening," Colette said, following closely behind her sons. "They wanted to say good night." She suddenly glanced with raised brows at the scene on the sofa. "What's going on, girls?"

"Oh, I was giving Paulette a hard time for not coming out with me tonight, telling her she never has any fun and won't ever catch a husband by hiding herself away night after night, and I suppose I upset her. I was just giving her my apologies." Yvette rose from the sofa with Simon in her arms. "Now, I think this young man needs to get to sleep." She handed the boy to Colette and straightened out her dress.

Grateful for the presence of the boys and impressed with Yvette's quick thinking and acting skills, Paulette struggled to put a neutral expression on her face and managed a weak smile. "I'm just overtired."

"So am I!" Colette agreed, looking a bit weary herself. "This week has been exhausting for both of us. You deserve to get some rest, Paulette." She turned to their younger sister. "And where are you off to this evening, miss?"

"I was going to attend the Sheridans' party, but now I think I may just stay in after all." Yvette gave a fleeting glance in Paulette's direction.

"Well, let me know what you decide to do. Come along, boys. Say good night!" Colette took Phillip's hand and they were serenaded by a chorus of good wishes for their sleep.

As soon as they were gone and the door closed, Yvette sat back down on the sofa beside her, her eyes full of worry.

"You don't have to stay home on my account," Paulette said, looking at her little sister all dressed up in her finery and now not going anywhere.

"I want to stay home with you." Yvette squeezed her hand. "Oh, Paulette. What are you going to do?"

"I need to check with a doctor first, I suppose. To be sure one way or another. Would you come with me?"

"Of course. But we can't go to anyone who knows us," Yvette mused. "And certainly not any doctor in town. Maybe we can go to Brighton under the pretext of visiting Mother. We could use a false name there and see a doctor in Brighton."

"That is a brilliant idea."

Yvette flashed her a smile. "I know you don't think so, but I do have them from time to time." She paused and their eyes met. Her expression suddenly turned serious.

"I can't believe this is happening. And to you. The sister least likely to be in this position."

"I can't either. But I suppose I shouldn't be surprised." Paulette released a resigned sigh. "This is what comes from doing everything with a man."

"Are you scared?"

"Terrified."

"I am here for you," Yvette promised, squeezing her hand tightly. "We'll figure this out together."

Feeling tears well up in her eyes once again, Paulette squeezed Yvette's hand back, barely able to whisper a faint, "Thank you."

Chapter 20

Details

"My advice to you, Lord Cashelmore, is to go back to Ireland and end this matter once and for all."

Declan stared at the man who sat in the chair across from his desk. He had hired the best criminal attorney in London, Mr. Sebastian Woods, three weeks ago to look into his case in Ireland as well as the matter of the threatening letters and so far he had turned up nothing more than what Declan already knew.

Someone in Ireland wanted him in prison or worse.

He also knew that it was time to go home and finally put an end to the accusations. He'd been gone long enough. He was innocent of whatever allegations they chose to heap upon him and he had to do something soon to defend himself against the serious charges Margaret's family were trying to trump up against him.

However, he wasn't ready to leave London just yet.

Mara was doing so well. Her nightmares had ceased completely. She was smiling and giggling more and more and she seemed lighter and almost back to her true self. He couldn't uproot her now. She was happy here in her new home in London. Bringing her back to the ugliness in Dublin could erase over two months of progress, he was certain of it.

And there was Paulette to think about.

He could not bring himself to leave Paulette, even though he had not seen her in weeks.

It was only his fear for her safety that kept him from being with her. He had no idea if the author of the notes planned to act out his cowardly threats, but it was not a risk Declan was willing to take with Paulette's life. Which was why he was pleased that Lucien Sinclair had seen to it that his sister-in-law was protected, unaware that there was a true need for her protection and safety. Someone was following Paulette and him and until he found out who it was, Declan could not have chanced Paulette being seen with him. It seemed to be working, too, for she had sent him word that she had only received one more of those letters since they stopped seeing each other. Declan, however, was still receiving them quite regularly. The most recent note arrived only yesterday and was more disturbing than the others.

You're a killer. So you will be killed, too. Time is running out for you, Cashelmore.

The letters angered Declan not only for what they said but for the distance they had placed between him and Paulette.

"I feel it is imperative that we follow the trail of these letters back to Dublin. There we can find out who is sending these outrageous notes and put a stop to this nonsense, as well as put these dangerous accusations against you to rest in a court of law," Mr. Sebastian Woods added, glancing over the latest letter. He was a tall and angular man, with shoulder-length blond hair that he let hang loose. He was not at all what one would expect a re-nowned solicitor to look like. But he was the best.

"Yes," Declan agreed with reluctance. "I will make plans to go back home before the end of October."

"I think that is the best course of action, Lord Cashelmore," Sebastian Woods said, rising to his feet. "I shall begin making arrangements to journey to Dublin with you."

Declan shook hands with his solicitor and saw him out, thinking of his home in Ireland. He had no wish to uproot his daughter and bring her back there so soon.

Yes, Mara was his main concern, but his thoughts kept coming back to Paulette.

It had been torturous for him not seeing her pretty face, hearing her soft voice, or touching her every day. He felt empty without her. All he longed for was to take Paulette in his arms and kiss her. He wanted to be with her. She was the only person he ever had confided in about the truth of his married life, and talking to her about his hellish union to Margaret had eased something in his soul.

He simply missed being near Paulette.

Each night he found himself dreaming about her and that scared him. He should not want her so much, should not think about her so much. About how he wanted her in his arms in bed at night. Wanted her home with him.

Sometimes he even thought of marrying her. But how could he involve her in the complicated mess that was his life? How could she marry someone who was accused of murdering his wife? Not that Paulette believed that about him, but she refused to tell her family about him. Her family would never accept him as good enough for her, and Declan agreed. He was a widower with a mute child. He was rumored to be a murderer, and was haunted by a past that would not let him be. What kind of life was that for Paulette?

Yet he could no longer imagine his life without her.

In the meantime he counted the days until the grand opening of the new bookshop. He hadn't been officially invited, but he figured there would be so many people in attendance, he could blend in with the crowd and at least see Paulette and tell her that he was leaving for Ireland. Besides, he didn't want to miss her opening day. She had worked so hard for the new store and he was quite proud of her for it.

He would surprise her at the opening of the bookshop.

Chapter 21

Mother

"*Quelle surprise!* It is such an unexpected pleasure to have my two daughters come visit me! *Quelle bonne surprise!*" Genevieve La Brecque Hamilton declared happily.

In her late fifties, the many lines on the face of the matriarch of the Hamilton family did not betray her beauty. She still possessed long silver hair that she swept into an elegantly styled knot behind her head and wore a fashionable gown of gray silk. Her blue eyes danced with excitement at the arrival of her daughters.

As Genevieve reclined on the divan in her cottage by the sea in Brighton, Paulette and Yvette sat in the parlor with her, exchanging guilty glances between them.

Paulette's head was still spinning from the news Doctor Brewster had just given her earlier that morning and it was difficult to listen to her mother.

"We're only staying the night, *Maman*," Yvette explained matter-of-factly. "The new shop opens next week and Paulette must get back to London."

"Oh, yes," Paulette agreed. "I've so much to do to get ready for it."

"If you are so busy then what brings you two girls to Brighton? I was not expecting you today. *Je ne m'attendais pas du tout à vous voir.*"

"We wanted to know if you were coming to London, *Maman*," Paulette answered. "We know how you feel about the bookshop, but it would makes us very happy if you could be there for the opening."

A look of displeasure appeared on Genevieve's face. "Oh, I find it insulting that you would think I would not attend the grand opening of my daughters' new bookshop. I don't know why you girls would think such dreadful things about me." Their mother pouted. "Honestly, what you girls must think of me! *Honnêtement mes filles, ce que vous devez pensez de moi!*"

"Oh, *Maman*, we didn't mean to upset you," Yvette cried with a little laugh. "We just know that coming to London is not on your list of favorite activities and you've never made a secret of your feelings for the shop."

"Hmmph." Genevieve crossed her arms, her nose in the air. "You exaggerate. I do not believe that. *Je ne le crois pas.*"

"Truly, Mother, we did not wish to insult you." Paulette wondered how she would ever survive the one night here with her mother.

"I will be there," Genevieve declared with great indignation. "I would not miss such an important event. You are my daughters. We are a family. Of course I would be there. *Bien-sûr que je serais là, nous sommes de la même famille.*"

"Thank you, *Maman*," they both responded in unison.

Genevieve La Brecque Hamilton had a somewhat tumultuous relationship with her five daughters, especially Colette. Growing up, their mother had made it known to all that she cared little for her husband's love of books and detested living above the shop. Genevieve and

Thomas Hamilton's marriage was not a happy one. While Thomas buried himself in books, Genevieve took to her bed, feigning illnesses and ailments, allowing her daughters to care for her. In essence, Colette, as the eldest, had become the head of the family, taking care of her younger sisters when their mother would no longer do so. After their father passed away, Genevieve tried to sell Hamilton's Book Shoppe against Colette's wishes but had not been successful. Then she moved to her little house by the sea in Brighton, where she demanded visits from her daughters and occasionally she ventured to London to see them.

Just then Fannie, their mother's housekeeper, bustled into the parlor, carrying a tray filled with lemon cakes and hot tea, and declaring for the dozenth time how fine it was to have the girls there.

"Thank you, Fannie," Paulette said, as the woman returned to the kitchen promising to cook them a special supper to celebrate their visit.

Then Genevieve turned her attention to her youngest daughter. "Now, tell me, what is new in London? Tell me everything. *Dites-moi tout.* Have you any interesting beaux, Yvette?"

As Yvette happily chattered on about the scores of young gentlemen who had fallen under the spell of her charms, Paulette's stomach churned. There was no longer any doubt.

She was going to have a baby. Declan's baby.

Cold fear coursed through every single fiber of her being. Complete and utter fear. What on earth was she to do? Sometime in May she was going to have a child! Her mind could not grasp the reality of that fact. While taking the train down to Brighton earlier that morning and wearing a small gold band on her finger that Yvette had somehow found for her, Yvette concocted a plausible story. She had been quite clever and thought of everything.

Paulette used the false name, Mrs. Livesey, and her "husband," John, was an artist in Paris, and she and her sister were on their way to visit him. But Paulette, suspecting she was carrying a child while en route to join him, wanted confirmation before she saw her husband again. She didn't know if the doctor, a rather dour and disapproving gentleman with cold hands, believed her story or not. It mattered little in the end when, after his examination, he confirmed Paulette's worst suspicions. She fought to keep from bursting into tears at the news. It was only the press of Yvette's hand in hers that kept her from sobbing in the doctor's office.

As they made their way to their mother's house, the two of them wanted nothing more than to take the first train back to London. But since they had told Colette that they were visiting their mother, they had no choice but to go and see her.

Now all Paulette could do was worry. What was she going to do? How would she tell Declan? What would he say? How would she tell her family? They would be so ashamed of her! Lucien would most likely kill Declan. She shuddered at the thought.

Good God in heaven, what was to become of her? She would be ruined! Completely and utterly ruined.

"And what about you, Paulette? *Parle-moi un peu de tous les hommes qui s'intéressent à toi.* Tell me about the gentlemen interested in you."

Paulette blinked incomprehensibly at her mother.

"Paulette! Are you asleep? Wake up! *Réveille-toi, petite marmotte! Je t'ai posé une question!*" Genevieve snapped her fingers, attempting to gain Paulette's attention. "I asked you a question. Can you not answer a simple question?"

"I'm sorry, *Maman*. I didn't hear what you said."

Her mother gave her a suspicious glance. "You are a beautiful young girl. Why do you not have a suitor? *Comment est-ce possible qu'une belle demoiselle comme toi n'ait pas de prétendants?* How can a beautiful girl like you not have a beau? At your age? You should be married by now, Paulette. *Pourquoi n'es-tu pas mariée? Qu'est-ce que tu attends?* You should have a husband and a baby. What are you waiting for? Are you going to spend your whole life in that bookshop, like your father?"

"How many questions are you asking me, Mother?" Paulette asked in frustration.

Genevieve gave her a determined look. "You know exactly what I am asking you."

"Let Paulette be, *Maman*," Yvette chimed in an attempt to calm them. "She's happy working in the bookshop for now and will marry when she's ready."

If Paulette weren't so consumed with dread, she would have laughed at her younger sister's defense of her to their mother. The roles were reversed. Usually it was Yvette asking the same questions their mother just asked, and Colette defending Paulette.

The day wore on and supper was an endless affair that evening and although Paulette was sure the meal Fannie had prepared especially for them was delicious, she could not stomach more than a mouthful or two. She had no appetite for food. In fact she felt terribly nauseous. She managed to add to the conversation enough so that she did not appear too quiet and pushed her food around on her plate to give the appearance of eating.

But she was grateful to finally climb into bed later

that evening. Sharing the bed with Yvette brought back memories of their childhood.

"It's been years since we've been in the same room, let alone the same bed!" declared Yvette as she snuggled under the covers. "Oh, it's so cold in here!"

Through the darkness, Paulette whispered, "Thank you for coming with me. I don't know how I would have gotten through this without your help."

"It's the least I can do. But I don't think you're through anything yet, Paulette. In fact, I'd say you're only just beginning."

"I know, but you've been such a comfort to me." Paulette felt tears well in her eyes again.

Yvette propped her hand under her head, her elbow on the pillow. "You need to tell Lord Cashelmore. He's sure to marry you once he knows. It's the only solution to this mess."

Paulette did not think that would be the case. Besides she didn't wish to force Declan's hand in marriage. "He never wants to marry again. He said so."

"Well, he hasn't much choice now, has he?" Yvette retorted rather matter-of-factly. "You're having his baby. A *baby*, Paulette! You *have* to get married!"

"I don't *have* to . . ."

"Unless you want complete scandal and utter social ruin you do!" Yvette was aghast. "And think of the child! What about the baby?"

"I could go away for a while . . ."

Yvette grew very thoughtful at Paulette's words. "Yes, you could. . . . We could tell Lucien and Colette that we want a trip abroad. Lucien has always suggested that we take one. I could go with you. We could stay in a nice villa in Italy somewhere until the baby is born and then we could return to London as if nothing happened."

In spite of the seriousness of their conversation, Paulette managed to laugh a bit at her sister's apparently well-laid scheme. "Have you planned all this out?"

"Well," Yvette answered a bit defensively. "It's not as if it hasn't been done before. I've read about it in a lot of novels. It's what girls like us always do when they're in your kind of trouble."

For the last week, Paulette had been thinking of nothing else but what girls should do when faced with this particular kind of trouble. Aside from marriage, taking a leave of absence was the only other socially acceptable alternative. "I was thinking more along the lines of going to stay with Juliette in America. She's coming to London for the opening of the store. I'll explain everything to her then and just go back to America with her when she leaves."

"Oh! That's an even better idea! Juliette will know what to do. Why didn't I think of that? It's much more plausible and would raise less suspicion."

"That's what I'd prefer to do, rather than hide away in Italy."

Releasing a heavy sigh, Yvette asked, "Is that really what you want to do?"

"None of this is what I want, Yvette, but I have very few options. And I feel like a fool."

"You're not a fool. You're a girl in love and that's why they have all these rules in society, you know. To keep the men away from us and to prevent us females from ending up this way." Yvette paused a moment. "Are you going to tell Lord Cashelmore?"

Paulette's first instincts had been to tell Declan as soon as she returned to London, but the more she thought about it, the more she believed it might be better to say nothing at all. If she told him about the baby,

Declan would feel obligated to marry her, just as Yvette predicted. But Paulette did not want to marry a man who was marrying her out of duty or a sense of guilt. If she slipped away to visit Juliette for a few months, no one would know about the baby, except Yvette and Juliette. She could think of what to do once she was in America. Juliette would know what was best and it would buy Paulette some time. "I don't have to tell him anything if I go to America with Juliette."

"I still think it's best to tell him," Yvette said with a bit of worry in her voice. "He'd marry you and you wouldn't have to run away."

"No."

"Now you're being foolish."

"Would you want to marry a man who was being forced to marry you, Yvette?"

After a quiet minute her sister grudgingly admitted, "No, I suppose not, but still . . . You're having his baby, Paulette. You already told me what a good father he is. Why wouldn't he want a baby with you? He has to marry you. At the very least he deserves to know about his child, don't you think?"

"I can't think about this anymore," Paulette cried, placing her hands over her face.

Ever since she suspected that she might be with child, she had been trying to picture Declan's reaction if she were to tell him about the baby. Her visions ranged from him being overjoyed and wanting to make her his wife, to her words being greeted with stony silence and disgust. Declan had so much to worry about. He was dealing with the charges being brought against him in his wife's death as well as struggling to help his daughter speak again. He certainly didn't need to take on the added burden of Paulette and a baby.

A baby. She dared not even let herself think of this child. Dared not think of loving it. Of imagining a life with this baby. It was too heartbreaking.

"I'm sorry," Yvette whispered in the darkness. "I can only imagine how you feel right now."

The lump in her throat kept Paulette from responding and tears threatened, stinging, like pin pricks behind her eyes.

Her sister's imagination wouldn't even come close to knowing how Paulette felt. Frightened. Embarrassed. Confused. Overwhelmed. Heartbroken. Worried. Dizzy. Faint. Foolish. Nauseous. The list went on and on. Only one word was not on her list of feelings. And that was regretful. She could not for one single minute regret any of the nights she spent with Declan Reeves. In spite of the consequences she now faced, she looked back on those times together with only joy and love. She had never been happier or felt more alive than when she was with him. Did she wish the precautions they had taken had worked? Yes. But she did not regret one moment of being in Declan's arms.

Under the warmth of the quilt that covered her she laced her fingers over her abdomen. The smooth cotton of her nightgown covered her, but she rubbed her hands gently across her stomach. One would never guess by looking at her that a tiny person was growing within her. A baby. Her baby. Their baby. Her heart fluttered with a strange excitement. A glimmer of hope.

"Do you know the terrible irony of this whole situation?" Yvette asked, settling back into the pillows.

"What?" At the moment Paulette could not think of anything more ironic than the fact that of all her sisters, she, the most practical and reliable one, was the one to find herself in the most irresponsible of all situations.

"Lisette."

Paulette's tears came full force then. "Oh, it's not fair." How could it be that her married sister, who wanted a baby so desperately, could not seem to have one and there was Paulette, not married and with child?

Yvette whispered, "We can't tell her about this."

"It would break her heart if we did." Paulette wiped at the hot tears that spilled down her cheeks and into her ears as she lay there in the dark.

Chapter 22

Dilemma

Yvette Hamilton knew she had to tell someone what was happening, but she was not quite sure whom to tell. Paulette had sworn her to secrecy, and Yvette couldn't break a promise like that to her sister. Not to Paulette of all people. After the confirmation from the doctor in Brighton, Paulette's plan to have the baby in America could work, but Yvette disagreed with it completely. In her heart she believed that this mysterious Lord Cashelmore simply had to marry her sister. It was the right and proper course of action for a gentleman. As if anything about this situation was right or proper.

This was the biggest problem that she had ever dealt with before. Riddled with fear and worry over her sister's situation, she knew that she and Paulette could not handle this on their own.

Which is why she chose to tell Jeffrey Eddington.

It wasn't really breaking a confidence, Yvette reasoned, since Jeffrey already knew about Paulette and Lord Cashelmore.

After Colette and Paulette left to go to the bookshop

one morning after their little trip to Brighton, Yvette ventured to Lord Eddington's townhouse.

Just as his butler had opened the door, Jeffrey had been descending the stairs and saw her.

"Yvette! What in God's name are you doing here?" Jeffrey could not hide the astonishment on his handsome face upon seeing Yvette Hamilton standing upon his doorstep.

"Is that any way to greet a lady?" she remarked, a bit put out by his curt welcome. Jeffrey was usually more gallant than that. His butler stood there dumbfounded, not sure what to do.

"Let her in, Dennings. It's all right," Jeffrey said to the older man who seemed at sixes and sevens. Jeffrey turned his attention to Yvette. Taking her arm and leading her from the grand foyer, he said, "Ladies do not come calling upon gentlemen at this hour of the morning without an escort, Miss Hamilton."

"They do when it's important and they need to speak with that gentleman privately," she said as she glanced around her with interest.

Yvette had never been to Jeffrey's townhouse before and found herself quite curious about it. As he ushered her through the house, she took note of the masculine feel of the place. Surprisingly, there was nothing surprising at all about it. The house was tasteful and understated in its décor. There was none of the fashionable knick-knacks and curios and heavily patterned wallpapers that were all the rage. Feeling a bit disappointed, she had expected something more . . . more . . . well, decadent about Jeffrey's home.

She had known Jeffrey Eddington since she was thirteen years old and he had become a part of their family when Colette married Lucien Sinclair. Aside from his acting as a protective older brother to all of them, Yvette had always liked him for treating her as if she were a lady. Even when she wasn't.

"What is the matter, Yvette? Has something happened to your sisters? Is one of them hurt?" he asked once they were in the privacy of his study, his blue eyes filled with worry.

"No, not exactly," she said, taking a seat on a leather chair, facing him. She arranged the long train of her satin damask bustle gown neatly around her. She loved the way the floral sprig pattern on the golden yellow satin caught the light, making it her favorite brand-new dress.

Jeffrey leaned against his large oak desk, watching her, his expression puzzled. "What is going on then, Yvette? What are you doing here? Aside from looking quite beautiful in that gown."

"Thank you," she murmured, feeling a bit flustered. That was another reason why she liked Jeffrey. He always noticed her and complimented her prettily, although this time she blushed a little under his regard. "Well . . ."

"Well?" he urged.

Suddenly feeling foolish for coming to his house to tell him what she had intended to tell him, she hesitated. Now she was not sure if she should confide in him. "I thought . . . that is . . . I came here to ask your advice on a matter of a very personal nature."

"Who is he?"

"I beg your pardon?" she asked, taken aback by his question.

He crossed his arms in front of him, eyeing her with keen interest. "Who is he? I assume that's why you're here. To find out more about your newest conquest. Hasn't he fallen in love with you yet?"

"Oh, no! It's nothing like that!" Yvette exclaimed, with a giggle and a dismissive wave of her hand. "How funny!

As if I needed your assistance with my romantic life! I'm not here on my own account!"

He cast her an odd look at her words. "Well, what is it then?"

She hesitated, patting her blond curls in place. "Now I'm not sure if I should tell you."

"You came all this way, Yvette. It was obviously important enough for you to seek me out. I can tell you're harboring some kind of secret, so you may as well tell me now."

He was right. She had come here for help, which she needed. Which her sister needed. She paused for a moment. "It's about Paulette."

Jeffrey immediately stood straighter, a look of anger clouding his handsome features. "Is it Lord Cashelmore? Has he done something to hurt her?"

That gave Yvette pause. Had Lord Cashelmore hurt her sister? "I'm not sure if hurt is the correct term I would use."

"Yvette, just say it." His voice was filled with determination and not a little anxiety.

"The reason I came to see you is only because Paulette told me that you knew of her . . . *friendship* . . . with Lord Cashelmore, so I knew you would be understanding."

"I won't be understanding for much longer," he growled, growing impatient. "The man has a dark reputation. I warned Paulette about him in the first place, but I was under the impression that they were no longer seeing each other."

Yvette hesitated again, a flicker of fear in her chest. "It seems there has been a bit of a complication that adds to the seriousness of the situation."

His expression darkened. "Damn it, Yvette."

Yvette just blurted it out. "Paulette's going to have a baby and someone is threatening to kill her!"

"Good God. You're not jesting." His eyes widened at the news, then he grew terribly somber. He shook his head in disgust. "I should have stopped it from the beginning. I knew no good would come of their association. I blame myself for this."

"Don't blame yourself, Jeffrey. They've been meeting in secret. No one even knows about them. She only told me two weeks ago."

"Is she sure? Has she been to a—"

"Yes, we visited with a doctor in Brighton last week."

"Who else knows about this?"

"Just me. And now you."

"Well, she's just going to have to marry him, that's all."

Yvette shook her head. "That's the problem. She won't marry him."

"What?" Jeffrey was incredulous.

"She says neither of them wishes to marry and she wants to go stay with Juliette in America and have the baby there," Yvette explained, beginning to feel like she made the right decision in coming to see Lord Eddington.

Jeffrey whistled low. "She's completely lost her mind."

"I know and it has me very worried. That's why I'm here. We can't let her run away to America. Lord Cashelmore needs to marry her. As soon as possible."

"He certainly does. Although I'm not sure I like the idea of your sister marrying a man suspected of murdering his first wife."

"Paulette swears by his innocence." Yvette looked at Jeffrey. "And I believe her."

Jeffrey paused, thoughtful. "She said the same to me, and as much as I would love to believe Paulette, I don't trust the man himself. She's in love with him and a woman in love will believe anything the man she's in love with has to say."

Now that was interesting. Yvette arched an inquisitive brow in Jeffrey's direction. "Is that so?"

"Yes," he responded matter-of-factly. "So Cashelmore knows nothing about the baby?"

"No. And she had no plans to tell him. Perhaps you can talk some sense into Paulette. Or even speak with Lord Cashelmore. I feel that if he knew about the baby, he would want to do the honorable thing and marry Paulette, as he should."

"Perhaps," Jeffrey said.

"She's in love with him, just as you said. She shouldn't have to flee to America and have her baby alone. It will break her heart, Jeffrey."

"Does he love her?"

"I don't know for sure, but who wouldn't love Paulette? He'd be a fool not to marry her."

"You have a point there."

"Paulette is already planning to leave with Juliette when she gets here and you know Juliette will do anything to help her. We have to stop Paulette from ruining her life. And the baby's."

Jeffrey remained quiet. A lengthy silence ensued and Yvette grew worried. Finally she asked, "You'll help her, won't you, Jeffrey? Please?"

"Yes."

"What will you do?" Yvette's heart pounded, wondering how Jeffrey would address the problem.

"I'm not quite sure yet." He flashed her his signature, charming grin and winked at her. "Aside from getting you home posthaste before we have another scandal."

Smiling, Yvette rose from her seat and took the arm that Jeffrey offered her. In spite of his flirty ways, she knew he would take care of Paulette's problem. "Thank you, Jeffrey. I knew I could count on you."

"You can always count on me, Yvette." Jeffrey paused as if something just occurred to him. His brows furrowed and he stared at her incredulously. "Did you say someone was threatening to kill her?"

Pausing to look at him, Yvette grimaced. "Oh, yes. About that . . ." She had almost forgotten the other part of Paulette's dilemma. Now she had to explain to Jeffrey what she knew about the threats.

He wasn't going to be happy at all.

Chapter 23

Family

As they arrived at the site of new bookshop for the grand opening, Paulette struggled to contain the terrible nausea that had been plaguing her day and night. Today it seemed worse than ever. On a day when she should be overjoyed and full of satisfaction, she could not bear even the smell of food, let alone eat any of her breakfast.

Unable to sleep, she knew she appeared weary and gaunt that morning. Tossing and turning in her bed each night as she wrestled with the decision she had to make sooner rather than later did her appearance no favors. She still had not told Declan about the baby although she knew that she should. Part of her yearned to tell him, but something held her back from doing so.

She had hoped against hope that Juliette would have arrived by now. Juliette had written that she and her husband and daughter would return to London in time for the opening, yet here it was the day of the event and there was no sign of them. Paulette longed to confide in Juliette and know what her thoughts were. She also planned on leaving with her sister on her return voyage to America. If Juliette ever got there, that was.

Paulette waited impatiently as the new shop filled with family and friends. Lucien and Colette were there with their two little boys along with Lisette and Quinton Roxbury, Yvette and their mother, Genevieve Hamilton. Even their estranged uncle and aunt, Randall and Cecilia Hamilton, had surprised them by arriving for the opening of the new store, along with their son, Nigel. Tom Alcott and his mother, Anna, and her fiancé, Jack Harris, were there as well.

Touched by everyone who made a point to share in their special day, Paulette glanced around the beautiful shop with pride. Feeling eyes on her, she saw Lord Jeffrey Eddington. She did not like the look he gave her. As if he knew she was in trouble. Guiltily she averted her eyes from his intense gaze.

Filled with the hum of voices and activity, the shop was crowded with guests who had been invited to the opening. Many were friends of Lucien and Colette. As the Marquis and Marchioness of Stancliff, they had a wide social circle. Quinton and Lisette Roxbury too had invited a number of his political friends. And surprisingly, a rather large crowd had gathered outside the store as well, much more than they had expected. But it barely mattered to Paulette, because the person she wanted to be there more than anyone in the world would not be there that day.

Raising his hand in her direction, Quinton motioned to her. "Come, Paulette. It's time. We're ready for the unveiling."

Paulette was the one who was to pull down the drapes revealing the sign bearing the name of the new bookshop. Everyone was looking forward to learning the name, which she and Colette had kept as a secret. She moved toward Quinton, and a dizzying wave of nausea washed over her. She willed herself not to be sick right there in front of everyone as she walked unsteadily toward her brother-in-law.

"Are you feeling all right?" Quinton asked in her in a discreet whisper. "You look a little green."

Swallowing, she barely nodded her head, grateful she did not have to be the one to give a speech this day. "I'm fine. Let's go."

They made their way out of the store and joined the gathering crowd on the street. Colette, Lucien, and the rest of the Hamilton family joined them as they climbed the steps to the small dais that had been built outside the shop and they took their seats. Colette stepped to the podium to begin her speech. Paulette pressed her fingers to her forehead, fighting another wave of dizziness, and breathed in the cool autumn air.

Paulette's eyes scanned the crowd, wondering at all the people who had come out on this crisp October day for the opening of a new bookstore in London. It was quite a spectacle. There were men and women of all classes in the crowd as well as children.

It was then she spotted him and a little thrill raced through her.

Standing amidst the spectators and holding his daughter in his arms so she could see over the crowd, was Declan Reeves, the Earl of Cashelmore. He looked even handsomer than she remembered in his dark suit and tall black hat. Her heart skittered in her chest and she could not help but smile at him. Had over a month really passed since she last saw him? Oh, how she missed him!

Declan acknowledged her with a warm grin and nodded at her, their gazes holding for a long moment.

A feeling of euphoria filled her at the nearness of him and she felt the nauseous feeling almost fade away.

Declan knew how important this day was to her and he had come to share in it.

Seated beside her, Yvette followed her gaze and gave her a little nudge. "That's him, isn't?" she whispered.

Paulette nodded with pride, still smiling at him, for Declan Reeves was truly a sight to behold.

"Oh, he is very handsome," Yvette said in her ear.

At that moment a large carriage made its way through the crowded street, stopping as close to the shop as it could get. Everyone turned to look. The door swung open and out stepped Juliette Hamilton Fleming, dressed in an elegant gown of stripped navy and white, a pert hat with a white feather perched upon her head.

"Wait!" Juliette called, waving her hand frantically. "Don't start without me!"

Then her husband, Captain Harrison Fleming, stepped down behind her, carrying their young daughter, Sara. Juliette came hurrying through the throng of people and up to the dais to join them.

"Juliette! You're finally here!" Colette cried with happiness, throwing her arms around her sister.

"I'm so sorry, but better late than never! We planned to be here sooner, but our ship ran into some bad weather. We only docked this morning and we raced across town, just in time I see!" Juliette laughed, as she was embraced by each of her sisters and her mother in turn. Another round of hugs was given to their brother-in-law, Harrison, and little niece, Sara.

No one was happier to see Juliette return than Paulette. She could barely wait to get her sister alone and confide in her.

"My daughter has come home at last!" Genevieve La Brecque Hamilton's beaming face expressed her joy at having all five of her daughters together again for the first time in over a year. "Oh, this is a wonderful day for our family! *C'est une journée fantastique pour notre famille.*"

As they all took their seats once more, Colette made a brief speech about the bookshop and the history of Hamilton's, mentioning their father's years of hard work and dedication to providing quality books to the community.

"My sister, Miss Paulette Hamilton, who has been instrumental in every aspect of the design and installation of our new location, will now reveal the name of our newest bookshop," she announced.

Paulette stood on shaky legs and Quinton handed her the silk cord. Momentarily forgetting her sickness, she glanced at Colette in excitement. All their years of hard work at their father's dusty shop where they had to pinch pennies and scrimp to make the needed changes had come to this momentous occasion. "Are we ready?"

Colette flashed her joyful smile. "Ready!"

With a forceful tug, Paulette pulled the rope, releasing the coverings that draped over the sign. The elegantly scripted words were etched in wood above the front window. In gold lettering on a black background was:

THE HAMILTON SISTERS' BOOK SHOPPE

As the crowd applauded, Juliette, Lisette, and Yvette exclaimed over the new name.

"Oh, that's just wonderful!"

"The Hamilton sisters!"

"Oh, how marvelous! *Oh, mes filles, la librairie est magnifique!*"

"It's perfect, just perfect!"

Paulette turned to the crowd and met Declan's gaze and recognized the look of approval in his eyes. A thrill went through her. She wished he could stand beside her on the dais with her family. She wished he could hold her hand and share in her joy.

Everyone stood admiring the impressive new store-front, exclaiming over its beauty and its ideal name.

Pleased beyond words with the name of the shop, their mother dabbed at the tears in her eyes. "I am so proud and happy. *Je suis tellement heureuse et tellement fière.*"

Caught off guard by their mother's unexpectedly emotional response to the new bookshop, the five sisters exchanged surprised glances.

"It is true!" Genevieve Hamilton declared. "You are even more successful than your father! *Je suis si fière de vous, mes filles. Vous avez réussi là où votre père n'avait pas pu le faire.*"

Filled with wonder, Paulette hugged her mother, grateful that she was there.

The whole group then filed back into the store where refreshments were served and people milled about the bookshop, commenting on its superior design and layout and congratulating the sisters on their accomplishment. Their newly trained female employees stood behind the counter in their neat green aprons, ready to assist customers in purchasing books.

The day become a blur of activity, so busy was Paulette greeting guests, giving little tours around the shop, and assisting customers with books. She was in her element, doing what she loved best and what made her happy.

Carrying a plate of Mrs. Alcott's shortbread biscuits, Paulette went to the large and brightly colored children's section of the shop, where she knew her niece and nephews were playing together. Phillip and Simon, handsome in their new suits, were seated at one of the small tables with their cousin Sara, their laughter filling the air. At three years old, Sara Fleming was an exact replica of her mother, Juliette. With long dark hair and mischievous blue eyes, she had an impish smile and an exuberant personality to match.

Paulette was stunned to see Mara Reeves standing beside her little niece. Sara was talking a mile a minute, not caring in the least that her newfound friend was not responding. Yet Mara listened to Sara with rapt attention, as Sara counted the books in front of her. The two young girls were a study in contrasts, one dark haired and talkative, the other fair and calm.

Glancing around, Paulette knew Declan was in the shop somewhere but she did not see him. The last time she spied him was after the unveiling outside the store. She assumed he had gone home then, for she had not seen him again. Now her heart raced at the thought of being so close to him. However, it worried her that Mara was unattended, for it was not usual for Declan to leave her alone. Yet Mara did not appear anxious. In fact she seemed most comfortable as she played with the other children, a bright smile on her sweet face.

Paulette moved to the little group, placing the plate of biscuits on the table, which was greeted with joyous cries from Phillip and Simon. She knelt down beside the two girls.

"Hello, Auntie Paulette," Sara said with a little grin.

"Are you having fun?" Paulette asked her niece.

"Yes. These books are all mine. All of them," she announced, possessively placing her small hand on top of the stack of children's books on the table in front of her. "I'll let Phillip and Simon each have one. Just one. And she can have two," she said, pointing a chubby finger at Mara. "But she won't tell me her name."

"Her name is Mara Reeves," Paulette explained, glad that the two girls had unexpectedly become acquainted. "Mara sounds just like your name. They rhyme!"

"Well, Mara can have two books, because I like her,"

Sara declared, taking Mara's hand in hers. She giggled in delight. "Mara. Sara. Mara. Sara."

Paulette turned her attention to Declan's daughter. "Hello, Mara. This is my niece, Sara Fleming. And these are my nephews, Phillip and Simon Sinclair. Are you having fun here with them?"

Mara grinned and nodded, her face beaming.

"I'm so happy to see you today," Paulette said. "Do you know where your father is? Is he here in the shop?"

Mara looked up with her green eyes, so much like her father's, and nodded her little head. Raising her hand she pointed toward the small reading room, which was designated to hold book-club meetings and discussion groups. The door was closed. Paulette wondered what on earth Declan could be doing in there. Perhaps he was waiting for her in there, where they could have a moment alone together? Filled with an excitement she hadn't felt in weeks, Paulette smiled in anticipation.

"Thank you, Mara." She glanced at the children happily eating their shortbread biscuits. "Now you all play nicely together."

With a sense of nervous delight, Paulette stood and went directly to the reading room. Declan had come to see her, to support her and share in her special day. She was touched by his thoughtfulness. He must have good news about the letters and he was waiting for her. She wanted to throw her arms around him, to feel his lips on hers once more. She would tell him about the baby. She would introduce him to her mother and sisters this very afternoon. Suddenly filled with hope that everything would work out the way she wanted it to, she couldn't wait to see him.

Placing her hand on the handle, she heard voices on the other side of the door. Male voices. Curious, she paused a moment, listening. Who was in there with

Declan? Definitely two male voices. If only the children were not giggling and chattering so loudly she would be able to hear what they were saying! She debated whether she should knock first, but reasoned that it was her shop and she could enter her own reading room if she wanted to. However, she waited another minute, straining to make out what was being said, sure she heard her name mentioned once, before she flung open the door. Paulette did not know what or who she expected to see when she opened the door, but she was sure the scene that greeted her had not been in her realm of possibility.

Declan Reeves was engaged in an intense conversation with Lord Jeffrey Eddington.

Paulette's heart almost stopped at the sight of the two men poised so seriously and the tension in the room almost knocked her off her feet. They both ceased speaking and turned to look at her, and, judging from the expressions on their faces, Paulette was quite certain that she had been the topic of conversation. She frowned in confusion.

"What's going on in here?" she managed to ask, noting that Declan appeared in a state of shock.

"Hello, Paulette," Jeffrey said, his voice low and his eyes shuttered. He stood with his arms crossed in front of him.

Paulette's eyes moved between the two men, trying desperately to guess the subject of their discussion. She rested her gaze on Declan. "What is going on in here?"

Avoiding Paulette's glance, Declan said, "Lord Eddington, can you give us a moment of privacy?"

"Certainly." Without another word and ignoring Paulette's questioning eyes, Jeffrey strode from the room, closing the door behind him.

"Declan?" she asked the moment they were alone.

"Please sit down, Paulette." He motioned to one of

the comfortable chairs upholstered in green velvet that had so pleased her when she chose the fabric.

Unable to read his mood, Paulette moved closer to him, wishing he would take her in his arms. But he did not. He did not make an overture to her.

"I don't wish to sit," she said. "I want to know what you and Jeffrey Eddington were discussing."

"Oh, I'm quite sure you can guess, can't you, darlin'?"

"No. No, I can't." Her heart beat wildly in her chest at the cold and sarcastic tone in Declan's voice. What in heaven's name had Jeffrey said to Declan? Had he warned Declan to stay away from her? Had Jeffrey offended Declan in some way? Perhaps it was about the threatening letters. Whatever it was, Paulette did not like the dark look Declan was giving her.

"Sit down, Paulette. Please. I need to talk to you." His mouth was set in a grim line and he looked just as forbidding and dangerous as he did the day she first met him. More so now, if such a thing were possible.

Staring at him, she lowered herself onto the chair and wrung her hands together. Something was terribly, terribly wrong. After not seeing each other for weeks, he did not seem happy to see her in the least. He did not embrace her or kiss her as she longed to hold and kiss him.

"Declan, please, tell me. What is wrong?"

"I think you are quite aware of what is *wrong*."

She blinked at him. This was definitely not about the letters. No, not at all. He would not be angry with her if it were about the letters. A niggling feeling of dread began to blossom in her chest. He couldn't possibly know about the baby, could he? The only person who knew anything was Yvette, and Yvette promised to never tell a soul. . . . Oh good Lord! Paulette's stomach rolled. *Yvette couldn't have told him . . . She couldn't have . . .*

Declan's words were brittle. "It has been brought to my attention that you and I need to marry as soon as possible."

Oh, dear God in heaven, Yvette *had* told Jeffrey Eddington! It was the only explanation. Paulette would throttle her sister later for opening her big mouth and betraying her confidence in such a horrific manner. At the moment, however, she could barely breathe, could barely think. "Declan, I . . . I was going to tell you—"

"No, you weren't," he interrupted, his eyes full of angry accusation. "You were going to leave for America with your sister and never even tell me about the baby. Our baby."

Paulette's face burned in shame as he spoke the words aloud. Her desperate idea of leaving London without letting Declan know about the baby now seemed quite reprehensible. "No, no, that was only a last resort plan, if I . . . if we . . ." She faltered, unable to explain herself.

"If we . . . ?" He prompted her to continue.

She hesitated. "If we did not marry."

"Oh, we're marrying, Paulette, you can rest assured on that count."

She should feel relieved. Declan was going to marry her. He'd just said so. She did not have to hide in America or give away her baby. She should rejoice. The man she loved had agreed to marry her. Instead she felt hot tears prick the back of her eyes. Somehow Jeffrey Eddington had gotten involved in her affairs and he more than likely coerced or threatened Declan into marrying her. Which was not how she ever wished for a man to ask her to marry him. And Declan did not even ask her. He simply said, *"We must marry."*

He did not truly wish to make her his wife. He had been clear on that point from the start. Now he was only asking her out of duty. Well, he needn't be so bothered by her circumstances. She did have some options available to her. She had resources and could very well go through with her plan. Maybe she would go to America with Juliette after all and never come back to London. Maybe she would open a bookshop there and raise her own child. She could put on that gold ring she used in Brighton and pose as a young widow. She need not wed a man who obviously did not wish to marry her.

And it was quite clear that Declan had no wish to marry her.

He had greeted her so warmly earlier that day, when she spotted him in the crowd. She had felt the pride and love in him then. But now . . . now that he knew he must marry her, he was so very distant and cold. He was obviously not pleased at the prospect of having Paulette for his wife, in spite of her carrying his child. There was no tenderness, no concern for her well-being or state of mind. There was no happiness. No words of love. No reassurances that all would be well.

There was just coldness from him.

Paulette blinked back the tears. She refused to cry in front of him or seem weak in any way. Rising to her feet, she gazed back at him just as coolly. With as much dignity as she could muster she said, "Thank you for your offer, but I think not. I've no wish to marry you, Lord Cashelmore."

"We will marry." He stated the words as fact, his Irish accent becoming a bit thicker in his anger. "It's bad enough that I had to learn the truth from Eddington and not from you, Paulette, but I swear to you that you will not take my child from me. Unfortunately that means marriage."

"I will not marry you." Her legs trembled and she needed to leave the reading room immediately, before she burst into tears in front of him.

His eyes glittered with bitterness. "What's the matter, Paulette, don't you wish to marry a wife killer?"

She gasped at his harsh words, but she threw back at him the only words that would hurt him as much as he had hurt her. "No, I do not."

With that, she flung open the door and hurried from the reading room as fast as she could, leaving Declan staring after her.

Chapter 24

Friends

Declan watched Paulette go, stunned. Completely stunned by the whole bloody mess. He should go after her and talk some sense into her, but he was simply too angry. Angry with her for not coming to him and telling him about the baby. Angry at himself for getting her into this position in the first place. It was all his fault and he accepted full responsibility for it. He'd told Eddington that as well, but he doubted the man believed him.

Although loath to admit it, he was also deeply hurt by Paulette. Hurt that she had not confided in him about her condition as soon as she knew about it. Her lack of trust in him was unbearable. She should have come to him! Having a baby was not what he had expected or planned, but he certainly knew a child was a possibility after all they'd done together no matter how careful he had tried to be and all the precautions he took. It was his fault, not hers, that she was in this situation. He would not have been angry with her. Had she feared him? Had she begun to believe the rumors about him? Was that why she now coldly refused his offer of marriage, when surely she knew she must marry him or face complete social ruin or a life in exile? Did the thought of marriage to him repel her that much?

Life with a man suspected of murder held no appeal and he could not blame her for that.

Filled with regret and self-recriminations, he was thankful he was leaving for Ireland tomorrow. He had to clear his name once and for all, for how could he ask a woman as lovely as Paulette to share it with him, when it was so tainted?

"Excuse me, sir?"

Declan looked up to see a beautiful woman who looked startlingly similar to Paulette standing in the doorway of the reading room. Although she was a little taller and her hair was black, the clear blue eyes and the delicate face showed a striking resemblance. He had seen her from afar earlier that day, during the unveiling, but up close there was not a doubt of who she could be. She was most definitely one of the Hamilton sisters and from what Paulette had told him, he guessed this must be Juliette.

She gave him a curious look.

"Yes?" he asked.

"Is this little blonde your daughter?"

Declan's heart lurched. Good God, with all that had happened he'd completely forgotten about Mara! They had been in the crowd that morning to witness the opening of the shop. He had wanted to be there to support Paulette and see the new shop. Hell, he had simply wanted to see her. He'd missed her terribly during the last month. So he had brought Mara along, and then on an impulse he had entered the shop with the rest of the guests and customers. Declan had wandered about the place, impressed by all she had done inside the new location. He'd even managed to stay out of Paulette's way,

and she had been so preoccupied with all that she had
going on that she had not noticed him when he took
Mara to the children's section. That was when Lord Eddington had pulled him aside, asking to speak to him privately. Declan left Mara seated at one of the little tables,
looking at a picture book. He thought he'd be gone only
a minute.

Now he felt awful for leaving Mara alone for so long.

"Is she all right?" Panicking, Declan hurried to the
doorway. "She's not hurt, is she? I was only in here a
short time, and I thought it would be okay."

"Oh, she's fine." Paulette's sister moved to the side
to allow him to pass by. "I didn't mean to frighten you. I
simply wanted to find out to whom she belonged."

Declan stopped short. Mara was not crying for him or
scared in the least. His daughter was playing quite contentedly with another little girl and two boys at the children's table just where he had left her. They all looked to
be near in age and were laughing and singing and looking at books like they were old friends. Mara was laughing, really laughing. Once again, Declan was stunned.

"I'm so sorry to have worried you," Paulette's sister
said, coming to stand beside him. "It seems that my
daughter has become quite possessive of your daughter,
saying she wants to take her home. They're all having a
wonderful time together."

"Yes, I can see that," Declan murmured in relief, fascinated by the scene in front of him. He recalled Paulette
once suggesting that Mara should play with children her
own age. He wished he had listened to her, for the
change in his daughter was quite astounding. The
younger of the two boys, a handsome dark-haired boy
who had to be close to three, reached over to take a book
out of Mara's hands. She held on to it quite firmly, not

letting him have it. "No!" she declared. The word was clear and the sound was music to Declan's ears. He wanted to cry with delight. It was a small step, to be sure, but Mara had spoken her first word in a year!

His daughter had said "no." Just as Paulette had said to him moments ago. The irony was not lost on him.

"I'm Mrs. Harrison Fleming," the woman beside him stated. "And that is my daughter, Sara, and those two are my sister Colette's sons, Phillip and Simon Sinclair."

"I'm Declan Reeves and that is Mara."

"*You're* Declan Reeves?" Her voice was incredulous as she gave him an assessing look and echoed again, "*You're* Declan Reeves?"

"Yes, I am." He smiled ruefully. "The one and only."

"Well, that explains a great deal, but I certainly wasn't expecting to meet you so soon."

He gazed at her wryly. "I gather your sister Paulette has mentioned me before?"

Juliette Hamilton Fleming gave him a knowing glance. "In a surprisingly short time, I've managed to learn quite a lot about you, Lord Cashelmore. It seems I've returned to London just in time."

"It's a little late to warn her away from me," Declan said quietly.

To his surprise, Juliette laughed and gave a little wave of her hand. "Oh, I've figured out that much on my own, Lord Cashelmore."

"So you know everything then?" he asked. Aside from his name and title, Declan wondered just what else Juliette Hamilton Fleming had managed to learn about him.

"You could say that."

"Is your family ready to kill me? Do I need to make a run for it?"

Once again, Juliette's laughter took him by surprise. "Since I just arrived in town, I don't know if you're in the clear yet, but it seems no one else knows about you, except Yvette."

"And apparently Lord Eddington knows," he added, recalling their conversation in the reading room. Eddington made it clear in no uncertain terms where he stood on the matter of Declan's relationship with Paulette. The man wanted to kill him.

"Oh, Jeffrey knows too, does he? I must say I'm not surprised to hear that."

"Oh, he knows."

"You must forgive Jeffrey. He tends to take on the role of our big brother and it is not unexpected that he's aware of the situation. He's probably being a bit overprotective given the circumstances . . . of your past."

"I did not kill my wife," Declan stated quite emphatically.

"I didn't say that you had." Juliette gazed at him levelly, her blue eyes understanding. "But if you didn't kill her, then who did?"

"I don't know."

"Paulette doesn't believe you did either."

"But you wonder about it, don't you?" he couldn't help but ask. "You're worried for your sister."

Again Juliette looked up at him, her gaze direct. "I'm worried for my sister, but not for that reason. Paulette would not be in love with you if you were capable of murder."

Declan grew quiet. Paulette was in love with him? Then why had she turned down his offer of marriage just now?

"And I trust my sister's judgment, Lord Cashelmore.

Paulette is the most sensible out of all of us Hamilton sisters. Besides, I think I like you already."

Confounded by Juliette Hamilton Fleming's candid manner, Declan could only say, "Thank you. I think I like you as well."

"So when are you marrying Paulette?"

Declan gave a rueful laugh. "I would marry your sister today, but she turned me down just now when I asked her."

Juliette shrugged her shoulders. "Well, then I suppose I should take back what I just said about her being the most sensible of us all."

Declan laughed aloud, throwing back his head.

"It wasn't that funny," Juliette remarked dryly.

"Now I know I like you," Declan declared.

"Well, thank you."

Juliette's smile was so like Paulette's it took Declan's breath away. "Do you all look so ridiculously alike?"

"Yes, we do. Variations on a theme." Juliette sighed. "But I'm the prettiest."

"And the most modest, of course," Declan added.

"Of course."

He laughed at Juliette's jesting manner. Paulette's sister was certainly bright and charming, but Declan thought that Paulette was far and away more beautiful than any of the sisters he'd met so far.

Sara Fleming came over to them, dragging Mara with her, their little hands clasped together. She looked up at her mother with beseeching eyes. "Mama, can Mara come home with us? Please?"

Juliette gave Declan an amused glance. "Leave it to my daughter. We only docked in London this morning and already Sara has made a new friend. The poor child has been cooped up aboard ship for two weeks with only adults for company and as you can see she is thrilled to find your daughter here. Phillip and Simon are fine, but a girl! Now that's a treasure! Lord Cashelmore, would you mind if I brought your daughter home to Devon House with me for the afternoon so the girls can play together for a little while?"

Although intrigued by the offer, Declan hesitated. "I'm not sure. I have some important engagements this afternoon and Mara hasn't been away from me—"

"Oh, but Devon House has the most wonderful nursery and playroom. Mara will have a delightful time, I assure you. And it might do her some good."

"You know about that, too?" Declan asked, surprised how much Juliette knew about him.

"Yes. Word travels fast in this family." Juliette smiled merrily, her eyes dancing. "Why, just look at the two of them together! Playing with a friend her own age will be good for Mara. I promise you that I'll keep a close eye on her. And Mara might just have to speak to keep up with my little chatterbox. Besides, you could use the time to talk some sense into the most sensible of sisters."

He'd already met Colette Sinclair and from what he knew of Paulette, the Hamiltons were not complete strangers to him. Still it seemed odd to send his daughter off with this woman he just met. Then again, Mara seemed very happy and at ease with them. Declan kneeled down to talk to her. "Mara, darlin', do you want to go and play at Sara's house this afternoon? I'll come get you whenever you want."

Mara seemed to weigh the matter over in her mind, looking between Juliette and Sara Fleming, and back at him. Then she smiled shyly and nodded her head. Declan didn't know who was more surprised by this development, Mara or himself.

"Well, then. You can go, darlin'. Be a good girl for

Mrs. Fleming and I'll be back to get you. I promise." He placed a kiss on her head and rose to his feet. He turned to Juliette. "Here's my card. If anything is wrong, please send for me immediately."

"I'm sure everything will be fine," Juliette said, pocketing the card with his address. She gave him an enigmatic smile. "And I'm quite certain Paulette would know where to find you in any case. Oh, here comes my husband!"

A tall man, with golden hair and a ruggedly handsome face bronzed by the sun, came to join them and Juliette made the introductions. Captain Harrison Fleming greeted him somewhat suspiciously, which was no surprise to Declan at this point.

Captain Fleming turned to his wife. "Is he the one?"

Juliette nodded. "Yes. But I've discovered I like him very much. We're taking his daughter home for the afternoon to play with Sara."

"Of course we are." Captain Fleming smiled in amusement, apparently used to his wife's whims, and shook Declan's hand in greeting. "Please forgive my wife and daughter, Lord Cashelmore. They can be quite willful."

"Oh, I think I understand completely," Declan remarked, already liking the man's good nature. He obviously loved his wife and daughter very much.

"It gives Lord Cashelmore a perfect excuse to come by Devon House later and meet everyone." Juliette gave Declan a most knowing look.

Yes, Declan supposed she was right. He would have to face Paulette's family sooner or later, and since he was going to marry Paulette even if he had to tie her up and kidnap her, sooner would be better. Although he'd had his fill of sisters-in-law with Margaret's family, he had a much better feeling about the Hamiltons already. He'd liked everyone he'd met so far. The Hamiltons seemed like a wonderful family, and the thought that his reputation could cause embarrassment to them filled him with regret.

Once he returned to Ireland he would end all the allegations for good.

Declan gave Mara one more kiss before he took his leave of the Flemings and went in search of Paulette.

Chapter 25

Sisters

Paulette hid in the upstairs office of the Hamilton Sisters' Book Shoppe until she was quite sure Declan Reeves had left the store. She and Colette now each had her own office on the second floor of the shop and Paulette's had been elegantly decorated. The long, velvet divan proved to be quite handy that afternoon, as she lay there and wept until she had fallen asleep. She crept back down at closing time while Colette was dismissing their staff, who had done remarkable work all day.

"Where have you been?" Colette asked when they were alone. "I haven't seen you for hours. I thought perhaps you'd left earlier with Mother and Yvette."

"I was in my office. I had a terrible headache, but I didn't wish to go home. I went upstairs to rest on the divan for a bit and I fell asleep." Paulette attempted to smooth her tousled hair.

Colette studied her face with concern. "Well, you don't look very well, I must say. It's a shame you missed so much of a great day."

"Yes, I know," she said with a tired smile. "But I'm so glad it was such a success!"

"Well, I am very glad that you're still here." Colette grinned conspiratorially, her eyes dancing. "I had planned on the two of us having a private little celebration before Davies takes us home. If you're feeling up to it, that is. You really don't look well."

"Oh, I'm fine now. Truly. I'd love to celebrate with you!" Surprised but delighted by the idea, she followed her older sister to the small kitchen area in the back of the shop. There Colette produced a bottle of champagne and two glasses.

"You and I worked very hard to make these two shops successful," she explained, as she poured the sparkling liquid into the crystal glasses. They sat at the elegant wooden table, draped in a pretty lace cloth. "Although I don't think Father would have approved of all the changes that we made, I do think he would be very, very proud of us today. And I don't believe any of it would have been possible without your help, Paulette. Especially in those early days. Do you remember staying up all night with me, painting the bookshelves with the paint I barely had enough money to buy?"

Paulette smiled, accepting the glass that Colette handed to her. Recalling that time fondly, she could almost smell that cream-colored paint again. "Yes. And I made all the little signs for the shop."

"Oh, you were quite proud of those signs! And I bought all that green ribbon from the clothes money Uncle Randall had given us. How determined we were to change the shop!" Colette sighed. "You were so little, Paulette, yet you worked harder than any of them, right by my side, always cheerful and determined to make the shop better. You were not even aware of how dangerously close we were to losing it."

"No, I knew. I had that habit of eavesdropping, remember?" Paulette had been very afraid of being thrown out on the street, as Uncle Randall had proclaimed would happen to them after their father died. Thankfully none of his predictions came true.

"Yes, it seemed you especially liked to eavesdrop when Lucien came around to visit me." Colette laughed softly at the memory. "Six years ago we couldn't even imagine a day like today, having a grand opening for a new bookshop, five times as large as Father's!"

"But we did it!"

"Yes, we did. So here's to you and me and these two bookshops we love so much. To the Hamilton sisters." Colette raised her glass.

Paulette raised hers and said, "To you and me, Colette," before taking a small sip of the bubbly liquid. She placed her glass of champagne on the table, not wanting any more, for her weak stomach could not handle it. She and Colette had worked very hard over the years and they deserved to celebrate their success. Paulette should have been overjoyed tonight. Inexplicably, tears welled in her eyes.

"Oh, Paulette, what is it?" Colette set down her glass, her expression concerned. "Please tell me what's wrong. You haven't been yourself for some time now."

"Well, I suppose you might as well know, since almost everyone else does now."

"What are you talking about?"

"I confided in Yvette first, although Jeffrey knew part of it, but then I think Yvette told Jeffrey and Juliette. And Jeffrey told him today. So it's really not a secret anymore."

"What isn't a secret anymore?" Colette's expression changed from concern to confusion.

"I'm going to have a baby."

Colette blinked. "What did you say?"

"I'm going to have Lord Cashelmore's baby."

With one swift motion, Colette downed the rest of her champagne. She stared at Paulette. "I heard what you said, yet I can't believe it. Are you sure?"

"As sure as one can be about these things. I visited a doctor when I was in Brighton." It was difficult to tell her eldest sister these things. Colette had been like a mother to her in more ways than their own mother had. She valued Colette's opinion higher than anyone's and the thought of disappointing her was unbearable.

"I see. At least I think I see." Colette still seemed stunned by the news. "So I take it that Lord Cashelmore came back to visit the bookshop more than that one time?"

"Yes," Paulette admitted ashamedly. "He came by quite often."

Her sister looked so sad. "Oh, Paulette, I wish you had come to me about this."

Before Paulette could respond, the door to the kitchen opened and Juliette, Lisette, and Yvette filed in.

"We knew we'd find you two here!" Juliette declared in triumph.

Lisette smiled broadly. "We decided we wanted to come and celebrate the new shop with you both!" She placed a basket in the center of the table, filled with chocolate and other delicious treats.

"Oooh, champagne!" Yvette exclaimed, eyeing the bottle and glasses with delight. "I can have some, can't I?"

"Yes, of course, but just a little." Juliette picked up the bottle and began pouring champagne into crystal glasses. "We're celebrating a few things this evening. The new shop named in our honor. My homecoming. The five of us being together again. And Paulette's important news."

"Paulette has important news?" Lisette's brows furrowed in confusion, and her pretty greenish-blue eyes stared at Paulette with interest.

"Oh, we'll get to that," Juliette said mysteriously. "Be patient."

Inwardly, Paulette grimaced. How on earth would she be able to face Lisette when she learned about the baby? Her sister would be heartbroken.

"Where's Mother?" Colette asked.

"We left her at home, resting with the children. While Lucien, Harrison, Quinton, and Jeffrey are off to their gentlemen's club," Yvette explained. "So this shall be our club!"

As the five women sat around the table bathed in the golden light from the gas lamps, they held up their glasses of champagne.

"To the Hamilton sisters and their new shop," Juliette announced. "And to all five of us being together again. Just the girls."

While they sipped their champagne, Paulette stared at her four sisters, so alike yet so very different in personality. Colette, brunette and serious, was the one who took on the responsibility of caring for all of them. Juliette, dark-haired and flashing eyes, was always seeking fun and adventure. Then there was auburn-haired Lisette, sweet and calm, who was the peacemaker of the family. And little Yvette, with her blond curls and love of all things pretty, was sharp and witty. Paulette loved them dearly and loved it best when they were together like this. They weren't above the old bookshop with their parents any longer, but it was close enough.

"Colette, you need to be careful with champagne,"

Juliette teased with a gleam in her eyes. "Remember what happened the first time?"

"I'm always careful with champagne now," their oldest sister remarked laughingly. "I learned my lesson that night with you and Jeffrey."

"What happened with you and Jeffrey?" Yvette asked with keen interest.

"Oh, never mind!" Juliette waved her hand. "That's a story for another night."

Lisette asked, "Now someone please tell me, what is Paulette's big news?"

The other four suddenly grew quiet. Paulette hesitated, feeling wretched at having to reveal her shameful predicament to Lisette. She simply could not bring herself to say the words aloud. Minutes ticked by.

"Somebody tell me!" Lisette cried in frustration.

Colette spoke up first. "Paulette is going to have a baby."

An audible gasp came from Lisette, her face stricken with disbelief. "You must be jesting!"

"I wish it were a jest . . ." Paulette finally said so softly.

"Don't look at me," Juliette offered helplessly. "I only learned of it this afternoon when I arrived."

"For once I knew about something important before any of you," Yvette piped in, happy to be the first one in on the secret for a change.

"So it's true?" Lisette asked, her worried eyes searching Paulette's. "You're really expecting?"

"Yes." Paulette reached her hand out to Lisette, who sat beside her.

Looking distressed, Lisette did not take it. "I don't understand any of this and I must say, you all seem very calm about the situation. Who is . . . Who is the father?"

"His name is Lord Cashelmore," Paulette responded,

feeling overcome with shame. "He's a widower from Ireland."

"Lisette, you met him briefly at Devon House a little while ago," Juliette explained. "He came by to pick up his daughter."

"I'm very confused," Lisette began. "Why was—"

"Wait a moment!" Paulette interjected. "Did you say that Declan Reeves was at Devon House? This afternoon? With Mara?" Paulette was stunned by this turn of events. How was such a thing even possible? How had Juliette and Lisette met him?

Juliette explained it all calmly. "Yes, Lord Cashelmore's daughter and Sara became rather attached to each other while they were playing in the children's section of the shop earlier, which is where I met Lord Cashelmore this afternoon quite by chance. Yvette had already filled me in about your relationship with him, you see. So he and I chatted for a while and then I invited Mara over to spend the rest of the afternoon with Sara. He agreed and came by later to pick her up. And the situation being what it is, I took the opportunity to introduce him to everyone."

"Introduce him as what?" Paulette cried, her heart beating wildly.

"As Lord Cashelmore, who else?" Juliette gave a little laugh. "It's up to you to introduce him as your fiancé, not me."

"Mother seemed to like him." Yvette nodded at her in affirmation. "I liked him, too. And you were so right, Paulette. He is *very* handsome. And such a divine accent! Although he does have that dark and brooding look about him, so I could understand where someone would think he killed his first wife."

"*WHAT?*" Lisette looked about ready to faint.

Paulette covered her face with her hands, completely

mortified. Things seemed to have spiraled out of her control today. When she was a little girl she used to believe that she could wish herself out of any situation. But no matter how hard she wished now, her tangled situation with Declan Reeves would not magically disappear.

Colette turned to Lisette to explain. "Yes, unfortunately our Paulette has gotten herself involved in a bit of a predicament. It seems Lord Cashelmore is under suspicion for causing his first wife's untimely death in a fire."

"How is it that do I not know about any of this?" Lisette eyed each one of them in turn.

"It just sort of happened little by little," Paulette began to explain slowly. "I met Declan Reeves at the bookshop one afternoon, and even though I knew about the rumors that followed him, and Colette warned me to stay away from him, I . . . I just couldn't. He's a good man, I swear to you. He's just plagued by these vicious rumors, but he had nothing to do with his wife's death. He's gentle, and kind, and a wonderful father and—"

"I'll attest to that part at least, from what I saw of him today with his daughter," Juliette interrupted.

"Thank you," Paulette continued. "He loves her and is trying to help her overcome the loss of her mother. Mara liked books so he kept coming by the shop and we spent more and more time together. Because Colette didn't approve of him, I assumed you would all feel the same way so I didn't tell any of you about him—"

"But she told me though," Yvette interrupted proudly.

Paulette gave her a sharp look. "Yes, but not at first. I kept the whole matter a secret, not ever thinking it would amount to anything so serious. But one thing led to another . . . and well, now . . . I told Yvette when I suspected about my condition, and I just told Colette, but I felt the worst about telling you, Lisette, knowing how much you want a baby and I just—" Paulette could not continue for she was about to cry again.

Lisette remained silent, eyes downcast. The others exchanged worried glances across the table and the room grew quiet.

Wracked with guilt, Paulette pondered the prospect of crawling into a hole in the ground somewhere and never coming out. Doing so might be a preferable choice to the mess she had just made of her life.

"Don't worry about my feelings right now, Paulette," Lisette murmured softly. "I'm fine and you seem to have other issues to worry about."

"But I do worry," Paulette protested. "It just doesn't seem fair that I should be with child, when you—"

"Stop, Paulette. Honestly. I'm fine." Lisette squeezed Paulette's hand and gave her a cheerful smile. "Now, I assume you are to marry him."

Once again the room grew quiet and they waited for Paulette to speak. "Well . . ."

Confused, Lisette said, "But he must marry you. You've told him about the baby, of course?"

Paulette turned to stare pointedly at Yvette. "No. Unfortunately I did not get a chance to tell him myself, because *someone* went and opened her big mouth and told Jeffrey Eddington and Jeffrey told Declan today in the bookshop!"

"Oh, Yvette!" Colette exclaimed in surprise.

Juliette rolled her eyes.

Paulette glared at her younger sister. "How could you betray my confidence like that, Yvette?"

Lifting her chin in defiance, Yvette defended her actions. "Yes, I told Jeffrey about the baby. But I had to, Paulette! I had to! This isn't a little secret about you being in love anymore. This is about your life! You're having a *baby*, for heaven's sake! And you weren't going to tell

Lord Cashelmore about the baby, but planned to run off to America with Juliette when she leaves!"

Four pairs of astonished eyes stared at Paulette.

"It really is quite difficult to believe that you are considered to be the sensible one out of the five of us," Juliette remarked dryly.

Colette's face was agog. "You weren't seriously considering that as an option, were you?"

Paulette could barely look her sisters in the eyes.

"She was!" Yvette confessed heatedly. "I thought she was making the biggest mistake of her life. I promised I wouldn't tell anyone about Paulette and Lord Cashelmore, but since Jeffrey already knew about them, I went to him for advice. He agreed with me that Paulette was being foolish and that Lord Cashelmore should be told. It's his child too after all. And then today I had to tell Juliette about Paulette's plan."

"Yvette did the right thing in telling Jeffrey," Lisette stated, her eyes on Paulette. "This is not a secret you can hide for long, Paulette. Lord Cashelmore must marry you!"

"Leave it to Jeffrey to become involved in this," Juliette laughed ruefully.

"This isn't funny," Paulette pointed out.

"No, it's quite serious." Juliette's expression suddenly grew somber. "Which is why you must marry Lord Cashelmore without delay."

"None of you care that he is rumored to have murdered his first wife?" Yvette asked.

They all turned to stare at Yvette.

"What? It's a valid question! It's the whole reason that Paulette kept him a secret in the first place."

Paulette sighed in weariness. "He's completely innocent of any wrongdoing involved with the fire that caused Margaret to die that night. I swear to you. He will swear to you."

"I believe him," Juliette said. "He told me this afternoon that he had nothing to do with her death and there's something about how honestly he said it that made me believe him."

Paulette reached across the table and squeezed Juliette's hand in gratitude. "Thank you for that. I knew you would understand."

Again Lisette asked, "So you're going to marry him?"

Paulette hesitated. "This afternoon I told him that I would never marry him."

"Why on earth would you say that?" Yvette cried in dismay.

Colette groaned.

Juliette downed the last of her champagne.

"I know what you're all thinking," Paulette began to explain, "but Declan never wanted to remarry after all the bad things in his first marriage. He's only asking me because of the baby. He doesn't really wish to marry me."

"It doesn't matter what he wants anymore," Lisette pointed out. "He has to marry you now."

"But I don't want a husband who doesn't want me," Paulette declared, knowing she sounded like a sulky child.

"Do you love Lord Cashelmore?" Juliette demanded.

Paulette grew thoughtful. Yes, she loved Declan. Which is why she couldn't force him into a marriage he didn't want. "Yes, I love him."

"Does he love you?"

"I don't know." Paulette paused. "There were times I believed he loved me, but he's never said so."

Colette's expression grew weary. "Don't be an idiot, Paulette. He said he'd marry you. It's the right thing to do. You love him. He obviously cares for you. Think of the child."

"Think of Mother," Yvette said ominously.

Covering her face with her hands, Paulette groaned at the thought of their mother learning of her situation. The humiliation was too much. "Oh, please, please don't tell Mother about this yet. I couldn't bear her knowing right now."

"Then think of your future if you don't marry him," said Lisette.

"Think of your future if you do," Juliette added, with a hopeful grin.

The room grew quiet.

"So you really think I should marry him?" Paulette finally asked in hesitation.

"Yes!" all four sisters said in unison.

"You won't hate him?" Paulette revealed her secret fear that her family would never grow to love the true Declan and would always remain suspicious and leery of him. She wanted them to accept him into the family.

"Of course not," Lisette said sweetly. "Why would we hate anyone you loved, Paulette? As long as he treats you well and is a good man, we will welcome him into our lives because of you. I'm sure we'll all grow to love him when we get to know him."

"I like him already and I've only known him a day," Juliette declared.

Her sisters wouldn't disapprove of him because of his notorious background after all. "I feel like an idiot," Paulette said, "about everything. And I'm so very embarrassed."

"Don't feel that way." Lisette patted her arm gently. "It's okay."

"It could have happened to any of us." Juliette gestured to her and Colette.

"Looking back now I wish I'd gotten with child and

had to get married to Quinton," Lisette remarked rather sarcastically, making them all laugh.

"You mean to say that you've all done *that* before you were married?" Yvette asked. Her eyes lit up with possibility and intrigue.

Holding up her hands, Juliette admitted without shame, "Guilty."

"We've already said as much to you, Yvette," Colette said. "Besides, just because we did, doesn't make it right or mean that you should do the same. Look at what happened to poor Paulette."

"Yes. Look at me," Paulette said, frowning. "I'm as sick as a dog and haven't eaten in days."

"You really don't look well at all." Yvette eyed her sister critically. "You had better marry Lord Cashelmore before you start to look worse."

That made them all laugh again, Paulette especially. "I love you, girls, and Juliette, I'm so glad you're home again."

Juliette grinned broadly. "I am, too. Although I always seem to arrive as something momentous happens!"

Chapter 26

Words

Standing on tiptoe, Mara Reeves gripped the railing of the great ship tightly in her hands, trying to peer over the edge. She couldn't see anything but the wooden railing. Suddenly Papa lifted her up in his arms, holding her close against his broad chest. A strong gust of wind buffeted them and Mara buried her face in his coat until it subsided before looking out at the expanse of gray sea that swelled beneath them. She clung to Papa as the huge ship rolled back and forth on the waves. The land drifted farther and farther away.

"We'll come back to London soon, Mara, darlin'. I promise," he whispered to her.

She didn't want to go back to Ireland, and she knew Papa didn't want to go either. His eyes were sad. But he said that they had to go.

Mara liked their life in London. She liked Mrs. Martin and their house there. She liked the little bookshop and pretty Miss Hamilton, who made Papa's eyes smile. And she especially liked the other children she'd met only yesterday. She'd had fun with Sara Fleming and her two boy cousins at Devon House that afternoon. Mara had hoped she could play with the children again, but she knew they left for Ireland the next day.

Mrs. Martin traveled with them, along with Papa's valet named Hobbes, and another gentleman, whom Papa introduced as Mr. Sebastian Woods, his attorney. After their ship docked, Mr. Woods stayed in Dublin and they boarded a carriage to take them home.

When they finally arrived at Cashelmore Manor, Mara was fascinated by a grand party happening at the estate. The house was filled with lots and lots of guests dressed in finery. Oh, and the music! There was so much going on. As Papa sent Mrs. Martin and Hobbes to see to their things, he carried Mara through the ballroom, searching for Uncle Gerald. She knew her father was upset, but Mara couldn't get enough of staring at all the pretty dresses. Such glittering colors and patterns as they swirled on the dance floor in time to the music. She had never seen a ball before and now she understood why all the adults wanted to have one. It looked like great fun!

"Declan, my boy! And Mara!" Uncle Gerald shouted, looking more ashamed than surprised as they were ushered into her father's private study. Uncle Gerald was wearing elegant black evening clothes, and his face looked very red. "I wasn't expecting to see you."

"So I can see." Papa's expression was grim.

"What are you doing here?"

"I live here. This is *my* house."

"Yes, of course! I know that, but I . . ." Uncle Gerald sputtered. "I . . . I meant to ask what has brought you home from London so suddenly? Has something happened? Have you had news from the courts?"

"Something like that." Papa's eyebrows furrowed and he motioned to the rather lavish party going on in their house. "What's happening here, Gerald? This is certainly not a welcome home party for me."

"Oh, it's just a gathering of friends to celebrate Alice's birthday. It's nothing." Uncle Gerald's face grew even redder.

A dark memory tugged at the back of Mara's mind, calling to her. She had very few memories of her uncle, even though he wasn't really her uncle. She knew that he was Papa's cousin, but she was told to call him uncle, so she did. Uncle Gerald had always been kind to her. He liked to make her laugh with funny faces that he made and give her sweets. But something . . . something about him frightened her. . . . She hugged Papa.

"It's a little more than a gathering of friends." Papa's voice was cold. "There must be two hundred people out there."

"Yes, well . . . You know how these things happen. . . ." Gerald's nervous laughter made Mara feel uncomfortable. "It started out as a small party, but then Alice just kept inviting more and more people. You know how wives are. . . ."

"I asked you to look after the place for me, Gerald, I didn't expect you to—"

"Excuse me, Lord Cashelmore, but there seems to be a bit of a problem." Mrs. Martin entered the study, looking very worried. Another woman, who Mara recognized as the Cashelmore housekeeper, hurried behind Mrs. Martin. The housekeeper, Mrs. Finley, looked distraught.

"What is it?" Papa asked her.

Mrs. Martin looked ill at ease. "Aside from Mara's rooms not being aired, all the other bedrooms are being used by houseguests at the party, and your rooms, my lord, the master's rooms, are occupied."

"My rooms?" Papa turned on Mrs. Finley, who looked ready to burst into tears. "My rooms are not to be used by anyone while I'm away. You know that. Who is staying in my rooms?"

"Good evening, Declan." Aunt Alice entered the study, dressed in dazzling scarlet silk and her black hair artfully arranged atop of her head with cascading curls down her back. Mara had never seen anyone dressed so spectacularly. "What a wonderful surprise! Welcome home! You're looking as handsome as ever, Declan. Oh, and sweet Mara is here, too. She grows more beautiful every day. She looks just like her mother, God rest her poor, tragic soul."

Alice smiled at Mara in that false way adults did when they didn't care for children very much. However, Mara couldn't stop looking at Aunt Alice's sparkly red dress.

"Good evening, Alice," Papa said through gritted teeth.

"I'm afraid we must apologize, Declan," Alice said smoothly. "We weren't expecting you, as you can see. And while we were here overseeing the estate at your request, we took a few . . . liberties, shall we say? I'm afraid that Gerald and I have been staying in the master's rooms. We didn't think you would mind, what with you being in London and us staying here. We will, of course, have all our things moved out immediately, if you wish. However, I don't think you'll be needing them."

"What are you talking about?" he demanded. Mara sensed Papa was not happy at all with the situation.

"Not now, Alice," Gerald warned in a low voice.

Alice ignored her husband and made a gloomy face at Papa. It looked like she was sad, but she really wasn't sad at all. "It seems that the authorities have been made aware of your return. I really don't believe you have much time before they arrive here and take you into custody."

"Alice!" Uncle Gerald cried out.

Mrs. Martin gasped, her hand over her heart.

Not understanding what Aunt Alice was saying, Mara worried about what was happening. She felt Papa's shoulders grow tense and suddenly a flicker of fear blossomed in her belly.

Papa said, "Mrs. Finley, find a room for me tonight. I don't care where. And send someone up to ready the nursery for my daughter." He then set Mara on her feet. "Mrs. Martin, why don't you try to get Mara some supper and ready her for bed. I'll be up to see her shortly. Be a good girl, Mara darlin', and go with Mrs. Martin now."

Her father was angry. She didn't like it when he was upset. It hardly ever happened so she could remember those times very clearly. Papa became terribly angry with Auntie Deirdre before they went to London a while back. And before that was the dreadful night of the fire. He was very angry with Mama that time. But someone else was, too. Someone had been angry with Mara that night. . . .

"Come along, sweetheart." Mrs. Martin held out her hand and Mara took it, clinging tightly to her.

Mara was glad Mrs. Martin had come with them to Cashelmore Manor, for she hadn't cared for her former nurse. She had been very strict and became cross quite easily. After climbing two flights of stairs, Mara still held Mrs. Martin's hand as they stood in the doorway of her nursery. It seemed colder and darker than she remembered and with all the furniture covered with dust cloths it looked quite spooky.

"Well, it's certainly a grand room," Mrs. Martin said in her cheery voice, even though Mara knew she was still worried. "Once we get a fire lit in here, and put things to rights, we will make it all cozy again for you."

And she was right. A couple of servants came in and began lighting the lamps and the fire, removing the dust cloths and unpacking her trunk and bringing her supper tray. The nursery and her bedroom were warmed up and almost looked as she remembered. At least they no longer looked spooky!

As Mara ate her supper, she wondered how long they would stay at Cashelmore Manor. She already longed for her flowered window seat in London, where she could look out and watch all that happened on the busy street below. When she looked out the nursery window here at night, she saw nothing but darkness.

Mrs. Martin got her ready for bed and then Mara chose one of her books for Papa to read to her when he came. It was the little toy book that Miss Hamilton gave her the day in the park, *Beauty and the Beast*. Mara sat on her bed, pulling the little tabs to make the pictures move and the beast dance. Suddenly Papa's valet, Hobbes, came running into the nursery. The man was clearly panicked and upset.

"Mrs. Martin! They've taken Lord Cashelmore!" he exclaimed. "He's been arrested!"

"What do you mean?" Mrs. Martin cried, her eyes wide, dropping the dress of Mara's she had been hanging up in the wardrobe.

The toy book fell to the floor, but in her hands Mara held the cardboard tabs that made the pictures move.

"They've taken him into custody!" The pitch of Hobbes' voice increased. "What do we do? What are we to do here in this country now?"

Mrs. Martin pushed him out of the room. "Hush. Not in front of his daughter, you fool! I'll be right out." She closed the door and turned to Mara with a worried expression. "It's time for bed now, Mara sweetheart."

Something was terribly wrong and a sick feeling rushed through her. Mara feared she might throw up on the floor. Papa was not coming to see her later. She knew it with a dreadful certainty. Somebody had taken him from her. She understood that much. Silent tears welled in her eyes and streamed down her cheeks.

"Now, now. Everything is going to be all right, you'll see." Mrs. Martin sat on the bed beside her and hugged her tightly. She smiled at her, but Mara could see the fear and worry in the woman's eyes. "Oh, don't cry, Mara. Hobbes was just confused. You know how silly he is sometimes. Your father is fine. He just had to go out for a little while to take care of some business. He'll be back as soon as he can, because he loves you so much."

Great, choking sobs wracked Mara's small body and she shook with pain. *Papa was gone! Papa was gone! They had taken Papa!*

And Mara desperately needed Papa to come back to her.

Suddenly the paralyzing fear that had gripped her little throat for so long finally snapped open. Mara found the words she needed again, as she began to scream for her father . . .

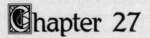

Chapter 27

Brothers

When Paulette hadn't seen or heard from Declan the day after the opening of the new bookshop, she began to worry a little. By the second day, she became concerned, and by the third day she was quite frantic. Had she so offended him by her remark that afternoon in the bookshop when she turned down his proposal that he no longer wanted to marry her?

Her sisters had led her to believe that Declan wanted to marry her and that they should marry. Paulette believed he would contact her and they would wed within the week.

Now she had nothing but doubts.

She loved Declan. But did he love her? Would they be able to have a happy marriage together? She was sure she could be happy with him, and that she would be a good mother to their child as well as to Mara. She'd been miserable this past month without him. She missed him and loved him. She needed to be with him now more than ever.

And she needed to tell him she was sorry.

Plagued by guilt, she recalled her cold words to him in the reading room. She knew she had hurt him terribly by saying she had no wish to wed him because of the rumors about him.

She spent the afternoon of that third day at home in her bedroom, wracked with nerves and too nauseated to work in the shop. Her mother had returned to Brighton. Colette and Juliette had taken all three children to the park and Lisette and Yvette were shopping. Left to her own devices, Paulette had nothing to do but think. And worry.

Why hadn't Declan come to see her yet?

Gathering up all her resolve, she decided that if Declan wasn't going to come to her then she must to go him instead. She had turned down his offer of marriage that day. Perhaps his male pride was injured and she needed to make amends. Wearing her prettiest dress of bright blue, which helped her still rather green complexion not appear so nauseous, she had Davies take her in the carriage to Declan's townhouse. She had never called on a gentleman so boldly before and she was a bit nervous when she knocked on the door.

"Oh, Lord Cashelmore is not in, Miss Hamilton," Roberts, the butler, informed her when she asked to see him.

Well then, she would just have to come back. Or wait for him. Paulette was determined to see Declan one way or another. She had to apologize for being so awful to him. "Will he be in later this afternoon?"

"I'm afraid not, miss," the butler said kindly. "He left three days ago. He's gone back to Ireland."

Paulette felt the world sway under her feet and all she could see was fading to black. Dizziness overwhelmed her.

"Oh, Miss Hamilton, are you well?" Roberts took hold of Paulette's arm to steady her. "Come sit down, miss."

Trying to regain her sense of balance, Paulette

stumbled to a chair in the foyer of the townhouse. A wave of nausea washed over her. Declan had left. He was gone. He had left her.

"Please just rest for a minute, miss," Roberts cautioned her, his face lined with worry. "Shall I send for a doctor?"

"No, no," Paulette willed herself not to vomit in Declan's hallway. She took a deep, fortifying breath. Good heavens, she was making a spectacle of herself! Almost fainting on his doorstep. Thank goodness Declan wasn't here to witness such a display. "I'm fine now. Thank you."

Roberts shook his head. "You don't look fine, Miss Hamilton."

"I am." She breathed in deeply again. "Did Lord Cashelmore . . . Did he happen to say when he would be returning to London?"

"He wasn't sure, miss, but he hoped he wouldn't be gone long. That's why he kept me on, to oversee the house here in the meantime. Please, miss, let me send for a doctor."

"No, that's not necessary. Thank you." Relief flooded her. He was coming back to London at some point in the near future if he kept the house. She rose to her feet. "I think I shall go home now."

"Please wait here one minute, miss. Lord Cashelmore left something for you in the event that you stopped by."

Paulette watched with wide eyes as Roberts hurried from the hall and returned holding an envelope. He handed it to Paulette. "He said I was to send it to you by the end of the week if you didn't come here yourself first."

With trembling hands, Paulette held the envelope tightly and wondered what Declan had written to her.

Meanwhile, Roberts went to the front door and motioned to Davies, the Devon House footman who

escorted Paulette everywhere. Davies immediately came
to assist Paulette back to the carriage.

Once in the carriage, Paulette tore open Declan's
letter, the words written in his sprawling hand.

Paulette My Love,

   *Mara and I have returned to Ireland. I must finally
put an end to the accusations against me. I need to clear my
name before I can ask you to share it with me, Paulette.
I love you and I want to marry you. I will be back for you as
soon as I can.*

Yours,
Declan

Trembling, Paulette's eyes filled with tears as she read
his note over and over. He did love her and want to
marry her. His words filled her with hope and love for
him. He was coming back for her, but she did not wish
to wait. Paulette knew instantly what she needed to do.

By the time she returned to Devon House, a plan had
formed in her mind. She went directly to Lucien's study,
where she found him sitting at his desk.

"Hello, Paulette." Lucien eyed her carefully as she entered his study.

Although she hadn't openly discussed her situation
with her brother-in-law yet, Paulette knew he had to be
aware of her condition by now. Feeling uncomfortable
about it and more than a little self-conscious, she began
hesitantly. "Do you have a few minutes, Lucien? I should
like to talk to you about something important."

His dark brows rose slightly, as he set down the pen he
had been writing with. "Of course. Come have a seat.
What is it?"

She lowered herself onto one of the chairs near his
large cherry wood desk. Her relationship with her

favorite brother-in-law had always been close. Lucien had supported her every decision about the bookshop and taught her a good deal about business. They had always been each other's allies since he was first courting Colette. "I need your help, Lucien."

"You're asking for my help now? Isn't it a little late?" He gave her a teasing smile.

Paulette's cheeks grew warm at his reference to her pregnancy. Ever since she had become involved with Declan Reeves, things felt a little uncomfortable between her and Lucien. She had been too embarrassed to confide in him what was happening with her and Declan. "I'm sorry, Lucien. I know I should have come to you sooner, but I . . . I just couldn't . . ."

"I understand, Paulette. Truly I do," Lucien said kindly, his expression sympathetic. "So, what can I help you with now? And this is just a wild guess on my part, but does this have anything to do with Lord Cashelmore?"

"Yes," she admitted in relief. "I need to go Ireland. Right away."

He gave her a surprised look. "And why is that?"

"Because Declan went home and I have to see him. I have to help him."

Lucien's expression grew somber. "He's in trouble, Paulette. I'm not sure how much you know, but I'm not going to lie to you. Jeffrey and I have been looking into his case to see what can be done."

Lucien's words frightened her. Just how serious were matters in Ireland for Declan? His troubles had seemed rather far away to her, something resolved rather easily. But now they seemed most urgent and the need to see him, to help him, was suddenly overwhelming.

A knock on the study door interrupted them. Lord Jeffrey Eddington came in.

"Ah, speak of the devil," Lucien quipped at his friend's timely arrival. "Come join us, Jeffrey."

"Talking about me again?" Jeffrey winked playfully at Paulette. "Good things I hope." He handed Lucien a sheaf of papers. "I just received a message from Dublin."

Dublin? Paulette's heart raced. "What message from Dublin? Is it about Declan?"

His expression quickly turning serious, Jeffrey sat on the edge of Lucien's desk. "How much do you know, Paulette?"

"I know Declan's in Dublin now. I know that I need to help him. I must go to him. He's innocent. I know he is. You have to help me to help him. Please." She pressed her hands together.

"We have tried, Paulette, I promise you," Lucien said. "Since the moment I found out about your . . . since the moment I knew you were to marry, I've been pulling every string I know and calling in favors for the last three days trying to get information. So has Jeffrey."

"You have?" Touched by their caring and concern for her, Paulette felt a lump in her throat.

Jeffrey nodded. "Yes, we have."

"Oh, you're both wonderful . . . Thank you . . ." Paulette whispered, overcome with emotion that they had gone to such lengths to help Declan, simply because she loved him.

"Lord Cashelmore has already hired himself the best criminal attorney in London to take on his case. A man named Sebastian Woods," Lucien explained, while glancing over the papers in front of him. "There's not much else we can do, Paulette. If he went to Ireland to fight these charges as you say, then there's a good chance he's been arrested and is in custody for the trial."

"I just got the telegram from my friend in the Dublin

office," Jeffrey announced grimly. "Unfortunately, that's exactly what happened."

"He's been arrested!?" Her stomach lurched at the prospect. Poor Declan! And who was with Mara? She would be so frightened without him! "I need to be there with him. And with Mara. Oh, Lucien, can you please help me make arrangements to sail to Ireland?"

Lucien smiled, seeming a bit amused by her request. "I can do that, of course. But I do think you'd be better off asking Harrison."

"Harrison?" Paulette asked in confusion. Juliette's husband was wonderful to be sure, but what would . . . "Harrison!" she cried in delight as she realized what Lucien meant. Her brother-in-law was a sea captain and the *Sea Minx* was a beautiful clipper ship. "He has his own ship!"

"Jeffrey, how do you feel about a trip to Ireland?" Lucien asked.

Paulette's head spun around. "Jeffrey?"

Lucien laughed. "Well, we're certainly not letting you go there alone."

"Yes, I think between Harrison and me we should be able to keep an eye on her, don't you agree?" Jeffrey said in mock seriousness.

"You would really come with me?" she asked.

"Yes. It's the least I can do," Jeffrey explained. "I feel like you're only in this mess because I didn't keep a closer watch over you."

"I'm not in a mess, Jeffrey, not really. I'm just in love," she explained to them softly. "And I'm not a child any longer, in case either of you hadn't noticed."

Both men remained silent, avoiding her eyes.

"I can't thank you both enough for helping me. And helping Declan. But there's probably something else you should know about." Paulette paused.

"What is it?" Lucien asked, looking concerned.

"I don't even want to guess." Jeffrey flashed her a grin.

Paulette took a deep breath before confessing. "Well, there have been these threatening letters."

"What are you talking about?" Lucien asked, his expression darkening.

Before Paulette could launch into an explanation, Jeffrey said, "Yvette already informed me of this as well."

Paulette shook her head. "Remind me not to confide in her again."

"Your little sister was right to tell me everything," Jeffrey defended Yvette with an emphatic nod of his head.

Then they explained to Lucien about the letters that she and Declan had been receiving and how Declan refused to see her until he discovered the sender of the letters.

Lucien's mouth set in a grim line. "So someone was threatening him."

"And Paulette," Jeffrey stated.

"Paulette, you really should have come to me with this right from the beginning," Lucien said, giving her a stern look. "This is dangerous."

"I know. And I'm very sorry about it. I wanted to tell you so many times, yet . . . The more involved I became with Declan, the more difficult it became to tell anyone what I was doing. It was a very romantic—"

"I've heard enough," Jeffrey interrupted. "We understand, Paulette."

She gave him a wry look. "I am one and twenty. I'm not a little girl anymore."

"I'm sorry, but we can't help but think of you that way," Lucien said kindly.

"It's true," Jeffrey added with his signature smile. "You and Yvette will always be little girls in my eyes, even when you're fifty years old."

Paulette gave her head a rueful shake. "You're daft but I love you both and I thank you for helping me, even if you don't think I'm old enough to be in love with Declan."

Later that night they made arrangements for her trip to Ireland as Harrison readily agreed to sail his ship, the *Sea Minx*, to Dublin, taking Paulette, along with Juliette and Sara. And of course, Jeffrey Eddington had decided to come along, too.

Chapter 28

Adversaries

Paulette stared with wide eyes at the massive estate that Declan called home. Cashelmore Manor sat upon acres and acres of rolling green land, its limestone and granite walls creating a towering portico with arcades on either side supporting square towers topped with carved pinnacles. The massive structure spread out on either side of the main entrance, with Tuscan colonnades leading to the stable courts. A long, straight driveway made a path to the great courtyard where the carriage carrying her and Jeffrey Eddington came to a stop.

Jeffrey let out a low whistle. "Well, take a good look at your future home, Lady Cashelmore." He gave her a knowing glance. "You may very well be carrying a son and the heir to this place."

"I'm not Lady Cashelmore yet." Unconsciously her hand slid to her abdomen and the baby within. Her heart raced at the thought of their child living in a place so grand. "When I met him he was merely Mr. Reeves, a handsome widower from Ireland. How did I know all this existed? I really had no idea what I was getting myself into." Paulette shook her head in wonder.

What would she find within the walls of Cashelmore Manor?

She recalled Declan saying his cousin was overlooking his estate for him, and together with the information that Jeffrey and Lucien had collected, she learned that Gerald O'Rourke and his wife, Alice, were staying at Cashelmore Manor. While aboard ship, Paulette had discovered quite a few interesting facts about Declan's family, as well as his late wife's, as she avidly studied the papers Lucien had given her regarding Declan's case.

The boat trip from London had been fairly smooth and she had handled the sailing of the Irish Sea surprisingly well. With her morning sickness being as bad as it was, she had anticipated a hellish time aboard ship. However, the sea air must have strengthened and calmed her spirit, for not only did she regain her appetite, but her nausea had lessened considerably. The same could not be said for poor Jeffrey, who spent the entire journey huddled in his cabin suffering the worst case of seasickness Captain Fleming had ever seen. He had been so ill that Paulette dared not even tease him about it. She loved Jeffrey all the more for making the journey for her sake, knowing how much he detested sea travel.

When they finally docked, Juliette and Harrison decided it was best if they stayed in Dublin with their daughter, Sara, until they had more information. Paulette and Jeffrey continued on to Cashelmore Manor, which was just outside the city of Dublin. Aside from seeing Declan, Paulette's first mission was to make sure Mara was being taken care of properly. With her father in custody, the poor child must be frightened and heartbroken at his absence. She also knew Declan would be frantic with worry over his daughter. She would not see him without being able to let him know Mara was safe and well.

Now she took a deep breath as they were helped down from the carriage by servants dressed in the Cashelmore livery. After giving their names, the butler, an ancient gentleman with not one hair on his head, led them into the main salon, where they were told to wait for Declan's cousin to join them.

Too nervous to sit still, Paulette wandered about the ridiculously ornate room. Her footsteps echoed as she paced the blue-themed room, with its twenty-foot ceiling and a white marble floor, admiring the formal portraits and fine china figurines and elegant vases on display.

It was hard to imagine Declan growing up alone in a house as cold as this, without brothers or sisters to play with. His parents died while he was a young boy, and he was virtually raised by nannies and tutors. The only blood relation he had left was his cousin, Gerald O'Rourke, and Paulette came here to see his cousin and ask what could be done to help Declan. However, she was a little uncomfortable with how to introduce herself and Jeffrey Eddington to Declan's family.

"This house is like a museum," Jeffrey murmured in distaste.

"Is it very different from your father's estate?" Paulette whispered back. For some reason she found it necessary to whisper.

"No, it's exactly like it," Jeffrey answered, shrugging carelessly. "But Father's place is a cold museum too and the reason why I don't live there."

Everyone knew that Jeffrey's father was the powerful Duke of Rathmore, a wealthy and imposing man, but the duke's wife had not been Jeffrey's mother. For all that he had been raised as the duke's only son in a world of privilege and luxury, Jeffrey could never inherit the title because he had been born on the wrong side of the sheets.

"I can't see you living in a place like this either," Paulette said. For that matter, she could not imagine any child ever living here. Including her own child.

"Good afternoon and welcome to Cashelmore Manor." A very pretty dark-haired woman entered the salon. Dressed in a stylish gown of deep burgundy, she posed in the doorway as elegantly as if she were a queen bestowing favors on her subjects.

Paulette and Jeffrey exchanged curious looks as they moved toward her and said good afternoon.

"I'm Alice O'Rourke, Declan's cousin. You must be Miss Hamilton." Her dark eyes raked over Paulette and then settled on Jeffrey. An odd smile spread over her face, as if a candle had just been lit from within. Her long eyelashes fluttered. "And you must be Lord Eddington. You're both friends of my cousin, I believe? Please be seated."

They all moved to sit upon the blue silk-covered chairs in the center of the large salon.

"It's such a wonderful surprise to have some of Declan's London friends visit us! To what do we owe the pleasure of your company today?" Alice O'Rourke said, her expression one of curiosity. "How may I be of help to you both?"

After a nervous glance at Jeffrey, Paulette began first. "Actually we were wondering how we could help you."

The woman looked completely puzzled. "Help me?" She released a throaty little laugh. "Why on earth would you think I need your help?"

"We thought perhaps you might need our assistance in helping Lord Cashelmore," Paulette said.

"Oh, I'm afraid there's nothing we can do to help him now." Alice O'Rourke frowned in a way in that looked a bit forced. "I'm sure you must be aware that the Dublin authorities have taken Declan into custody." She paused dramatically. "They believe he's responsible for his wife's death."

"We don't believe that," Paulette asserted firmly. "Surely you don't either?"

"Well, it doesn't make a difference what I believe, now does it?" Alice O'Rourke stared sweetly, her brown eyes full of innocence. "May I enquire why any of this is your concern in the first place?"

Jeffrey caught her attention. "Lord Cashelmore informed me of his decision to marry Miss Hamilton just before he returned to Ireland. She is his fiancée."

The woman could not hide her shock at this development. Her eyes grew very wide. "I thought he had ended things with you weeks ago! I had no idea that Declan had any intentions of marrying anyone! How could we not know of this?"

Giving Alice O'Rourke a triumphant look, Jeffrey said, "It seems your cousin did not think it necessary to inform you of his plans, now did he?"

"Well, unfortunately he's not in a position to marry anyone at the moment, is he?" said a rather round, red-faced gentleman with gray hair, who strode into the room with a drink in his hand.

"Oh, this is my husband and Declan's cousin, Gerald O'Rourke. Gerald, these are Declan's friends from London." Alice waved a hand in their general direction.

"So I've gathered. And you are his rumored fiancée?" The man turned his bloodshot gaze on Paulette.

She nodded. "Yes, I am his fiancée and we've come to see how we can best help Declan. We hoped to see Mara as well."

Gerald chuckled ruefully and took a sip of his drink. "I don't believe there's much you can do in the way of helping my cousin at this point, but you can try. We've done all we can on our end. It's out of our hands and up to the courts now, but I must say it doesn't look too good for him. And as for Mara . . . she's fine, simply fine. She's up in the nursery. I'm sending her to live with her mother's family. It's best for all concerned this way. Her aunts can take better care of her than Alice and I can."

Shivering, Paulette recalled all that Declan had told her about Margaret's two older sisters and how he had fled Ireland to keep Mara away from them. Declan would be devastated at the thought of Mara in the hands of his late wife's sisters.

Paulette stared at these two people who lived in Declan's house and yet would so callously give away his daughter. She was developing a strong dislike for Declan's cousin and his wife. They seemed not at all concerned with helping Declan's cause or worried about him in the least.

"May I please see Mara?" Paulette asked abruptly.

"Of course you may see her, if you like. Would you care to join us for supper this evening or do you need to return to Dublin right away?" Alice asked, clearly hoping they would decline the invitation to stay.

Paulette had no intention of staying with these people any longer than necessary and was about to refuse the half-hearted invitation.

"We would love to have supper with you." Jeffrey suddenly favored Alice O'Rourke with his most devastating smile, the one he used when he wanted to charm a woman.

It seemed Alice O'Rourke was not immune to Lord Eddington's allure. Once again her thick eyelashes fluttered. "That would be wonderful. I'm sure you're a most entertaining supper companion, Lord Eddington."

Growing a bit annoyed, Paulette rose to her feet, wondering why on earth Jeffrey agreed to stay for supper. She asked Gerald, "May I please see Mara now?"

Gerald stood, obviously as eager to end this visit as Paulette was. "Yes, I'll ring for a footman to escort you to the nursery."

"Jeffrey." Paulette gave him a pointed look. "Are you coming with me?"

He waved a dismissive hand at her, his eyes still on Gerald's wife. "I'll wait for you here, Paulette."

With an annoyed huff, Paulette followed the footman as he escorted her down the wide hallway and up a massive staircase that made the one at Devon House look small by comparison. They walked along another hallway, then ascended a more normal-sized flight of stairs, until they reached the nursery. It was another unnecessarily large room with tall windows, which at least let in some natural light, as the October sunshine spilled in the room. Carpeted with thick oriental rugs and heavy wooden furniture, there was nothing about the room that indicated it belonged to a little girl.

Paulette hesitated in the doorway, looking about and unsure what to do. It was then she saw Mara, at the far end of the great room. She sat on the floor, in a blue dress, her golden hair like a halo around her sad face, a few books and toys scattered on the carpet beside her. Paulette knew the instant that Mara sensed her presence, for the child stood up immediately, her eyes wide with recognition.

"Papa!" she cried, as she fairly flew across the room.

Paulette sank to her knees and Mara ran into her arms, clinging to her so tightly she almost couldn't breathe. The little girl sobbed and sobbed, saying over and over again. "They took Papa away. They took my papa."

"Oh, it's all right." Shocked that the child actually

spoke, Paulette held her close, whispering soothing words to her. "It's all right, Mara."

"Oh, Miss Hamilton, it's you!"

Turning at the voice, Paulette recognized Mrs. Martin right away. The woman smiled at her with relief. Slowly Paulette rose to her feet, still holding Mara in her arms. "Yes, I've only just arrived."

"I'm so happy to see you here, you've no idea."

"Mara's talking now?" Paulette asked.

"I guess you could say so, yes." The days of concern and anxiety cleared showed on Mrs. Martin's face. "But that's all she says. She just keeps asking for her father, the poor child. And who can blame her? But I've no idea what to say to her because I don't know what is happening with Lord Cashelmore."

Paulette smoothed her hand over Mara's golden hair in an attempt to calm the girl and moved to sit on the nearest chair, settling Mara on her lap. "Everything will be all right, Mara. Your father will be back with you very soon. He loves you and misses you very, very much. He wouldn't want you to worry and cry over him this way. He needs you to be a very brave girl for him right now."

Sniffling, Mara looked at her and nodded in understanding. She wiped her eyes with the back of her hands.

"Good girl, Mara." Paulette placed a kiss on the girl's head. She then turned her attention to Mrs. Martin. "I'm afraid I've not much more information to share with you either, but my family is trying everything they can to help him."

"Oh, Miss Hamilton, it was terrible the day they took Lord Cashelmore. They didn't even give Mara a chance to say good-bye to him, oh and she was just beside herself when she realized he was gone. It took me all night to calm her down, and she kept calling for him over and over. It just about broke my heart. And now his cousin says that Mara is to go and live with her Aunt Deirdre to-morrow and I know Lord Cashelmore wouldn't be happy with that arrangement at all. And what's to become of me? That horrid Mrs. O'Rourke dismissed me as soon as Lord Cashelmore was gone, but I couldn't bear to leave Mara here alone. Where would I go anyway? I'm stuck in this country without enough money to get myself back to London. And they sent Lord Cashelmore's valet packing that very night. Poor Hobbes. I don't even know where he went."

"Oh, we'll see that you get home safely, Mrs. Martin. With Mara as well," Paulette promised. "Lord Cashel-more would not be pleased with any of this, I assure you."

"What are we going to do?" Mrs. Martin asked.

"I'm not entirely sure just yet." Paulette hesitated. "Mara, do you want to go stay with your Aunt Deirdre?"

"No. I want Papa." Mara's words were perfectly clear between a hiccupping sob. "I want my papa."

"I know that, darling." Paulette smiled at her, happy that the child was speaking. "Would you want to come stay with me, perhaps? While we go and get your father?"

"Oh, yes, please." Mara hugged her.

Mrs. Martin frowned. "They'll never let you take her from the house."

"I'm sure you're right about that."

Paulette worried and wished that Jeffrey had come up to the nursery with her. He would be sure to know what to do about Mara. Whatever was he doing down there anyway flirting with that horrid woman? He chose the worst time to become smitten with a pretty face. Paulette knew if she asked the O'Rourkes if Mara could stay with her, they would refuse. And honestly, who was Paulette to waltz into Cashelmore Manor and demand the earl's daughter anyway? She was carrying Declan's child and would soon be Mara's stepmother but no one else was fully aware of that fact yet. She had no proof of her claim until she saw Declan. All she knew was that she had to protect Declan's daughter, and there was only one way she knew to do it.

She had to get Mara out of the house without being seen.

"Mrs. Martin, would you be willing to help me?" she asked.

"If it's the right thing to do, why yes, of course." The woman nodded.

"Lord Eddington and I have agreed to stay for supper this evening. While we are dining with the O'Rourkes, do you think you could manage to get Mara and yourself out of the house without anyone knowing? Once it's dark enough, just wait for our carriage along the drive and we'll pick you both up and take you back to Dublin with us."

"Miss Hamilton!" The petite woman's eyes grew round in astonishment. "Are you sure? That sounds very dangerous for us all. If Mr. O'Rourke or his wife find out . . ."

Yes, it was quite dangerous, but the little girl Paulette held in her arms had come to mean a good deal to her and she had to protect her for Declan's sake, if nothing else. "I don't know what else to do. I can't let Mara's aunts take her. We'll sort it all out when we get back to Dublin and see Lord Cashelmore. Mrs. Martin, do you think you could get out of the house without anyone realizing you're gone?"

Mrs. Martin thought for a moment, considering the urgency of the situation. "Yes, I believe we could. Those two don't ever come up to see Mara and in fact, they haven't since I've been here. Since I refused to leave, they are letting me stay on and have dismissed the other servants who are supposed to work up here in the nursery.

I don't think anyone would notice we were gone until they call us down tomorrow when Mara's aunts arrive."

"Well, then," Paulette said, "we shall just have to hope that you're able to escape without anyone finding out about it until we're safely away from here."

Paulette had no legal grounds to take Declan's daughter from her relatives, but she was convinced she had the moral right to keep the child safe and follow her father's wishes as best she could.

"Mara, sweetheart, I'm going to take you to see your father in Dublin," Paulette explained to her. "So I need you to listen very carefully and do just as Mrs. Martin says. Will you do that for me?"

Mara's green eyes filled with gratitude. "Yes, Miss Hamilton."

"Your father will be so happy to hear that you are speaking again." She smiled at Mara before saying to Mrs. Martin, "I shall have to return downstairs to have supper. But I will meet you both again at the far end of the drive, just as soon as I can. Bundle up good and warm, for it's getting cold out."

"Don't worry. You can count on me," Mrs. Martin promised, squaring her shoulders in determination. "I shall have us both ready to travel. And lightly."

"Thank you," Paulette said, hugging Mara to her one last time before rising to her feet.

"No, I think I need to thank you," Mrs. Martin said, her eyes welling with tears. "I don't know what I would have done tomorrow when her aunts arrived and took poor little Mara away."

Paulette hugged the woman, wondering how in the world she had become involved in such a complicated situation. With promises and good wishes, Paulette left the nursery, making her way through the massive house back to the main salon where she had left Jeffrey.

However, somewhere, she must have taken a wrong turn. More than a little lost, she found herself wandering down a long corridor on the ground floor. She felt she had been heading toward the main salon, but she must have veered left when she should have turned right at the bottom of the staircase. Now she needed to retrace her steps. Wishing she would see a footman or a parlor maid to show her the way, she wondered at the lack of servants visible in a house of this size.

It was then that Paulette heard the voices. She paused at the sound, coming from behind one of the doors. There were two voices, male and female, and they were definitely raised in argument. She inched closer to the source of the voices, knowing it was wrong to listen.

Ever since she was a young girl, she had had a little problem with eavesdropping. Her parents and her sisters were always scolding her for her terrible habit of listening in on conversations that did not concern her. Over the years Paulette had tried and succeeded at controlling her temptation to eavesdrop. Now, however, she gave in completely to her old vice, for the voices sounded as if they belonged to Gerald and Alice O'Rourke. She didn't think twice about whether what she was doing was wrong or not.

She tiptoed silently to stand even closer to the door, listening intently. Declan's cousins intrigued her for she suspected they were not as worried about Declan as they should be.

"You were flirting with him, Alice! I saw you with my own eyes!"

"No, I wasn't. I was merely trying to find out more about him."

"I don't need my wife behaving like a common trollop! You might as well have sat on the man's lap!"

"Oh, Gerald, really! Get a hold of yourself. You're acting like a jealous fool!"

"Yes, maybe I am a fool for marrying you and thinking you could become the wife of an earl and comport yourself as a lady!"

She goaded him. "Well, you're not the Earl of Cashelmore yet!"

"And you're not the countess!" he taunted back.

There was a pause, and Paulette had a moment to take in all that she was hearing. They were acting as if Declan were never coming back and Gerald had already inherited the title.

"Now, now, darling," Alice began in a more conciliatory tone. "This bickering is getting us nowhere. I'm not interested in some middling lord from London. You know I want only you."

Gerald mumbled something Paulette could not hear.

Alice continued. "It's just a matter of time now. Cashelmore Manor is already ours for all intents and purposes. Everything has worked out just the way we wanted it."

"As long as they don't find out I was there," Gerald said, his voice tense and worried.

"No one is going to find out. We've been over this before, Gerald. The child is still not even speaking. Come, darling. We must return to our guests. . . ."

Hearing the rustle of fabric, Paulette's heart raced. She spun quickly and hurried from the door, down the long hallway until she ran smack into a male body.

"Oh, Jeffrey! It's you," she whispered in relief.

"What have you been doing?" he asked, sensing her fear.

"I heard them arguing about you. He thinks she was flirting with you."

Jeffrey smiled mischievously. "She was."

"You're terrible."

"It was helpful in gaining some information." He shrugged. "How was Mara?"

"She's fine, but let's hurry back into the salon. They're coming now. I'll explain everything later!" Paulette pushed past him into the ornate blue salon and settled herself on a silk-covered chair. Jeffrey eyed her with curiosity, just as Alice and Gerald O'Rourke entered the room.

"We're going to dine in the small dining room this evening," Alice announced, her pointed gaze lingering on Jeffrey. "It's much more intimate since it will just be the four of us."

Paulette suffered through the excruciatingly awkward and tense meal. Alice O'Rourke continued to flirt shamelessly with Jeffrey while Gerald sat glowering and growing angrier and Jeffrey flirted back without a care in the world. Paulette worried all the while if Mrs. Martin and Mara were able to get out of the house without being discovered. Then she fretted about their safety, walking down the long driveway in the cold and dark.

Paulette almost danced a jig of pure happiness when Jeffrey finally announced that it was growing late and time for them to take their leave. He also graciously declined Alice O'Rourke's rather bold invitation to spend the night at Cashelmore Manor. Paulette wanted to be out of this house even more than Gerald probably wished them out.

Breathing a sigh of relief when she and Jeffrey were ensconced once again in their hired carriage, Paulette instructed their driver to go very slowly and be on the watch for a woman and a little girl.

"What are you up to?" Jeffrey asked in concern.

Paulette peered out the carriage window, searching

for two figures in the darkness. "Shh, just look out your window for Mara and Mrs. Martin."

"You're jesting, aren't you?"

"Not in the least." Paulette kept her eyes on the window. "We have to get Mara out of here. The O'Rourkes are planning to give Mara to her aunts, who despise Declan. I can't let that happen to her."

"We can't simply take the Earl of Cashelmore's daughter from her home!"

"Declan would want me to do just what I'm doing. I know he would," Paulette asserted with conviction.

"I certainly hope so," Jeffrey muttered, shaking his head.

Just then the carriage slowed to a halt. With bated breath, Paulette flung open the door. Mrs. Martin rushed to them, handing Mara up to her. Without a word of protest, Jeffrey assisted the two new passengers into the carriage. Paulette drew Mara to her side, hugging her tightly.

"Are you both all right?" she asked as the carriage continued to move quickly away from Cashelmore.

Mrs. Martin nodded with relief. "Yes, now that we're on our way."

Jeffrey asked, "Did anyone see you?"

"Not that I noticed."

Smiling, Paulette looked down at Mara. "Are you ready to go see your father?"

The child gazed up at her with a face full of hope. "Yes."

Chapter 29

Surprises

Declan paced the confines of the small room for the millionth time. He had been held a prisoner for days now and he was going to go mad if he wasn't released soon. He'd seen nothing but the inside of these four white-washed walls and he was losing his mind with worry. Although his solicitor, Mr. Sebastian Woods, assured him it was just a matter of days and he would be freed, Declan was beginning to have his doubts.

It had been too long already.

The one positive note in all this was that they had not confined him to the misery of the gaol at Kilmainham. Because of his wealth and position, and the nature of his case, he was given special consideration by the magistrate and confined to comparatively luxurious accommodations at a building near the Four Courts. He had decent meals, access to newspapers, and even a desk. The fact that there was one tiny window and an armed guard outside the locked door prevented him from forgetting that he was not in a cell. Declan wasn't going anywhere until he was released.

He felt completely helpless, and his worry for Mara gnawed at him day and night. His daughter was sure to be beside herself with fear and anxiety at his sudden disappearance. He had not even been able to explain to her that he'd be back or even say good-bye. In her childish eyes her father had simply vanished. He hoped Mrs. Martin was able to calm her and tell her that he would return quickly. His only comfort was that she was safe at Cashelmore with his cousin Gerald and not with Deirdre or Ellen Ryan.

Which brought up worries of another kind. Something about his cousin Gerald plagued him. He hated to suspect his only living relative of greed, but he had not liked the way Gerald and his wife had taken over Cashelmore Manor. Alice knew the authorities were coming and Gerald did not seem the least bit concerned when Declan had been hauled away that night.

Over the last year or so Declan had dismissed his misgivings over certain things that Gerald had said and done, attributing it to his own grief and anger with Margaret. Declan simply didn't want to believe that the one person whom he had trusted and confided in his whole life, in truth, wished him harm. It just wasn't possible.

Was it?

He'd asked Gerald to keep an eye on things while he was in London, never dreaming that Gerald would move into his house, into his very rooms, taking over the estate as if it were his own. His cousin had quite a lot to gain if Declan were permanently out of the way. So did his wife, Alice. If Declan were sent to prison or hanged for murder, then Gerald would become the Earl of Cashelmore, inheriting the title, the wealth, and the lands. Gerald had never seemed as if he desired those things before, yet the grand house party he hosted at Cashelmore Manor and his careless manner regarding Declan's incarceration caused Declan to reconsider Gerald's aspirations.

He had not imagined the look of guilt on Gerald's face when he and Mara arrived.

Somehow, Alice had sent a message to the authorities, assuring he was arrested that night. He had been betrayed by his own family in his own home.

And then there was Paulette Hamilton.

Paulette. God, how he longed to hold her in his arms again! It had been ages since he had kissed her. He regretted the way both of them spoke to each other that last day at the shop. She must be apprehensive about her situation and worried about the baby. The more he thought about it, the more he wanted to make Paulette his wife, wanted to make a family with her. He loved everything about her. And Mara loved her, too. He wished he hadn't left London without seeing her and saying good-bye. The minute he was taken into custody, he'd written to her, explaining what had happened and how much he missed her. But he had yet to hear back from her.

And so he waited. Alone. Powerless. Frustrated. Angry.

The turning of the key on the other side of the door caused Declan to stop pacing and face the door in anticipation. Mr. Woods had arrived, and hopefully he came with good news.

The tall, rather angular man sat upon the one of the two chairs in the tiny room. Running a hand through his long mane of blond hair, Mr. Woods grinned. "I think you're going to be very happy today, my lord."

"Am I free?" Declan held his breath.

"You're a free man," Sebastian Woods announced. "I have a carriage waiting downstairs for you."

Exhaling with relief, Declan could not hide his joy. He was finally free to go. He would have that carriage take him directly to Cashelmore Manor. He had to see Mara. Then he was going to London and marry Paulette Hamilton as soon as he could.

"It seems that you have some very powerful friends pulling strings for you, my lord. I've been instructed to take you directly from here to this address." Sebastian Woods handed Declan a slip of paper.

Declan's brows drew together in confusion. Someone was pulling strings for him? Powerful friends? Just about everyone he knew in Ireland thought he was guilty and the friends he once had shunned him. He had no idea what his solicitor was talking about. "Who instructed you to do this?"

"I'm not quite sure. I thought you would have an idea. I received a letter this morning, enclosed were your release papers and these instructions to have you brought to this house. The charges against you have been dismissed. That's all I know. But someone wanted you set free and had the influence to make it happen."

"The charges against me have been dismissed? Just like that?" Declan could hardly believe it. A minute ago he was facing the possibility of life in the gaol or a hanging if he could not prove his innocence. Now it was all over. Relief coursed through his veins.

"Yes. Completely dismissed. It's finally over." The man nodded in satisfaction. "You're a free man."

Not willing to question his sudden good fortune, he would discover the rest of the answers he needed later. Right now he wanted to get out of that miserable room more than anything. Declan smiled for the first time in days. "Well then, let's go."

After a ten-minute carriage ride, they arrived at the address to find a pretty townhouse in an elegant part of Dublin.

"Do you know who lives here?" Sebastian Woods asked as the carriage came to a stop.

"I've not a clue. It seems I know only as much as you do." Burning with a combination of curiosity and impatience, Declan leapt out of the carriage and ran up the steps, with Sebastian Woods following behind him. Before he could knock, the front door was opened by a butler who clearly expected and welcomed their arrival. The man ushered Declan into a small study, explaining that Mr. Woods was to wait in the parlor.

Declan looked around the room, wondering to whom it belonged. Growing more tense and impatient by the second, he'd had enough of waiting for this mystery savior and he strode to the door, determined to leave. It wasn't locked, thankfully, and he flung open the door.

And there she was.

Paulette Hamilton, looking more beautiful than he pictured in his memory, stood before him in the doorway. His anger evaporated in an instant. Stunned and surprised, he simply stared at her. He couldn't believe his eyes.

"Declan!" she cried and before he knew it, she was in his arms.

He held her tightly, finding it difficult to believe that she was truly there with him. Then he cupped her face in his hands and kissed her, the feel of her sweet lips like the rain after a drought.

"What in heaven's name are you doing here, lass?" he asked finally, staring into her blue eyes.

"I came to see you."

He laughed and kissed her again, still confused, but thrilled that she was there with him. "I don't understand . . . How did you get to Dublin? Whose house is this? How did you manage to get me released today?"

She smiled up at him, her arms around his neck. "Didn't you know I would do anything to find you?"

Declan pulled her back into the study with him and shut the door. He kissed her thoroughly then, his mouth covering hers, their tongues intertwining. God, but he had missed her!

He finally released her and he asked one word. "How?"

Paulette still clung to him as she explained. "I came by ship with Juliette and her husband, Harrison, as soon as I got your note that you'd left for Ireland. When I learned you'd been arrested, I had Lucien and Jeffrey Eddington help. They've done everything they could to get you released and they know some powerful people. And this house belongs to a friend of Lucien's, who lent it to us."

Stunned, Declan shook his head in disbelief. "Thank you, Paulette. I don't know what else to say except that I love you more than you will ever know."

Tears welled in her eyes. "I love you, Declan, and I'm terribly sorry for what I said to you that day at the shop. I didn't mean it. And I'm sorry for not telling you about the baby myself, and I'm sorry for—"

"Stop," he interrupted. "You have nothing to be sorry for, lass. I love you, Paulette Hamilton, and I want to marry you, whether there is a baby or not. The fact that you're having our baby just makes me love you even more." He kissed her to prove it. "I don't care about anything else right now but you and Mara. I have to go to Cashelmore and get her."

Paulette smiled up at him in triumph, her blue eyes sparkling. "Oh, but I already did!"

He stilled. "What?"

"I went to Cashelmore Manor the first day I got to Dublin and took her with me. She's here, in this house.

Just upstairs in the nursery and fairly bursting to see you. She's been missing you, Declan."

Mara was safe. *She was here with Paulette.* Relief coursed through his body. He stared at Paulette in amazement. If this woman could have been any more perfect, Declan couldn't imagine it. Moved beyond words at all that she had done to help him, he stared at her. "Thank you, love," he whispered. All he could do was kiss her.

"Come see her now." Paulette spun toward the door.

Declan stopped her. She turned to face him and he drew her back into the circle of his arms. "If I thought I loved you before I knew you got Mara for me, now I know I will love you until the day I die." He lowered his head and kissed her again, kissed her so thoroughly it left them both shaking. Then he grinned at her. "Let's go see Mara."

He followed Paulette up a flight of stairs and then another. On the third floor of this house was a pleasant nursery. Two little girls played on the floor, a sea of dolls around them. Instantly he saw Mara, her lovely gold hair spilling down her shoulders. She sat across from a dark-haired girl he recognized as Paulette's niece, Sara Fleming. The two girls laughed and chattered away. Declan froze in surprise as he realized that Mara was talking. He glanced at Paulette and she nodded in confirmation. He turned back to Mara, who still had not noticed him. The murmur of the two childish voices, so charming and so typical, thrilled him.

"Mara, darlin'?" he called to her.

Her little head spun around and she stood up in the same moment she heard his voice. Then he heard the sweetest words in the world.

"Papa!" Mara ran to him. "Papa's home!"

He scooped her up in his arms and twirled her around,

tears welling in his eyes. His daughter was talking! *She was talking again.* It was all he could think of. And she was here safe in his arms once more.

"Oh, Mara, darlin', I have missed you so much."

"I missed you so much too, Papa."

"Have you been a good girl?"

She nodded, her little face growing quite serious. "Yes, and very brave."

"I imagine that you have been, and I thank you for being a brave girl for me."

Mara placed her forehead against his. "Don't go away again, Papa."

"Never." He squeezed her tighter. "Never, love."

From the other end of the nursery Sara called to her, "Mara, come back and play!"

"Want to play with Sara and me?" Mara asked him with a bright smile.

"I'd love to, darlin', but I have to discuss some important things with Miss Hamilton first." Declan set her down carefully. "You can keep playing though."

Her green eyes worried, Mara looked up at him. "You won't leave?"

"Not without you," he promised his daughter.

Again Mara nodded her head and scampered back to play with Sara and the dolls.

Declan turned to Paulette, beaming with happiness. "She's talking. I can't believe it."

"Isn't it wonderful?" Paulette grinned. "Mrs. Martin said she first spoke the night you left. She called for you."

He thought it quite ironic that he had stayed by his daughter's side to protect her and calm her fears in the hope that she would speak again, but as soon as he was taken from her, then she found her voice. In any case, he was relieved that Mara was safe and with him again. "Where is Mrs. Martin?"

"She's here, too," Paulette whispered. "She's been wonderful, Declan, and she took excellent care of Mara while you were gone, even though your cousin dismissed her. They dismissed Hobbes that night and we didn't know where he went, but we found him yesterday and he's here, too. When I learned that Gerald was going to send Mara to live with Margaret's sisters, I had Mrs. Martin and Mara sneak out of the house under the cover of darkness so we could take them here to Dublin instead."

More was wrong at home than he'd even imagined and his heart fell at the confirmation that Gerald was at the cause. "This was all Gerald's doing."

Frowning, Paulette placed her hand on his arm and drew him from the nursery. "Let's go join the others and we can explain everything we've learned."

"The others?" he asked.

"Yes," she said, walking toward the staircase. "Juliette, Harrison, Jeffrey Eddington, and your solicitor. They're all downstairs in the parlor waiting for us. We have some news for you."

He stopped her and pulled her into his arms. She looked so pretty in her gown of dark green, her figure slightly fuller, her fair skin aglow. "Paulette Hamilton, you are an amazing woman, and I love you. I don't know how to thank you for all you've done."

She leaned up on the tips of her toes and kissed him. "You don't have to thank me. I love you and I love Mara. I would do anything for either of you. Now, let's go."

Hand in hand, he and Paulette descended the stairs and made their way to the parlor.

Declan was greeted by Paulette's family as they all

sat around a table, discussing the facts of the case with
Sebastian Woods.

Declan too learned that her family had done a great
deal in assisting his release. Apparently, Lord Eddington's father was a powerful duke, who wielded his influence over the matter. Coupled with Lucien Sinclair's
plea as the Marquis of Stancliff and the strong defense
that Sebastian Woods had presented to the court, Declan
Reeves was no longer considered the cause of his wife's
death.

"The most damning claim against you, Declan, was
your own words," Sebastian stated. "A number of the servants heard you that very night, saying that you would
kill Margaret."

All eyes turned to him. Declan faced each one in turn.
The curious looks of Juliette and Harrison Fleming, the
suspicious glance of Jeffrey Eddington. But the eyes that
mattered most were Paulette's and it was to hers he
looked. The trust and honesty he saw within her blue
eyes filled him with hope. "Yes, I said that. I was angry
that night, angry enough to say those terrible words to
my wife. But I was not angry enough to kill her. I called
her many other names though, which she deserved. But
when I left her bedroom door she was alive and screaming right back at me. Then I went to my own bedroom
and drank myself into a stupor. The next thing I knew the
house was in flames."

"It almost seems as if you were set up," Harrison Fleming pondered out loud. "You're angry, you threaten her,
and your threats come true."

"You could be right," Declan mused. "Everyone knew
our marriage was not a happy one."

"It comes back to proof," Sebastian Woods explained.
"We know the fire was deliberately set and not an accident. Someone set that fire. No one can prove you

started the fire, my lord. But no one can prove that you did not."

The room grew quiet.

Sebastian Woods continued, "The charges against you have been dropped, but the rumors and suspicion will persist until we know who is to blame."

"Margaret's family hated me so much and the rumors and suspicion grew from them, I'm sure," Declan said. "I was easy to blame."

"Who benefits most from your blame?" Jeffrey asked.

Declan began slowly, "My cousin Gerald would inherit everything, but I hate to think that of him. He wasn't even in Galway that night and—"

Paulette's next words chilled him. "I believe that your cousin did have something to do with the fire."

A tight knot formed in Declan's stomach. He had not wanted to believe his cousin guilty of betraying him in such a horrific manner.

Paulette continued, "When we were at Cashelmore Manor I happened to overhear a conversation—"

"You just *happened* to overhear a conversation?" Juliette arched a quizzical eyebrow at her sister.

"Fine. I admit it." Paulette sighed in resignation. "I was purposely listening outside the door. I could hear Gerald and Alice arguing, so I listened. They said something about the night of the fire. I thought it was very odd."

"What did they say?" Declan asked, but not sure he wanted to know.

"Well, at first they were arguing because Alice was flirting outrageously with Jeffrey."

Juliette laughed aloud and rolled her eyes. "Of course she was."

With a grin, Jeffrey gave a helpless shrug of his shoulders. "I was learning some useful information. She's a clever woman and quite ambitious. She doesn't love her husband and only married him for the prospect of becoming the Countess of Cashelmore."

Paulette continued eagerly, "Yes! They talked about Gerald soon becoming the next Earl of Cashelmore and how everything had worked out well for them since the night of the fire as long as . . . no one finds out."

"As long as no one finds out what?" Juliette asked the question on everyone's lips.

"That they were there the night of the fire, Declan. At the house in Galway. Because it was the last part of what I heard that gave me chills . . ." Paulette paused for a breath. "They said no one would find out because . . . the child was still not talking."

The room grew deathly silent and the implications were clear to everyone.

The knot in the pit of Declan's stomach turned to icy fear for Mara. His daughter had seen something else the night of the fire. As if watching her mother burn to death was not horrifying enough.

Had Mara seen Gerald there? Or Alice? Or both of them? Had they threatened her not to talk? Was that the reason why his daughter was rendered mute for a year? Declan felt sick to his stomach. "Dear God. It all makes sense."

Paulette took his hand in hers. "But Mara is talking now," she whispered.

"We still need to have proof of this," Sebastian Woods pointed out. "We need something more significant than an overheard conversation and the word of a traumatized child. Just as the proof against you was nebulous, my lord, the proof against your cousin is just as unsubstantial."

"Then I will get proof," Declan said, filled with anger at what his cousin's greed had cost his daughter.

"I'm positive he's involved," Paulette protested, her expression full of worry.

"We'll go to Cashelmore tomorrow morning and confront Gerald and Alice face to face. They won't know yet that I've been released. Let's surprise them and catch them off guard."

Chapter 30

Together

As the clock ticked midnight, Paulette waited with mounting impatience until the Dublin townhouse was quiet and everyone was asleep for the night. Silently she slid out of her warm bed and tiptoed from her room and down the hallway to the bedroom she knew Declan was staying in. She rapped lightly on the door. It opened and she slipped inside, the door closing softly behind her.

Declan pulled her into his strong arms. "You shouldn't be here, love, but I'm glad you are," he said in a hushed tone. He was bare-chested, and his skin was like warm velvet.

"It's a little late to worry about 'shouldn't,' isn't it?" she whispered into his mouth just before he kissed her. His warm lips covered hers and she melted at the touch of his hands pressing into her back. Wearing nothing but her night rail, she was as scantily dressed as he was.

He lifted her in his arms and carried her to the bed. They lay together in the darkened room. The only light came from the fire that burned in the fireplace to ward off the autumn chill.

"I can hardly believe you're here with me, Paulette."

"I've missed you so much, Declan," she murmured in his ear. "These weeks have been dreadful without you."

"And I've missed you more than you know, lass."

Again his mouth, hot and demanding, covered hers and a thrill coursed through her body. He moved over her, his weight settling on top of her, and the heat emanating from his muscles filled her with longing for him to touch her.

She was here in his bed at last. Declan was with her and a tranquil sense of peace filled her heart. Paulette caressed his face, the stubble that covered his jaw pricking her fingers, reminding her that he was real and not one of her many dreams about him.

Their hands explored familiar territory, reclaiming their brands on each other's bodies after such a long absence.

His kisses made her want more of him and she arched her back, pressing herself into him.

Her hands splayed through his dark hair and she breathed in the familiar scent of him, clinging to him. He continued to kiss her, his tongue plundering her mouth. His hand slid over her chest, squeezing her breast through the cotton of her nightgown. Anticipation of what was to come caused her to shiver when he slowly tugged her nightgown up the length of her body. She helped him as he lifted it over her head, leaving her naked beneath him. His hands moved over her, touching her, sending shivers of delight all over her.

"I love you, Declan," she murmured in his ear as her hands skated down the length of his back. His muscles were taut beneath her fingers.

"I love you, my beautiful Paulette." His hand stilled as it moved over her abdomen. "And I love this baby for making us a family."

She covered his hand with hers, feeling tears threaten at such tenderness from him. "I do, too."

"You know I'm marrying you before we go back to London."

Happy that they were to finally going to be married, she smiled. She wanted to be Declan's wife and raise their child together. "That is perfectly sensible," she agreed.

He laughed low in his throat. "None of this makes sense, Paulette." Then his tone grew quite serious. "Not you here in Dublin with me. Not everyone accusing me of killing my wife. Not my cousin betraying me. Not you having to steal my daughter back. Not your family having to help release me from prison. None of it makes any sense at all. Except you. You make everything perfect."

"We're perfect together, Declan."

"In my whole life, I've never had anyone believe in me, except you."

She smiled at him, touched by his words. "I'm an excellent judge of character."

"Yes, you are." He placed a kiss on the tip of her nose.

"I think Mara was happy when we told her about the wedding," Paulette said, thinking of Mara's little face when they told Declan's daughter that they intended to marry.

"Of course she was happy," he said. "She loves you."

"And I love her."

"I can't get over that she's talking again." His voice was full of disbelief.

"It's so good to hear her voice."

"I can't thank you enough for going to Mara first. I would have gone mad if Margaret's sisters had gotten their clutches on her."

"I know you would have. And that evening at Cashel-more I didn't know what else to do but take her. When

Mara agreed to come with me, there was no other choice. Although Jeffrey thought I was daft."

"It shows how much she trusts and loves you that she left with you willingly," he said. "And I owe a great deal of thanks to Eddington and to your brothers-in-law for all of their help in getting me released."

"They were working on things even before I asked them for help. They love me, so they were happy to help you."

"You have an incredibly loving family, Paulette. I couldn't have dreamed up a better family than yours. Watching you and all your sisters on the opening day of the bookshop made me feel lucky and proud just to know you. Mara already loves your sister Juliette. And Sara too, of course. Now that I am to be a part of this family, I am truly humbled."

Paulette grew quiet at his words. She had been lucky to have grown up in a loving and close family. She knew nothing else. Yet Declan lost his parents at ten years old, had no siblings, and the only relative he possessed, his cousin Gerald, had betrayed him in the most horrific of ways. Paulette could not imagine such heartache. When things were difficult for her, she could count on her sisters and brothers-in-law for support and guidance. That Declan was awed by her family's warm and caring unity, which was something she often took for granted, touched her deeply.

"I am very fortunate to have such a family," she whispered, realizing how true her words were. The last few months Paulette had been so fearful to let them know of her feelings for Declan, afraid that they would disapprove of her or be disappointed in her. Their opinions meant so much to her. Yet when they found out, they did not behave as she had thought they would. No, they all had done everything in their power to assist her in helping Declan. "I am very, very blessed," she said again.

"Yes, you are," Declan agreed. "I think we both are."

"But now you and Mara are a part of my family."

"I was part of Margaret's family once." He laughed a little ruefully. "I was a bit leery at first when you mentioned you had four sisters because my previous experience with sisters-in-law was not a pleasant one."

She said knowingly, "So I gathered."

He smiled at her. "But your sisters are all wonderful and lovely. I found Colette to be bright and charming the day I spoke with her in the bookshop. I met Lisette and Yvette only briefly, but I'm already fond of Juliette."

"Yes, she's quite unique, our Juliette."

"And Harrison Fleming is a good man. Of course, I'm now partial to their daughter, Sara, for befriending Mara so quickly, but your nephews Philip and Simon are quite the little gentlemen. And Eddington . . ."

"What about Jeffrey?" Paulette asked.

"I admit I was not overly taken with him at first. He made it clear he disapproved of me from the start," Declan said. "He did not trust me where you were concerned, and he was right to distrust me. But he's since proven to be an admirable fellow."

"I told you that Jeffrey is like a brother to us and probably more protective than a real one in some ways."

"Those were his exact words to me in the bookshop, when he told me about the baby. I sensed then how much he cared for all of you. Do you know I tried to find you that day after we quarreled? I was ready to apologize then and marry you. I was hoping I would see you at Devon House later that evening when I went to fetch Mara," he said. "Where did you run off to?"

"I was hiding from you, and everyone else, upstairs in

my office," she confessed. "I'm so sorry I behaved like an idiot."

Leaning on his side, his hand still covering her abdomen, he began caressing her. "Don't be sorry. I too acted like an idiot. I was just hurt that Eddington was the one to tell me about the baby and not you. I was hurt that you didn't trust me enough to tell me yourself."

"I know. . . . But you had made it clear that you didn't wish to wed again, and I didn't want you to feel forced into marrying me, so—"

"You would rather have run off to America with your sister and never told me about the baby?" he interrupted.

"Well, I had that idea as a last resort sort of plan. . . . I don't think I could ever have truly gone through with it." Paulette kissed him, realizing just how much her foolish plan had hurt him. "I was simply overcome with fears and doubts. Please forgive me."

"I'm sure you were worried out of your mind, and that's all my fault. I apologize for getting you into this situation in the first place."

"Oh, don't ever be sorry, Declan!" she cried, placing a finger over his lips. "That negates all that we shared together. I don't regret a single one of those nights with you."

He stared at her in wonder, placing a soft kiss on her lips. "Ah, Paulette, I don't know what to do with you, lass."

She smiled back up at him knowingly. "Yes, you do."

"Sure and I do." He grinned back at her. He moved his body over hers and his mouth came down on her lips, hot and demanding.

Paulette relished the weight of his body covering hers. He made love to her with infinite tenderness for hours and still she could not get enough of him.

Chapter 31

Confrontation

Gerald O'Rourke's head pounded and throbbed as the effects from too much whiskey the night before laid him rather low today. What he needed was a little more whiskey to take the edge off. He'd just managed to drag himself out of bed and the sun was already high in the late October sky, the light from outside pouring through the tall bedroom windows of the master's suite almost blinding him.

"Close the damn drapes!" he bellowed to his valet, who scurried back to the windows to correct his third mistake of the day. His first had been waking Gerald to say that he had rather important guests waiting for him in his study. His second mistake was telling him he didn't know who the guests were. "You damn idiot," Gerald grumbled again, pressing his hands to his throbbing temples. "Where's Alice?" he asked next, realizing that his young wife was not in their room.

"I'm not sure, my lord." The man rushed about the room, handing Gerald his robe and pouring him a glass of whiskey. "I think she's in with her dressmaker."

Gerald gratefully swallowed the drink, the liquid burning his throat on the way down. Of course Alice was with the dressmaker. Where else would she be? Apparently she now required a brand-new dress every blasted day. He handed the empty glass back to his valet, indicating that he needed another.

Gerald's hands shook as he struggled to get into his robe. Who the hell was calling on him at this time of day, declaring themselves there on a matter of utmost importance? His stomach roiled, rebelling at the whiskey he just dumped in it.

"Bring me some coffee, too," he demanded as he took the second glass of whiskey, gulping it quicker than it took to fill the glass. He wiped his mouth with the back of his hand. "And you have no idea who is here?"

"No, my lord. Gregson just said it was most urgent that you come down right away."

"Are you sure they are not here to see Mrs. Hanlon or Mrs. Hollingsworth?" Margaret's two sisters had been fit to be tied when they arrived at Cashelmore to take Mara and found her missing. They screamed all sorts of vile names at him, demanding to know the whereabouts of their niece. Of course, Gerald felt like a complete fool because he had no idea where the child had gone to, but he made up some story that he had her sent to Dublin to acquire a new wardrobe. Deirdre and Ellen had not been pleased by this at all. In the meantime he'd sent a few of the Cashelmore footmen into Dublin to see what they could find out. He had his suspicions of where the woman who claimed to be his cousin's fiancée must have taken Mara with her when she left.

"I am sorry I don't know, my lord," his valet mumbled in apology. "Gregson would tell me nothing."

"Jesus Christ, you're all a bunch of morons. Give me

the coffee, help me get ready and then go fetch Alice immediately."

"Yes, my lord."

Gerald loved being called "my lord." It had a nice sound to it and as soon as Declan had been arrested, he was technically the lord of the manor. So he ordered all the Cashelmore servants to address him only as "my lord." Gerald belonged here, in this grand house. He'd known that fact his whole life. It wasn't his fault his mother had been the older sister to the heir and then had foolishly married beneath her station.

His mother, Lady Victoria Reeves, had fallen in love with a poor, untitled scholar, named Francis O'Rourke. As the beautiful daughter of the Earl of Cashelmore, Victoria could have married anyone. But no, his mother had not cared for material wealth and went and married a man with no prospects. Her family should have disowned her, but the old earl, his grandfather, loved his daughter too much and didn't care that she had married beneath her.

Luckily for Gerald, he was not raised in poverty, for his grandfather had supported the young couple. It still was not the life of luxury and lavishness Gerald should have been entitled to. Meanwhile, his young cousin Declan, ten years younger and born to his mother's younger brother, had everything handed to him on a silver platter. After the old earl died leaving Declan's father the title, Declan's life of privilege as the heir only improved, while Gerald looked on from the outside, as the poor relation, asking for handouts.

When Declan was only ten years old, his parents were in a devastating carriage accident and both died of their injuries days later. Gerald's own parents had passed away of a fever the year before. That left Declan and Gerald as the only surviving members of the great Reeves family.

As the elder male, Gerald made it his duty to look after his younger cousin who lived at Cashelmore Manor. Declan had readily looked up to Gerald and grew to depend on him for advice.

Not quite sure exactly when the idea took hold of him, Gerald knew that if something happened to Declan, the Cashelmore title and estate and all that entailed would naturally fall to him. Not that he planned any harm to Declan, for he had been the sweetest of boys and Gerald was genuinely fond of him.

But as Declan grew older, Gerald became obsessed with the notion that Cashelmore belonged to him just as much as it belonged Declan. They were both legitimate grandsons of the earl. Why should an accident of birth ruin his whole life? Simply because Gerald had been born to the daughter of the family and not the son, why should he be excluded?

When Declan foolishly married Margaret Ryan, Gerald saw his claim on Cashelmore slipping further away. If Declan had a son, all would be lost. His relief at Mara's birth had been tremendous, for as he knew all too well, a daughter was not an heir. He waited in anxious uncertainty, but Margaret did not have another child.

In the meantime, he knew he should marry and continue the line on his side, just to be safe. Meeting the enticing and clever, if somewhat common, Alice Kennedy changed everything for him. Alice understood right away how things stood and all that Gerald had to gain if only Declan Reeves were out of the way.

Smart enough to realize that suspicion would naturally first fall to Gerald if anything out of the ordinary occurred to cause Declan's demise, Alice hatched the brilliant plan to implicate Declan in the death of his wayward wife. The strife in their marriage was known to everyone and it was easy enough to let people believe that Declan had been the cause of Margaret's death.

Thier plan had gone perfectly until the cursed night in Galway and Gerald had watched everything almost unravel completely in front of his eyes.

It had been worth it though.

Now that Declan was imprisoned for starting the fire, it was merely a matter of formalities before everything legally belonged to Gerald. Cashelmore would then be his forever. Gerald deserved it after all he had been through.

Finally dressed and presentable enough to meet the mystery guests who awaited him in the salon, he wondered again where Alice was as he made his way downstairs. The throbbing of his head had eased somewhat. That third glass of whiskey did the trick. Too preoccupied with his own thoughts, Gerald did not notice the anxious faces of the Cashelmore servants, huddled in corners whispering and scurrying out of his way as he walked the hallways.

Reaching the earl's private study, he tried to steady his shaking hands as he opened the door.

Shock raced through him as he stared at Declan Reeves, the Earl of Cashelmore himself, seated at the wide oak desk in the center of the study. There were others in the room as well. That pretty Hamilton girl and the English lord whom Alice had made a complete fool of herself over the other evening were seated on one of the sofas. An unfamiliar gentleman with long blond hair stood against the bookshelves with his arms crossed. Strangest of all, Mara Reeves sat beside that determined nurse of hers on the opposite sofa along with Ellen Ryan Hanlon and Deirdre Ryan Hollingsworth.

His shock quickly gave way to a sickening feeling that flooded through his entire body and he thought he might empty the contents of his stomach right there on the floor. Something was not right. How had Declan been released from the gaol? What were these people all doing at Cashelmore?

"Declan, my boy!" Gerald called, unable to hide the surprise in his voice. "How are you? What's happened? You must have good news! Have you been released?"

Declan did not smile and his tone was quite cold. "Gerald, so nice of you to finally join us. We've been waiting for you all morning. Yes, I can imagine your surprise at seeing me. I was released yesterday due to lack of evidence, so I came straight home to tell you the news." He paused briefly and stared at him. "It seems they have discovered the true identity of the person who started the fire in Galway."

A shooting pain gripped his chest and Gerald found it difficult to breathe. "That's wonderful news. I am delighted to hear it."

"I thought you might feel that way. Please sit down," Declan ordered. "I'd like to share this information with all of you." He motioned to Margaret's two sisters, who managed to look most displeased and intrigued at the same time.

"I would be happy to," Gerald said as he began making a move toward the door, "but I know Alice will want to hear this news as well. Let me have her join us." If he left right away, he and Alice could be in Dublin and board a ship out of the country by nightfall. He had some money stashed away, but they would have to hurry. He'd go anywhere in the world at this point.

"Oh, don't worry about Alice," Declan said with a grim smile. "She already knows all about it. She's waiting in the adjoining room and will join us after we've spoken to you."

A cold sweat broke out on his brow and Gerald's legs shook. What had they told Alice? And more importantly, what had Alice told them? That pressing sensation near his heart increased. He had to get out of this room, but now that strange, long-haired blond gentleman stood blocking the doorway.

"Sit down, Gerald." The command in Declan's voice brooked no argument.

Gerald cast a worried glance in the direction of the blond stranger as he lowered himself unsteadily onto the only empty chair left in the room.

Declan began, "I'd like to start by introducing you to my solicitor, Mr. Sebastian Woods. He's one of the most skilled criminal attorneys in all of England. Mr. Woods, this is the cousin I've been telling you about, Gerald O'Rourke."

Unable to speak, Gerald gave a slight nod to the imposing man. Between the throbbing in his skull, the tightness in his chest, and the shaking of his hands, Gerald could barely hold up his head. He dreaded what was about to happen. And most of all he avoided the haunting green eyes of little Mara Reeves.

Sebastian Woods cleared his throat, his sharp eyes honing in on Gerald, and his words were harsh. "I have some important questions for you, Mr. O'Rourke. Before I ask them, I am first going to ask one question to someone in this room and I would like everyone else to remain absolutely silent."

The man moved to the sofa and kneeled in front of Mara and his demeanor changed completely. He smiled kindly at her, his voice calm and soft.

"Mara, I know you remember that terrible night that your mother died and I know you don't even like to think of it. But I have a very big favor to ask you. Your truthful answer is very, very important. It can help your father and your aunts. No one will be angry with anything you say." Sebastian Woods paused, but never took his eyes off Mara.

Everyone in the room grew still.

"Mara, do you understand that you need to be very honest and tell the truth?"

"Yes." Her voice was a soft murmur.

Stunned that the child was speaking again, Gerald's hands grew clammy and underneath his suit perspiration dripped down his back and under his arms. When had Mara started talking? What had she said? He wiped the sweat from the top of his lip with the back of his hand. Keeping his eyes downcast, he didn't know where to look.

"Good girl," Sebastian Woods said. "Well, I know you have been very brave this week while your father was away and I need you to be brave a little longer. Can you do that?"

She nodded. Mrs. Martin patted her arm.

"Mara, can you tell me who you saw at Kenmare House the night of the fire?"

Her expression serious, she nodded once more.

"Who?" he encouraged her.

"Papa."

"Yes, that's right." Sebastian Woods grinned. "Your father was there with you. Was anyone else there that you knew?"

Gerald thought his heart would seize right then and there. He tried to look away, to look anywhere in the room but at Mara. But he couldn't. His eyes drifted to the little girl seated on the sofa dressed in pink, her golden blond hair like a halo around her face. He hadn't ever meant to hurt her. She was a sweet thing and he hadn't meant to hurt her! If only the girl had stayed asleep in her own bed!

She should have been fast asleep at that time of the night, not wandering the house all alone, getting in the way of things. Getting in the way of his plans!

After successfully lighting a small fire in the room directly below Margaret's, Gerald should have fled the scene. Everything would have been fine if he had done that. However, at the last moment, panic and remorse over what he had done overwhelmed him. Instead of fleeing the house, he had snuck up the back staircase to get Margaret out of that room before the fire reached her.

But it was too late.

The fire spread faster than he ever could have possibly imagined. When he reached Margaret's bedroom he could already hear her screams and smoke spilled from under the door. He reached to open the door but the knob was mad hot and the door was locked, and that's when he froze. Mara Reeves came running from the opposite end of the hallway, calling for her mother. She stopped short when she spied Gerald standing there. Startled by the child, Gerald screamed at her. "Go back to bed, Mara. You're a very bad girl!"

Margaret's shrieks pierced the air and the smell of smoke burned his nose. Frightened out of his wits at this point, Gerald didn't know what to do. He wasn't even supposed to be in Galway and not a soul had seen him there.

Except the terrified little girl in front of him.

Another shrill scream from Margaret, like that of an animal caught in a trap, pulled at his heart. Mara ran toward the door, frantic to help her mother. Gerald shoved her backward, as hard as he could, and the child fell to the floor, as he yelled, "Bad girl! Go to bed! Get out of here!"

Margaret must have finally unlocked the door for it suddenly flew open and a whoosh of flames shot out of the room. Gerald was lucky to only get singed as he jumped out of the way, falling to the floor and huddling in a ball. He saw Margaret come out, her nightgown already in flames, and she was shrieking in pain. Her long silver-blond hair had begun to burn. Bursts of flames lashed across the hallway blocking his path to Margaret and Mara. Now they were both screaming, the fire spreading quickly toward him. He could not get to either of them without crossing a wall of fire. It was then that his survival instinct kicked in and Gerald fled in the opposite direction, down the back stairs and out of the house as fast as he could go.

The rest of that night was a miserable blur. He managed to find his horse, which he had hidden in the fields, and he rode until he almost passed out, the horror of what he had just done driving his every step. He'd been lucky to get away unharmed, he told himself. But he worried about Mara. How had he left her there alone and defenseless in that inferno? He could think of nothing else until he finally learned the next day that she had escaped the fire unharmed.

Now Mara sat before him, with all eyes on her. Gerald knew in that moment it was all over. Everyone would know what he had done.

Again Sebastian Woods asked in a quiet tone, "Was there anyone else there you knew that night besides your mother and father?"

Mara nodded her head slowly and her green eyes met Gerald's. "Yes. Uncle Gerald was there. He said I was a bad girl."

A pin could have dropped in the study. Tears spilled from his eyes. Gerald could not stop them. "I'm so sorry, Mara, sweetheart, I'm so sorry . . ."

"You are a good girl, Mara. Thank you for telling the truth," Sebastian Woods said. He stood and gave a hard look at Gerald.

Immediately Declan rose from behind the desk and went to his daughter, gathering her in his arms and hugging her tightly. "You are a very brave girl, Mara darlin', and I love you very much." He then set her down. "Mrs. Martin, why don't you take Mara upstairs and give her a special treat and perhaps let her paint or read."

"Of course, Lord Cashelmore," the woman, who was quite shaken, said with a forced grin. She rose and took Mara by the hand. "Let's go, dear. The grown-ups have much to discuss."

Once they were gone, the atmosphere in the room quickly became charged. Gerald reached in his pocket and retrieved his handkerchief. Weeping like a child in shame and remorse, he wiped his eyes. He looked up to see all eyes, full of recriminations and outrage and pity, staring at him. Paulette Hamilton looked aghast. The two Ryan sisters were appalled. That Eddington fellow looked fit to kill. The solicitor sported a satisfied grin. And then there was Declan. The look of hurt and betrayal on his face was unbearable to Gerald.

"I didn't want to believe it was you, Gerald," Declan said, his voice full of disappointment and disgust. "I truly didn't. I never would have believed you capable of something like this. You let Margaret die. If I hadn't found Mara when I did, she would have perished along with her mother."

Gerald desperately wanted another whiskey. The pain in his chest increased to the point he could barely speak. "I'm sorry . . ."

Paulette Hamilton rose from where she had been sitting on the sofa and moved to Declan's side. He placed his arm protectively around her shoulder.

Sebastian Woods knocked on the door to the adjoining room and called, "You can bring Mrs. O'Rourke in now."

One of the burliest Cashelmore footmen entered the study, escorting a very reluctant Alice. His wife was absolutely furious.

"How dare you treat me this way?" she demanded angrily, until she saw Gerald sitting there, blubbering like a baby. Then she rolled her eyes at him in abject disgust. "Oh, dear God in heaven. You've told them everything, haven't you?"

Gerald hadn't, but he knew they knew. It was over. He and Alice had lost everything they'd planned for so carefully.

"Have a seat, Mrs. O'Rourke," Sebastian Woods said, rather obligingly. "We've just had a very interesting talk with your husband."

Alice flounced to the sofa recently vacated by Mara and Mrs. Martin. She crossed her arms and began tapping her foot with impatience. "Well, what is it you need me for then?"

"We have a few questions for you," Sebastian Woods answered, eyeing her critically. "Did you know of your husband's plan to set the house on fire?"

"Yes, of course. Do you think he thought of it on his own?" She laughed in derision.

Great tears spilled down Gerald's cheeks at his wife's cruel words.

Mr. Woods continued to question Alice. "Were you there that night as well?"

"No, I wasn't," she snapped. "Had I been there it would have been done correctly. None of them would have survived."

Gerald sobbed aloud as he sensed Alice's utter contempt for him.

Sebastian Woods continued his questions. "Who sent the letters to Miss Hamilton and Lord Cashelmore?"

Alice shot an angry glance in Gerald's direction. "We both did. We had a man in London, keeping an eye on Declan. We wanted him to come back to Ireland to be tossed into prison or flee the country for good. We were hoping the letters would scare him into doing one or the other, but they didn't seem to do much but break up their little romance." Alice cast a disparaging glance at Declan and Miss Hamilton.

"I'll need the name of your man in London," Mr. Woods said.

"Jesus, leave him out of it, will you? He's my little brother and he was only doing me a favor," Alice said, bristling with irritation. "I don't want him going back to gaol!"

"Well, your brother faces some charges in this case as well," the tall solicitor stated with satisfaction. "He might have to go back to gaol. As will you."

Declan added, "We figured out it was you sending the letters because Paulette said the day she came to Cashelmore, you knew about her and me, and I had never told a single soul about my friendship with Miss Hamilton."

Gerald sobbed, unable to look at Declan or Alice for the shame that consumed him.

"Gerald, after all you said to us about Declan and you were the one who killed our sister?" Ellen Ryan Hanlon suddenly blurted out, eyeing him with confusion.

"You made us believe from the start that it was Declan's fault!" Deirdre Ryan Hollingsworth echoed, wringing her hands with worry.

Gerald could say nothing in his defense. He merely sobbed louder and shrugged his shoulders helplessly.

"I don't understand how this happened!" Ellen wailed in distress.

Still confused, Deirdre asked, "But Declan, who are these people? Who is this woman?"

"Paulette Hamilton is the woman I love," Declan announced to the room. "And this beautiful woman, unlike everyone else who supposedly knew and loved me, believed me when I said I had nothing to do with Margaret's death."

Placing his hands over his face, Gerald sobbed uncontrollably.

Chapter 32

Wedding

Papa was marrying Miss Hamilton!

Mara was so excited she had trouble standing still, even though Mrs. Martin had instructed her very carefully about how she was to behave in the chapel. Mara rocked from one foot to another, wearing the pretty, white ruffled-lace dress they had just purchased for her in a fancy Dublin shop. Filled with pride at being a part of the wedding, Mara tried to hold still to be the little angel Papa said she looked like in her new dress. But she was just so joyful because she knew that Miss Hamilton made Papa happy and besides, she loved Miss Hamilton, too.

Miss Hamilton was kind and thoughtful and never cross with her, and she made Papa's eyes smile again. Now she would get to go to the magical bookshop whenever she wanted to and she would always be able to play with Sara Fleming. Tomorrow they were all going back to London on a grand ship. Sara said it was her father's ship and that she and Mara would be able to play together for the whole journey!

As they waited for the wedding to start, Mara stood

holding Papa's hand in the little chapel. A nervous flutter raced through her when she saw everyone seated in the pews looking at her. Papa said it was a small, private gathering but Mara thought there were still a lot of people there watching them in the chapel. Mrs. Martin grinned at her with pride. She had never seen Mrs. Martin dressed so fancy before and wearing a little hat with a feather, too! Her best friend, Sara Fleming, giggled at her and stuck out her tongue only to get scolded by her mother. As soon as they were married Sara would be her cousin! That made her excited, too. And Mara had already been instructed to call Sara's parents Aunt Juliette and Uncle Harrison. Mara marveled at the prospect of having an aunt and uncle who did not frighten her.

Her eyes glanced at her other aunts, Deirdre and Ellen, who were there in the chapel as well, still dressed in dark black with serious faces. They usually frightened Mara with their harsh words and strict manners. They were quite different from Aunt Juliette, who was high-spirited and always smiling. Miss Hamilton told her she had other sisters, too, who would also be her aunts and Mara would get to meet them again when they returned to London. Mara couldn't wait to go back to the grand house and play in the nursery with Sara, Phillip, and Simon once more. She now had a big family!

Just then a lady seated at the harp in the back of the chapel began playing softly and everyone stood up. Papa grinned at Mara and gave her hand a little squeeze. Mara felt a bubble of excitement in her chest.

Then Miss Hamilton entered the chapel, on the arm of that nice Lord Eddington, who gave her some peppermint sticks yesterday. Oh, but Miss Hamilton looked so beautiful! Mara couldn't help the little gasp that escaped her at the sight. Miss Hamilton's long gown was white silk with a few ribbons cascading down the back and her blond hair was atop her head, adorned with a crown of white roses. Her face glowed with happiness. Mara thought she looked just like a fairy-tale princess, like the one in the *Sleeping Beauty* storybook she had. Miss Hamilton smiled brightly at Papa as she walked down the aisle toward them. Then her eyes met Mara's and she smiled again, and Mara felt warm inside.

When they reached the altar, Lord Eddington kissed Miss Hamilton's cheek and moved to sit in the pew with the Flemings. Miss Hamilton then took Mara's other hand as Mara stood between her and Papa. The chaplain began talking. He was quite old and had no hair on his head. It seemed as if he talked for a very long time, going on and on about love and something called "holy matrimony."

Mara held very still, like a good girl, but she found it very hard to listen and her thoughts drifted.

Last night, Mara, Papa, and Miss Hamilton had a long talk together. She was glad because Papa said that now Mara could call Miss Hamilton "Mama." She missed her own mother very much. But since her mother had gone away, it would be good to have another mother to look after her again, especially one as wonderful as Miss Hamilton. She wanted a new mother and if she had to pick anyone in the whole wide world to be her mother, it would be Miss Hamilton.

Papa also explained to her that Uncle Gerald was going away, because he started the terrible fire. Mara felt sad to think of Uncle Gerald. She didn't understand why he would do such a dreadful thing. He'd always been kind to her, until the night of the fire, when he was angry with her, but Mara hadn't meant to be a bad girl by getting out of bed that night. She'd just had a bad dream and wanted to see Mama.

But Papa also told her she didn't ever have to think

about the fire again. Mara liked that idea best of all. Those memories were becoming fuzzier and more faded and that suited her just fine.

She had two people she loved best in the world right there beside her now.

Finally the old chaplain stopped talking and Papa and Miss Hamilton kissed each other. Mara giggled a little. She tried not to but she couldn't help it. Then they both leaned down and hugged her before Papa lifted her up in his arms. He carried her with them to a small room behind the altar where Papa and Miss Hamilton used ink pens to sign some papers with the chaplain. When they were done, they kissed each other again. And Mara couldn't help but giggle once more.

Then Papa asked Mara, "So, what did you think of your first wedding, darlin'?"

She smiled at him. "Oh, it was grand! And now I have a new mama."

"Good," he said, giving her a squeeze. "Because I thought it was grand, too."

She like that Papa was so happy. Mara knew how glad it made him that she was talking again, too. She liked talking again, too. It only felt the tiniest bit strange to talk aloud after being silent for so long.

Miss Hamilton took her aside and put her arm around Mara. Miss Hamilton always smelled like a flower garden. "I'm so happy to marry your father, Mara," she said in her soft voice. "And the most wonderful part of all is that I get to have the best daughter in the world, too. I know we talked about it last night, but you can call me Mama or Paulette."

"I want to call you Mama."

"That touches my heart." Miss Hamilton's eyes filled with tears, but she looked happy, placing a kiss on Mara's cheek. "You are a very sweet little girl."

"Can I choose any book I want?" Mara asked softly.

Miss Hamilton laughed prettily, wiping her eyes. "Yes, of course, and you can have as many books as you like."

"I feel bad because my toy book with the dancing bear broke."

"Oh, I'm so sorry, but I can get you another one. You can even help me choose children's books to buy for the store. Would you like that, Mara?"

"Oh, yes!" Mara nodded eagerly. It would be great fun to be in the bookshop all the time and help Miss Hamilton, her new mother.

Papa came to where Mara sat with Miss Hamilton. "Now I have the great honor of taking the loveliest ladies in Dublin to our wedding breakfast."

Mara giggled in delight and gave a kiss to Papa and her new mother. Not only were they having a celebration today and she was allowed to have two pieces of cake, but also tomorrow they were all sailing to London together!

Mara couldn't help but think that it was just like the happy endings in her book of fairy tales.

Chapter 33

Homecoming

"So, you're the one," Lucien Sinclair, the Marquis of Stancliff, said as he shook Declan's hand in greeting.

Paulette watched in amusement as Declan finally met her brother-in-law. Thrilled to show her handsome new husband and stepdaughter to her family, she beamed with happiness when they arrived at Devon House. In celebration of her marriage to Declan, Colette hosted a wonderful party in their honor.

Declan smiled at Lucien with a slight nod of his head. "Yes, and so it would seem."

"You had us all worried there for a while," Lucien continued to say.

"Not half as worried as I was," Declan responded. "And I thank you for all that you did to help my case."

"I wouldn't have done anything less for my sister-in-law," Lucien said, patting Paulette's shoulder.

"I'm just happy that she's married," Yvette added with an impish grin. "I was afraid she would never find a husband."

Declan chuckled at the youngest Hamilton sister.

"Well, I suppose she more than made up for that now, didn't she?"

"Yes, for now she has a new little family!" Yvette exclaimed. Then she lowered her voice and added, "And if I hadn't become involved and told Jeffrey, Paulette might be on her way to America!"

"I wasn't really going to go!" Paulette protested.

Declan gave Yvette a hug. "Then I must thank you, Yvette, for helping Paulette to see the sense in marrying me."

"I'm happy someone recognizes my good intentions!" Yvette quipped.

Returning to London with Declan's name finally cleared for good and Mara speaking again, Paulette knew they could put the past behind them and move forward with their lives. Although the events of the last few weeks had been more than a little overwhelming, Paulette welcomed the change from a young woman working in a bookshop to the wife of an earl, the mother of a four-year-old daughter, and a mother-to-be with a baby on the way.

Happy to have her family around her, sharing in the joy of her own new little family, the only thing left for Paulette to do now was to apprise her mother of her impending condition. With a heavy heart she crossed the room to where her mother sat in an alcove of the parlor.

"How could you marry someone I had only met once before? How could you marry without me there with you? How could you not tell me? *Comment ne pouvais-tu ne pas me le dire?*" her mother demanded to know, a look of hurt on her face. "How could my daughter marry without telling her mother first? I ask you! It breaks my heart that you would rush off and not tell me anything."

"There is a very good reason for that, *Maman*," Paulette attempted to explain as she sat beside her. She had dreaded this moment since she had last visited her mother in Brighton and learned the truth of her condition.

"I should love to hear it." Her mother gave her appointed look. "I would love to know how this marriage came to be. Explain it to me please. *S'il te plaît, explique-moi. J'aimerais entendre chaque mot.* Why was I not part of this?"

Paulette hesitated briefly then just blurted it out. "I'm going to have a baby in the spring, so Declan and I thought it best to marry as soon as possible."

Paulette then braced herself for the expected emotional outburst from her mother, demanding to know how Paulette could have let such a thing occur, how she should know better, what a complete disgrace she was to the family, and how Lord Cashelmore could not be any kind of gentleman to allow this to happen to her daughter. Her mother would probably feel faint from the shock and need to lie down.

Instead her mother stared at her for a moment or two, her pale blue eyes looking intently into hers. Then Genevieve La Brecque Hamilton did a most astonishing thing. She placed her hand over Paulette's hand and said most calmly, "Yes, then that was the wisest course of action, *ma petite.* That was a very wise decision. *C'était une bonne decision à prendre. Oui, vraiment, une bonne décision.*"

"*Maman?*" Paulette managed to ask in surprise.

"No. Say no more. I understand completely. Do not explain. *Il n'est pas nécessaire d'en dire plus.* It is clear that you love him, and now you are married. I am happy to have another beautiful grandchild on the way. *Et un autre beau petit-enfant en route.*"

"I love you, *Maman.* Thank you for understanding." Pleasantly surprised by her mother's reaction to her news, Paulette relaxed a little.

"I understand all too well. Do not tell your sisters.

Never tell them. *Ne le dis à personne. C'était pareil entre ton père et moi.* But it was the same situation with your father and me. We too had to marry quickly."

Paulette's jaw dropped.

"Close your mouth. *Je comprends tout à fait, ma chérie.* It is not a new story and many a marriage has begun that way. *C'est la vie.* Although I have a feeling you shall be happier in your marriage than I was. *Je t'aime.*" Her mother kissed her forehead, then sat up straight.

Startled by her mother's admission, Paulette was too shocked to say anything else. She never could have imagined such a thing of her father and mother!

"Now," her mother commanded, "bring him here to me."

At her mother's request, Paulette caught the attention of her new husband, who was on the other side of the room talking with her brothers-in-law and Jeffrey Eddington. Five very charming and handsome men stood there talking as if they were old friends. And with the exception of Declan, they all were. Declan and Jeffrey were beginning to move beyond their mutual distrust and become friends and already Declan seemed a part of them, and Paulette's heart swelled with pride at the sight. Her husband was the handsomest by far, looking very tall and broad, his green eyes flashing with merriment as Jeffrey told some joke. She knew he would fit in with her family and they would grow to love him for his own sake, not simply because she loved him.

As the men in her life laughed together, Declan returned her gaze and Paulette signaled for him to come join her. With a smile, Declan excused himself from the group and came to Paulette's side to face her mother.

Genevieve looked him up and down. "So Lord Cashelmore, you are the one who has swept my sensible and serious daughter off her feet. Yes, I can see why that

would happen. *Vous êtes vous-même un belhom...*
clair à present. You are quite handsome. Ah, I u...
everything now."

To Paulette's surprise, Declan's face grew slightly red
at her mother's words. Her husband was blushing and
did not know how to answer her.

Genevieve continued, disregarding her son-in-law's
embarrassment. "But you must be good to her. *Occupez-
vous bien de ma fille.* You must take very good care of my
daughter."

Declan said, "I intend to do nothing but take good
care of her, Mrs. Hamilton."

Genevieve nodded her head in approval and favored
Declan with a smile and motioned to Paulette. "All of my
daughters are special, Lord Cashelmore, but this one,
she is a treasure. You are lucky to have her. *Elle est sensa-
tionnelle.* She is magnificent."

"Mother!" Paulette protested.

"Oh, I know that already, Mrs. Hamilton. That is why
I married her." Declan placed his arm around Paulette's
shoulder.

"That is a good thing. I am happy. *Je suis heureuse.
Quatre filles mariées, il ne m'en reste plus qu'une.* Four
daughters married and only one left. Now we wait for
that one, eh?" Genevieve motioned toward Yvette, who
stood talking with Lord Jeffrey Eddington.

Watching her younger sister, Paulette laughed a little.
"Knowing Yvette, she'll be married before we know it, and
in the most lavish wedding ever. That's if she could ever
make up her mind which of her many suitors to marry!"

Epilogue

As Declan held the baby in his arms, Paulette smiled at him. "Is he asleep?"

"I don't think so . . ." he whispered with a shake of his head. "No, not quite yet. He just opened his eyes again and looked up at me. He has your blue eyes, you know?"

Their son had Declan's facial features and was still too bald to determine his final hair color, but Declan kept insisting that the child had Paulette's eyes. In either case, he was a darling baby and Paulette was ridiculously in love with him. He slept like an angel all night long and had such a calm temperament. In other words, he was a complete and utter joy. She loved motherhood even more than she could have imagined.

"Ah, there he goes now. At last. I think he's finally asleep," Declan said softly.

Paulette watched her husband place their sleeping baby in his cradle with great tenderness and for a moment she thought her heart might overflow with all the love she felt for them.

Declan returned to their bed and drew Paulette into his arms. "Oh, and he's a fine Irish boy."

"That's because he has a fine Irish father," she said.

She snuggled into him, not caring about the warmth of the June evening. The birth of their son, Thomas Hamilton Reeves, named after her father, a month ago had brought Declan much joy. Paulette already knew what a good father he was to Mara but she delighted in watching him handle an infant so gently. He wasn't afraid or awkward holding a baby as some men were.

"And the most beautiful mother in all the world." He placed a kiss on her lips.

"I'm just happy he's healthy and sleeps when he's supposed to."

"Mara certainly loves him!" Declan said with a laugh.

And indeed, Mara had taken tremendous pride in her baby brother and had been a great help in caring for him. She would kneel at his cradle and sing little songs to him.

"Everything has turned out so well for us, Declan. What a year it's been!"

"Certainly a lot of changes," he remarked dryly.

"A year ago I didn't even know you. Then there you were, with Mara. Your name has been cleared for good. And now we have Thomas. I couldn't be happier."

"And don't forget the bookshops."

The bookshop was doing well and Hamilton Sisters' was doing even better. They had a full-time staff at both locations even though Paulette and Colette still oversaw the business and went to the shops almost daily. They were thrilled that the Hamilton bookshops had become the premier booksellers in the city.

Declan paused for a moment, his tone growing serious. "I am proud of you for all that you and your sisters have accomplished. But I do need to return to Cashelmore soon."

Paulette tried to hide her reluctance at his words. Aware that this day would come eventually, she had bided her time as they spent the remainder of her pregnancy living in Declan's townhouse in London so she could be near her family. The thought of making Cashelmore Manor their permanent home weighed heavy on her heart. The house was too big, too cold, and too filled with memories she did not wish to recall. But she and Declan were the Earl and Countess of Cashelmore and the grand estate would belong to their son one day. It was their duty to live there and care for it.

"Yes, I know," she said.

"We've been so preoccupied with preparing for the baby, we haven't really discussed our plans for a home. But I was thinking we could leave at the end of the summer, spend the fall in Ireland at Cashelmore Manor, and then come back to London again to be with everyone here at Christmas," he suggested.

"That's a wonderful plan. And that's just when Lisette is due to have her baby! So I would love to be here for her." Paulette smiled at her husband, although the thought of living away from her sisters was difficult to bear. In truth she would become accustomed to the distance between them, especially knowing they would all visit often. It was being away from the bookshops that hurt the most. She would miss the day-to-day running of the shop. However, she knew her duty as Declan's wife and as the Countess of Cashelmore and all that entailed.

"We can make any changes we want to Cashelmore Manor," Declan added thoughtfully. "It needs to be updated, which is something I never had any interest in before. You can make it however you like it, Paulette, so it feels more like a home and less like a museum."

The house certainly needed to be updated. It was Declan's ancestral house, and now her son's. Paulette would do all that she could to make it a warm and inviting place. "I would love to make it our home."

"We don't have to live there all year. We can spend half the year here and half the year in Ireland." Declan paused and cupped her chin, tilting her face up to look at him. "And I thought that might suit you more if you had a bookstore to take care of, so I purchased an empty shop for you in Dublin."

Paulette sat up, her heart racing. "What?" she cried, then she lowered her voice, afraid of waking the baby. "What did you say?"

"I think it is high time the Hamilton sisters opened one of their bookshops in Dublin, don't you?"

"Oh, Declan!"

"What? Do you not think it a good idea?"

She threw her arms around him and hugged him tightly to her, this wonderful man who loved her enough to make her the happiest woman in the world. This man she loved with all heart. She loved his green eyes, his handsome face, every dark hair on his head, the lilt of his voice, the touch of his hand, the purity of his soul. She loved him more every single day.

"Thank you, Declan. Thank you so much. I would love to have a bookshop in Dublin. I'm sorry I didn't think of it myself. But you did and I love you for it!" She kissed him.

He captured her face in his hands and stared in her eyes. "It's the least I can do. You rescued me, Paulette, when I didn't even know I needed saving. When I met you, looking so beautiful in the bookshop, I was buried in grief and an unwillingness to deal with the circumstances around me. Your spirit and absolute faith in my innocence saved me. I love you and there's nothing I wouldn't do for you."

Placing her hands over his, she gazed back in his eyes. "I love you, Declan Reeves, and I don't think I can thank you enough."

He grinned wolfishly at her, his eyes filling with desire. "Oh, I think you can."

"I might just at that." She giggled, and he kissed the laughter from her lips.

"You can spend your life trying," he said low.

She kissed him back. "I promise I will."

Dear Readers,

I hope you enjoyed reading *To Tempt an Irish Rogue* and loved Paulette and Declan's story as much as I did!

Which leaves us with the youngest Hamilton sister's story still untold. I must admit that I feel a little sad to be writing the last of the Hamilton series.

With her four older sisters married, what will happen to Yvette Hamilton? Will her romantic and dramatic personality bring her happiness? Oh and of course, what of the dashing Lord Jeffrey Eddington? Will these two end up together? You'll have to read the book to find out, but here's a little preview in the meantime. Enjoy!

Thanks for reading!
Kaitlin O'Riley
www.KaitlinORiley.com

Yvette Hamilton laughed seductively as she favored the handsome, hazel-eyed gentleman before her with a smile. Her most charming smile. The smile that melted male hearts with ease and had more than one suitor declaring his undying love for her. She had perfected the maneuver over the years and had become quite skilled at using it. Well aware of its power, Yvette employed it sparingly and only when she wished to captivate a special someone.

Yvette was no longer wasting her time. She had a life-changing goal to meet before the end of the year. This was her third Season after all. She should be married by now or at the very least engaged to be married.

It wasn't from a lack of offers. No. That was most definitely not the case. She had been the toast of her first Season and even her second. She had been swimming in proposals from fine young gentlemen from good families with excellent prospects, and even a few from those of questionable standing in society. She should have been satisfied with any of them.

But she was not.

No, Yvette aspired to something better.

Not content to settle for just any husband, she had her sights set on a far loftier goal. Determined to make the most brilliant match possible, only a duke would do for Yvette. And her goal was to be affianced to him by Christmas. That gave her only three more months.

She wasn't bold enough to think she could snare a prince, even though two of Queen Victoria's sons were still unmarried. But as luck would have it, earlier that summer she met Lord Shelley, the gentleman in front of her whom she now favored with her stunning smile. He had been traveling abroad for the past two years, and having just returned home, he was now in the market for a wife.

And Yvette would make the perfect wife for him.

One day he would inherit the title of Duke of Landsdown and Yvette intended to be his duchess. The competition for his attentions had been quite fierce all summer long, for a prize such as Lord Shelley was rare indeed, but as summer turned to fall, Yvette had emerged as his favorite.

"You are looking quite beautiful this evening, Miss Hamilton," Lord Shelley said.

"So you've already told me." She cast a flirtatious eye around the ballroom, as if she had tired of him, and fluttered her new lace fan. That had been her strategy with him from the start. Lord Shelley was a man used to having women fall at his feet. Yvette refused to be one of them.

He whispered to her, "That is because I can think of nothing else when I look at you."

Yvette tallied his compliment to the growing list she kept in her head and felt a slight surge of victory. One by one, the other young ladies vying for his attentions all summer had fallen out of favor with him, leaving only Yvette and her greatest rival, Lady Louisa Fairmont, to battle it out. Yvette was positive that she would win him in the end.

She turned and stared into his knowing, hazel eyes. Fair-haired and charming, Lord Shelley was a good looking man. He had straight teeth and a well-proportioned nose. At thirty years old, he was of average height, but his title gave him the air of a much taller man.

"You are very kind, my lord." She glanced away.

"May I get you some punch?" he asked.

"Oh, that would be lovely. Thank you." Such a coup! He was fetching her some refreshment. He'd never offered to do that before. Inwardly she gloated a little.

"I shall return immediately." Lord Shelley walked off toward the refreshment table.

As he left, her dearest friend, Lady Katherine Spencer, joined her. "So, how is your quest progressing?"

Yvette grinned, pleased with her evening's endeavors. "I believe quite well, Kate, quite well."

Her friend gave her a quizzical glance, her freckled face wrinkled with disgust. "I don't understand why you wish to marry him so much. He's a terrible bore. Let Lady Louisa have him."

"He's going to be a duke." That settled the argument as far as Yvette was concerned.

Kate's soft expression darkened a bit. "Still . . . he's not romantic in the least. I don't believe you'll be happy with him."

"I shall be quite happy being a duchess, I can assure you. It will make up for any supposed deficiencies in his character." Yvette confirmed with a nod of her blond head. When she was a duchess her life would magically change for the better. She simply knew it.

"If I were you, I'd go after Lord Eddington," Kate said in a voice full of longing. "He's the most dashing gentleman I've ever met. You should try to marry him."

Yvette laughed at the utter absurdity of such a prospect. "Lord Eddington? I could never marry him!"

"Why ever not? He's devastatingly handsome, he's rich, and he makes all the ladies swoon . . ."

"Putting aside the fact that he's been like a brother to me, he's . . . he's . . ." Yvette struggled to find the proper words. Oh, Jeffrey Eddington was indeed all the things Kate had said. Yvette also knew him to be charming, funny, sweet, and unfailingly loyal. In fact he had grown quite dear to her. Even she had to admit that he had a special place in her heart. But as for marriage? It was completely out of the question.

"I know you used to be sweet on him, Yvette."

Perhaps she had nursed a childish infatuation for Jeffrey years ago, but as a mature woman she had quite outgrown such silliness. "Well, I am not sweet on him any longer. Besides, he is not marriage material."

"Because he's a . . . a bastard?" Kate asked in a furtive whisper.

It was common knowledge that Lord Eddington was the illegitimate son of the Duke of Rathmore and a stage actress. Yvette wanted more for herself in life than that. "I can't very well marry Lord Eddington if I wish to become a duchess, now can I?"

"Are you enjoying the ball, Yvette?"

At the sound of a very deep familiar voice, Yvette's heart raced as she turned in his direction. There stood the subject of their gossip, Lord Jeffrey Eddington, and by the look on his face, he had heard everything she had just said.

More by Bestselling Author
Hannah Howell